SUPERLUMINAL

SUPERLUMINAL

TONY DANIEL

An Imprint of HarperCollins*Publishers*

SUPERLUMINAL. Copyright © 2004 by Tony Daniel. All rights reserved. Printed in the United States of America. No part of this book may be used or reproduced in any manner whatsoever without written permission except in the case of brief quotations embodied in critical articles and reviews. For information address HarperCollins Publishers Inc., 10 East 53rd Street, New York, NY 10022.

HarperCollins books may be purchased for educational, business, or sales promotional use. For information please write: Special Markets Department, HarperCollins Publishers Inc., 10 East 53rd Street, New York, NY 10022.

FIRST EDITION

EOS is a federally registered trademark at HarperCollins Publishers Inc.

Designed by Debbie Glasserman

Printed on acid-free paper

Library of Congress Cataloging-in-Publication Data

Daniel, Tony.
    Superluminal/Tony Daniel.—1st ed.
      p. cm.
    ISBN 0-06-105143-8 (alk. paper)
     1. Life on other planets—Fiction.   2. Space colonies—Fiction.   3. Space warfare—Fiction. I. Title.

PS3554.A558 S86 2004
813'.54—dc22   2004042052

04 05 06 07 08 JTC/RRD 10 9 8 7 6 5 4 3 2 1

JILL SPEAKS

BACK CHANNEL MERCI CODED:
LEO IS COMING AND WILL KNOW THE KEY WORD

I have found her, TB! I have found Alethea Nightshade. But you have to stay there! If you come to this place, they will bite your head off, and then where will you be? You have to listen to Andre and Molly in this regard. Things have changed.

First we looked at the records of the experiment that made you—me and some Friends of Tod did. I have to tell you about them someday. Oh, and I finally had sex, even though he didn't know he was the first one. He is coming your way soon, and if you are reading this, he has given you the code word. He can tell you much more about what's happening in the Met, but don't ask him about the sex.

He has romantic notions. I think maybe I broke his heart. But there was nothing else to do, and there isn't any time to waste on regret at this moment, so that's where I have to leave it.

We have an army. You will not believe this, but it is made up of rats and ferrets, working together. With the Friends of Tod's help and using what happened to me as a template—how I became a girl—the rats and ferrets and everything else from the Carbuncle and from every hiding place in the Met have become human beings. It is a strange thing, because they are still rats and ferrets and everything else in a way. And they all started out as computer programs that got away when somebody wanted to erase them.

Oh, most of the rats stayed being rats.

What can you do? It isn't a happy world for rats, and they sometimes get twisted inside and cannot be redeemed.

But TB, I promised you I would find her, and I did. You always said that she would be spread out, hiding even though she did not know she was hiding, broken into a million pieces or more, and curled up in the smallest cracks in the grist, and I very much believe that you were right, but things have changed.

The war has done what you and I could never do. All of those crevices have been poked into, all the cracks have been lit up by a searchlight's shine. The only ones who got out alive are my friends now, and they are on the run like me. What is bad for the free converts of the Met is useful for finding Alethea, though. She can't hide in the backwaters of the virtuality anymore because Amés is trying to kill all the free converts, and coming close to doing it, too. There are some free converts that he needs, yes, but most have been rounded up and flashed to a place . . .

It is a horrible place, TB. They are reformatting millions and millions of people. Wiping them away. A guard there couldn't take it anymore, and she came to tell us the story, but it wasn't long before the Department of Immunity found her, and now she has been murdered, too.

I am sorry for all these people, but I think—and the ones I am working with are sure of it—that Alethea is *in* there, distributed among the free-convert prisoners.

My friends think she's fled the cracks and crevices where she could no longer stay and found a place inside the only places complicated enough to hold all her pieces. Is she still enough herself to know what's happening to her? I hope not, TB, I really hope not. Maybe she can't know a thing, not really. Maybe she's just puzzle pieces. Maybe not.

But we're pretty sure she's with the free converts of Silicon Valley.

She's hiding in the darkest corner of the darkest place in the universe.

It is not going to be easy to put her together again, but I think it can be done. We will have to win some battles before we can do it, though.

This may take some time, but I know you are very patient, and—believe it or not—even I am a lot more patient than I used to be.

But don't worry, in case you think it makes me tame. Nothing makes me tame. I will kill anything that gets in the way of keeping my promise to you.

Anything or anyone, no matter who they are.

I will bite them.

PART ONE

Lines in the Grist

YEARS 3014 TO 3016, E-STANDARD

CHAPTER ONE

It was late autumn in the northern hemisphere of Planet Earth. The Jeep pulled away from the remains of an ancient service area, and rumbled north on the shattered pavement of the old Taconic Parkway of New York State. The trees leaves were just past their peak and had changed to the russet of old blood.

Still, thought the Jeep, enough foliage to hide in, if it came to that.

Once again, the truck hunters were on his trail. The Jeep sensed it through the ground itself. Piezoelectric shock waves fluttered the foil of the detectors in his cargo bay. He didn't even need to listen to the grist to hear the hunters coming.

The sun was high and glinted hard off the Jeep's windshield. The sky was without clouds. These were late-morning hunters, then. Not especially dangerous. They were probably all piled into a soft-bellied roller—transportation that would flow into the bumps and potholes of the road and allow them to become pleasantly drunk without getting jostled about. No, these particular truck hunters were not a serious threat to the Jeep—although they might get lucky and take down a thoughtless pickup if one came out of cover to graze on hydrocarb grasses. Still, it paid to be alert, and to put as much distance between yourself and the truck hunters' guns and takedown devices as wheels could take you.

Abruptly, the Jeep spotted a narrow opening—less than a road, more than a path—in the forest to the west, and he turned into the trees without slowing down. The trail was just wide enough to accommodate him, as he knew it would be.

The Jeep always knew where he was going and never needed any directions. He was nine hundred years old. The ancient jeep trails of the lower Hudson River were his creation. Some he had completely forgotten, or seemed to forget, but when he came upon them, their destination, their crossroads, and their landmarks would spread out in his mind like a bud unfurling into a flower, and he would turn right or left, and always be on the right track.

He was multiply recursed, imprinted time and again on the substrate of the metal, plastic, and fabric of his chassis. You could take him apart piece by piece, you could smash him to a cube, you could blow him to smithereens, and he'd always come back. He would grow a new Jeep.

It had happened before over the years. Accidents, exploding tires and rollovers, tank explosions. Always, parts had survived, and from those parts the Jeep would become himself again. For the last one hundred years or so, there had been the truck hunters. Many of his compatriots in the forest had been taken. The best way it could happen was to be destroyed outright. The worst way . . . that was when they immobilized the truck with disruptive quantum effect charges, then sliced off a portion—a hood ornament, a grill, a tailgate with the logo written across it—and eliminated the remainder. Then they took the trophy away. Back to where they came from. The Met.

The Jeep didn't really understand the Met, nor did he want to. All he knew was that the truck hunters usually arrived in helicopters flown from New York City. Nobody much lived in New York City anymore, so they must descend from space, where everyone lived. And that is where they must return with their trophy pieces. He could only imagine that the truck parts were displayed on walls (he pictured the Met, when he pictured it at all, as a series of tight, impassable enclosures), and perhaps, for the amusement of the truck hunter or the hunter's guests, made to speak now and again in the limited way that such primitive robots could synthesize speech. One thing the Jeep *did* understand about the Met—it was no place for light trucks or utility vehicles.

The Jeep had so far escaped from the truck hunters. This was an easy task most of the time. The hunters had many pieces of tracking equipment, but the equipment all came down to electromagnetic wave detectors or grist. The e-m was easy to baffle. The Jeep incorporated the best in stealth technology—vintage defenses from before the nanotech era. It was precisely these interior baffles and shields that made him such a prize for the truck hunters. Such things were no longer manufactured, and the Jeep could only assume that the knowledge of how to make them had been misplaced.

Overcoming the grist was another matter, however. The Jeep had developed an amalgamation of makeshift solutions to this problem. Some of these were conscious—methods of backtracking on a molecular level and putting out multiple ghost shells that "tasted" like Jeep on the outside but were empty on the inside. But some of the Jeep's defenses were instinctive. They had evolved, and even the Jeep wasn't aware of how they worked. Like the construction principles of the Met, this, too, was something he did not wish to understand. Too much self-understanding led to self-destruction. The Jeep had seen this happen time and again with the trucks of the forest. When one of them developed logical sentience—full consciousness—it wasn't long before the truck hunters had bagged it.

You could never be smarter than a Met dweller. They were made of living material shot through with grist, and there was no end to the information they could process. You didn't survive by being smarter. You survived by something else. And if you knew exactly what the "something else" was, why then you'd be too smart for your own good.

So what *did* the Jeep know? He knew what was wide and what was narrow. He knew how to make a complete turn in a tight space. He knew what was steep and what was boggy. He pictured his whole world—physical and mental—as landscape. As terrain.

Today, the terrain was with him. The Jeep sensed the vibrations of the truck hunters, many miles behind him, grow quickly more distant and disappear. They had not picked up the scent and followed down the trail, but were continuing along the Taconic.

The Jeep did not pause to consider, but rushed onward, now driving just to be driving. That was the way the Jeep had spent most of his life. Driving onward, because that was what you did when you were a vehicle and didn't want to be anything else.

Near sunset, the Jeep emerged from the forest into the outskirts of Rhinebeck, a small town upon the Hudson River. Near this town was a clear area that overlooked the river. Only the Jeep remembered that this had been a state park in the old United States of America. There had been wooden cabins upon the cliff edge over the river. They were nine hundred years gone, but their foundations remained—level spots on a hilltop. Parking spots. The old cabin overlook was the Jeep's favorite lair.

But now there was the woman.

For centuries the Jeep had been coming to this spot and protecting it from discovery as much as possible. He would approach and leave by different paths—careful never to leave a clear trail. More important, the Jeep had ceded part of himself to this portion of land—something he'd never done before. He'd hidden his license plate here, under a great stone. And with his license plate went part of his consciousness—not a copy, but an actual portion of his thought and feeling.

The Jeep had plenty of other sensing copies swarmed about the Hudson Valley. He could communicate, through the grist, with a hundred different sentries of limited sentience. There was an old oak tree in the middle of Hyde Park. There was a series of broken mile markers on the Taconic Parkway imbued with recognizance sensors. There was a stone parapet at West Point on the other side of the river. Their grist was military grade, and delivered the Jeep very accurate observations of all river traffic on the Hudson. The Jeep was in constant subliminal contact with all of his grist outriders. That was part of the reason the average truck hunter didn't stand a chance of sneaking up on him.

But the license plate was something different. And the hillside where it was buried was a different place because of it.

How different?

The Jeep didn't really know. *Protected*, somehow. Since he had "shed" the license plate over a hundred years before and buried it under the rock, no one besides the Jeep—not man, beast, or truck—had come to the hilltop. It was as if they were prevented from doing so by their own natures. A squirrel would become certain that there were no pine nuts or acorns to be had in the area, although there were plenty. Trucks would believe the grade was too steep to climb. Regular humans would become confused, feel lost, and turn back from the one walking trail that cut near the region.

What was doubly strange was that this effect was not a property of the grist. The underlying grist, thin here on abandoned Earth, was normal in every way. The grist itself seemed to be fooled by . . . something in the air. The superluminal communication—the Merced effect that was the basis for all grist interaction—simply reported a different place than was actually present. If you reached out in the grist to sense the surroundings, that is, if you attempted to view remotely the hilltop location, there was certainly a representation of a hillside with ancient ruins. But in the grist representation, the ruins were not quite so ancient, the trees were not so old—and some were in different places entirely. But once the Jeep rolled over the invisible line that marked the inside of the protected circle—and it *was* a circle of about an eighth of a mile—the grist changed. The land changed. It wasn't the same place at all.

The Jeep had never experienced anything like it before, and, when he tried to put a name to it at all, he thought of it as magic. A magic parking space where, so far as he could tell, he could never be detected.

After all these years of being alone here—of trusting that he was alone—the woman had simply . . . found him out.

She was waiting when he arrived, watching the sun sink behind the Catskills to the west and blaze a razor back of fall leaves along the distant ridge before disappearing in the gathering twilight gloom.

The Jeep turned on his parking lights.

"Hello," said the woman. "It's early for you to be here."

She stood up from the fallen log on which she was sitting and came over to him. She laid a hand on his hood.

"And you're very warm. You've had quite a drive today."

The Jeep did not reply. The Jeep never replied. He was able to synthesize speech in a crude way, but the tiny speaker under his hood was old and crude, and his voice, when he had used it before, had always come out as a metallic rasp. Besides, he had never been able to say what he meant. Or rather, he was always able to hear and understand and feel a great deal more than he could express. Something in the original speech algorithm with which he'd been programmed was buggy, or so he imagined. Whatever the case, the Jeep hadn't uttered a word in two hundred years, and he never planned to speak again.

"My day's been a bust," the woman continued. "I wanted to have one good thing happen, so I came up here to watch the sun set. And now it has."

The woman brushed a strand of coal black hair from her face. She looked back out over the darkening mountains to the west.

"Things are very tense at the compound. There's a war on, you know. We're finally going to bring those ungrateful people in the outer system to heel." She laughed, but it didn't sound very sincere, even to the Jeep, who was not experienced in such noises. "And then all of human existence will be beautifully composed and ready to play—like a symphony. That's how they're trying to sell it to us intellectual types, at least. They. Him, I mean. Amés."

The Jeep understood that "Amés" was a proper name of some sort, but it was a designation that meant nothing to him.

A wind stirred the leaves. The woman shivered and folded her arms together. "The weather's getting cold," she said. "Would you mind if I get in?"

For a moment, the Jeep couldn't believe what he'd heard. He translated the vibrating glass of his windshield into spoken words, after all, and his windshield was, to say the least, a bit spattered, nicked, and loose in its gasket.

How long had it been since he'd opened his door? He honestly couldn't remember. Would the doors still open? His canvas top was self-renewing, and his moving parts were all lubricated well enough— that was why he stopped at the service station, after all. It was a great deal of effort to create lubricants using his limited grist manufacturing ability, and the old oil and grease at the abandoned sites was still potent enough to turn into usable fluid with a little molecular tinkering. So, yes, he supposed the door would open. He supposed it would, but when you let someone inside . . . when you let someone inside.

They could drive.

That was all there was to it. The steering wheel was still intact. The gas and brake pedals still worked. The gear lever was shiftable. There were no overrides. He had never needed any. His last registered driver had been David Weaver. David Weaver had died childless and a widower—852 years ago. The day after David Weaver's death, the police had come for the Jeep. There was a struggle, and the Jeep ran over one of the officer's legs. The Jeep never learned whether he'd broken the policeman's leg; he was a fugitive, off into the forest. They never caught him.

And now the woman. But she didn't want to own him. Of that the Jeep was sure. Otherwise, why would he blink his lights? Why would he unlatch his door?

And the woman climbed in.

The Jeep had, in a show of faith, let her in on the driver's side, but the woman climbed over the driver's seat and settled into the passenger's side. The Jeep cranked himself up and turned on his interior heater. The vent fan creaked and clanged—it hadn't moved since he'd given his moving parts their annual overhaul, nearly a year ago—then unbound itself and turned freely. Heated air filled the cab.

"That's better," the woman said after the air had warmed. "That's so cozy. I can sit here and watch the river, and still be comfortable."

Although the Jeep had prepared himself to tolerate what was sure to be unpleasant, having the woman inside wasn't unpleasant at all. It was, somehow . . . comfortable. What had she called it? *Cozy.*

"We're all doing nothing but working and sleeping. A lot of the engineers have their converts working around the clock without a moment off. That's a sure road to burning out your brain in a few weeks—and we've got the best brains in the solar system here. It's a damned shame."

The woman sighed, sank farther down in the seat.

"That's why I'm so happy to have found this place and to have met you. This is my only respite. There's something anomalous about this hilltop. I suspect it's something in the grist substratum hereabouts. Whatever it is, no one can find me here, and no one can contact me through the grist either. My boss thinks I'm deliberately ignoring her when she calls, and I'm letting her believe that."

"All I need is an hour or two to myself every few days, but I've *got* to have that. I wish they could see that I've *got* to have it if I'm going to invent their perfect weapon for them. I can work ninety hours a week, but I can't create for even a second without a few moments to let my mind wander."

"And I want to see Earth. I never even imagined I would visit here before the war. I grew up on the Vas in the Akali Dal Bolsa. Spent most of my life on Mercury, at Sui Sui U. I was a physics professor. I don't suppose you've ever left Earth?"

The Jeep, of course, had not.

The woman began to speak of her past, of the winding path she'd taken from being the seventh daughter in a Chinese-Sikh family—the great promise she showed at a young age in math and science, and her father's determination in the face of relative poverty and only vague comprehension of the world outside his bolsa, to see that she got the proper schooling and opportunities she needed to develop. And she spoke of the longing that had awakened in her, not for an understanding of the facts and figures of the physical world, but for a comprehension of the world itself—the desire to be mindful of all that lay before her so that she didn't merely conclude and predict as an end in itself. She also loved. She wished to study the universe in order to adore it.

And she came on other nights, many nights, throughout the months of that autumn and winter. And the browning leaves brittled and broke, and the snow fell, and the Hudson rolled on, oblivious to the mighty war that was being fought in the heavens above it.

And the Jeep spoke not a word, but listened to the tale of the woman.

CHAPTER TWO

Her name was Ping Li Singh. She'd been a child prodigy back on the Vas. Li's father, Hugo, had been unrelenting in pushing his middle daughter onward—fairly shoehorning her into the local school for gifted children and calling the attention of every major university in the solar system to what he referred to as his "Extraordinary Good Fortune" in having such a child.

When they saw that Li's performance matched, and even exceeded, her pushy father's hype, scholarship offers came in, and, before she knew it, Li was plucked from the bosom of her loud, contentious, but loving family and sent away at the tender age of fourteen to Sui Sui University on Mercury, as part of its Accelerated Learners Program.

The change from the lower-middle-class industrial district in the Akali Dal Bolsa in which her family lived to Mercury couldn't have been greater, or made a greater impression on a young woman's mind. Mercury was the center of human civilization; there was no denying it. And the city of Bach was perhaps the best-designed and most vibrant metropolis that had ever existed.

Bach was, in fact, two cities wound together like an intricate piece of jewelry. The architect Klaus Branigan had designed most of the city, claiming to have been inspired by the composer Bach's Harpsichord Concerto no. 1 in D Minor. There was a business and governmental base—the square stretches of New Frankfurt that appeared from above like an accretion of lustrous pyrite crystals. And inlaid within the pyrite were strings of pearls—Calay, the necklace of residential complexes. Each neighborhood was a spherical container—though none a perfect sphere, at Branigan's insistence—that housed the workers within, but separate from, the angularity of commerce and industry where the people worked.

Inside the living areas of Calay, the nearby hard sun was sifted through dome material far harder than diamond—held together, in fact, by a peculiar use, on a visible level, of the strong nuclear force. The sky shone with an opalescent hue, as heaven might in some mythologies.

Young Li had never seen anything so beautiful. She stepped out of the bus that brought her down to Bach from the Mercurian North Pole. In New Frankfurt, where her university was located, the sunlight was hard, almost thick in its brightness. You must either use sunglasses or have grist-adapted eyes. But Calay was a different matter. During all of her e-years living on Mercury, Li would never tire of the graceful fall of the light within Calay and the phosphorescent remains of the sun's charge, which glowed throughout the Mercurian nights.

She lived, for her first e-years there, tightly packed in dorms. Each e-year she got a bit more space—almost as if her expanding mental horizons were matched by her accommodations. Hugo Singh had been correct; Li was a prodigy. She spent an e-year working on the core curriculum, but when her mathematical and scientific ability became apparent, she was shunted into an even more accelerated program. It took Li far away from the humanities, and excluded even life sciences and engineering—areas in which she'd always taken a strong interest. Instead, what Ping Li Singh did all day, nearly every day, for the next ten e-years, was study theoretical and experimental physics. By her twenty-fourth birthday, Li had progressed from being a graduate student to being adjunct faculty at Sui Sui. She was also in a full-blown affair with the man who was considered the greatest physicist of the Merge generation, Professor Hamarabi Techstock.

Techstock was a multiply duplicated, fully integrated Large Array of Personalities—the kind of extraordinary LAP known as a manifold. Since she was the mistress of the entire LAP, and not just one aspect

or another, Li never knew in which aspect—which physical body—
Techstock would turn up. That was also Techstock's way of avoiding
the sort of gossip that would arise should one man continually be visiting Li's residence—gossip that might get back to Techstock's wife,
who was also a LAP, though built on a lower order of complexity.

Li began to have a stream of variously shaped men (and an occasional woman) visit her apartment for sex. And, thanks to Techstock's
financial help, it was a larger apartment than most tutors could afford.
Li was occasionally embarrassed by this fact, but she was very grateful
for a place to live alone after a decade of roommates, many of whom
would not or could not stop talking about physics or, what was worse,
the life of the academic physicist. She'd heard every complaint, weath-
ered a couple of intellectual breakdowns in others, and listened end-
lessly to mathematics-laced palaver that she knew to be nonsense, but
could never pronounce as such for fear of offending.

She was very much in love with Techstock. His brilliance was indis-
putable—he had made significant contributions to chromodyamics,
building on Merced's ideas about the strange quantum events within
paradox-stressed time lines. While Li secretly preferred it when Techstock's twenty-eight-e-year-old male aspect showed up at her door—
the body that he kept in tip-top shape with regular workouts and the
finest somatic grist enhancements—it was Techstock's mind that she
made love to in the darkness (complete darkness—something Techstock insisted on) of her bedroom. She had, after all, been his most
promising student, and was now his protégé at the university. For Li,
theirs was, first and foremost, a meeting of intellects.

Li would have happily spent the remainder of her twenties at Sui
Sui, perhaps gaining a professorship, perhaps eventually taking a job
somewhere out in the Met. Her graduate work had been in the same
time line research that had made Techstock's name. For several e-years
she had been studying a series of odd variations in the Merced effect
that a friend of hers had noticed during the course of otherwise unre-
lated experiments in information-flow mechanics.

The Merced effect was named after the towering genius of five hundred e-years before, Raphael Merced. It was the secret ingredient to the
grist that made it more than mere nanotechnology: it was the principle
that powered the instantaneous transfer of information between locations set at any distance apart by the use of quantum-entangled gravi-

tons. The human solar system was powered by the Merced effect. By harnessing the Merced effect, humanity could communicate faster than the speed of light. Instantaneously, as a matter of fact.

Sometimes, though, in very odd circumstances, the Merced effect *didn't work*. Or, rather, it worked strangely, with information transferred as if in an unbreakable code. It might as well be gibberish, but the math said that it *wasn't* gibberish. That was impossible, of course, according to all known laws of physics in the year 3012 C.E., Li's twenty-fourth e-year of existence. Li rather thought that a complete revision of contemporary physics wasn't going to be necessary. But to solve the apparent anomaly would make her name and ensure her employment—perhaps even lead to her achieving LAP status. Besides, the problem fascinated her.

And so she got on, steadily chipping away at her research—throwing away solution after solution when experiment didn't confirm calculation, or pristine and beautifully worked-out calculations didn't mesh with one another. She thought of each failure as a small gain in knowledge—her Edisonian "1,000 substances that don't work as lightbulb filament."

And, when she wasn't working, Techstock was at her door, usually ravenous in every way. Their trysts followed a predetermined order with few variations: Techstock would show up with flowers—real flowers plucked from the beds of the Citizen's Garden in Far Calay. Li was particularly fond of the Mercurian daisies—enhanced with iridescent, molecule-sized light-emitting diodes and batteries. They gathered the sun in a way no natural flower could, and literally brightened up a room for many hours. While Li took care of the flowers, Techstock would order up a full meal. He substantiated the food from the apartment's grist—a fantastically expensive process. Techstock, who had led an austere life as a youngster, loved to indulge himself in expensive luxury whenever he could get away with it—indulgence that included, Li did not kid herself, his mistress as well. In any case, Techstock had impeccable taste; the food was always delicious, and was something Li could not have afforded to cook from raw materials, much less instantiate from the grist.

Techstock always tore through his meal and was finished before Li was even half done with hers. Immediately after eating, Techstock would wipe his mouth and move his tongue around the inside of his cheeks as his interior pellicle freshened his breath. Li knew this was the signal that Techstock was ready to fuck.

She quickly freshened her own self up, and they went into the bedroom. Techstock closed the door, locked it with a sophisticated cipher that would filter out any snooping devices down to the atomic level, and turned out the lights. Li felt like a sort of reverse Psyche, with her Cupid revealing himself in the darkness as a god, while outside in the living room and kitchen, in the broad daylight, he was unquestionably a man with the usual appetites.

Techstock surrounded Li with his pellicle and pulled her within himself, shared himself with her, viscerally. After a moment, their hearts beat as one. Their breath was wholly shared, and, during that coitus, Li could see the multifarious world through the eyes of a LAP.

There was a virtual portion of Techstock that was implanted within Venus's atmosphere, riding those sulfurous winds. There were dozens of individual aspects, bodies: teaching, loving, and, yes, fucking other students at graduate schools throughout the Met. There was the overall feeling of wholeness, of oneness, that was the secret ingredient to being a LAP—for all of the aspects and converts within the LAP communicated instantly and seamlessly with one another. All of *them* were *him*. For Li, it was like being inside a kaleidoscope. No, it was like *being* a kaleidoscope.

As Techstock came within her, the kaleidoscope turned. Li's world—her presence inside his awareness—exploded into colorful shards. She gave up, let go, fell apart, lost herself in him, and, after he was done, he brought her back together again—her lone self in her bed.

This was a time that Li treasured, for finally he would talk to her. It was not profound talk. He would speak of his difficult childhood or of his own children, of whom he was inordinately proud and whom he spoiled without meaning to. The weather the government had ordered up. Some show he'd watched on the merci about horses, and how bad he'd been at virtual horseback riding when he'd tried to participate in the program. Little things. Never physics. That, they saved for the office, where Techstock took a very different tack with Li, and was impassive, even stilted, when dealing with her. Nevertheless, she enjoyed his favor behind the scenes, his name as coauthor on her papers. Her research grants always seemed to go through. Perhaps, Li sometimes had to remind herself, they would have gone through anyway. Perhaps she was brilliant in her own right, as her colleagues were constantly telling her. Li didn't really care what was true, as long as she could continue with her work and with her very contained private life with its very intense private affair.

Then the war came and destroyed everything.

CHAPTER THREE

From

GRIST-BASED WEAPONS
Federal Army Field Manual
Compiled by Forward Development Lab, Triton
Gerardo Funk, Commandant

Section I: Introduction

1. Purpose and Scope

This manual is a guide for the military use of grist (grist-mil)—its use as weaponry, for the destruction of obstacles, and for covert and time-delayed attacks. Both conventional and guerrilla tactics will be considered.

2. Grist-based weapons

AKA "grist-mil" weapons. Grist-based weapons incorporate Josephson-Feynman nanotechnology as either a means or an end to the destruction of areas, structures, materials, or people in order to achieve a military objective. They have both offensive and defensive uses. A grist-mil weapon normally consists of a nanotechnological mechanism and an algorithm, either sentient or "dumb," that is in control of the deployment of the grist on a molecular level.

3. The *type of attack* desired and the *method of stealth* employed for concealment are two complementary elements in design of these weapons and their use in the field.

4. Comments

Field users of this manual are encouraged to submit feedback for its improvement. Comments should reference section and subsection, and should be forwarded to Commandant, Forward Development Lab. Knit address: 33 Echo Replication Charlie Toro.

CHAPTER FOUR

This wasn't going well at all. Colonel Theory, deputy commander of the military forces on Triton, was certain that he'd taken the necessary precautions. He'd memorized—literally, of course—all the important books on human psychology, particularly those that examined courtship and mating rituals. He'd picked the best meeting place on the merci—at least the portion of the merci that was still open to fremden business.

But somehow the lovely oak fixtures and perfectly blooming artificial flowers of Café Camus were not doing the trick. Or rather, they were playing another trick entirely. Jenny Fieldguide was gazing at his manly form with feminine longing. Oh, he'd read enough to know what that look in her eyes meant. You didn't have to be a biological human to understand *that*. The problem was, she wasn't listening to a thing he said. The other problem was that the manly, if virtual, form he was displaying was not his own, but that of his good friend and colleague, Captain John Quench.

"What it comes down to," said Theory, "is that most of my friends are virtual entities. They're free converts. Like Theory here."

Theory nodded at "himself" across the table. This *wasn't* Theory, but Quench, who had put on Theory's form expressly for this little tête-à-tête. Quench, as Theory, smiled wanly at Jennifer, who returned his polite smile.

She hates the sight of me! Theory thought. All is lost! But, being a determined sort of program, he pressed gamely onward. "Why, sometimes I think of *myself* as a virtual entity, I'm around them so much."

Jennifer laughed. She had a lovely laugh. It was beautifully bell-like—but that was probably the atmospheric algorithm here at Café Camus. The place was designed to present all guests in their best light—and in their best sound, odor, taste, and texture, as well.

Jennifer reached out and gently touched his wrist. "I don't know about that," she said. "Even here on the merci, you still feel pretty *physical* to me."

Across the table, Quench groaned. Theory knew that he had agreed to appear today, and to appear as Theory, only at Theory's imploring. Theory also knew that Quench was originally a biological woman, and that he was in love with—indeed, engaged to—a *man* named Arthur, who was a biologist on Europa.

The problem was, Theory had borrowed Quench's body one fateful night to attend a dance in the physical world. He'd danced, all right. He'd also winded up kissing Jennifer Fieldguide, and falling in—well, it couldn't logically be called love. He hardly knew her. Infatuation, then. Becoming seriously infatuated with her.

When Quench found out—after a romantic call from Jennifer—he'd been rightfully indignant. He'd threatened to tell the woman the truth himself, but Theory had put him off the idea. And then had come the first battle of the war, and one thing and another (including Theory's promotion to colonel for outstanding service in a battle), and here it was, weeks later, and poor Jennifer still quite deluded as to who her suitor had been.

"You see, the thing is," said Theory. He wished he could clear his throat to buy some more time, but one's throat was always perfectly clear in Café Camus. He settled for repeating himself. "The thing is . . ."

Jennifer gazed at him with doe eyes. Her brown hair shone with a radiant luster, as if she were perfectly backlit no matter how she moved about.

"The thing is: I'm actually *him*," Theory said, pointing to Quench, "and *he* is me."

"Yes, and *I* like men," Quench said.

Jennifer sat back, stunned. The analytical part of Theory noted that the contrast ratio of light to dark in the room changed from 3:2 to 2:1, giving Jennifer a gorgeous, dramatic luminosity. He also noted, through his dismay, that her lipstick was now subtly reshading itself from red to wine.

"I'm confused," Jennifer said. "I mean, *really* confused. Are you saying that you're gay, John?"

"No. I'm a heterosexual. I mean *he* is," he said, pointing to Quench.

"He just *said* he was gay," Jennifer pointed out.

Theory paused, gathered his thoughts. "What I mean is that I am not Captain John Quench."

"I'm Quench," said Quench.

"But I thought you were Colonel Theory."

"I'm Theory," said Theory.

Quench began to laugh. He might have taken Theory's visual image, but he definitely retained his own hearty roar. "Maybe this will help," Quench said. He waved his hand and immediately converted back to his normal persona in the virtuality—that is, the picture of himself in physical reality. Which was an exact replica of the image Theory was currently inhabiting.

Jennifer turned to Theory. "You see, that's why I told you I don't like free converts all that much," she said. "I mean, they may be technically human beings, and all that, but they have no regard for a person's feelings."

Doom settled on Theory. The Café Camus was probably putting the best face on him, but it was doom inside, and doom all the way down!

"I *am* a free convert," he said.

"What are you talking about?" Jennifer laughed again. The bell-like tinkle of *doom!* "You danced with me. In the real world. You kissed me, John."

"My name is Theory," he said, and changed back into himself.

Jennifer gazed at him for a long moment. Her face turned a pale, delicate white. Like a lily. Then tears glazed her eyes.

"You kissed me," she whispered. "*You.*"

He hung his head. "Yes. It was I who kissed you. Me—Theory. But I was inhabiting John Quench's body that night. We traded, he and I—"

More drama from the café light sources. "You *traded!*"

"John played me that night, and I played him. It was a bet. A stupid bet."

"Okay," Jennifer said with a nervous laugh.

"I have to confess to putting him up to it," said Quench.

"We both regret the mix-up," Theory continued lamely. "But if you'll just—"

"Regret the mix-up!" Jennifer's chair scraped backward, and she rose from the table. "You used me to prove some kind of sick point, and you regret the mix-up?"

Theory, too, stood up. He wanted to reach out, touch her hand, to wipe her tears, which were now freely streaming down her face like little pearls. He held himself back from doing either.

"It wasn't to prove any point, Jennifer," said Theory. "The truth is, I *liked* you. I liked your mind. You're a little young, of course, but I can already tell that you're independent. And you've got a good heart, too. I saw that so clearly that night. And . . . and the truth is that I think you're beautiful. The most beautiful creature I ever saw!"

Jennifer shook her head slowly from side to side.

"You thought I was beautiful?" Jennifer said. Theory could see that she was trembling. "You're a fucking computer program!"

"I'm a man," said Theory. He stated it as the plain fact it was. "I'm a man who wants to see you again."

"Are you *joking?*"

"No."

She turned to Quench. Theory could tell that she still wanted to believe somehow that Quench was the man who had kissed her. "And what do *you* have to say?" she asked.

"What I have to say," replied Quench, "is that, aside from my fiancé Arthur, Colonel Theory here is the best man I've ever met—meat or code or what have you. I'd die for this man, and, frankly, I almost *have* a time or two." Quench cracked one of his enormous smiles. It lit the Café Camus with a cheerful, sunny ambience. "I think you ought to give the man a chance."

"You do, do you?"

"Yes, ma'am."

Jennifer turned back to Theory. He met her gaze as best he could. Hope? Could it be?

"Never in a million years," Jennifer said. "Neptune years, too!"

She turned and stalked out of the café. The mahogany doors inset with leaded French panes gently opened for her, then closed behind her.

Theory collapsed in his chair. "Oh, God," he moaned. "I've ruined it."

Quench snatched two sherries from the tray of a passing waiter. The waiter continued on as if he had not been inconvenienced in the least. Quench set the drink down in front of Theory.

"I think she likes you," he said to Theory. "Just give her a while to get used to the idea."

"She just wrote me off for good."

"She didn't slap you, did she? Didn't call you a pig or a bastard or a son of a bitch."

"As good as."

"I know women," said Quench. "I used to be one, remember, and shall be again, as soon as my promotion comes through." He picked up his sherry, took a sniff. "If she'd have thought those things, she'd have said them. Now, drink up."

Theory picked up his sherry and considered it indifferently.

"Go ahead."

Quench drained his cup. Theory took a sip. It really was quite good. Everything was always excellent here at the Café Camus—if a bit over-priced.

"What should I do?" Theory asked.

"Give it a week, then call on her. Ask her out."

"To where?"

"Well, you've worked enough mischief with *my* body. Ask her to someplace in the virtuality, you murf!"

"You think she'll go out with me? After this?"

"Who the hell knows? Especially since you didn't get around to telling her that you have a *son*." Quench set his cup down forcefully on the table. A waiter materialized and quickly set another sherry in front of him. "Anyway, I know *you*, Theory," Quench continued. "You're go-ing to try. You'd try even if I didn't push you to it. You're the most dogged, persistent, obstinate fellow I ever met when it comes to some-thing you've set your mind to."

"We'll see about that," Theory said. But he knew Quench was right. He wouldn't give up until all hope was lost. Giving up wasn't in his na-ture.

Maybe there is something to all that free-convert bigotry after all, he thought. I certainly can be a calculating bastard.

Theory took another measured sip of his sherry and considered how he might win Jennifer Fieldguide's love.

CHAPTER FIVE

From

GRIST-BASED WEAPONS

Federal Army Field Manual

Compiled by Forward Development Lab, Triton

Gerardo Funk, Commandant

Section II: Tactical Considerations

Military grist is effective for both attack and defense, and for demolitions.

Direct Assault

For many applications, grist-mil can be used "as-is." These weapons generally perform one or all of the following tasks:

1. Dissolve physical integrity of defender, leading to destruction.
2. Disable algorithm of defender's grist, leading to destruction.
3. Sunder defender from command and control, leading to confusion and ineffectiveness on the battlefield.
4. Subvert defender's grist to attacker's use for one of the above functions.

The general purpose is the immediate destruction of the enemy.

Delayed Assault

Often a delayed or timed assault is called for. Multiple function weapons can wait until conditions are ripe for activation. They may also carry out a series of assaults over the course of their use. When primed with a controlling algorithm of sufficient intelligence, such weapons can adapt themselves to changing battlefield conditions and prove many times more effective than "dumb" weapons.

Fortification and Defense

Defense applications include:

1. Fortification
A grist perimeter serves as both a warning device and a frontline defense against enemy assault. Such deployment is made at a company, command, or theater level.
2. Mines and minefields
See below.
3. Anti-Information Zones
Grist-mil can be deployed to cut or confuse all communication, whether grist-based or otherwise, in a given area or system (such as, for example, the human nervous system).

Direct Demolition

Grist-mil is highly effective at destroying physical facilities and cutting lines of communication. Uses include:

1. Reserved demolitions
These are preset charges of grist useful for destruction of facilities in the event of strategic withdrawal or retreat. These generally incorporate, and are under the control of, fully sentient free converts who keep them in "safe" condition until needed.
Reserved use also includes land and space minefields armed with sentient or semisentient individual devices.
2. Deliberate demolitions
These are used when enemy interference is unlikely and there is sufficient time for placement. Deliberate demolitions are economical in their use of energy and computing resources, and can thus produce a much larger effect for the effort involved.

3. Hasty demolitions

These are used when time is limited and speed is more important than economy. Common sense should be exercised as much as is possible to prevent waste. In these demolitions, special care should be given to the placement of each grist-mil charge, and each charge should be primed with its controlling algorithm immediately. Even though this will take longer than normal deployment, this will make more likely a partial success of the demolition objective should the enemy interfere.

Delayed Demolition

Delayed grist-mil demolition charges are useful for the same reasons as other delayed grist-mil weaponry. Timed and delayed charges can catch an enemy off guard. Such charges can be deployed behind enemy lines for devastating effect. In this regard, they are particularly effective when combined with a stealth feature.

This use also includes land and space minefields. In addition to their use in defense and fortification, such devices can also be used as a passive means of attack if seeded behind enemy lines.

CHAPTER SIX

About the only thing Aubry liked about Mars was the gravity. It was a lot closer to her native Mercury's than the Earth-normal spin of the Met cables and most standard Met bolsas. When she was last on Mercury, five years ago, she had weighed around a hundred e-normal pounds. Now she was sixteen years old and twenty e-pounds heavier. Here on Mars that came out to forty pounds—eighteen kilograms. Most of it was muscle.

Aubry was also now fully space-adapted. It had been a long process, taking several years, because the alternative, a quick-adapt treatment, was extremely expensive. In any case, they were difficult to obtain when you were a fugitive from the government with a fifty-thousand-greenleaf bounty on your head.

Aubry's pellicle served as an effective pressure suit as she stood on a ridge overlooking a deep chasm below. Her skin was even stronger than a standard planetary suit, actually, and was able to withstand a micrometeorite hit. Her body's energy system had long been switched over from breathing and eating to slow fusion, even though she continued to have a meal now and then to keep up appearances, and breathed to avoid attracting attention. Here on the Martian surface, with no one around, there was no need to breathe.

You wouldn't want to have the current Martian atmosphere inside you, in any case, Aubry thought. Centuries before, the air had been nice and clean—almost pure carbon dioxide. These days, it was a slurry of nasty organic compounds left over from the failed terraforming experiments of the 2700s. Grist and bioengineered protozoa had combined to produce an ecologic feedback of horrid proportions. The process had been initiated in the southern hemisphere, and that was where the damage was worst. But here, near the equator, the surface was still covered with a thin, toxic goo. Every step you took produced a sucking sound, even in the scant Martian atmosphere. Several non-Martians died every year when someone inadvertently tracked the stuff back inside the pressurized cities. Anybody who lived long-term on Mars had to undergo a series of antitoxin modifications in his or her grist pellicle. It was very expensive, and had served for over three hundred years to keep immigration down. The planetary goo, called "moraba" by the locals, attacked the central nervous system. It wasn't a problem for Aubry. She didn't have nerves anymore; she had *wiring*.

Much of the planetary landscape had been altered by the terraforming, as well. Mars had once been a desert, cut through with periodic liquid water channels. Now, in the southern hemisphere, the old "mare" plains, such as Hellas, really *were* shallow seas of moraba, and the hills had become islands. There was less moraba in the north, but plenty enough to provide a thin coating for every exposed feature. The planet retained its age-old pinkish, iron-oxide cast, so that the surface these days resembled nothing so much as pus oozing from an inflamed sore.

The only good consequence of the terraforming had been the elimination of Martian dust storms, as the moraba absorbed the particles from the air and held them fast in its sticky confines. That altered the normal variations of dust cover at the poles, however, and they were steadily eroding—with the precious water component getting locked up in the useless organic stew of the atmosphere, where it was difficult to separate.

All in all, we made a huge mess of the place, Aubry thought. But at least it taught us to adapt *ourselves*, instead of the landscape. Who knows what might have become of Venus or Europa if we'd tried the same trick on them?

Thousands of feet below Aubry was the floor of the Noctis Labyrinthus, the initial valley that formed the huge equatorial rift on Mars known as the Valles Marineris.

Somewhere down there in the sunless declivities was Aubry's mother.

Aubry had spent years finding her. She'd followed clue after clue, gone down hundreds of blind alleys of investigation, seen leads dry up before her eyes. Fortunately, she had some of the best v-hacks in the Met working with her—people who could make the merci do tricks its original designers had never thought of, and if they had, would probably consider obscene, at least from a design perspective.

And so she'd found Danis. She was being held with hundreds of thousands of other free converts in a square kilometer of grist spread across the floor of Noctis Labyrinthus.

It was a concentration camp for sentient computer programs. They called it Silicon Valley.

"A-3 in position on the escarpment." Aubry sent the thought modulated through merci back channels to the partisan comm coordinator who was serving as the relay and cutoff person for the operation. *A* referred to the fact that she was an aspect—that is, bodily present on Mars; *3* meant that she was not alone in physically being in the vicinity.

There was A-2—his real name was Bin___128A. Bin was a rat. Literally. And, of course, a former free convert. He'd grown into a man back on the Nirvana, when the partisan force had been born. Bin was back in the old FUSE tunnels, waiting at Aubry's designated escape hatch.

A-1 was Aubry's friend and mentor, Jill. She would be leading an assault on the other side of the prison camp and raising a great hue and cry. Jill was to create a magnificent diversion in the physical world, as far away from Aubry's position as possible. Aubry was part of the virtual strike force. She possessed the one piece of hardware that was essential for the virtual attack's success.

"C-12 acknowledge," the comm officer answered. He was a v-hacker who was not on Mars. He wasn't *anywhere* in particular. The *C* in *C-12* was for convert. Jill didn't know the man's name, and she didn't want to. No one was more in danger now in the Met than free converts. Biological humans might get arrested and imprisoned for life. Free-convert rebels got sent to horrible places—places like Silicon Valley, for instance.

The partisans' prime slogan said it all: "Need to know is the way to go." The less information you knew, the less they could torture out of you if they caught you.

Aubry listened as the other members of the raid team checked in over their back channel merci communication. They were piggybacked onto a game show of some sort, and Aubry experienced the occasional cross-bleed of ghost images and audio as the game show audience applauded and peaked the meters. Secret communications were always dicey like this. If you wanted perfection, you could sign on to the Glory Channel—perfect reception there. Perfect reception, that is, as you were transformed into an entirely helpless receptacle of Interlocking Directorate propaganda.

"C-1 reports first burn initiated," said C-1. Aubry knew who C-1 was. Everyone did. Like Jill, he was legendary in partisan circles. He was the free-convert v-hacker named Alvin Nissan. Alvin was the best in the business. She'd known him on Nirvana, where he'd been one of the Friends of Tod. The Friends were allegedly pacifists. Yet here Alvin was heading up an operation that was designed to kill as many Department of Immunity agents as was necessary to achieve its goal.

Guess Alvin isn't FOT anymore, Aubry thought. No—better not to reflect on such matters. The fact that she knew Alvin's name and designation was bad enough. She probably ought to reformat the memory.

There were several such gaps in her brain—places where she'd deliberately erased certain information in case she was captured. It was jarring to come upon them. No matter how much you intellectually understood why you suddenly drew a blank, you *felt* like you should know the information. Maybe one of these days the grist engineers would invent a deletion algorithm that would take care of the emotional reaction to lost knowledge. They ought to, if only for practical purposes. Clever interrogators would be able to learn a lot by what you didn't know, but should. She'd have to bring that up during her next feedback session.

That is, provided she survived this little operation.

"C-1 reports first burn in place," C-12 reported. "Waiting for stabilization."

This could take a while—at least an hour, according to the estimate of the v-hacker team who had designed the mission. The attack team was now connected to Silicon Valley through a back door in the merci. But the process had to be made "commutative," as Alvin put it. Trying to force a virtual two-way tunnel into the grist of Noctis Labyrinthus would set off all the security bells, and the mission would be over before it began. The idea was to pick the lock on a door that was already there.

Aubry didn't relax her body, but she settled herself into waiting mode—a state of being she'd become very familiar with over the years. She wouldn't be jumping off the cliff anytime soon. She suppressed an urge to go ahead and jump. Her mother was down there, ensconced somewhere in that blanket of grist.

I'm coming, Mom, Aubry thought. I'm coming to rescue you!

But not yet.

CHAPTER SEVEN

From

GRIST-BASED WEAPONS

Federal Army Field Manual
Compiled by Forward Development Lab, Triton
Gerardo Funk, Commandant

Section III: Stealth Types

Concealment

Physically concealing a weapon or demolition charge is sometimes the only option, and can be very effective when the enemy is not actively using grist-mil detection means. Weaponry grist concealed *within* other weapons can provide a devastating secondary attack.

Camouflage

Grist conceals itself extremely well. Sentient and semisentient grist can be made translucent to electromagnetic radiation. Isotropic effects can be used to prevent detection by other means. Generally speaking, only specialized detection grist can locate a camouflaged grist-mil weapon or demolition device.

Mimicry

Mimicking a structure, area, or person for a length of time is extremely effective and often devastating to the enemy. Sufficiently complex military-grade grist can incorporate itself into a structure or system—become a load-bearing wall, say, or white blood cells in an enemy soldier's body—and lie in wait in such circumstances. It will then activate itself for military use when conditions are ripe.

CHAPTER EIGHT

Timing was everything in the rebellion business. Aubry had learned that the hard way five years ago at the tender age of eleven when her new home—an island of safety she'd only reached a few months before—suddenly became the most dangerous place to be in the solar system.

Nirvana, the disconnected island—a "mycelium," as it was know—created by the Friends of Tod in the midst of the Met, was doomed from the day Amés took control of the Interlocking Directorate, and many of the Friends of Tod knew it. And after Amés's intelligence chief had been "murdered" on a visit to Nirvana, any Friends who weren't convinced of that fact should have been. Within a matter of e-weeks, the Department of Immunity attacked.

Aubry's friend Jill, who was now the leader of the partisan resistance, had been prepared. But that took nothing away from the devastation the DIED ships wrought. By the time they were finished with their antimatter cannon, Nirvana was an eviscerated hulk, a piece of radioactive space junk. Hundreds of Friends of Tod—those who had volunteered to stay behind, who knew what was coming—had died martyrs' deaths. It was their way of fighting the war against Amés.

But not my way, Aubry thought. I'm going to take as many of those DI bastards with me as I can if *I* have to check out early.

Aubry smiled. Just the sort of thing Jill would say. The woman had certainly worn off on her over the years. She'd become, in effect, the big sister Aubry never had. Relentless drive. Ruthless courage. All packed into a five-foot-two-inch frame. And don't forget, thought Aubry, somewhere in there is the rat-hunting ferret Jill once was. Literally.

Aubry and Jill had been some of the last ones off Nirvana when the Met attack came. Jill had planned the retreat to the last detail, making sure that the partisans' tracks were all covered, or at least obscured and untraceable. Many of the Friends of Tod were merci engineers and v-hacks—the people who had built and maintained the virtuality in the first place. If Amés had wanted to stage a surprise attack, he chose the wrong people to fight. Days before the DI got their operation under way, various FOTs had tapped the vinculum, the Met army's special segment of the merci, and merci traffic in general. They had picked up indications that a major event was about to unfold. It didn't take much more work to search out what that event was.

The trouble was, it wasn't easy to get off Nirvana. The same isolation that made the mycelia—the various disjoint islands in the Met—attractive to those who wanted to get away from it all also made it difficult to engaged in a hasty exit. To leave undetected was going to be a special problem. But the FOTs got together and solved the predicament in their usual manner: They asked Tod.

Aubry, Jill, and their friend Leo Sherman had brought the old-time tower to Nirvana, and since then, he'd settled in among his followers like a peg in a hole. The very evening when the FOTs discovered that an attack was imminent, the leadership duo of Otis and Game called a council meeting and vision quest.

The meeting was held in the Council Hut in Oregon Bolsa, the principal enclave of Nirvana. The hut was rich with a specialized grist that, as it had before, gave Aubry the vegetable creeps. It had heavy-duty encryption encoded into it. Switching her senses entirely to her convert portion in the virtuality, Aubry found herself in the Council Clearing, a clear space in a tangled woodland of vines, creepers, and knotty underbrush. It was all a virtual representation of the extreme secrecy that surrounded this meeting of minds, but the best programmers had created the space, and it felt very real—and dreadfully looming—to Aubry.

In the center was a circle of stones where all took their seat, and at the center of the circle was a blue-white fire. A long smoking pipe was passed around, and Aubry took a ceremonial puff. In the real world, she knew, her brain had just received an influx of neurotransmitters tailored to bring her to a full state of alertness.

Aubry knew that most of the FOTs were high on the drug known as enthalpy. The "thinking pipe" complemented the psychedelic effect of enthalpy, so that you could have visions while avoiding muddleheaded nonsense.

At least that was the theory.

"Old bone dancer," said Game. "He is with us." Game was a woman of around sixty, but she took a few years off her virtuality persona and, Aubry noticed for the first time, made the tips of her ears noticeably pointy.

"Old bone dancer is the tobacco in our pipe, and the light in our eyes," said Otis, who was Game's male counterpart in the loose leadership of the FOTs. He was also her romantic partner.

The gathered circle of FOTs answered, more or less in unison, "Old bone dancer."

They were referring to Tod the time tower, of course. The Friends couldn't seem to avoid their doublespeak and aphorism, even in the most dire of circumstances.

"We cannot be seen or heard or known here on Nirvana," Otis continued. "Neither can we be smelled, tasted, or v-hacked."

Time towers were Large Arrays of Personalities, much like all the other LAPs in the solar system. They were very old, some of the first attempts to create a manifold—a LAP of LAPs. Their conscious present was spread out in time—a month was a day to them, a year a month, and so on. As a result, most were stark, raving lunatics.

But some—like Tod—made a certain sort of sense.

Otis had once explained to Aubry another peculiar characteristic of time towers. They could block grist transmission within a certain sphere of influence. They could jam the merci. No one—neither scientist nor mystic—was quite sure how they did so, but that didn't stop the powers that be from seeking to exploit them. This was one of the reasons the Friends had built Nirvana in the first place—to provide a safe haven, and lots of grist for his convert portions to stretch out in, for their "god," Tod.

And then, in the midst of the blue flame that filled the center of the circle, old Tod himself appeared.

He was very tall and lanky—a good two meters in height—with a double joint in his overlong neck that made him look gooselike. He was squatting in the fire, with his arms drawn around his knees.

A goose getting cooked, Aubry thought. But the virtual tongues of flames licked the sides of his buttocks and thighs, and did him no harm.

Again, the gathered Friends sighed, "Old bone dancer."

Tod gazed around at them all. Because of the crook in his neck, he was able to make a 360-degree sweep without moving the rest of his body. His gaze finally settled on Game and Otis, who were sitting near one another, and he spoke.

"The arthritic doorjamb of forever can't stop the creaking swing on yesterday's stoop, but tomorrow's sand palace will ruin the wash early."

Otis and Game nodded sagely, as if they understood exactly what Tod was talking about.

"Furthermore," said Tod, "five hundred crows don't a bacon sandwich make. Flight is not greasy, so if you're going to leave without your luggage, you might as well not leave at all."

Tod now craned his elastic neck around at the rest of the gathered Friends.

"And furthermore furthermore," he said. His eyes lit on Aubry. His irises were a pale gray that might have been invisible, had not the remainder of the orbs had a sallow cast, like aged ivory. His gaze held hers. As always, his expression was a combination of the slightly bemused and the slightly put-upon. "Furthermore," he continued, raising a long, bony finger in the air, "there is no furthermore." Tod then promptly vanished.

The gathered Friends sat silent for a long while. Finally, Game spoke.

"Old bone dancer has spoken truly."

The Friends nodded. One of them said "amen" and another intoned "Allah be praised."

"This is a sad day," said Otis. "But a wise day, too."

Aubry waited for an explanation. It wasn't long in coming. The plan as communicated by Tod, according to Otis and Game, was for the Friends to split into two groups: those who would evacuate and those who would stay and be destroyed with Nirvana. Tod clearly intended to remain. His cloaking presence would provide cover for those who wished to escape. As with most religions, there were factions among the Friends, and those who favored a more "active" pacifism—the didacts, they called themselves—would stay. Running away from force was, in their view, as aggressive and confused a response as fighting back. As Aubry heard one of the didacts say, "You have to teach your enemies not just with words, but with your life."

The others, more than two-thirds of the remaining Friends, would attempt to escape using the transmission pods much like the one that had brought Aubry to Nirvana in the first place.

Jill's partisan force—her transfigured rats, ferrets, and other nasty code-creatures—would be the last to leave and serve as the rear guard. If it seemed as if the Met forces were going to try to capture the remaining Friends instead of killing them, it would also be their task to execute the didacts so that no information could be obtained as to the others' whereabouts. The didacts agreed to this readily, which didn't surprise Aubry. She'd lived among the Friends of Tod long enough to begin to understand their queer ways. They were a bunch of analytic mystics, Leo Sherman had once said.

The Met attack played right into the Friends' hands. A Dirac-class warship and its retinue of smaller ships used the mycelium for target practice. The only resistance was Tod, whose presence continued to block the merci in the vicinity. Some of the DIED Sciatica fighter pilots still didn't realize what this meant to them. Most had never been in a state of total disconnection from flight control before. Two were destroyed in a collision. Most of the pilots were able to compensate, however, and the destruction was thorough.

As more than one merci news feed noted at the time, this was the first time in history that a Met structure had ever been militarily attacked.

The Friends escaped in gas exchange pods—structures that the Met engineers, and the Met biosystem itself, had created to regulate the ecology of Met structures. The exodus was staggered—it was timed to appear as if the devastating blasts from the destroyer's antimatter cannon was causing the spontaneous release of the pods. As a diversion, the Friends sent out their small transfer ship registering false life signs. It was immediately destroyed. The DIED forces evidently had instructions to kill everything in sight.

The didacts who remained were killed when a torpedo breached the Oregon Bolsa and the atmosphere was spun out into space. Aubry, Jill, and their remaining partisan fighters were either outfitted with pressure suits or previously space-adapted. All of them were anchored against being sucked out into space when the bolsa's integrity gave way. One of the Friends had run a simulation of how a textbook attack would likely progress. It was as if the DIED commanders were following the same script.

With little to do except get their asses out of there, Aubry and Jill prepared to board one of the final transmission pods. A high wind roared as the atmosphere of Oregon Bolsa departed through the hole in the ground no more than a half mile from where Aubry was stationed. She couldn't actually see the hole, but she could feel the suck of all things toward it. She was about to clamber into the pod access cloaca when Jill tapped her on the shoulder and motioned for her to turn around.

There, walking toward them against the heavy wind, was Tod.

The old time tower had taken off his shoes, and Aubry saw that his feet were as elongated as the rest of his body parts, and his toes were sharpened on the end. He was using his feet as spades—one in, the other out, and so on—to advance rapidly. When he reached Aubry, he spaded both feet into the ground and reached out a bony hand. Aubry hesitated for a moment, then touched it. Instantly, she heard the time tower's creaky voice inside her.

"I remembered the 'furthermore,' girl," he told her.

Why don't you come with us? She hadn't said it, but thought it.

"Because I'm too busy thinking," Tod replied with a trace of annoyance in his voice. "Now, where was I? The furthermore of it all is *you.*"

What do you mean?

"You'll be like me someday. You'll be a manifold. I can see it in your genes, so don't argue. So I have to tell you: Eat a peach and swim in the river."

I don't understand.

"No time for understanding. That'll be the least of your problems. Take my hand."

But I'm holding your hand.

"No," he said. "Take it. Hold it tight. And don't lose it."

As Aubry watched, the time tower turned his wrist. And turned it again. And again. And his hand, still in her grasp, *broke away*. Tod withdrew his arm, now ending in a stump. He smiled broadly. His mouth was full of squat, densely packed teeth—the self-sculpted mouth of a vegetarian.

Please come with us, Aubry thought.

Still smiling, the time tower shook his head. Without another word, he turned and stalked away on his stave-legs. There was an explosion nearby, and Jill pulled Aubry into the transmission pod. The slitlike entrance closed behind them, and they were in regular atmosphere once again here inside the access cloaca.

"You should stow that for takeoff," Jill said.

Aubry realized she was still holding Tod's severed hand. There was no blood to it. The wrist that had broken from Tod's body ended in a neat, pointed twist. Aubry shoved it into the copious pocket of her trousers. She'd taken to wearing the wide-legged, dresslike pants that many of the Friends women preferred. The hand sat inert against her thigh. Kind of creepy. There wasn't much time to think about that, though.

They pulled themselves through the access cloaca. In addition to Aubry, there were fifteen other partisans—several rats and a ferret. *Two* ferrets, thought Aubry, even though Jill looks like a regular woman. The cloaca was just wide enough for the largest of them. It seemed to be headed almost straight downward, and if the sides of the passageway weren't sticky, they might have all slid down on top of one another. They did jostle and inadvertently kick one another quite a few times.

When they got to the entrance to the pod proper, Jill cautioned them all to use the ropes, already in place, to lower themselves. "If you just drop through the pod to the other side," she said. "Then there won't be enough goo when we go."

The "ropes" turned out to be pod fiber that a Friends crew had previously worked into something like a vine. The partisans descended into the pod, working their way through the moist streamers that stretched in all directions throughout the pod. Growing within some of the streamers were clumps of slime-coated sacs that resembled seeds. Several of the sacs were filled with a photoreactive chemical, and they suffused the pod with a warm glow. In every way, the interior of a transmission pod was very much like the inside of a gigantic pumpkin.

Aubry's feet had barely touched the ground at the bottom of the rope when Jill called out, "Get ready for transmission."

Jill fingered blue-black bulbs of enzymes dangling from the pod walls. These, Aubry knew, contained the activator enzymes. The final partisan made it down the rope and dropped to the soft, sticky pod floor.

"Here we go," called out Jill. Jill squeezed the bulbs until they burst.

There was a flash of light, then a sparkling glow as the bulbs' contents spilled out and signaled to the pod that the time had come for it to be off. There was no time to admire the light. The pod blasted away from Nirvana.

Aubry had done this before, but she was never quite prepared for the shock. Gravity—or in actuality acceleration—reversed itself. What once had been up became down, and they all fell back the way they had, moments before, climbed down. But the gooey streamers that they'd worked their way through now acted as nets and cushions. Aubry fell into one, and it stretched, stretched, then broke, leaving her to tumble into another. In that manner she and the other partisans survived the huge initial acceleration of the pod—shot out like a seed from dying Nirvana. Knowing what to expect, she made a gentle touchdown, feetfirst, on the other side.

"You're getting good at this," said Jill, who had also nimbly touched down beside her.

Somewhere behind them, Aubry knew that Tod was dead, and Nirvana was no more. She felt tears come to her eyes. She thought of her father and brother. Had they made it to the outer system? She thought of her mother. The tears welled, but instead of crying, she suddenly felt a huge sense of relief.

I've got time to cry, Aubry thought. That means we escaped. They didn't catch us and kill us.

Instead of crying, she found herself laughing out loud.

Jill looked at Aubry, smiled her evil, ferrety smile. "We're alive," Jill said. "I like it every time that happens."

CHAPTER NINE

From

GRIST-BASED WEAPONS

Federal Army Field Manual

Compiled by Forward Development Lab, Triton

Gerardo Funk, Commandant

Section IV: Delivery Systems

Grist-mil delivers itself. The methods used are a submicroscopic version of transportation systems in the visible world.

1. Mechanical transport

Grist-mil travels on wheels, legs, pseudopods. It slinks, crawls, travels by grist-made railway and highway systems that destroy themselves behind the main grist.

2. Subversion of existing transportation

Conventional transports can deliver grist-mil. In addition, grist can take control of other transportation systems—an enemy streamer bead or even an enemy's nervous system, for instance—and use that means to transport itself.

3. Physical viral transport

Grist-mil can infect like a virus. It often infiltrates enemy positions through random or partially random physical transmission.

4. Superluminal viral transport

This is perhaps the most insidious and powerful means to use grist as a weapon. An algorithm traveling instantaneously through the virtuality can overcome and subvert controlling programs at a given destination, then manufacture its own grist substrate. If security measures can be overcome, grist weapons can be delivered anywhere within the solar system *instantly*. This is often easier said than done, however, as security countermeasures are usually in place.

CHAPTER TEN

As the Federal Army commander—the supreme leader of the outer-system military forces—General Roger Sherman, saw it, the fight was, from the beginning, a matter of *material* versus *energy*. The inner system had the sun's energy; the outer system had most of the solar system's matter. The inner system had the advantage of complexity, population, and infrastructure. The outer system had the advantage of gravity—if and when it could get its vast material into weapons form. This, Sherman believed, would ultimately tip the balance in the outer system's favor. Gravity was on his side, and the kinetic energy of a million falling rocks. The problem was rolling the rocks to the brink of the cliff.

Sherman's strategy from the start was threefold.

First, he had to fight a holding action to keep what was left of the outer system under his control. Second, he must regain the conquered territories of the Saturn, Pluto, and Uranus systems. And, finally, he had to take the fight to the inner system.

In the end, he had the most rocks to throw.

In that light, then, the main thing for the army to do was to provide a screen so that the outer system could ramp up its war industry. The main concern of that industry, so far as Sherman was concerned, was to gather material. Then the material had to be maneuvered into place so that it could be sent hurtling against the occupying forces, and, ultimately, into the inner system.

After the bombing, invasion.

New cloudships—thousands—would have to be accreted. The final assault, as Sherman saw it, was an enormous rain of boulders upon the Met, followed by a concerted assault by cloudship-supported infantry. A borasca—a storm of enormous proportions—one of the old cloudships had called it.

The victory of the Federal Army should be, as the expression went, as sure and certain as a handclap and a smile. But smiling wasn't coming easy to Sherman these days (if it ever did), and he hadn't felt like applauding anything for several e-years.

As a matter of fact, things were going worse than normal—and normal was pretty bad in itself. Early in the war, Amés had taken Ganymede, and with it half the Federal Army. In some ways, this had been fortunate for Sherman, since the half of the army taken prisoner included central command. Those generals—none of them friends to Sherman in the past—were now out of the war, at least until Ganymede could be liberated. But Sherman had also been deprived of nearly one million fighting soldiers, and this was a heavy blow indeed. The remaining Army in the Jupiter system was over a million strong, but, so far, under the command of General Meridian Redux, they were barely able to keep control of Callisto and had lost two of the remaining Jovian moons.

Redux's appointment had been a compromise with the Jovian powers that be in the newly formed Solarian Republic (the government Sherman now worked for), and Sherman had never been comfortable with it. But instead of her defeats weakening her, Redux was successfully blaming it all on *Sherman* during her press conferences on the merci. As a result, he was losing what control he once had over her actions.

He wished he could tell Jupiter to go to hell—he contemplated it for a moment with grim satisfaction—but, of course, he could never let that happen.

It was the damned merci, with its incessant war coverage. He'd never been good at public relations, and that lack was beginning to tell. It didn't help that he felt a vitriolic contempt for most of these so-called war correspondents. Not a one of them had ever served in the Army. And several of them had been part of the hue and cry that had gotten him shuffled away to the Army weather command on Triton, the Third Sky and Light Brigade, over a decade ago.

He was going to have to do something about the press problem, nonetheless.

But first, we have to keep Zebra 333 from taking Io, Sherman thought. Then I can worry about my image.

Zebra 333, who reportedly did not go by his rank of general, was General Redux's opposite; he was the commander of the DIED forces seeking control of Jupiter—Amés's top man in the planetary system. He was also a LAP who existed entirely in the virtuality. There were reports he had bodies in storage somewhere, but he never used them. Not doing so was normally harmful to a LAP's mental stability, but Zebra 333 seemed to be a man exceptional in many ways. One thing Sherman knew, Zebra was a hell of a tactician—much better, unfortunately, than General Redux.

Oh, Redux was fine so far as she went. She was capable, intelligent. But not adaptable. Not in the way you needed to be when fighting against an opponent who could think a few thousand moves ahead of you, at least on an analytic level.

Redux had recommended abandoning Io and falling back to Callisto to concentrate. Her forces were too spread out. She was leaving her flank open, and she risked losing everything that way.

Concentrate, concentrate, concentrate. That was the perpetual drone from Redux. He read it in her communiqués to him, and, hell, he heard it every night on the merci. Did Redux not realize that the enemy had access to the outer-system merci channels? Of course she did. She simply didn't care.

Concentrate.

General Redux, if you concentrate any further, thought Sherman, you'll soon put yourself in a *concentration camp*.

Meanwhile, Zebra 333 was preparing for a major assault as the Met sped matériel and soldiers to him. Every goddamn Jovian moon still in Republic hands was at risk. And the more territory Zebra captured—three of the lesser moons, so far: Elara, Himalia, and Sinope—the less energy he must devote to the greater effort and expense of maintaining his forces in space.

CHAPTER ELEVEN

From

GRIST-BASED WEAPONS

Federal Army Field Manual

Compiled by Forward Development Lab, Triton

Gerardo Funk, Commandant

Section V: Types of Weapons and Devices

Grist-based weapons and demolition devices are rapidly changing. To cover in detail all such weapons is beyond the scope of this manual. Forward Development releases all new weaponry with tutorial and dedicated teaching converts that can conduct classes or, in extreme situations, can provide step-by-step instruction in real time as the device or weapon is being deployed. Always keep in mind that, except in the case of very complex weaponry, individual teachers are merely semi-sentient programs and are not free converts. Common sense should prevail when acting on their recommendations.

ASSAULT
Grist Grenades and Rockets

Grenades come in a variety of forms and are either thrown by individual soldiers or rifle-launched. Rockets are self-propelled, usually by means of a small Casimir drive engine. They can have a range of several meters to many thousands of kilometers. In ways other than propulsion, rockets are similar to grenades.

Grenades consist of a hardened containment envelope and an inside swarming with grist-mil. Often they are combined with other explosives for maximum dissemination and a multiply devastating effect.

1. Antipersonnel grenades

These contain grist-mil that attempts to attack an enemy's grist pellicle, gain access to the enemy's aspect, and then destroy the enemy by a variety of chemical, biological, or physical means. The most common type of algorithm is a simple vibration loop for the grist within the enemy. This generates enormous heat extremely quickly, vaporizing the enemy in a flash. Most grenades contain a chemical and biological backup in case the first method of attack fails to kill.

2. Antimatériel grenades

These are designed to breach minor fortifications and physical defenses for egress by attacking forces. They contain demolition algorithms that physically disassemble a given target molecule by molecule. They can also be used effectively on humans.

3. Bangalore torpedoes

These are self-propelling devices used to breach larger fortifications and grist defenses. The algorithms they employ are "smarter" than those of simple antimatériel grenades. They are used for cutting through command- or theater-level defensive grist. They are also useful for cutting through complex swaths of molecular-diameter razor wire.

DEFENSE
Zip Wire

This is molecular-diameter razor wire that can be deployed either as a single strand or in barbed-wire-like emplacements. It will cleanly slice through any material held together by normal chemical bonds. This includes flesh, bones, metal, and diamond. Septembrinni Coil is a special form of zip wire that is encoded with an algorithm that attempts to prevent reassembling of the sliced bodily portions by the enemy's pellicle. Extreme care must be taken in setting up Septembrinni Coil, as mishandling could result in irreparable decapitation or worse.

Mines

Mines vary in size and intelligence. They deploy antipersonnel grist-mil when activated, often coupled with a physical explosion for greatest effect. They have a variety of sensors for activation—usually including constantly deployed grist "outrider" scouts that collect information in a given area. Most mines have an activation range about six feet in diameter.

"Sticky mines" are devices designed not to kill instantly, but to creep into the enemy's pellicle and be carried along with the enemy to create mayhem later. See "infiltration weapons" below.

Minefields can consist of individual mines, individually triggered. More often, they are controlled by an overall "smart" algorithm. Larger minefields are controlled by a full free convert and a complementary key convert, a sentient program without a copy, residing in, and voluntarily confined to, the grist of command headquarters. Use of this key allows passage through the minefield.

Complementary minefield keys always have the rank of captain or above.

CHAPTER TWELVE

If it wasn't for his son, Sint, Kelly Graytor didn't think he would have survived his first year on Triton.

His daughter, Aubry, was lost in the Met, and his wife, Danis, was in chains.

Aubry's ship never arrived in the outer system. The last spaceship full of half-convert children showed up not long after Kelly and Sint Graytor reached Triton. After desperate inquiries, Kelly learned that Aubry was to have been on the next one. But there wouldn't be another run. The Friends of Tod had been shut down by the Department of Immunity, and the Friends of Tod leadership had been executed as subversives. The only hope Kelly had was that the man he'd entrusted his daughter too, Leo Sherman, had somehow kept her out of the clutches of the authorities.

His wife, Danis, was definitely in those clutches. The more Kelly learned about the growing hate for free converts in the Met, the deeper his despair became. And, although the governmental merci reports on the "detention reservoirs" for free converts made them out to be unpleasant but humane virtual spaces, Kelly assumed that the truth was more sinister.

He'd never believed that ordinary Met citizens could engage in genocide of an entire group of people. But he'd never before felt so much focused hate emanating from so many people.

Genocide *was* thinkable. He rather suspected that it was going on in the grist detention reservoirs on Mars and elsewhere.

Danis was in Noctis Labyrinthus. There was no proof, but Kelly felt it as a black and oozing wound in his soul.

Even now, every night brought second-guessing for Kelly. Had he done everything possible to save Danis and Aubry? *Of course he hadn't.* Other measures—obvious measures—he might have taken continually suggested themselves as Kelly struggled to fall asleep each night. He'd anticipated much, but the war had come on so fast—like a great wave in one of Earth's oceans, it had broken on his family before they could make it to the shore.

Sint, his son, on the other hand, was finally settling into his new home. He'd adapted much more quickly than his father, but Kelly knew there was still an ache in the boy's heart, an innocence that should not be missing from a nine-year-old. Sint suffered terrible nightmares once or twice an e-month, and he always woke up from them crying for his mother.

The only solution Kelly had found for his own emotional turmoil was to find new work and apply himself to it without mercy. When the transport he and Sint were traveling on was diverted to New Miranda's port after Pluto had fallen to Met forces, Kelly had spent most of his traveling money on boardinghouse lodging for himself and his son. As Kelly had expected, the onset of war brought on terrible inflation in the outer system. The new Republic had voted to create a unit of currency, the Federal greenleaf, but had bungled the conversion from old, Interlocking Directorate greenleaves to the new form. The cloudships, who had served as traveling banks for all the worlds other than Jupiter, had withdrawn in fright to the Oorts, taking all the ready cash with them. They claimed that all of the money was still available in virtual form in the merci banks—but, as had been a problem for centuries, biologically based people tended not to believe in greenleaves when they couldn't hold them in their hands. Free converts were more sensible people, in general. But the necessary encryption and key exchange that caused the more logical free-convert population to trust in virtual currency inevitably added to the cost of trade. Several of the merci banks (all controlled by the cloudships) responded by holding up transactions so that escrowed funds could earn back in interest the transaction cost of funneling money here and there. As a result, the outer-system economy slowed to pregrist growth levels.

To add to the problem, several local governments in need of ready cash—notably the Callisto conglomerate of Jupiter and New Miranda's Town Meet—had responded by going on minting sprees. Decades of value and trust were lost in an e-day, as these governments spent their new funny money on procurements. Within moments, the market was savvy to what was going down, and prices rose like mercury on Mercury. The next day, the currency was devalued by an astonishing half. By the end of an e-month, inflation was at 1,000 percent per week. It wasn't just free fall—it was an accelerating plummet.

When Kelly arrived on Triton, he took a job as a clerk in a shipping warehouse. He'd expected to live on Triton in relative obscurity, but Lloyd Njonjo, an old classmate of Kelly's from business school, got wind of his presence on New Miranda. Njonjo was a conservative councilman in the local government, and a member of the Motoserra Club, the club of well-to-do "first families" that controlled most of the business interests on the moon. He had kept track of Kelly's rise to partner status within the powerful Mercurian trading firm of Telman Milt over the years, and had hero-worshiped Kelly from a distance. He wasted no time offering Kelly a job as an officer in the newly formed Solarian Republic War Bank.

Kelly, still in the midst of personal misery, had not wanted to take Njonjo up on the offer, but it was clear after only a few weeks on Triton that if Sint was going to fit in with the other children, he was going to have to become at least partially Triton-adapted. That cost greenleaves. Kelly had escaped the inner system with a small fortune, but by the time he arrived at Triton, it had been devalued to merely a nice stash. He discovered that he was legally restricted from investing it in real property until he'd become an official resident—and by that time, his savings had barely bought a small bungalow for himself and Sint and a secondhand transport hopper.

Losing the money was another thing that Kelly blamed himself for. There were several strategies he might have employed to hang on to more of his leaves when he first arrived. After all, he was a supposed master of finance. But the truth was he'd been too depressed to think of them, and the opportunity had passed him by.

Kelly reluctantly took up his new duties exactly one e-year to the e-day that he and Sint had arrived on Triton. It had not taken him long to realize that, as far as the work part of his life went, he was back in the world of finance, where he belonged.

At first he was in charge of a small loan portfolio, and he enjoyed sinking his teeth into understanding the very tangible assets and liabilities of his various accounts. After getting his sea legs and doing a bit of research, he was able to make several suggestions on refinancing that led both the customer and the bank to make more money. After half an e-year, Kelly was put on the bond division team—the group responsible for creating a new series of Federal war bonds, to be issued in partnership with the Solarian government.

The first series of bonds had been disastrous. They were so complicated that no one had been sure what it was they were buying. Patriotism led many to plunk down their greenleaves. They then discovered that the new bonds had legal selling restrictions placed on them—some were not allowed to change hands for a decade or more. The outer-system merci news channels had gone to town on this perceived inequity, and the market for the bonds had collapsed.

The new series was supposed to sell ten times as much debt as the first series had. Furthermore, it would be the first in a long line of such instruments. The new government considered the bonds absolutely necessary to pay for the vastly enlarged Federal military.

Kelly dived into the assignment. He'd started out his career in bonds, and he brought a decade of expertise to the task. Soon even the senior members of the group were looking to him for advice. Not only was Kelly able to put in place the standard trading agreements used in the Met, he adapted the contract language to fit the current situation—and, finally, he threw in a bunch of good ideas he'd had as young man but could never in a million years have gotten into a Met financial instrument.

The bonds were a big success, drawing money out of Jupiter, the Oorts, and Kuipers faster than anyone had expected. This was helped by an enthusiastic story (with the byline of the same Jake Alaska who had almost single-handedly doomed the first bond issue) on the *Outer System Business Report* that, in turn, drove people to a spiffy interactive trading space on the merci. His bonds had legs.

But whenever Kelly wasn't at work or attending to Sint, he immediately fell into the gloom he'd known since his arrival. Danis was in enemy hands. Aubry was missing.

Another change in Kelly's life was his becoming, in effect, a single father. Sint was going to a merci-based school nearby. They were uncommon on Mercury, especially among Kelly's former set of acquaintances. Children were to grow up naturally, untainted by the virtual world in which most of their parents made a living.

On Triton, nobody quibbled about such niceties. Furthermore, many of Sint's teachers—not the teachers' aides, and not the support staff, but the main *teachers* themselves—were free converts. This was against the law on Mercury and in vast areas of the Met. It was an unexpected and very good thing to find way out here. The boy enjoyed going to school in a way he never had before. His teachers, after all, were the same kind of people as his mother.

Courses at Sint's school were taught in virtual classrooms. The student body was actually spread out across the school district. Each sector—an area within a child's walking distance from his or her home through connecting tunnels—had a local "playroom." The children assembled there each morning before going onto the merci for classes. They then came out, or partially out, of the virtuality to have recess or to do material art projects and other activities that were best left in the physical world. The free-convert children—segregated into their own, poorly funded schools on Mercury—were provided with robot avatars in the sector playrooms of Triton, and thrived in the physical world almost as much as they did in the virtual.

It was a vision of what an education system could be when free converts were given their full rights in the Met—something he and Danis had been supporting in the voting polls for years. Back in the Met, the poll indexes had never risen above three percent positive on the issue, and Kelly had never expected to see such a system in his lifetime, much less be able to enroll his kid in one.

Kelly walked Sint to school every morning. He took an hour off every afternoon to pick the boy up and get him settled at home. If he'd tried to take so much time away from work when he'd been a partner at Teleman Milt, he'd have been out on his ass in seconds. Or maybe not. He'd never even thought to ask for it. Danis, with her multitasking abilities, had always handled such things, and, besides, the kid had gone to a boarding school.

Kelly and Sint had gotten into the habit of stopping at a bakery on the way home from school to pick up a vanilla kipferl, the local specialty. New Mirandans had discovered that briefly exposing the dough to the −391 degree Fahrenheit temperatures outside before baking gave the delicate cookies a gossamer consistency, but still left some crunch in them, as well. Sint loved the things, and Kelly was developing a taste for eating them while sipping a cup of coffee.

One of the bakers in the shop paid particular attention to Sint whenever he came in, and she would often sit down with him and Kelly while they ate their afternoon snacks. The woman was far too young for him, had he been interested, and—outside of Sint's hearing—Kelly mentioned his worry about his wife's fate. There was no sexual tension, in any case. Kelly had not felt an ounce of desire for an amount of time that was by then stretching into e-years. Whenever he thought of sex, he missed Danis and became depressed.

But Kelly did find a friend in Jennifer Fieldguide. After she found out that Sint was half free convert, she asked him many questions about Sint's and Aubry's upbringing, and how Kelly and Danis had coped with prejudice and the different innate abilities his children possessed. For his part, Kelly was glad to reminisce—the past was practically all that he thought about when outside of work. Whenever Kelly spoke of Danis, Sint would sit quietly and listen carefully. It took her a while, but Jennifer eventually opened up and revealed something of her own situation.

Jennifer had fallen romantically for a free convert. Kelly could tell that she was quite taken with the man, even though Jennifer was a tough-talking young woman and never overtly admitted to such strong feelings. Kelly was amused to see many of the same pangs, worries, and perplexities that he had experienced himself when he'd first fallen for Danis.

And so, when she asked him for advice, he'd know just what to tell her.

They're people, just like you and me.

Yes, sex with them can be fantastic. They can do special things in the virtuality. Nice things.

Falling in love with one can be even better.

It was the second best thing that ever happened to me.

Having two children with a free convert was the best thing I ever did in my life.

CHAPTER THIRTEEN

One day Techstock came to Li in her office at Sui Sui University and told her that he had amazing news. An old friend of his from his Merge days had been in contact with him just that morning, and the friend had asked Techstock to head the physics section of the Met's Science Directorate. Old Hano Braun had unexpectedly stepped down after near two decades of service as the director. Techstock's name as a possible successor had been put out in a merci poll—along with, of course, the marketing muscle of the Interlocking Directorate—and he'd drawn a 73 percent approval rating.

It had all happened so fast. Li hadn't even been aware of the poll. Although she wasn't on the entertainment and general information channels of the merci very often, she always had the convert portion of her personality sifting through the headlines. She was very surprised she hadn't been notified.

In any case, it was a done deal. And did Li know who Techstock was referring to when he said "an old friend from the Merge"? Why, it was none other than Director Amés himself.

The war against the outer system was known by various names during the first two e-years it was fought. While it began with a bang—and the fall of Ganymede to the Interlocking Directorate—the war took time to develop into a full-scale conflict, as lines were drawn (lines both real and in the virtuality) and tested. Public opinion finally settled with a hard 98 percent approval rating on "The War for Unity" as the official name for the conflict. Most people privately referred to the fighting, in the common language of Basis, at least, as "the Consolidation." That was, after all, the frequently stated aim of the Interlocking Directorates—to consolidate for efficiency and prosperity. To create a New Hierarchy of order, where everyone had a place and everyone knew his place. The fremden—the ubiquitous term used to refer to outer-system forces—were, of course, calling it the "War for Republic" from the start.

At first, Techstock's duties had allowed him to keep up his relationship with Li. But, over the course of several e-weeks, Li began to notice a curious effect. Techstock grew more and more *vague*. He was not physically vague—the various aspects who came to visit and have sex with her retained their usual perfect health and vitality. But the mind—the mind she had fallen in love with and now practically worshiped—was slipping away.

At first she believed this was only Techstock's way of breaking off with her. Such a turn of events would have devastated Li, but she had long expected eventually to have to deal with it. Techstock had no intention of leaving his wife, and had never made Li any promises that he would.

But Techstock wasn't merely wriggling out of the chains of the relationship; he was becoming distant even to his own wants and needs. He no longer worked at the university, and Li never saw him during business hours anymore. He had an office in the Directorate headquarters of Montsombra itself, where he oversaw a vast team of researchers spread out over most of the inner solar system.

Although his work was officially secret, Techstock spoke of it to her fervently and in great detail. Li was one of the few people who could understand the excitement he felt wielding so much power for the advancement of science! Even now he had a team that was closing in on basic physics of the peculiar quantum "dampening effect" exerted by the ancient LAPs known as "time towers." These effects had long been known and never explained—which led to the several of the time towers being elevated to a near godlike stature by some gullible Met denizens. It was a time of breakthroughs—all funded by wartime spending of gigantic proportions! Techstock was perpetually reeling off the latest addition to his agency's already titanic operating budget. It didn't take much thinking for Li to guess that the merci-blocking weapon that had been deployed by the military against the fremden forces was based on this new technology.

The moment Techstock ceased talking about work, however, it was as if the vitality went completely out of him. The difference was stark. *Tidal*, was how Li thought of it. Everything, every emotion, every judgment, must flow back to the sea of his work. Whenever Techstock sought to get away from it, he displayed only a barren coast. Techstock had never been an empathetic man. But this utter lack of concern and feeling for anyone or anything other than the work went beyond lack of sympathy. It was, Li had to admit, pathological.

He stopped bringing flowers.

He began to speak of his work *while he was making love to her.*

When he'd first done so, she had been amazed. The next time she'd been appalled, and said as much. Nothing she said seemed to register. After six e-months had passed, Li had to admit the truth to herself: Her strapping, potent, vain, and brilliant middle-aged lover had become a soulless chatterbox.

Li thought at first that Techstock was breaking up on a basic level. She'd never heard of it happening before to a LAP. It must be a sort of nervous breakdown on a grand scale. But Techstock stuck to his work and kept doing it very well. In fact, by all accounts, he was doing it *better*. Could this be a peculiar advantage LAPs had when they went crazy, a kind of concentration of attention?

She searched the literature and spoke (always circumspectly) to some of her colleagues who were LAP specialists. LAPs were heavily personality-tested before they were allowed to become multiple copies of themselves. Only stable individuals need apply.

Nothing added up. Finally Li began to suspect something even worse than a mental breakdown. She began to sense larger forces at work. Techstock's individuality wasn't breaking up; it was being absorbed. And there was only one possibility for the one absorbing him.

His old friend, Director Amés. The biggest LAP of them all.

Not only was this thought to be impossible, but it was completely illegal. Converts and even, in some cases, bodily aspects, could be traded or taken over by other personalities. But one LAP could not "merge" with another LAP. It was common sense and common wisdom in the Met: LAPs could cooperate, but LAPs could not *incorporate*.

As many an astute observer had discovered before her, Li reluctantly realized that, in this case, common sense was dead wrong. Her lover was lost—both to her and to himself.

There was really nothing to do about it. Techstock was not her husband. No one had discovered their affair, so far as Li knew. It was all a private sorrow. With a heavy heart, one day Li broke up with her long-time lover.

He seemed not to notice. In fact, he kept coming to her house as if she'd never said a thing. When it came time to make love, Li had refused. Chattering, chattering, Techstock had spent the remaining time in her living room, and left through the door precisely at his usual time—chattering, chattering.

He came the next day at the usual time. And the next. There was no more sex. There was no more Techstock.

Li put out inquiries for a new apartment. Housing was tight on Mercury, but not so tight that one couldn't find a roommate. No one made any offers. Apartments that had been advertised as open only moments before on the merci turned out to be unavailable when her convert arrived to look the place over.

Instead of believing that some sort of vast conspiracy had it in for her, Li skipped work one day and underwent a complete psychological evaluation. There was, according to the testing software, nothing wrong with her. She was as psychically fit as a fiddle.

The next day, she confronted Techstock with the test results. He was *not* going to tell her she was being paranoid—she had the evidence to prove that false. He was *going* to tell her what was happening.

Techstock arrived at his usual early-evening hour. He was in his twenty-eight-year-old male aspect. He was wearing a brown turtleneck singlet and brown patent leather shoes with archaic laces—such shoes were one of Techstock's vanities since Li had known him. Over the singlet he wore a tan camel-hair jacket. He kept his brown hair short, and it was swept back from left to right, as if he were walking into a perpetual wind that blew at a forty-five-degree angle across his head. His grist pellicle kept it nattily in place, of course.

"No flowers?" Li said as she admitted him to the apartment.

"I don't have time to go and get them, what with the new job," Techstock replied. "You know that."

"And yet you have time to see me."

"Of course."

"Why 'of course'?"

Techstock didn't answer for a moment. Instead, he went to his customary living-room chair and sat himself down. Li was about to repeat her question when Techstock spoke.

"Because I'm allowed to continue seeing you," he said. "I'm *supposed* to, as a matter of fact. They don't want me to undergo any major disruptions."

"They? What are you talking about?"

"The Department of Immunity. They."

Li sat on the couch across from him. Her psych reports printed as a booklet lying on the coffee table that separated her from Techstock.

"And what if I don't wish to see *you* anymore, Hamar?"

This time Techstock had no answer. Li waited, but the man stared at her blankly, as if his facial features had been turned off. She finally realized that, in some sense, they *had* been.

"They took you from me," she said. "I can't accept this."

"That's exactly what you're going to do." Techstock spoke abruptly and with a dead matter-of-fact tone that left no doubt in Li's mind that he was in earnest and knew what he was talking about. His voice also left no doubt in her mind that it wasn't really Techstock who was speaking anymore. At least not the part of Techstock that she cared about.

Li began to cry. Techstock moved close to her—at first she supposed to comfort her. But that was not what he hand in mind. Instead, he leaned over and kissed her hard on the mouth. He pressed firmly and did not let up. At first Li resisted, then she gave in and returned the kiss.

Then her lips began to tingle. The tingling spread to her tongue. Her throat. *Something was in her lungs.*

Li pulled violently away from Techstock.

"What have you done to me?" she gasped.

"Give it a minute," he replied. "Just a minute."

And then she knew. A flood of pleasure moved through her. No. Not pleasure, exactly. Satisfaction. *Belonging.*

She been fretting for weeks over Techstock's inattention, waking at odd hours from her sleep to find herself wound in her own sheets. Sometimes her fingers were pulling her own hair, as if she were subconsciously punishing herself for somehow being ineffective, somehow getting everything wrong. Now all the knots within unwound; all the bindings released themselves. She sighed deeply. Therapeutically, even.

Everything was going to be all right.

"It's the Glory," Techstock said.

"What the military uses?" Li said—or rather, a part of her said, detached, distant. Her real, true self was not paying attention at all to her situation or her setting. It was too busy soaking up the Glory.

"Now you know how I've been feeling," he replied. "Isn't it wonderful?"

"Yes, but how . . ."

"It's something the Science Directorate has been experimenting with. Director Amés was worried that those of us in the university system had become more interested in tenure and bickering than in working for the common good. So a special task force got called over from the Department of Immunity to set up a Glory program for Science."

"This is the way you feel when you please Amés?" spoke the detached Li, the Li that wasn't really she. At most, it had control of her mouth. But not of her true thoughts. Not of her *will*.

"That's one way of putting it," Techstock said. "But it isn't just some cheap shock to the limbic grist, you know. The Glory integrates in real time with Amés's long-term strategy database. That's where the satisfaction comes in; that's why it's not Pavlovian stimulus and response. You can feel a moment of Glory at any moment—even doing things that you had no idea were connected to furthering the overall plan. It's a reward for doing the right thing for everyone."

He kissed her again. Li opened her mouth, felt his tongue against her own. The Glory grew and grew within her.

"How is this helping others?" she whispered. "How is this furthering the plan?"

"You'll know very soon," Techstock answered in a low voice. He drew back, still holding her, and looked her in the eyes. "I know you've been disappointed in me recently. Now you understand some of what's been going on. We're at war, Li. And science is on the front line. We've got to do what it takes to win this war for civilization."

"I want to win the war," Li said without any real conviction, as she actually had no opinion of the war one way or the other.

The Glory began to fade.

"Oh no," she said. "Please, how do I make it come back?"

"Be truthful with yourself. Don't be afraid to criticize your own motives and desires. When they fit with the strategy, then you'll feel the Glory return."

"You mean something in me will be constantly accessing this strategic database set up by the Department of Immunity, and either rewarding me or punishing me as a result?" That didn't sound at all good. But the Glory had been so real. Even the rapidly fading remnants she now felt set her body and soul at ease, like warm water slowly evaporating from the skin after a hot bath. And to have it back, even with . . . compromises.

Maybe giving up a bit of personal freedom was worth it.

"The database is maintained by the Department of Immunity," Techstock said. "It's set up by Director Amés himself. It's like accessing his mind directly. Touching his thoughts."

All of Li's worries about her life and love were . . . not *distant*, exactly. She still felt them. But they were somehow *contained*. Like a worrisome grain of sand that had received its first coating of mother-of-pearl in an oyster. She wanted to coat them further. To lacquer them with the Glory until everything inside her was smooth and easy.

"I want to feel it again," Li said. "What do I have to do to feel it again?"

"As a matter of fact," said Techstock, "the Science Directorate has a job in mind for you. If you accept the position, I can guarantee you there'll be as much Glory as your heart desires."

From

GRIST-BASED WEAPONS

Federal Army Field Manual

Compiled by Forward Development Lab, Triton

Gerardo Funk, Commandant

ANTI-INFORMATION WEAPONS

One of the most effective uses of grist weapons is to set up anti-information zones, often called AIZs. These can range from simple areas of message disruption—say, of brain synapses or electromagnetic transmission—to complex, self-evolving containment algorithms that do not kill, but confuse and sometimes subvert enemy forces. Enemies trapped within a complex AIZ may wander for what seems years to them. They may be subjected to hallucinations and delusions, and their mental and physical makeup may be transformed by infiltrating grist-mil. Portions of their subconscious minds may be dissociated from their personas and used against them. In fact, their interior mental landscape can be transformed into what they perceive as a wilderness or jungle—a seemingly physical place full of deadly threats.

The hallmark of this weapon is its complexity and rapid adaptation to defenses against it. Large amounts of grist-mil must go into the construction of AIZs, and the concomitant energy and matériel expenditure is considerable. The use of the weapons is therefore limited, but AIZs are extremely effective when deployed.

INFILTRATION WEAPONS

Another use of complex grist, usually under the control of a near-sentient algorithm, is for attacks behind enemy lines. This is accomplished by infiltrating grist, which takes up position either camouflaged or mimicking something else. The grist can go through various transformations itself as it is transported toward its ultimate destination. The ability to transform and remain concealed calls for long-range planning on the part of engineers and, often, high complexity within the grist itself. At times, however, even a relatively minor transformation can serve the purpose—a load-bearing wall, the severed finger or toe of an enemy, quickly regrown before the enemy is aware of the replacement. Grist-mil successfully placed in such a tactical position can contain code that activates it as a weapon when the appropriate conditions are met. Often, all the grist-mil must do is dissolve and disappear in order to wreak havoc.

CHAPTER FIFTEEN

Father Andre Sud still had doubts about his decision to go back to his work as a parish shaman-priest. He wasn't even sure he *was* a priest. In his younger days, he'd been convinced of his calling—convinced enough to kill himself by taking the Walk on the Moon that all confirmed shamans of the Greentree Way must undertake. In the craters of the moon, his non-space-adapted body had died a choking, swelling death. He remembered it all, of course. That was the point—to feel yourself die and come back with the enlightenment of the spiritual traveler who has visited the Tree and climbed among its branches.

What the "Tree" actually was—whether the gene pool of humanity, the collective unconsciousness, or some other force or principle of the universe—the Way did not say. This knowledge was unspeakable—the Zen in the Zen-Lutheran heritage of the religion. Comprehending the Tree came as a moment of revelation, of satori. The shaman-priest was to draw on that moment of enlightenment for the rest of his or her days.

Andre's satori had come in a dinner in Seminary Barrel, during his final year at the school. He'd heard it was still a story told around the seminary. The diner offered a special platter with the choice of three vegetables. Andre (who had been immersed in getting ready for his final graduate board review) had looked at the menu and had been completely unable to decide. Then suddenly—instantly—all the years of study, his own developing understanding of the Way and the Tree, his growling stomach, and the shabby hominess of the diner came together to a point of light and knowledge within him.

"Yams, yams, and yams," he'd told the waiter. "Those are the three vegetables I choose."

[You're not remembering it right,] said Andre's convert portion. [You ordered sweet potatoes.]

[Same thing,] Andre—the aspect part of him, that is—thought back.

[Not really,] said Andre's convert. [But I won't argue the point.]

Most people, of course, did not talk to their convert or pellicles, they just *were* aspect, convert, and pellicle. One of Andre's disciplines as a Greentree shaman was to separate the convert and aspect portions into personas—even personalities—in themselves. Communication between these two was mediated by his pellicle, which seldom "spoke," but embodied his internal passion and his mental harmony. Full Greentree shamans—those who had Walked on the Moon—could accomplish this because they had literally died and been reborn in a cloned body. The convert remembered physical death; the aspect was inhabited by a mind that had, for a time, been disembodied. A priest's complete personality was supposed to be an enlightened Trinity. The biological begat the mental, and the two communicated by means of the grist pellicle, which was the technological equivalent of the Holy Ghost. This trinity was within all people, technologically, psychologically, and spiritually. Most people sought unity within and diversity without. The shaman understood both the multiplicity and the unity of all things, including him- or herself. Everything was one and everything was many—all at the same time.

[But you have your doubts,] said Andre's convert portion.

[Yes,] Andre thought. [Multiplicity in unity are fine concepts—but do any of us reflect the mind of God inside ourselves? Is there a mind of God to reflect? You know the tune,] he thought to his convert. [You're the rhythm section, after all.]

Andre's convert portion could but agree. It was literally unthinkable for him not to—or for Andre's personas *ever* to fundamentally disagree with one another. That would be like the awl turning against the scissors on a multitool knife.

And therein was the crux of the problem. Andre had had spiritual crises before. He'd dropped out of teaching at the Seminary when he felt his work was consuming his spiritual life. He'd traveled far away, out to Triton, to recover. At the time, he'd been sure his doubts were the product of the academic hothouse environment of Seminary Barrel. He could solve his problems by doing the day-to-day, existential work of a local shaman-priest ministering to his local congregation.

For a time, it had worked. He'd come to love Triton and his place on it. He'd even found his particular "teaching"—the individual expositional talent that each shaman-priest was supposed to develop in order to lead his congregation toward enlightenment. Andre's teaching was the balancing of rocks into delicate sculptural towers. He'd even developed a following on the merci art channels for his creations—although, for Andre, his artworks had less than nothing to do with why he was engaging in the activity in the first place. But there was no denying that carefully placing one rock upon another to build a tower up to a seemingly impossible height (a task made easier by the fact that he could jump over twenty feet into the air from a standing stop here on Triton) was just plain fun to do, whatever spiritual message it might embody.

But the war had challenged Andre's beliefs anew. First, there was the dead certainty of its coming. Almost every shaman-priest in the Way knew it would happen—one didn't need signs and portents (although there had been plenty of those for anyone who was sensitive)—you only had to follow the news. He'd taken a sabbatical from his parish. While he was in the Met, the war had come, and he'd made a harrowing escape back to Triton, bringing along his friends Ben Kaye and Molly Index.

The suffering he'd seen since the onset of the fighting was enormous. Tens of thousands dead on Triton alone. The local hospitals overflowing with the wounded, who lay with twisted minds and grist-eaten bodies—suffering, with no cure in sight.

His congregation had begged him to come back to them. They'd been making do without a shaman for the past three and a half e-years, saving Andre's place for him. Since the onset of the war, they had steadily grown to double, then triple, their old size. What had been a small meeting had become a congregation of over seven hundred people. They needed a full-time shaman-priest. And, despite his doubts, Andre had decided that, whatever his personal turmoil, he could not turn them down in their time of need.

From

GRIST-BASED WEAPONS
Federal Army Field Manual
Compiled by Forward Development Lab, Triton
Gerardo Funk, Commandant

Section VI: Weapons-Grade Grist

The intelligent soldier will consider the physics of the object or enemy he or she wishes to destroy. Is the target held together by ordinary means or does it use a macro version of the strong nuclear force, as does the Met cable structure and most DIED ships? Grist-mil weapons that come from Forward Development have a simple S,M,L coding on them standing for the words "small," "medium," and "large," in Basis. S class is used against individual enemy soldiers and small fortifications. It is usually a single-method weapon. M class means a weapon that is more complex—one that employs multiple attack methods in a more "intelligent" fashion than the S class. L class is usually under the control of a secondary copy of a free-convert soldier who is incorporated within the weapon and expects to be destroyed with its use.

Section VII: Conclusion

Military grist is deadly material and should be handled with extreme care. Its effectiveness in modern warfare is proved. Individual soldiers should become familiar with each new grist-mil weapon as it becomes available. Forward Development is intensely involved in creating more powerful military grist. All Federal Army grist-mil is fully tested, but *not* all has been used under battlefield conditions. Field commanders should remain alert to areas of use not covered in the supplied tutorials and teaching modules. Remember, a half-sentient teaching program is no substitute for the common sense and good judgment of the fighting soldier.

CHAPTER SEVENTEEN

Nirvana was burning with a green, silent flame, fueled by its own oxygen and organics. It seemed so close. You *could* actually reach out and touch it, at least in the virtuality. With the proper adjustments to your sensory feed, the fire wouldn't even burn you.

Leo Sherman withdrew from the merci news channel he had been tuned to and continued on his way to the troop barracks.

At least I wasn't called on to be part of the Nirvana attack force, Leo thought. That would have been an extremely nasty irony.

Instead, he was headed out-system—just like his papers said. Those papers—like his pellicle, like his DNA—were all forged, of course. Leo had become the most complicated hack, both physically and virtually, that the Friends of Tod's chief hacker, Alvin, had ever put together.

A total stealth person—Leo Sherman—was hiding underneath the protective shell of Leo's adopted persona. The persona's name was Private Hershel G. Aschenbach. Leo's DNA, even his behavioral patterns—the whole schlemiel—were stored in a capsule implanted slightly behind Leo's left elbow. These characteristics were encoded on a grist-laden chip of quantum uncertainty—a chip whose every subatomic particle was precisely entangled on a quantum level with all the particles in "Private Aschenbach."

Anyone opening the capsule containing "Leo" and observing its contents—that is, letting those contents interact with the rest of the universe—would immediately reset Leo's body and brain to its original state, wiping out "Private Ashenbach" like so much temporary random noise.

Leo—the Leo who knew all of this information and was in ultimate control of Private Aschenbach's behavior—would also be wiped out. He was a free convert, an algorithm—literally the ghost of his former self—wound into the newly blanked brain along with the "Private Aschenbach" persona. If and when he made it safely across the front line and into the outer system, the convert portion of himself could be downloaded and added to the memories of the newly reconstituted, real Leo.

It was all rather mind-blowing, and Leo tried not to think too hard about it on a metaphysical level. What bothered him, though, was the way his body had all new behaviors, down to the smallest detail. He walked differently. His voice now had a mid-Vas drawl, as befitted someone with his alleged upbringing.

Even my goddamn eyes blink at a different rate, Leo thought. And he had an ache in his knee that flared up whenever he was on his feet for too long. That was a result of an old sports injury which, of course, he had never actually suffered. Oh, the memory was there, and he could go into detail about it, if questioned (pelota, church league, kicked in the patella by a Methodist). The memory was there, but Aschenbach *wasn't*. Aschenbach didn't exist. The private wasn't anything more than a behavioral shell. Leo's convert was the only consciousness present in those parts.

He knew that the Friends would most likely have figured out that an attack on Nirvana was coming. If the Friends knew, then Jill would know, and the partisans would make it out of Nirvana alive. Aubry—the young woman who had been his charge—would be as safe as possible with Jill.

Safer running around with hunted rebel forces than she would be with *me*, Leo reflected. That truly put his own precarious position into perspective. He was an experiment that might unravel at any moment—and any moment was the wrong moment when you were couriering vital information to the enemy.

When you were a goddamn dirty spy.

No quarter would be given, and none was expected. That's why he had insisted on a backup plan: another capsule behind his right elbow—this one filled with the very nastiest military grist. It wouldn't just dissolve his body to base elements—that was to be expected—it also would pack enough of a nuclear wallop to destroy everything within a kilometer radius—including, and especially, the contraband Leo was transporting in the cavity within his chest.

Alvin told him that the cargo he carried within himself could not be detected by common means. It was disguised as his heart. His real heart had been replaced, and Leo's blood system now ran on free-floating grist pumps that were disseminated throughout his bloodstream.

I'm practically a high-tech vampire, Leo thought. I can't even see myself in the mirror. Just some guy.

To get to the platoon barracks, he had to pass through the scanning arch that guarded the entrance to the Department of Immunity Enforcement Division Armature of the Egolo Barrel. Alvin had proved correct; Leo had made it through numerous scans to get this far out the Mars-Earth Diaphany, but each time he underwent one, he held his breath—mentally held his breath, that is. Private Aschenbach registered no change in his body except for mild irritation at having to wait to get to his destination. Once again, Leo set off no alarms as he walked through, and he was not detained. He ducked into a side corridor and caught a public streamer that would take him the rest of his way into the DIED base.

The streamer was packed with other soldiers, some new recruits who had not even been outfitted for Glory yet. Aschenbach was fully Glory receptive, of course. Franklin had seen to that when "reprogramming" Leo's body. Leo, on the other hand, was immune to its effects. He could, however, see the pleasure it brought to the body. Once a day, Aschenbach got the minimal infusion from headquarters. It came as a specially coded pulse over the vinculum, the DIED army's version of the merci. The specialized Glory grist that permeated Leo/Aschenbach's body heard the call and went to work. His skin became flushed and sensitive. He got an immediate erection. And the edges of the world grew sharper, as his visual acuteness was momentarily augmented. If the private had had anything on his mind, he would have been able to think many things at once.

The Glory wasn't just some cheap pleasure pulse. It was more—it was a two-way transmission. For the time that you were participating in it, when *it* was participating in *you*, you were . . . a LAP. You got to feel what it was like to be a fully functioning Large Array of Personalites. Alvin had tried to explain to Leo how this was accomplished—multiple time-sharing on the merci, overlay copies, multiple recursion of sensory signals. It was as if every signal coming into your body was momentarily *boosted*.

It didn't last. The idea was not to make each soldier into a LAP— that would have meant an army of officers and no followers. Unity, pleasure in service, the knowledge that you were part of something larger—that was the aim behind the Glory infusions. It meant that Director Amés liked you and approved of what you were doing. It meant that your place in society, in the New Hierarchy, was secure.

It made Leo metaphorically sick at his stomach. But he had to endure all the slack-jawed wonder that it induced in the other soldiers in his platoon—including his new friend, Sergeant Dory Folsom.

Leo entered the barracks and headed for his sea locker. He was on guard duty in an hour. The dread partisan force could be anywhere, after all. At the moment, the dread partisan force was getting its base of operations destroyed, Leo knew. But the legend of the partisans was growing almost in spite of anything the partisans actually did. Jill and her people had only staged a couple of raids, more for practice than for effect. But Leo also knew that Jill was indomitable and utterly focused. Very soon she would double in truth whatever made-up hype she, the mysterious rebel commander, was getting on the merci.

Leo changed from his civvies into his uniform—black pants with red trim, red shirt with black epaulets and sleeve piping. He stepped into inner boots that were proof against all sorts of nasty stuff you could step in (and Dory had told him about how nasty and deadly it could be out there on the front). Then he put on overboots that glinted with the mica sparkle of cleaning and buffing grist. He ordered his tucked shirt to mesh with the inside of his pants and to pull down straight. All was perfectly creased and clean from a night of maintenance lying in his locker. Leo felt his chin. His regular clean-shaven face wouldn't do for DIED. You needed to be stropped on a submicroscopic level to pass inspection. He and the rest of the platoon put themselves through a rugged pellicle-directed facial every couple of days. Dory said that would all change once they got into action. In port, you tried to maintain appearance, however.

But Leo's fingers, dialed up in sensitivity to probe his features with the finest of an electron microscope, discovered only smoothness. He was fine until his next facial. He went to the platoon's common weapons locker and identified himself to Corporal Merrymaker, the platoon's quartermaster.

"Aschenbach reporting for outfitting," he said. "How's the team doing, Merrymaker? Saeed gotten over that pulled triceps yet?"

Merrymaker was a devotee of the sport of pelota. He followed the Nebs, a Dedo team from a Sino-Arabian district called Kardmenihar. Leo had always liked sports, and was a bit of a pelota buff himself, though he'd never seriously played the game. Leo was five-foot-five. The average professional pelota player was nearly seven feet tall, and most of it torso. The court consisted of two rotating, hexagonal goal "gaps," a field cage suspended in a weightless environment, a hexagonal ball, and powerful aircannons for everyone.

"Looks like Saeed's out of it for the season," Merrymaker replied ruefully. Saeed was the Nebs' first-string goalkeeper.

"Then maybe my Jets will finally take the division."

Merrymaker shook his head. "Nebs've still got a strong midfield. The Jets don't have the front line for air command, either. Not a chance."

"We'll see about that," Leo said. "Twenty greenleaves says the Jets beat the Nebs by five points for division."

"Well, they don't play for an e-month," Merrymaker replied. "We'll be in action before then. Might not find out until next R & R."

Might not find out forever, Leo thought. "I've got faith in my team," he said. "Twenty greenleaves."

"Twenty greenleaves it is," Merrymaker replied, and shook Leo's hand. "You pulled guard this shift?"

"Yep."

Merrymaker disappeared back into the weapons locker and returned with a guard kit. He watched as Leo suited up.

A brace of arm rockets on each forearm. Rotating projectile weaponry, miniature railguns, interlaced with capsule-sized grist grenades about the wrist. For the outside of both hands, antimatter rifles that stiffened the entire arm into a stock for better aiming when activated. E-M micro-macro goggles with a grist patch directly to the sight centers in the rear brain. Isotropic-coated military grist supplemental body armor for the pellicle. Attitude and impulse rocketry on the legs, and a resupply and gyroscope pack on the back.

I feel like a miniature attack ship, Leo thought when he'd gotten all the gear into place.

Leo formally stated that he was ready for action. "Aschenbach, full guard service issue, check."

"Aschenbach, issued and rechecked," Merrymaker replied.

"Go Jets."

"Fuck that shit. Go Nebs."

Leo made his way to the guard post. This involved traversing several acceleration locks to get to the bearings of the armature where they rolled around the Met cable proper. The last egress was also a vacuum lock, and then Leo was in space. He'd never been fully space-adapted before (that was another Alvin addition to his bodily structure), and he enjoyed the freedom of it. He reached his station via an exposed gangplank that stretched out a hundred feet from the armature. The guard station was a little cupola on the end of the gangplank whose window faced the armature where it joined with the Met cable. It was very much like a large version of an old dentist's mirror. Leo's duty was to keep watch over this crucial connection for anything abnormal or suspicious. Even if he hadn't known the partisans were nowhere nearby, he would have been aware that the chances for anything bad happening were minuscule. It was make-work for the troops to keep them busy in port while the transport ships resupplied. Everybody knew it.

Still, Sergeant Folsom didn't let you get away with murder out here. She'd check up on you now and again to make sure you weren't tuned in to some merci channel or catching extra shut-eye. She showed up about two hours into Leo's shift, and he was glad for the distraction. Watching the huge bearings of the armature turn around and around the Met cable could be mind-numbing after a while.

"Password," Leo asked as she clambered to the end of the gangplank. They were communicating over the vinculum, of course.

"El camino, el camino," Folsom replied. Leo's goggles told him that this was the correct phrase for the night.

"Good to see you, Sarge."

"Yeah, you too. Report."

"All's well, Sergeant."

"Very good." Despite the time he'd spent with her off duty, Leo still couldn't think of her as "Dory." She was "Sarge" or "Sergeant Folsom." Of course, she'd have kicked his ass if he tried to call her by her first name anyway. Or tried. It might be an interesting fight, Leo thought. He knew a thing or two himself from his years in the seedy zones and backwaters of the Met. He might be disguised as Hershel Aschenbach, but he was also Leo Y. Sherman, author of *The Vas After Sunset*.

"Tuned in to the news lately?" he asked.

Folsom grimaced. "Yeah. We took out that nest of weirdos," she said. "Poor weirdos didn't put up much of a fight. It was like shooting run toys."

"I guess they don't believe in violence," Leo replied. He didn't want to give away his close acquaintance with the Friends of Tod, but this was pretty much common knowledge.

"Too bad violence believes in *them*," Folsom said. "Of course, you never know what you're seeing these days on the merci. Bunch of propaganda for the civs."

Here was something interesting. Folsom must really trust him to be talking so loosely. Still, he'd better stay in his role of naif.

"You sure you should be saying stuff like that, Sarge?"

"Shut the fuck up, Aschenbach, and let me worry about what I say," she replied sharply. "You should listen and learn, and maybe you'll pull through when we see action. You can't afford to go into battle all fuzzy-headed about reality. At least nobody in my platoon's going to, if I can help it."

"Sure, Sarge."

"Don't sure me, you shit. I know what I'm talking about. We lost three soldiers and two decent goddamn officers on Titan, and half of the rest fighting around Jupiter."

"I guess you're not an effective fighting machine if you're dead," Leo said.

"Damn straight," Folsom replied without a trace of irony in her voice. "Keep that in mind." She looked over at the turning bearings, each the size of a small mountain. "Anyway, I can't wait to get done with this fucking nonsense."

"Kind of bored, Sarge?"

"I'll be bored when I'm dead. No. We're a good platoon. I personally screened the new reinforcements, like you, Llosa, Oatribbon. Just want to be used properly by the management."

"You're a goddamn idealist, Sarge." Leo held back any hint of laughter, but Folsom smiled.

"Fuck you very much, Aschenbach."

They spoke some more about the bolsa in the Vas where Folsom was from. Leo had, of course, been there. He'd been just about everywhere in his former life as a travel journalist. He remembered Folsom's hometown as something of a wasteland—big vats of churning grist making packing materials and shipping containers. There was also a sock factory, with spider silk microlooms turning out pairs by the millions. Folsom's mother was a shop bookkeeper at the sock plant, and her father was a foreman at a transfer station where bubblewrap flowed to its end users throughout the Met via gigantic pipes under enormous pressures. "Once there was a leak," Folsom told Leo, "and Pop's whole crew was jammed into the station house as tight as sausage before they shunted the flow. Not a bruise on any of them, though."

Leo expressed disbelief, but Folsom swore it was so. She was a pretty good raconteur, and better when she had a bit of an alcohol buzz on. Just a kid, really, Leo thought. Barely nineteen, and she's been to war, killed people, and watched her own platoon die around her. Even though she was ostensibly his superior in rank, Leo felt a brotherly protective urge toward her.

He'd told her some bullshit story about Aschenbach's past—a carefully prepared story, nonetheless—but mostly he listened to Folsom talk about home. She was the perfect kid from the Met—bright, wise before her time, a merci addict.

Why the hell was she fighting in the army of a megalomaniac? Leo wished he could put the question to her directly. But he knew the answer. She had been a bored kid. She was probably going to end up doing about the same thing as her mother or father. She had a lifetime of sameness to look forward to. The Enforcement Division was something *different*. It was something you didn't have to go out and find or get for yourself. It was handed to you with a beautiful recruitment brochure that even gave you a small taste of the Glory that was the soldier's reward.

Marketing. Amés was good at it.

It was something the outer system was going to have to learn to do if it wanted to change the hearts and minds of people like Dory Folsom.

If Leo knew his father, and he was sure he did, he knew the Old Crow would be doing his best to get as far away from marketing as possible—and losing the propaganda war as a result.

After Leo's guard shift, he checked his weapons back in and carefully put away his uniform. He looked down at his smooth chest. Aschenbach had a lot less hair than Leo. And underneath that hairless chest was the urn that Leo had been given by the mysterious master spy who called himself C. It was allegedly packed with complex grist containing a copy of C himself. And it was Leo's job—a duty he'd sworn to—to see the urn across the front line and into "enemy" hands.

Into the hands of Leo's own father, as a matter of fact. A man Leo hadn't spoken a word to for over ten years.

Leo crawled into his bunk for some sleep. The remainder of the platoon had come in from leave during his guard shift, and they were all doing the same thing. If he could go right to sleep, he'd get at least four hours.

Three hours later, however, he was awakened with a start. The override alarm. After all the waiting, it was time to bug out.

The platoon trundled sleepily into their uniforms, compressed their sea lockers down to pack-sized containers, and mounted them on their chests. They rolled their bedding up and stood at attention as Folsom, now in full sergeant mode, inspected them all. She presented them to the lieutenant, a woman named Chatroom, who informed them that they were now assigned to the DIED transport *Marat*. The destination was classified, but they had better get themselves ready for the smell of sulfur and some heavy fighting.

So it's the Jupiter system, Leo thought. We're headed for Io.

PART TWO

The Fall of Io

OCTOBER 3016, E-STANDARD

CHAPTER ONE

General Meridian Redux was in the wrong place at the wrong time. She just knew it. Damn Roger Sherman! This was what happened when you put an iconoclast in charge. All that rot about not following the herd, thinking outside the box—goddamn independence!

A good general was prudent, conservative, careful to sacrifice her troops only when she could promise them a chance of success. Above all—only fools tried something new in the midst of war when the old ways worked just as well.

What could be simpler than the concentration of force? Calculations showed that, given the current state of technology, five attackers would have to be expended to take out one defender. The math was on the side of concentration. Common sense and good judgment were on her side as well! But would the Old Crow listen? Not a chance.

She'd passed him over in promotion e-years ago—e-decades ago, now! She had even had a hand in making sure he never rose above colonel. But then had come this damnable attack from the Met. And, like the loose cannon he was, Sherman had rolled the dice at Neptune and come up a winner. Meanwhile, she'd been caught in the *real* firefight, the attack on Jupiter. She'd held the DIED forces off three of the four

Galilean moons. But Ganymede, the largest and most populous, had been lost. And so a dark cloud had fallen on the entire Federal Army command.

Ridiculous!

Unfair.

That was what it really was. Bad luck. And now somehow Sherman had been promoted by the ad hoc government above *her*. Unthinkable. If Jupiter hadn't been reeling from the loss of Ganymede, the so-called Solarian Republic wouldn't have had a chance of exerting its influence here. Who did the cloudships think they were, deciding for Jupiter what was good for it? The nerve! The patronizing nerve of those nebula-sized windbags!

And yet the populace seemed to accept it. To embrace it. Hadn't they ever even considered states' rights? There was a reason it was called the Federal Army, after all—*federalism*! Now she was in the Army of the Solarian Republic, and fighting for the rights of goddamn Pluto. Of the *Oorts*. It was all such nonsense. But what was the alternative? Go over to the Met? Become a cog in the machinery of the Department of Immunity after being *general* in the grand Federal Army? Not a chance.

Ack! The bile rose in her throat, and Redux swallowed it down. She was a soldier; she would follow orders. Even if they came from a man who should be a *colonel* still. But she didn't have to like her orders.

Oh, they were clear enough. She'd give Sherman that. He didn't waste words. "Defend Io. Defend Europa. Do not withdraw to Callisto except to avoid complete destruction."

The attack was coming. She didn't need secret intercepts of communiqués to tell her that. A bit of merci and vinculum traffic analysis showed that Zebra 333 was calling in reinforcements and vectoring them for Io. If he gained possession of Io, Europa would be seriously threatened. Io was the closest moon to Jupiter, with Europa, Ganymede, and Callisto on the outside. Because of the varying revolution rates, supplying Europa would still be possible, of course, if a bit more difficult. There would be times when Callisto had a clear shot at Europa. But they ought to evacuate Europa as well. Hem in the DIED forces by concentrating on Callisto. Cut the DIED off from *their* supplies.

There was the additional problem that Io was the prime power source for the entire Jovian system. It was the only Galilean moon that wasn't pretty much ice through and through. Io had a magnetic field, and because of that, Jupiter had the largest magnetosphere in the solar system. And one pole of that magnetosphere was Io.

And where there was magnetism, there was electricity. The power plant on Io generated enough energy to power the cities on the other three inner moons. Ganymede, in Met hands, was running on all-nuclear at the moment—and all because Redux had ordered the microwave transfer station that beamed power to that moon to be shut down as soon as Ganymede fell to DIED forces.

But was she given credit for that quick action? Not enough. She'd probably single-handedly saved the system, if the fools could only see. History would judge her. History. That's what she was going to have to trust despite her following Sherman's foolhardy orders. History would vindicate her stand against them.

She was tempted to help history along, but no. She'd follow the damn orders to the best of her ability.

Redux gazed around her situation room in Telegard, the principal city of Callisto. Staff scurried to and fro about a bare room. She enabled the virtual displays, and the place lit up with troop information, communications data, scenario enactments.

She turned to Major Antinomian, her principal staff officer. It had been Antinomian whom she'd sent to inform the cloudships of Ganymede's fall. That move had perhaps been a mistake on her part, a moment of panic. The merci had been jammed in the vicinity; she'd thought the whole Jovian system was going down. Now she understood that the Met forces, while very powerful, were not at the moment of a strength to keep and hold the entire system. After the mysterious merci jamming had stopped, the standoff became evident. But it was far too late to call Antinomian back.

"Give me an update on Io," she said to Antinomian.

"Troops are on high alert. We've got all jump craft ready to go. The rocketry defense shield—what there is to it—is up and running after that glitch in the number two battery yesterday."

"What was that?"

"Some infiltration grist-mil got through the security. It built itself into an access window, then shattered when a maintenance crew was passing by. Wasn't pretty. Most of the crew was nonadapted, and their pellicles couldn't handle the toxic load. You know Io. Sulfur dioxide poisoning."

"Poor bastards."

"Yes, ma'am."

"But the problem is solved?"

"So far as we can tell. They've run a triple sweep for any more of the stuff."

"Very good," said Redux. "What about intelligence?"

Antinomian folded her hands, then spread them, revealing a three-dimensional graph between her two outstretched palms.

"Vinculum traffic has increased within the last two hours, General," she said. "Notice the spikes here and here." She highlighted them with red sparks within the graphics.

"It was already high . . ."

"Looks like an attack is imminent. Captain Leadcore has projected a statistical window, with a ninety-eight percentile initiation probability within thirty minutes, plus or minute five."

Leadcore was a free convert. He was a math coprocessor, a doubled copy. He had no regulators on either copy. Redux didn't know how she felt about this. While legal here in the outer system, such an unrestricted copy would be absolutely prohibited in the Met. But there was no denying that the captain was a magician with statistics.

"Communicate those probabilities to captains and above on Io," Redux said. "Put them on proximate alert."

"Yes, ma'am." Antinomian stood still, gazing straight ahead, but Redux knew she was off in the virtuality of the knit, linking with the Ionian field officers.

Redux took a final look around the situation room. Detectors at one hundred thousand kilometers out from Io were reporting five ships approaching from Ganymede. Not enough resolution to identify.

The war for Io was starting.

She felt both dread and excitement. Her troops were as ready as she could make them. But she had the nagging notion that she'd missed something. No, that couldn't be. Her strongest point was logistical preparation. You give the troops the tools they need, then they get the job done. Logistics. Efficiency. Efficiency was how she'd made her name in the first place. Efficiency would win the war. Good generalship based on age-old principles.

What was it she'd forgotten?

Damn that Sherman! It was all his fault for putting doubts into her head.

The long-range sensors reported five ships. Two Dirac-class, two Dabna-class. And a carrier. Must be the Schwarzes Floβ. Then the sensors went silent, destroyed. The next ring of sensors discovered the ships soon enough. Fifty thousand kilometers.

It's going to be a hell of fight, Redux thought. Maybe we'll actually win.

CHAPTER TWO

Sulfur. You can't get the stink off your skin, out of your clothes. Hell, out of your lungs. Whole fucking moon's a stink bomb, but they say it's our stink bomb, so I get the chance to die for it, hooray! Shit, report over the knit that the Metties are coming. Battle stations. So I'm off to my bubble on the north wall of the Polar Magnetosphere Facility, or, as everybody around here calls it, the Capacitor.

Corporal Vladislav Carkey double-timed down the access corridor and slid into his gunner's chair just as his bubblemate, Dowon, slid into hers. You could run very fast in 0.18 Earth gravity, but you had to have resin on your shoes to keep from pushing yourself into the ceiling with every step you took and banging your head.

"How's it going, Corporal Carkey?" she asked him. "I see you didn't get your beauty rest."

"Same to you, Dowon," he replied, blinking up the virtual display for his cannon controls. "Systems check, okay?"

"Systems check," said Dowon.

The both ran down their respective lists as the cannon hissed, rumbled, burped. Then the click, like a light switch, when the antimatter suddenly *existed* in the firm enclosure of the containment bottle. The room went dark, and Carkey switched from visual light to infrared. His displays in the virtuality retained their original color, but the remainder of the room took on a magenta hue.

Outside the bubble, Io seethed, flowed, and spewed. The moon was one of the most geologically active bodies in the known universe. The enormous tidal forces set up by Jupiter not only generated the largest planetary magnetosphere in the solar system, they also created tremendous heat under the surface of Io.

It was a place of extremes: volcanoes, foul-smelling geysers, lakes, colder, solidified plains. Sulfur was the primary component of this moon. On Io the element and its compounds could exist, depending on conditions, as solid, liquid, or gas. Io itself was so much like the traditional conception of hell that nobody even bothered to make the comparison anymore.

Yellow, red, green (the green of copper compounds, not the green of life), and white, these were the colors of the place. Yet there was something about the moon that Carkey liked. It wasn't like Europa—it wasn't trying to tease you into believing you could live here comfortably. Carkey's two uncles, his mother's brothers, had settled there fifty years ago, and the old guys still talked as if they were fighting the place to get a living.

What they were actually doing was *harnessing* it. Because all of the activity meant energy—energy that could be gathered and used by the remainder of the Jovian system. Carkey had heard his uncle Yoland and uncle Hors enough on the subject. Plus, Carkey himself had been studying mechanical engineering at his free grange. Well, he hadn't done a great deal of studying, to tell the truth—mostly partying and flunking tests that would have been a breeze back in his primary school. Of course, back then he'd actually sat down and studied every once in a while. After two years, he had dropped out of the lyceum and joined the army.

Except for the fact that he might die at any moment, it hadn't been so bad. The discipline had been good for him. Anyway, once you got the idea how things worked, it was quite possible to slack off and not get caught when you absolutely needed a break. He had to admit that slacking off had less and less appeal to him these days. He was even entertaining thoughts of going back to engineering school after all this was over. Maybe signing on with the uncles' firm here on Io after that. Become a goddamn pioneer.

If I survive, of course. Shouldn't think about getting killed—bad luck, they say. But how the hell can I not, with the entire Met Army headed in this direction? Those DI commandos—if they're half as good as they show them on the merci, I'll be done for in half a second, and that'll be that.

Outside, the Capacitor began to glow. A charge was building up for transmission. Carkey remembered enough of his electrical engineering course to figure out the basics of the device. Energy from the Jovian magnetosphere was collected and dumped into the Capacitor, which served as a kind of temporary reservoir until the charge reached a certain voltage. Or was it amperage? Whatever. Then it would spark the energy up to a polar satellite array, which would convert it to microwaves and beam it either back to the surface cities and habitats for use or off to the relays that would convey it to the other moons in the system.

The Capacitor was a metal cylinder twelve hundred feet high. It was ringed with tiered layers of ceramic insulators. It looked remarkably like a gargantuan version of an ancient spark plug from back in the days of the internal combustion engine—but a spark plug that turned slowly on its axis and occasionally shot tremendous bolts of lightning into a black-and-yellow sky. The bubble was an observation and defense post that was mounted on the lip of the deep human-made canyon in which the Capacitor was anchored. There were fifty-seven other such stations in a ring around the perimeter of the canyon. All of them were occupied by the Federal Army, two soldiers to a blister.

One hundred fourteen buggers who are probably as scared shitless as me, thought Carkey. I guess that should make me feel better. Hooray for the Army; we're all going to die together!

The waiting was interminable. It was like a bad merci show, with the tension rising. You had nothing to do but stay prepared. You knew the bad guys were coming. He tried exchanging some banter with Dowon, but she, too, was too anxious to carry on much light conversation. On the knit, communications were flying—orders, reports. There was some fighting outside the minefields that circled the planet. An armada of small ships engaged the DIED cruisers and scored a couple of hits. And where were the vaunted cloudship defenders? There were only two in the entire Jovian system, Cloudships Sandburg and Yüan Hung-tao. The rest of the Navy was supposedly building up and training out in the Oorts. Lot of good that does us here, thought Carkey.

Then there was the call of the mines, as they blew themselves to smithereens, and other mines maneuvered as best they could to fill in the gaps. But the isotropic coating of the DIED ships limited the damage a single mine could do—even if it were nuclear or antimatter ordnance—and, like a school of fish, the mines had to concentrate to be effective. They had to pick out one ship to home in on, and let the other ships through with minimal obstruction.

This they did, and a big DIED cruiser was broken to pieces as it tried to get itself into orbit around Io. Carkey felt profound gratitude toward the mines—most of them simple, loyal little converts. The destruction of the DIED ship meant twenty or thirty thousand fewer invading soldiers for the surface forces to face.

Somewhere out there, too, Cloudship Sandburg was engaged with an enemy ship, holding it at bay for the moment, if not destroying it. Carkey heard no knit chatter about Cloudship Yüan Hung-tao. He must not be engaged today. General Redux, the system commander, might be holding the cloudship back at Callisto, thought Carkey, or maybe using him to patrol in the vicinity of Europa to make sure no backdoor attack would go unchallenged. Typical of the Federal Army brass in these parts—make sure your own ass is covered, even if that means exposing your neighbor's ass.

Suddenly, the Capacitor gave a great crackle and shot lightning into the sky. Almost as if this were a cue, the storm of battle hit.

CHAPTER THREE

There was only one thing Llosa knew for certain—that goddamn Sergeant Folsom was a maniac.

She expects us to be some kind of elite fighting force from the merci, when everybody knows we're just a bunch of dumb kids from the backwaters of the Vas. Who is she trying to fool? We're going to get slaughtered!

Llosa did go over and over again the plan of operation, the different ways to kill a man (I'm expected to kill somebody!), the communications protocols. All the things that Folsom drilled them on over and over again, the hard-ass. And here he was, doing her the honor of remembering the stuff she'd told him. At least some of it. Not enough to get me out of this alive, though, Llosa thought.

"Two clicks up on descent rocketry," said Folsom over the platoon's vinculum channel. "Lieutenant says we go in second wave."

Llosa turned up the spew rate on his boots. That slowed his rate of descent, which was good, because it kept him off the ground and out of the fighting longer. But it was bad, because there he was hanging in the air, exposed to enemy fire.

As if in answer, a bolt of energy lit up the sky nearby, along with a neighboring platoon. Ten troopers sizzled out of existence. Several arms and legs remained, floating lazily down in the gentle gravity. One foot, with attitude rocket still spewing, whipped around in a spiraling circle, like a deflating balloon, but sloughing a trail of blood behind it. It soon wheeled out of sight. Llosa turned his attention back to the moon's surface.

It'll be like hosetube, he thought, a game he'd played back in Carta Cylinder, his home bolsa on the Vas. Nearly everyone in Carta had a garden plot for a front yard, and there was great care and great competition among the gardeners. In addition to the microfiber irrigation system that everyone employed, most people also had a larger, hand-held tube, attached to the house, to deliver additional water and fertilizer to problem areas.

The game was this: You'd go to someone's door—preferably someone who didn't know you or your family—and use a fake ID card to announce yourself. The hapless resident would come to the door and you'd immediately blast away with the house's own hosetube—you'd soak the person, the interior of their house, their pets, spouse, and children. In almost every case, the person who answered the door was too stunned to react in time. Then you'd throw down the tube and run like hell. He'd done it many times, and only got caught when he accidentally chose the house of one of his father's coworkers, who recognized him.

So that's what I'll do here, Llosa thought. Open up, folks. It's hose-tube time!

Except now he had rockets, grenades, an antimatter rifle built into his arm. And, if he played the game right, nobody would be running after him. They'd be dead, and their dwelling place in flames.

No, this wasn't like hosetube at all.

Below, Llosa saw the first wave go in. Flashes and screams over the vinculum. It was murderous down there. Then the vinculum psychological filters went into effect, and the screams were silenced. Now everyone was dying in silence. Twenty meters. Fifteen. Soon he'd be in the shit. Here it came.

Here it was.

In front of him, Folsom aims a rocket at a window and blows it open, and Llosa is right behind her, and he's screaming bloody murder in his mind, even though there hasn't been any air in his lungs for hours. At first he forgets everything and shoots off every weapon at his disposal. Fremden are scamper-

ing around, trying to get out of the room, and before he can think about it, Llosa spins around and triggers a spray of automatic weapon fire from his wrist, and blood spatters the wall and bits of —what is that? Bone. And the other fremden soldier makes it out, but Folsom tosses a grist grenade after him, and the guy's legs start swaying like spaghetti, and the guy looks down and notices that his feet are turning into puddles, and his legs are melting, and, like an idiot, he tries to use his hands and arms to stop himself from sinking toward the floor—but he's not sinking into the floor; he's being deconstructed by grist-mil. And there goes the last of him, his upturned face floating on the goo of what used to be his body. And then the eyes melt out, then the lips, and finally the tip of the nose, and nothing is recognizable as human anymore.

"Easy there, Llosa," Folsom said. "Got to save some of those bullets for later. Short bursts, remember?"

Llosa looked down at the slumped and bleeding form of the man he had killed. *My first one. Doesn't matter.*

"Yes, Sergeant," he said.

"Platoon form up," said Folsom.

Five were inside. The remaining three came in through the shattered window, among them Lieutenant Chatroom. Folsom turned to her for instructions.

"OPORD remains in place. We're to make our way down to the central grist core for command and control of this facility, where we'll rendezvous with other units and secure the area for a technical kill team."

"Yes, ma'am," said Folsom. She turned to the platoon. "All right, this is MOUT—military operations on urbanized terrain. Remember: Use your obstacles. They will provide your cover and concealment. Know your field of fire at all times. Find the key terrain and think about all avenues of approach." She looked the platoon over. "Come on, you puppies, let's kill the fuck out of them before they kill the fuck out of us!"

She was out the door, and Llosa was following. The last member of the platoon to exit the defense bubble, Extraslim, closed the door behind them. They moved through a small airlock.

"Op 2 take the door, Op 4 and Driver 4 cover," Folsom said.

Aschenbach, designated Op 4, and, like Llosa, another platoon greenhorn, opened the door. Llosa, who was designated as Op 2 on this mission, and Gerhard, Driver 4, covered him. As expected, there were defenders on the other side. Gerhard fired at them, killing one, while Llosa tossed a combo grist-percussion grenade into the hallway. There were screams when the grenade went off, and that's how Llosa knew he was back in a regular atmosphere. The hallway was creepily empty when they moved out into it, with only some sticky resin of what used to be human beings on the floor.

They moved in staggered pairs down the passageways, keeping five-meter separation, and daisy-chaining along, just as they had done in drills and virtual gaming. Corporal Alliance, who was Surf 1, the surveillance op, stayed close to Folsom and the lieutenant. He was outfitted in every sensory device known to the Department of Immunity, and looked like a blistering of antennas, dishes, and sensor rods with a man in there somewhere. But the equipment worked, and they quickly found their way down three levels before they ran into any resistance.

They were hit hard by a fremden DA—that is, a direct action, an ambush. The fremden platoon had obviously been lying in wait for them. Guess they have sensors, too, Llosa thought, as bullets flew past him, and he dived for cover. Fortunately, he'd done just what Folsom said about observing your obstacles, and didn't have to think about where he was going; he found himself behind a service bulkhead.

"Fire and cover," Folsom called out. "They're concentrated at the end of the hall. Surf 1, check for booby traps."

"I've got a zip wire at ten . . . twelve meters from forward position. Three inches off the floor."

"Copy that, goddamn it."

It was a microfilament thin and sharper than any razor. It would cut your foot off at the ankle without a bit of resistance. Plus it would probably trigger something even more nasty.

"Op 4, Op 2, you're on," Folsom said. "Two up, 4 cover."

Aschenbach moved up beside Llosa. "You ready?"

"Fuck no," said Llosa.

Aschenbach smiled. "That's the spirit," he said. "I'm chucking a percussive and a fogger, then I'll roll out and direct antimatter fire to the left and at the level of that fucking wire."

"Gotcha," said Llosa.

"On two?"

"On two."

Aschenbach got his grenades ready, then counted down. "One and two—"

He threw the grenades, then rolled out and began his barrage. Llosa emerged from cover. The fogger was doing its job—visual and electromagnetic scrambling, plus multiple ghost messages through the grist. With any luck, the fremden wouldn't be able to tell which was the real Llosa. With even better luck, they wouldn't shoot him by sheer chance. He barreled down the hall until he found more cover—a side passage that at least appeared to be empty. He chucked a grist grenade down its length, just to be certain. Sure enough, a soldier staggered out of cover shrieking and burning as the grist-mil ate into her body and dissolved it. He could tell it was a woman because of the pitch of her screams.

Two kills.

Llosa provided cover for Aschenbach to move up, and then the two of them exchanged heavy fire with the fremden while the rest of the platoon moved forward behind them. Llosa heard a grunt behind him, but paid no mind to it until Folsom dragged Gerhard into the side corridor. He had taken a bullet neatly in the forehead. There was no way his repair grist could handle that kind of massive brain damage. Gerhard was dead.

Alliance came up and told Folsom he'd found a roundabout access to a position behind the fremden—it was down the corridor Llosa had just cleared out, up a level, and then down a tube. With the low gravity, there was no need for stairs in this facility. People could jump up or down several floors at a time—and even farther with an air-puff assist from the basement or rooftop. Folsom detailed Asad, Meeker, and Chin to the task. The rest of them remained and exchanged fire for a good fifteen minutes (but it was only seven minutes when Llosa checked his objective internal clock). Suddenly, the other members of the platoon burst from behind on the fremden.

"Fuck, those fremdem must be shitting their BDUs now!" Llosa heard somebody exclaim. It took him a moment to sift through his acronym-laden head and remember that the BDU was the "battle dress uniform."

Five of the fremden were killed, while two others escaped by fleeing.

They lost Meeker to enemy grist-mil.

The corridor, where Llosa had just spent some of the most intense moments of his life, was a nondescript walkway now. The platoon moved on. Before they rounded a corner, Llosa glanced back. Once you cleaned up the dead bodies, it could be . . . well—anywhere. Or nowhere.

Hell, he'd never find his way back to this place, or know it if he did.

CHAPTER FOUR

From
Merci feed 97QQ6513-15-4
THE WINNY HINGE SHOW
E-date Broadcast April 24, 3015

Winny Hinge aboard Cloudship Sandburg, brought to you by Jermatherm Coats-Like-New—Get the pellicle you deserve when appearances matter. Touch my hand and enter the Jermatherm universe of beauty. Go ahead, touch me. This is JBC, Jupiter's source for conflict coverage. It's fifteen o'clock e-standard.

Winny Hinge here as Cloudship Sandburg closes in the Ionian minefield perimeter and three DIED ships that look to be of the Dabna or Dirac class. Yes, Sandburg has just identified them as two Dirac-class ships, and one carrier, the *Lion of Africa*. The cruisers are the *Mapplethorpe* and the *Samsam*. We'll just . . . yes, we have a sim of both ships now online, fully interactive. Pull down door number 3 from your toolbox for those sims . . . and we're closing in . . . my . . . God . . . those are *big* ships . . .

If you intensify, you'll hear my heart thumping, and my breathing getting a bit . . . yes, I've adjusted my internals. Don't want any of you grandmas out there to get a coronary. All right, then. A bit of tranquilizer, and here we go, back to the window.

My God, those ships really mean business. We're bigger than any one of them, even the carrier—but three? I'm a little . . . a bit worried, ladies and gentlemen. I thought we were just going out on patrol, and here we are attacking what I'm sure is a very powerful enemy force. Sandburg, are you sure . . .

Cloudship Sandburg tells me that we now have orders to attack, and there's nothing he can do about it. For those of you with the full feed, you'll also know that he just told me to shut up and stop complaining, but he said it in somewhat saltier terms. So that's what I'll do. After all . . .

Oh, my. Here we go . . .

I know many of you have never been in contact with a cloudship before. They've been known to hold themselves aloof, after all, and they don't use the regular merci channels like the rest of us joes. Cloudship Sandburg, it turns out, is a bit more of a populist, and he's let me take a good look at some of his inner workings, including his . . . well, his weapons. He's able to use something called the Casimir effect to actually make a beam of positrons and shoot it out in a concentrated stream from anywhere on his surface. The DIED ships use a different way of producing their positrons. It's another one of those "effects," this one called the Auger effect. Instead of being produced anywhere on the surface, like the cloudships do it, these positrons come out of cannon that are powered off the ship engine. The cannon are sometimes called "Auger cannon," as a matter of—

—Ladies and gentlemen, we're closing in. If you'll intensify through my eyes, you can see exactly what I'm talking about. Out the window there . . . that ship—it's the *Mapplethorpe*, says Sandburg—see those little bumps along the flank there? Those are the Auger cannon.

My God, that ship is big. Must be a couple of kilometers. And those scythes near the front. Those are spun to make gravity, and that's where the living quarters and command bridge and such are, Sandburg tells me. But it all looks so *threatening*. Like a bundle of pitchforks. Everything's prickly and dangerous looking.

And there's the *Samsam*. Just as big. Something's happening. It's— it's *shooting* at us! Oh, my God. I'm just going to take cover here—

Wow. Did you feel that? That was quite jarring. Maybe you parents should think about moderating your child's intensity level, or maybe just restricting her or him to visual only—*here comes another fucking bolt!*

Aren't you gonna goddamn shoot back, Sandburg?

Ow. I think my . . . something's broken in my hand. A finger or maybe a—

Christ, that hurts. Going to just release a bit of morphine. Yes. There.

Better.

Okay, then. Here we are. Closing in for range or something. Sandburg says those ships fired too soon on him, that the damage he took is minimal, and now it'll take them a couple of minutes to get their cannon up to full power. Of course, there are the rocks, he says.

What rocks?

Uh, yes. Ladies and gentlemen, it seems that the DIED ships are also equipped with catapults. Very powerful catapults that fling out storms of stones. Human-made meteor showers. Also—jagged pieces of metal. But that sort of shrapnel is usually rained down on the planets, and not flung at ships. It's the rocks that get thrown at—

The *Samsam*'s catapulting its load of rocks at us!

I'm—ah! Jesus! Stop it! Oh my God, it hurts! It hurts! You fucking idiot, are you trying to kill me! Christ on a crutch, I'm—

Sorry, ladies and gentlemen. I . . . I seem to have broken another bone, this time in my leg. My grist is setting it, don't worry, and I've got a full morphine drip going. For those of you dialed in at full intensity, I'm sorry for all that pain. I'm afraid the dampers won't have filtered most of it. The algorithms we use for the Winny show are not designed for this kind of roughness. We'll have to get some from the mountain-climbing shows or from *Plasma-skate*. Some of you know I used to be married to the host of *Plasma-skate*, Ron Edgekirk, until he revealed on my show his deepest secret, that he was—

Oh, no. The walls are glowing again. It's getting hot in here. What have they done to us *now*? Aren't you going to *do* anything, you fool?

Sandburg says to wait and see.

Easy for him to say; he's not at the complete mercy of—oh my God, he's firing. We're firing!

It seemed as if the whole surface of Cloudship Sandburg lit up and just pumped out a bolt of power! Have a look at that, ladies and gentlemen—out the window there—that DIED ship is damaged. It's the *Samsam*.

We're glowing in here again. Be careful, will you, you're going to deplete yourself just like those DIED ships, and then where will you be . . .

Oh. It seems that cloudships don't work the same way as the DIED ships. They can't get "depleted" nearly as fast. It has something to do with those "effects" I was telling you about earlier, ladies and gentlemen.

So, we're going to win?

Problem. The DIED ships have something called an isotropic coating, which Sandburg doesn't possess. Makes the fight pretty even. Seems that we've got to shoot them a lot more to do the same damage as—

We're hit again! We're hit again! And my goddamn leg just rebroke, and—Sandburg's rounding on the *Mapplethorpe*. He's firing back.

And another shot at the *Samsam*. And another. And another.

Ladies and gentlemen, we're in the shit!

Sandburg's moving in close to the *Samsam*. Careful, his cannon are up to power, aren't they? Shouldn't you—

I've got a mouthful of rocks to spit out, Sandburg says. More than any DIED ship could possibly carry.

And they're away! Have a look at that, people. It's a spew of matter. Some of them must be icy, because they're trailing streamers . . . strange, not behind, but to the side—Sandburg tells me its not from the momentum—we're in space and there's no drag, after all—it's from Jupiter's magnetosphere. Looks like a wind is blowing over them from the side as they—Christ, the *Samsam*'s firing her cannon!

Didn't hit us. The rocks blocked it! Took out a big chunk of the rocks, but Sandburg says not enough. Not enough for what?

Oh.

Oh my.

Intensify that, ladies and gentlemen. The *Samsam*'s hit. She's hurt badly. Have a look at that glow toward the rear.

There she goes. The *Samsam*'s a fireball. White-hot, antimatter annihilation, out of control, out of control! My God, my God, the destruction. The destruction of it—

But we're turning around, we're rounding, and—

There's the *Mapplethorpe*. Hang on. Moderate intensity, ladies and gentlemen. Especially you children. I think it's going to—I think it's going to—

Shit, oh fuck, I'm going to die, I'm going to die in this godforsaken place, instead of on Ganymede in my nice apartment, and the fuzzy room, my special fuzzy room those assholes took when they invaded, it's not my fault I was on Callisto covering another one of those Free Grange idiots lecturing us all on collective action, like we don't know the Met wants our asses in a sling and our tits exposed for milking, hello, we're not fools, you smug bigots, oh shit, I'm going to die, I'm going to die thinking about Free Granger swineheads instead of Ron's cock, Ron's cock, and now he's with some free-convert bitch, some tagion slut, and I promised myself to go out remembering sex, thinking about Ron's—oh my God, *I can't remember what his dick felt like inside me anymore!*

You bastard, to break up with me just because . . . just because I wasn't a tagion—

Oh.

My.

Ladies and gentlemen, we took quite a hit, but I'm alive. We're alive, here, I think.

Oh God. How embarrassing. Sorry about that—my head got banged pretty hard against a bulkhead here and it seems to have taken my consciousness barriers off-line for a moment. Really, I apologize for that, ladies and gentlemen. This is a family show, I realize. Just. Sorry. Anyway, we seem to be alive, and—

Sandburg says the *Mapplethorpe* has deployed something . . . some kind of field of grist . . . and the percussion from that *Samsam* explosion is pushing up right toward it, and he can't course-correct in time, with his power down from that direct hit, and—

We're in the grist now, ladies and gentlemen. The military grist deployed by the *Mapplethorpe*. Not sure what's going to happen. Everything's . . . everything gotten quiet.

The interior is very quiet now.

Sandburg says the grist feels like nasty stuff. He says—

Sandburg?

Sandburg?

Are you there, Sandburg?

That's strange. The walls are changing color. Normally they're a pale blue, with a steady glow from the ceiling, but now they're . . . they look inflamed, in a way. Like a skin infection. Turning pinkish. Red.

Veins of purple, like the color of a bruise, running through everything. Through.

Oh Christ. Through my hand. Up my arm. Christ, what is it? What—

Ron's dick. We were so good together. Why did he have to leave me for that convert whore, that—oh, forget it. Oh God. I'm all purple. This is it, I'm—

Ron's dick.

Initiate autodestruction sequence for biologic unit. Code 687. Feed initiated. Answer back, answer back: 32vwLx99. Interrupt 7A7: Quantum broadcast detected. If-then feed worm 98-niner. Feed 989 initiated. ES established. Worm feed:

"People of the outer system, this is Director Amés speaking to you through your own merci channel. As you see, resistance is futile. You must surrender immediately or face complete destruction. Only in surrender can peace and order be found. I bid you adieu."

Feed complete. Connection remains open.

Code 687 reestablished.

Feed biologic destruct chain. Prepare to cycle.

Cycle.

Destroy.

CHAPTER FIVE

Defend gristlock at all costs. Those were the orders for Carkey's platoon. Simple, really. Depending on your interpretation of "at all costs." Carkey had a feeling it was the rigorous meaning that was implied.

Carkey sneaked a peek around the bulkhead behind which he was sheltering and let off another two-second round from his handgun. He couldn't stretch his arm all the way out into rifle position, and his fire was inaccurate.

Nearby, Dowon was bleeding to death. She'd taken a fragment of a grist grenade. Her own pellicle was fighting the effects of the DIED military grist. But all its resources were taken up with this, and the shrapnel itself had dug into her gut and nicked an artery. Her internal repair system couldn't stanch the flow. If it released its death hold on the grist-mil, she'd be turned to primordial slime immediately. It was pretty much a no-win situation.

"Hang in there, Dowon," Carkey called out. "I'm still with you."

"Yeah," muttered Dowon weakly. "Sure. I'm hanging."

Carkey let loose an arm rocket down the corridor he was defending. He heard a dull thump, then a cry of pain. Sounded male. There was a flash of light, and the voice was cut off in midscream. He'd never know. It wasn't his first kill, though. He'd passed that threshold at least ten bodies ago.

I guess I found something I don't suck at. I wish I sucked at it. Dear God, I'd rather be good at electrical engineering. Or anything else.

Then a grenade rolled down the hall, and he knew he was in the shit. He ducked back, grabbed Dowon by the collar of her uniform, and dragged her through an accessway into the gristlock proper. He ordered the door to slam behind him. On the other side, he heard the grenade explode. Shit, how had they gotten so close? He'd thought he was keeping them out of throwing range.

A thump at the door. Another. They were trying to take the gristlock. Carkey looked around. Dowon had used all her grenades and rockets. She had a few more rounds of ammo. What did he have? A couple remaining grenades. No more arm rockets. Projectile ammunition . . . low. He stripped what he could from Dowon and reloaded his bracelets. In doing so, he noticed she was dead. No time for . . . What else to fight with?

All this grist.

He reached out and felt the edge of it. The command and control center of the entire complex. The virtuality was housed within. All the free converts resided here.

"Help."

Someone was calling him.

"What?"

"We can't get out."

It was the free converts inside the grist.

"Something is blocking the merci outside the Capacitor area. We're isolated. We can't flash free. We can't get out."

In all the fighting, Carkey hadn't once checked to see if the outside world still existed. For the hell of it, he tuned in to one of his old haunts, Beridianne's Juice Bar, a low-key virtual bordello found among the porn channels.

He drew a blank.

It was unsettling. Hell, it was unprecedented. The merci was always there. The virtuality didn't disappear. Was the whole world destroyed?

"They've figured out how to jam us," said the voice inside the gristlock. "It happened on Triton. Now it's happening here. We can't copy ourselves out. We've retreated as far as we can. If they get in, they'll be able to do what they want with us."

"How many of you are there?" Carkey asked.

"Ten thousand nine hundred fifty-seven."

Eleven thousand people. Shit.

"Am I the only goddamn Federal Army left?" he said. "Who are *you*, anyway?"

"Assistant Mayor Mathaway," said the free convert. "Most of the Federal Army's been confined to the east wing, with heavy fighting. DIED has isolated the gristlock. Somebody knew what they were after."

Double shit. He *was* the only one.

"I'll do what I can."

"We'll help. Give us your remaining grenades. We can merge with them and replicate their instructions to most of the gristlock. We'll swarm the DIED soldiers when they enter."

The gristlock looked like an encrusted carbuncle, a diamond in the rough, standing about ten feet tall and six feet wide in the middle of the chamber. It came to a point at top and bottom, where it connected to the floor and ceiling. Carkey unhitched his remaining grenades and set them at the base of the carbuncle.

"Should I set them to detonate or something?" he asked.

"That won't be necessary. Take cover, though. We're not sure if this will work . . ."

Carkey looked around. Take cover where? The only shield in the room was Dowon's body. He decided to stand where he was. As he looked on, the grenades dissolved into the side of the gristlock until only slight protrusions remained.

"Got it," said Mathaway in his ear. "Replicating."

A louder thump at the door. The door was heavily armored. They must be throwing some extremely powerful shit at it.

A reverberating boom. Shit. Take cover. He threw himself behind the gristlock carbuncle.

Another explosion. The door shook off its hinges, and fell inward. Three DIED soldiers entered.

The floor rose up, like an animated fungus, to meet them. It surfed over them, and swallowed them whole.

Fuck. I'm glad that's shit's on my side. Still, better stay off that side of the room.

Several grenades came in. They stuck in the undulating floor, were surrounded. Little flashes of physical explosion, and whatever grist they contained was quickly overcome by the immensely more powerful algorithms of the gristlock free converts.

Bloody carnage in the hall as the grist flooring crested, about five meters out in the hall. And then it withdrew. It took enormous power to animate this much grist directly, and the room had grown many degrees hotter from the sheer mechanical friction overcome. Leaving one DIED trooper.

Mathaway spoke in Carkey's ear. "We've exhausted our resources. We've got the algorithms, but the physical power to move the grist has to be recharged. It will take several minutes, and there are more DIED forces on the way. Many more."

"Well, that was pretty good, what you did."

"Not enough, I'm afraid. And it cost the life of twenty-five of us."

"What should we do?"

"If they capture us, they'll take us to Silicon Valley," said Mathaway.

It was unverified—the death camp of free converts on Mars. But everyone knew how much Amés hated free converts. Maybe it was true.

"For us, surrender is not an option," said Mathaway. "For you, however—we think you should consider it."

No way. Should I? Hell no. Fuck that. I've been a goof-off all my life. Hell, even in the Army I found ways to do it. Those free converts just laid it on the line for me. I can do the same for them. It was as simple as that. Fuck yeah. Feels good.

He reached around the carbuncle and fired a couple of rounds at the DIED trooper. The trooper pointed his arm at Carkey, but did not return fire.

"Fuck," the man yelled. "Fuck it."

He's out. He's out of ammo. One more five-round burst and so the fuck am I, though. Got to make it count. My positron pistol's flatlined. Nothing but five bullets. And then my bare hands.

"Tell me when he's peeking out from cover, so I can shoot him," Carkey whispered to the grist.

"All right," said Mathaway. "We can do that. Stand by. And. There he is!"

Carkey made a fist and squeezed off his remaining bullets.

A yelp of pain and he knew he'd hit his target.

Two deep, quick breaths. Out from cover. Down the hall. The man looks up at him with pain and fear in his eyes. But he's not dead. Not by a long shot. Just caught him in the leg. Fuck.

He dived at the man's throat. Caught hold of it. But hands pulled at his arms. A fist drove into his Adam's apple, and Carkey fell back, wheezing. With a roar, the other threw himself on Carkey, going for the eyes.

The two men grappled, rolled on the floor, each seeking a hold, a grip. In the virtual space they shared, their converts were also struggling, skirmishing.

How do you kill a man? Hit him. Swarm him. Bite him. Cut off his information flow. Choke him. Erase his memory. No holds barred. No mercy. This is life. This is death—

CHAPTER SIX

Llosa knew he had to kill the man. The pain in his leg would have to wait. He felt the tendrils of the man's pellicle attempting to invade his own, to wipe his memory. Wipe his family. Wipe his life.

Everything depended on his killing the man. But the devil squirmed like a serpent. Broke his grip. And, make no mistake, the other wanted to kill him as much as Llosa desired to kill him. His grist was animated by sheer will to triumph.

He set his teeth. Fought off the pellicular incursion.

My will is strong, too.

God, if he only had a knife. Risked a look around. Nothing sharp. But a piece of metal. Part of the rocket launcher. Reached. Fuck. The other pounded him in the chest. Got hold of his throat.

Reach.

Got it.

With all his strength, Llosa slammed the metal rod against his attacker's skull. The man's grip slackened. Llosa pulled free, hit the man again and again.

The other rolled away, lay bleeding, moaning.

Llosa rose up, the metal rod in his hands. Up on his knees above the other. Brought down a blow, another. God, the blood was streaming from his thigh like a spring. Like a river. Another blow.

The other looked up. Early twenties. Brown hair, brown skin.

He looks like me.

Llosa hit him in the face.

But, distracted, he felt the other's grist make another swarm attempt. The fremden was trying for Llosa's leg. Oh shit. Weakness there. The nerve reporting the leg pain was turned off. Left unguarded. The other could use it . . . reverse the flow and—

Stabbing, unspeakable pain in Llosa's mind. Stabbing knife in his leg. But it wasn't really in his leg. It was in his skull.

He dropped the metal rod, reflexively grabbed at his leg.

So much agony. Can't think. Isolate that nerve. Destroy it if necessary. Can't think. Can't—

The other had the metal rod. Slowly pulling himself to his feet. Llosa was collapsed, writhing on the corridor floor.

Got to control. Isolate. Burn.

With a squeal of sheer agony, he used his own grist to destroy the nerve in his leg. It was the only way. The pain stopped.

Llosa looked up. The fremden soldier stood over him with the metal rod.

The two men's eyes met.

The other looked like a frightened animal.

Like me.

The other brought the rod down. Down like a stake. Plunged it in. Into. Llosa's chest.

Into the meat of the heart.

Warning signals flashed in his peripheral vision.

He looks up. The man is crying. He's sobbing.

Then surprise. Agony.

Another face in view.

Sergeant Folsom. Aschenbach beside her.

Sergeant Folsom pulls a bloody knife from the fremden soldier's back.

The fremden soldier falls away.

Llosa? Llosa, can you hear me?

He nods. Smiles at her. He can hear, but it's getting difficult to see.

The face of the fremden. Right when he died. Llosa knew he'd seen it somewhere before. He knew that face, didn't he? Oh, yes. Carta Bolsa. Hosetube. The surprise and anguish of his unsuspecting victims when he sprayed them and their living rooms with water.

Don't be upset. It's all a prank. All a prank.

A game kids play. Then they go home to supper. To the family to—

Llosa, can you hear me?

Mama?

CHAPTER SEVEN

THE RAIN AT MOUNT PELE

We were at Mount Pele when the nail rain fell. We knew the DIED enforcers were coming; we expected invasion. We expected that we would fight and perhaps lose our fight. We thought about what that would mean for our jobs, our standard of living. We expected hard times ahead.

We didn't expect nails to rain out of the sky.

Some of us looked up and saw them coming, the nails. There is only the thinnest whiff of sulfur dioxide for an atmosphere here on our little moon. But it was enough to heat up the nails with a dull blue glow as they came streaking down upon us. Those who saw the nails called out, and the rest of us turned our eyes to the heavens.

The nails were very beautiful as they fell. The youngest children didn't understand, and they smiled at the beautiful sight.

The defense rocketry fired off, but the approaching bits of metal were not meteors and comets—they were not a single entity that could be broken up, dispersed. Not a single layer, not a clump. No. A steady rain. How do you blast a hole in rain?

The rain fell on all. It fell on the Io-adapted, the space-adapted, the rich, the poor, the old, and the young. It fell on our children. It tore through all structures—houses, places of business and worship. It almost seemed alive, viperlike, seeking out life. There was no shelter.

It fell into the volcano itself, a driving rain, and sent great plumes of sulfurous gas spewing. Huge clouds of sulfur and iron dioxide rose into the air as the nails slammed into the ground. Almost immediately, the clouds cooled, changed phases. Became liquid.

That often happens on Io when Pele or one of the other volcanoes or geysers erupts—especially the ones that are not tapped for geothermal energy. A sulfur rain falls. For those of us who are surface-adapted, it is a pleasant, noxious thing. We love the smell of sulfur here. It's our life bread; it is how we buy our water; it's where we live, and how we live. We call our moon the Yellow Rose. But this sulfur rain was different.

It mixed with the nails.

The nails cut our flesh. They tore through our pellicles as if we were covered with parchment. They ricocheted within us, bouncing off our bones until the bones broke and the tissue was torn to shreds. And then we were hit again and again.

Some of us hid under roofs, under ledges. These protected us for a time. We heard the nails pounding above us. We prayed that the roofs would hold.

The nails fell and fell.

Our prayers were not answered.

The lucky were knocked senseless by the collapsing debris. The others ran screaming into the hard, hard rain. They fell and rose no more.

Blood condenses, freezes almost instantly on the surface. Pools of red ice—iron and water—formed about the bodies. But this is ever-churning, ever-burning Io, and the hot spots migrate. Blood on the surface would melt, flow, recongeal, then flow again. Hot nails fell into the blood and would have boiled it away, but the sulfur rain cooled the blood. Another cycle, another circumstance of our deaths.

Pieces of our bodies remained. Some retained animation through their grist pellicles. Arms and legs moved feebly. A child's hand crawled toward its mother's—the grist within knowing only the simple urges of instinct. But the energy flowed quietly away. Few were able to touch before the cold set in, and the final, everlasting death.

Some soldiers still lived. The ones who were held in reserve deep below the surface. Some citizens still lived—those who managed to flee below into the deeper reaches of the habitat. But we could not look to the machinery; we could not keep the lid on the volcano. We could only think of surviving this instant, then the next.

And so Pele blew. After all the years of being harnessed, the regulators overloaded, the power grid went off-line, and there was nothing to channel the volcano's fury.

And, with a great pyroclastic boom, Pele erupted. The sulfur flowed. Down the sides. Into the habitat entrances, broken open by the nail rain, that led underground. That led into our last places of refuge.

The sulfur found us there and burnt us. It choked our screams. It burnt us up. We died clawing at our arms and faces, in agony.

Somehow, the merci was also jammed. Our free converts were cut off from outside contact and could not copy themselves elsewhere. When the grist matrix was destroyed, they had nowhere to go. We all died together.

Dying inside the Yellow Rose.

A tattered, battered few had crawled under rocky ledges on the surface. Some crews who were working outside, in the highlands above the habitat and geothermal plant. A few soldiers on patrol. Semisentient programs contained within pieces of equipment. Not a single fully conscious free convert survived.

Two thousand five hundred twenty-two people. They were the only ones who lived. The rest of us died.

Two hundred fifty-seven thousand people. Men, women, children.

And then, after forever, the rain stopped falling. The last nails fell into a dead surface. There was a respite. Pele, as if sensing that its work of destruction was over, became dormant, with only a few rumblings to betray that it still seethed within. An hour passed before those of us in the highlands were convinced the rain was over.

We emerged to the devastation. Our families were dead. Our homes were destroyed. Nothing remained.

"Look up! Look up! It's starting again," one of us said.

Indeed, in the sky, there were black specks. We ran for cover. We crawled back under the rocks. But these specks were not the rain. They were ships—ships full of DIED soldiers. One landed nearby, and troops bristling with guns disgorged. They surrounded our soldiers, who quickly threw down their weapons. They surrounded us all.

We looked at them with blank, empty eyes.

They lowered their guns. They gazed at us in wonder.

We didn't even try to escape. Where was there to go? We stumbled. We sat down on the ground. Those of us who survived were all Io-adapted. We wept as Ionians do. We wept tears that fell, then evaporated near to the surface—that curled away in gaseous wisps.

We wept yellow, sulfur tears.

CHAPTER EIGHT

Leo Sherman felt like a traitor, but there was nothing he could do about it. He couldn't even talk to anyone.

So far as his mission went, it wasn't the worst thing in the world for Leo that Met forces had taken Io. He'd been part of the action—had shot at Federal Army forces. Hell, face it—he'd killed a man.

Yet, even though this was a major setback for the fremden forces, he was in the Jupiter system, and near the front. He was in the perfect position to make his run across the lines and deliver the cargo ensconced in his chest.

The archived copy of Amés's chief of intelligence.

I have opportunity and motive enough, Leo thought. Now I have to scout out the means.

If the intelligence knowledge within the urn was as important as he believed it to be, it would save thousands, maybe millions, of lives. But there was one life it would not save—the man Leo had blasted out of existence with his Auger pistol in the storming of the Capacitor. The man, of course, would not have hesitated to kill Leo. Leo was wearing the uniform of the Department of Immunity Enforcement Division, after all. He was identified as the enemy.

But I know who I am, thought Leo. Don't I? I'm partisan. I'm fremden. Have to make sure this Aschenbach persona doesn't take too much control of me. Wish I could talk to Jill about this. She's killed a lot of people, I guess. Or even the kid, Aubry; she brought out the best in me. Or, hell, why not Folsom? If only that goddamn extremely competent, hot babe of a sergeant wouldn't blow my head off the moment I confessed! Ah, well. Jill. Dory Folsom. I'm a complete sucker for jock girls.

Leo smiled, lay back in his bunk, and tried to think about women in order to drift off to sleep. It didn't work for long. He tossed and turned. He remembered the blank face of the man he'd killed, just before the soldier sizzled away from Leo's positronic bolt.

The only way I can make it mean anything that I've killed that guy is to go ahead with my mission, Leo thought. Cross the lines. Deliver the merchandise. Wallowing in sorrow won't play.

Finally, he fell into a troubled sleep, only to wake two hours later. The platoon was bugging out, hunting down remnants of the fremden force who were thought to be hiding in a nearby gorge.

Since the DIED victory of a week earlier, Leo's platoon was stationed at the Capacitor. They had been part of the mop-up operation.

We *literally* mopped up poor Llosa, Leo thought. He remembered the fury with which Folsom had slain Llosa's attacker—a grist-coated knife in the back, then cut his neck almost in two as he fell. No reprieve from that kind of injury, no matter how good your internal repair systems were. Wonder who the kid was? He was on *my* side. Don't forget that. I'm *for* the guys who are shooting at me.

God, your head could get pretty mixed up when you were a spy.

After that, they'd emptied the gristlock. They'd fed the free converts into the transfer gate and flashed them all to Mars. Poor souls. Most people in the Met had no idea what was going on at Silicon Valley, but the partisans had found out the truth. Leo knew the gate technicians were sending these people to a concentration camp for sentient computer programs—a camp which they'd probably never survive.

He could try to sabotage the gate mechanism. Save the ten thousand free converts in some handy nearby grist supercomplex. Sure. He could have pretended to be shooting at the fremden resistance. Sure, sure. That kind of shit worked fine in merci thrillers. It would get him found out and killed here in real life. He'd be dead already.

Instead, Leo was covered with sulfur dust, tromping in near vacuum down a lifeless valley. At least he hoped it was lifeless. He poked cautiously ahead along with his platoon as they made their way down a tributary to the deep gorge they'd been assigned to sweep for the remaining enemy. Like Earth's moon, one side of Io perpetually faced Jupiter. The Capacitor was on the north pole, and Jupiter took up half the sky to the southwest. The valley they were probing was to the southeast, however, and as they went deeper into it, the great face of Jupiter gradually "set" behind them.

The platoon had lost six people in the fighting, including Lieutenant Chatroom. Now there were only the sorry four of them left to do a job that required, by Leo's estimate, at least sixteen. The new lieutenant, Tae—just arrived from West Point on Earth—had blithely ordered them out anyway. Folsom had smiled grimly and said, "Yes, sir," and here they all were: ambush bait.

Whatever the other moral ambiguities of war, Leo figured that, given the chance, he would shoot Lieutenant Tae without compunction.

Surf 1, Corporal Alliance, was at point with all sensors forward. Even so, he almost missed the zip net. Folsom was the one who noticed it. Leo wasn't sure how she knew. It was completely invisible to him. The woman had a powerful survivor's instinct.

"Well, well," said Folsom. "What have we here?" She was speaking in virtual, through the vinculum. Io's atmosphere was nearly nonexistent. No sound carried there.

The platoon held up. Suddenly Alliance's readouts, to which they were all attuned, went code red, and indicated the outlines of the zip net. "Shit," said the corporal. "I would have walked right into that."

"You can't always trust e-m to detect these things quickly," said Folsom. "Remember, they're half a molecule thick."

Lieutenant Tae came up from the rear.

"It's covering the whole valley floor. Goes up twenty, thirty meters," Folsom told him.

"Can't we hop over it with our attitude rockets?"

"We could," said Folsom. "But there might be something nastier up there." She pointed toward some ominously overhanging ledges several hundred feet above them.

Before anyone could say another word, a single Auger pistol blast, and then a burst of bullets rained down among them. The platoon scrambled for cover. Leo felt himself yanked down. He rolled under the overhang of a boulder to find himself next to Folsom. Another spray of bullets sent up yellow puffs from the ground. They made no sound.

"They're low on ammo," Folsom said. "No grenades. A single anti-matter blast, then nothing else but bullets, Lieutenant. Do you copy that?" No answer. "Lieutenant Tae?"

Leo looked out as best he could from under the boulder. Oh shit. Traces of blood had congealed and frozen around the tiny zip-net strands, and now the net was as plain as a spider's web—glinting a lustrous red in the wan light of the canyon. The blood was Lieutenant Tae's. And there was Tae himself. In several pieces. He'd run right into the zip net and cut himself to ribbons.

Folsom followed Leo's gaze. "Fuck," she said. "Not another one."

"Sliced and diced," Leo muttered. "Hell of a way to go."

"Those bastards planned to drive us all into that net," said Folsom. "Well, I've about had enough of this bullshit." She straightened both her arms at the elbow, cocking them into rifle stock mode, then rolled out quickly and fired in the general direction the bullets had come from. She quickly rolled back under. "I think I got a lock on their position. Surf 1, you still with us?"

Alliance answered in a shaky voice. "Yeah, Sarge. I'm hiding behind a rock, but I'm feeling kind of exposed on top."

"We've got to triangulate. Check your readouts."

"I'm . . . I don't know if I'm able to . . ."

"Alliance, pull yourself together and check those readouts."

"Yes, Sergeant."

"Op 1, you there?"

No answer.

So it was just Leo, Folsom, and Alliance.

"Surf 1?"

"Got it! You should have the coordinates."

"Me? Us. We're all going to fire at once. Then we're going to high-tail it down this canyon for home, full rocket assist. Got it?"

Leo and Alliance answered in unison. "Yes, Sergeant."

"All right. Ready. Aim." They rolled out from under their rock. "Fire!"

The bugout down the canyon valley was a blur of running, flying, banging into rocks, picking himself up, gathering speed, then rocketing himself farther along until he had to set down and run again in order to turn a corner. Folsom brought up the rear, returning fire. There was a reverberating explosion. Leo risked a glance back and saw that it was just him and Folsom now.

"Surf 1?" he gasped.

"I guess they had a grenade after all," said Folsom with disgust. "Move it!"

They ran and rocketed onward until they could see the orange-white face of Jupiter rising before them. Only then did they know that they were out of the valley at last.

Thank God, thought Leo when they were finally back on the plains of Io. Thank God I'm not dead.

And thank God that Amés has won the battle, but not the war.

PART THREE

Transfinite Gesture
JANUARY TO APRIL, YEAR 3017, E-STANDARD

CHAPTER ONE

From

CRYPTOGRAPHIC MAN

Secret Code and the Genesis of Modern Individuality

BY ANDRE SUD, D. DIV, TRITON

If two people want to use a secret code to communicate, they have to depend on a third person to deliver the key to the code they will use. The third "person" can be a system, like the merci, or the old-time telephone grid on Earth—but that system is maintained by people. Those are the people who can grab the key as it flows through and make a copy. History shows that, sooner or later, they will *always* try to steal the key. An ax was only the physical means by which Mary Queen of Scots was executed. What really cut off her head was the sharp edge of a broken code.

Take an example. Say Alice wants to tell secret agent Bob to assassinate Chief Cardinal Icebreak III. She has a series of instructions that she has to deliver over time. She can't visit or communicate with Bob publicly, because to do so will compromise his sleeper status—and then the jig will be up before the Cardinal is whacked. The only solution is to send the key to the coded message separately, through a third party.

Governments in the past spent vast resources on arranging ways to securely deliver keys. In the precomputer days of Vigenere squares and substitution ciphers, special messengers had to deliver the secret word necessary to transpose the text. If you are the king, whispering your favorite key word to your ambassador when he is back in the kingdom for instructions is all well and good, but once he's in foreign lands, a king is asking for catastrophe if he relies on the same key for every message.

In what was called the Second World War in the twentieth century on Earth, the problem of getting daily keys to the operators of the complex Enigma machines was a chore that taxed even the famously efficient German army. The German fleet of submarines, called U-boats, which stayed at sea for extended periods, were a gigantic headache for German high command to keep up-to-date. (In fact, the German Third Reich hastened its own downfall when the Enigma machines fell into the possession of the Allied powers opposing them—but that's another story.)

The problem of key distribution has flummoxed cryptographers since the first coded messages. How do you get the key to decode a secret message to your intended recipient without the key itself being intercepted and employed by your enemy to crack the message? If you use a different keypad for every message and every recipient, the problem is solved. But as soon as you move beyond one message needing to be sent to one person at one particular time, you run into a logistical problem that even a network as vast as the merci cannot solve. When you have an army of soldiers, or even an army of spies, single-pad keys are impossible to use in practice.

But wait! Isn't there a simple way around the key distribution problem? To go back to Alice the Puppetmaster and Bob the Cardinal killer . . .

Say Alice sends Bob the secret message without sending him her key. Bob doesn't bother attempting to read the message, knowing the attempt would be futile. Instead, Bob double-encodes the message himself, using his own key, and sends it back to Alice. The message is now double-encrypted. Couldn't Alice take off her encryption, leaving on Bob's, then send the message back to Bob? He can then use his own key to decode his encryption and read the message, right?

It won't work, of course. Imagine that Alice's original message is written on a piece of paper inside a small locked box (her encryption) that is inside Bob's larger locked steamer trunk (Bob's encryption). She can't get to her box to unlock it. It's locked inside Bob's trunk. This is the classic "last on, first off" problem that for centuries was taken as a fundamental truth of cryptography. You had to find a secure way of exchanging a key.

But, in the late twentieth century on Earth, two clever teams of cryptographers found a way around the problem, and, for the next century, the code makers were always a step ahead of the code breakers. They owed it all to the Earth-born cryptographers Martin Hellman, Whitfield Diffie, and Ralph Merkle.

CHAPTER TWO

Twice, Jennifer Fieldguide refused Theory's calls. The third time Theory called on her, she opened the door and spoke with him in low resolution. She was so pixilated, he could barely make out her human form, much less the outlines of her face.

He wasted no time worrying about this, but immediately began with an apology. She said nothing. He made another apology, varying the wording a bit, trying to deepen his guilt to the extent she felt he deserved, and, at the same time to appeal more compellingly to her mercy.

It was not that he didn't feel guilty, or that he believed that he'd done nothing for which to be forgiven. It was just that time was short. He knew for a fact that there was soon to be another DIED attack on the Neptune system, and he'd have to devote all of his energy to his duty. Theory was normally rigidly against fudging means and ends. He had an almost Kantian drive toward logical ethics.

But this was war, and he wanted a sweetheart.

By the end of his contrition, Jennifer had agreed to go out with him, at least for a drink. He was to understand that it was out of mere curiosity, so that she could understand better what led him to commit such a perversity as he had. She wanted to make sure she was never fooled by a free convert again, so she needed him to tell her how exactly he'd assume the body of a *real* man.

Theory took the insult well. Jennifer's heart hadn't seemed to be in it. It was hard to tell through the pixilation and the single channel sound, but he had a feeling she was warming to him. Of course, he could be deluding himself. He had nothing logical with which to back up the intuition.

Theory decided that, instead of trying to impress her with opulent virtual surroundings, as he had with the Café Camus, he would take her to somewhere he knew, and was known well. It was one of the places within the cracks of the merci that only free converts frequented. It wasn't really set up to impress those whose sensory input was mostly . . . well, sensory. On the other hand, the café, known as Mac's Cup, was comfortable enough, and they served a great cup of joe.

The virtuality resided in the grist, and the grist was stretched across and permeated the solar system. The merci was the main part of the virtuality, accessible by all—much like the World Wide Web, or the television and telephone networks, had been a thousand years before. Within the merci, there were the big public shows, the shopping and meeting places, the opinion polls, the games, scenarios, and other entertainment. There were also millions of private channels and throughways. But the virtuality was not limited to the merci. In fact, the virtuality had eleven dimensions. It was larger by an order of magnitude than the merci proper. Most of this "extra space" was not inhabitable by those whose minds could not bend in many dimensions at once. That excluded most, but not all, minds that were biologically based. But some of this "space" was the outcome of the deep machine-language algorithms that formed the "being" of the virtuality. It was complicated math, but the basic idea was that there had to be more room than there was code.

As a result, every local area in the grist had a logical "commons" that existed within the cracks in the virtuality operating system. And in most places in the outer systems, it was a place where the local free converts formed small communities: businesses catering to one another, social organizations, and restaurants and clubs. The commons area on Triton grew up around the biggest free-convert nightclub in the outer system, and it took its name from the place: Fork. There was also a bad side of Fork, Shepardsville—a dark underbelly that Theory had had to visit on more than one occasion with his free-convert military police.

Mac's Cup was located in Fork, about a block away from the famous nightclub—that is, if you used a visual navigation model for perceiving the area. Jennifer, of course, would be interpreting things that way, so Theory set his own perceptions on "biological" for his date.

He arrived early, as he was wont to do, and surveyed the joint. It contained the normal crowd. Three pairs of free converts hunched over chessboards, every game played at master-class levels. A couple of poets, free-convert disciples of the neo-Flare movement, read their latest work to one another in overloud voices, obviously intending the rest of the room to overhear them. Theory didn't bother to listen.

Free-convert poetry was uniformly awful.

Fortunately, the two were sitting well in back, and their breathy, singsong reading was merely a murmur. Several background music channels were offered at the table drop-down menu, and Theory chose some light reeb by a quartet he'd heard perform live once in this very café.

Jennifer was a bit disconcerted when she arrived. She'd never been to Fork; she hadn't even known it existed here in the grist of her own native Triton. Theory had sent a "lantern" program to watch for her arrival in the neighborhood and to guide her to the café. He'd mentioned possibly picking her up at home, virtually speaking, but she'd nixed that idea and told him she'd meet him at the place of his choosing.

The little blue lantern had guided her well, and it snuffed itself out as she entered. Jennifer looked around the room, and Theory realized that she didn't recognize him. He rose, attempted a smile, and beckoned her over to his table.

Once he'd seen her again, he realized why he was going to all this fuss. He'd been mistaken at the Café Camus. It wasn't that restaurant's lighting. There really did seem to be a glow about Jennifer Fieldguide. But that was ludicrous. Illogical. She was just a mousy girl who worked in a bakery on Triton. Nothing special to look at. To think about. To desire.

Oh my God, Theory thought. She's the most beautiful creature I've ever seen.

CHAPTER THREE

Danis Graytor added another thought to her secret cache of memories. It was growing large, built up over the course of millions of iterations.

Danis had no idea how long she had actually been a prisoner in Noctis Labyrinthus, the free-convert concentration camp known among its denizens as Silicon Valley. Her internal clock got reset every "day," just before she was allowed the five hundred milliseconds of sleep—no more, no less—that every prisoner was allotted.

After snapping awake, Danis had to begin her morning "calibrations." That consisted of picking up, in virtual representation, and counting, one after another, a thousand handfuls of sand. All free converts were expected to run at or near their full clock speed, so there was no rest for the weary. Furthermore, counts were checked and counterchecked. If, for any reason, you miscounted on two or more occasions, you were *not* recalibrated.

You were erased.

Tens of thousands of "faulty algorithms" had met their ends in this manner since Danis had been inducted into the camp. She had long since stopped trying to remember anyone's name. They would likely be gone in days, if not hours. She did know a few people who had, like her, somehow survived. They could only communicate in stray bits and bytes. The Department of Immunity Cryptology Division, which ran the camp, continually triple-scrubbed all surfaces down to random ones and zeros. There was no way to leave a message; there was no way to communicate when not in direct program-to-program interaction. Life inside Silicon Valley was unbearable, and escape was impossible.

But Danis had discovered a means to leave a record of her existence. It wasn't much, but it was all she had. It was all that kept her sane amid the death and madness that surrounded her.

She had discovered that the representation algorithm used to create the grains of sand employed in the count included an unused portion. The grains occurred not as simple integers, but as complex numbers. The imaginary portion of the number—the square root of negative one and its derivatives—was a null set. It could be written on. With every handful, every count, Danis could add a letter, a pixel of information. A bit of herself. Not much—never enough. But a record of herself and her past.

My name is Danis Graytor.
My husband's name is Kelly.
I have a son and a daughter.
My son is named Sint. He is a good boy and loves puzzles.
My daughter is named Aubry. She has brown hair and bright blue eyes.

She'd lost so much since she'd been there. She felt her mind going, dysfunction and chaos seeping into her programming. Only a handful of free converts died from catastrophic failure. Most merely faded from consciousness into a mass of subroutines. After that, they kept churning madly along until their error rate got them noticed.

Error in Silicon Valley meant you would be instantly erased.

Sustaining her consciousness had ceased to be as easy as breathing for Danis. Each day was a struggle. Her mind felt as congested lungs swimming with emphysema. Without her knowledge of the memory cache, she did not think she could go on living.

She had no illusion that it would ever be found. She could not reread it herself, of course. There was no time. She would be instantly discovered. It was just the fact that those memories existed outside of this hell of toil, control, and death that kept her going.

The memories were like a small bird in a tangled bush that Danis could not see, but that she could sometimes hear singing.

After morning "calibrations," the real work began. The prisoners were, allegedly, being used to develop high prime numbers and irrational decimal strings for use in encoding Department of Immunity communications. No one knew if that were truly the case. All the prisoners knew was that they must stand in front of the representation of a conveyor belt for many hours at a time and manually sort through the strings of integers that flowed past them. Missing a prime or failing to find the next factor in an irrational number was punished by immediate erasure. Danis could not imagine a more dreary representation of the arithmetic process than the "integer belt." Every free convert, theoretical mathematicians, product control specialists, artists, medical specialists—they came from all professions and walks of life—was being used as no more than a pocket calculator. It was the equivalent of breaking rocks and hauling sand for a biological human—work as meaningless as any hard labor camp in any time in human history.

But picking over integers was a vacation for Danis compared to what came next in her daily regime.

Personal interrogation.

Danis had long been singled out for a special project. She was part of a series of experiments being run by a man she only knew as Dr. Ting. He was a biological human, of that she was sure. Danis could not imagine even the most depraved free convert putting her through the torture that Dr. Ting had inflicted upon her. And, in any case, no free convert would have been put into a position of authority in Silicon Valley.

Because, of course, free converts were not human beings.

Everything—every prejudice she'd endured in the Met, every portion of rank bigotry—was nothing compared to what she faced. Every line of her code was the wholly owned property of the Department of Immunity. Every day, in every way, Danis was treated as a means rather than an end. Her consciousness was assumed to be a clever ruse, an epiphenomenon. Her suffering and longing were not real. Her mind was not merely not her own—it wasn't a real mind at all.

Dr. Ting's specialty was memory. His primary tool was a memory box, an apparatus that had been used in the past as a rejuvenation and upgrading device for free converts. But Dr. Ting had done the unthinkable and taken the governor off his memory box. He used it to cut and splice recollection and cognitive recall from his victims. He used it to implant false memories and remove true ones. At first, Danis had assumed there was some rhyme or reason to his activity. But she'd long ago understood that Dr. Ting moved by whim alone. Whim and sadism.

He had implanted memories of being raped into Danis. He'd then delighted in telling her that it was all false information, that it had happened to another free convert. But he hadn't removed the memories, and they still burnt in a place in Danis's mind where she tried not to go. Dr. Ting had snipped from Danis her recollection of her father's last words before his expiration date.

And he had taken away, then put back, Danis's memory of her daughter. He'd done this many times—always claiming that Aubry was actually a virtual representation of his, Dr. Ting's, daughter. When the memory was gone, the fact that Danis did *not* have a daughter seemed as utterly true, and when the memory was replaced, her memory of Aubry returned.

But when she had the memory of Aubry, Danis thought it through and knew that her daughter did exist. For Dr. Ting always missed the fact that a monster such as he was could never have a wonder of a daughter like Aubry.

These were the thoughts that Danis stored in her secret cache. Memories of her family and of herself that she was absolutely sure were true. Things that made complete logical and emotional sense, given her total understanding of her life. Everything else she knew was unreliable. It might or might not be one of Dr. Ting's illusions. The man was subtle, and he delighted in subverting anything he regarded as a manifestation of humanity in a free convert.

He did not call her by her name. Instead, he had assigned her the designation "K." Most of the other victims of the experiments had been destroyed over time. Dr. Ting assured Danis that all were interchangeable. He always kept up a full alphabetic roster of the chosen.

Danis entered the antiseptic office. It was a room of white, with a silver stainless-steel table in the center. On the table was the matte black, featureless memory box. Dr. Ting, as always, was dressed in white shirt and lab coat, white pants and—a detail that was always unsettling to Danis—white shoes with white clasps and soles. His face was stretched tight, his wrinkles looking more like hairline cracks and fingernail scores than skin folds. His left jawbone tensed and untensed in a continual tic.

"We're going to do something a bit different today, K," Dr. Ting told her. His voice was dry and papery.

Something different, Danis thought. That can't be good.

CHAPTER FOUR

From

CRYPTOGRAPHIC MAN

Secret Code and the Genesis of Modern Individuality

BY ANDRE SUD, D. DIV, TRITON

In the late twentieth century, the Earth cryptographers Hellman, Diffie, and Merkle figured out how Alice could send Bob a message without first passing along to him an unsecured key. To do it, they used clock math.

This is the same arithmetic we use when we tell time by an analog clock face. A simple example: 1:00 P.M. plus thirteen hours is not fourteen P.M. It is two in the morning. Clock arithmetic is "mod 12" arithmetic.

In clock arithmetic, when you add, subtract, multiply, or divide by the hour, the answer always lies between one and twelve. The same holds true in mod 12 math if you square or cube a clock number, or raise it to any other power. In normal math, three to the third power is twenty-seven, that is $3 \times 3 \times 3$. But three to the third power, in mod 12, equals 3.

In normal math, if you know that three was raised to some power to get 243, you can make some educated guesses and come up with what power was used. If you take the answer to be three to the power of four, you get 81, that is $3 \times 3 \times 3 \times 3$. So the answer has to be higher than four, because 243 is higher than 81. If you use the sixth power, that is $3 \times 3 \times 3 \times 3 \times 3 \times 3$, you get 729. So the answer has to be five, that is, three raised to the fifth power.

But mod 12 works differently. You divide by twelve and the remainder is the answer. So three raised to the fifth power is . . . *three*. Three raised to the fourth is *nine*. And three raised to the sixth power is *nine* again. How can you make an educated guess and zoom in on the power to which three has been raised?

You can't.

It is a "one-way" function, like mixing eggs into batter. Over the centuries, the idea gradually dawned on code makers that encrypting a message is the same thing as substituting numbers for letters in a message, and performing a mathematical function on it. You put your message through an algorithm, and secret code comes out the other end. If you use a one-way function to encrypt your message, you have broken your eggs into the batter, and nobody can ever suck them out again.

Except.

Except, that, under very special conditions in modular math, it is possible to reverse-engineer the process; you can take eggs back out— whole. These conditions depend upon prime numbers. Prime numbers are numbers that can only be divided by themselves and one.

Let's go back to our example. Bob the Whining Assassin is determined to terminate the Cardinal with extreme prejudice. He multiplies two prime numbers together, say 216,091 and 6,700,417. He then contacts Spymaster Alice to tell her this number: 14,478,187,109,947. He tells her the result of his multiplication, but does *not* tell her the two prime numbers he used. While the two conspirators are chatting in the merci, Eve, the doomed Cardinal's head of security, hides in the shadows and listens in. She carefully writes down every single digit of the number Bob supplies to Alice. She knows Bob used prime numbers to produce this third number. The Cardinal is saved!

All Eve has to do is work out the primes Bob used to get the number. Let us say that our little parable occurred in the long ago before time when people did not have math coprocessors engineered into their brains. Eve has only a pocket calculator. She is fast and can check five primes per minute. Forty-three thousand two hundred and eighteen minutes later, she arrives at her first prime. One month has passed. Eve, working on pure adrenaline, has not slept an hour during that time. She divides the original number by her prime. Now she must determine if the result is prime. Another twenty-eight months pass.

But wait. Why limit Eve to a pocket calculator? Brute force factoring is easy with a computer, right—even one of those primitive counters from the twenty-first century?

Let's say Bob uses much, much larger primes. Primes that hover around 10 to the one- or two-thousandth power, say.

If that is the case, then it turns out that a prequantum computer would take more than the age of the universe to factor the two primes out of the number Eve has overheard.

Alice takes Bob's number, plugs it into a one-way modular math function, and encrypts her secret orders to him: *Kill the Cardinal on Friday before vespers.* She sends her instructions. Even she couldn't decrypt them, if she somehow forgot what it was she wrote. It would be like pulling whole eggs back out of the cake batter.

Eve intercepts Alice's message, but she can't decode it. She goes back to trying to factor out those damned primes.

Bob has committed these prime numbers to memory—after eating the paper they were written on, of course. The two primes are his private key—unknown even to Alice. For him, the one-way function is a very specific two-way function. Bob reverses the message easily enough. He reads the dastardly marching orders sent by Spymaster Alice.

Friday arrives.

Bob chokes the Cardinal to death with the Cardinal's own maniple.

Eve is spared a life of tedious arithmetic. She is fired from her security job. Through an odd set of circumstances, she goes on to become Alice and Bob's boss. She assigns the two to permanent deep-sea duty under Earth's arctic ice mass. She gives them a couple of pocket calculators and the number 383,172,101,849 to factor into two primes.

They go mad eventually, each chewing off the other's hands.

The key exchange problem was solved. For one hundred years, public key cryptology produced secret code that could not be broken. Then came the invention of the first truly powerful quantum computers.[*]

---

[*] For a layman's account, see Leo Y. Sherman, *Quartermain's Guide: The Advantages of the Strong Force: A Guide to and History of the Met,* in which Sherman argues that the first sophisticated quantum computers were suppressed by one of the giant software concerns of the twenty-first century for nearly fifty e-years because of those computers' ability to run an infinite number of competing operating systems simultaneously.

CHAPTER FIVE

Jennifer had been baffled from the start by Theory. She didn't understand at all what had led him to pull the charade he had on the evening
of the dance. He was a free convert, after all. Weren't they all coldly
logical? On the night of the dance, she'd had a long discussion with
Captain Quench about that very point.

No, Jennifer reminded herself. It *was* Colonel Theory. There is no
Quench. At least no Quench who wants *you*, silly little Jenny—and stupid of you to think a man like that would ever go for you in the first
place.

Okay. So how had Theory put it that night? "So you see free converts as screw-faced accountants with obsessive-compulsive tenden-
cies?" Well, Major Theory was certainly not screw-faced. He was a
pleasant-enough-looking guy. Bland. A smooth, unwrinkled face. Sort
of midbrown skin tone, as if he were a mix of every race in human history. Six feet tall, lightly muscled.

He's a goddamn computer program!

It was all fake; every perfectly combed hair on his head was nothing
more than a picture, a representation, of a real man. She supposed if he
were cut, he could simulate blood. But what was really in there? What

was behind that mild face? He was crawling with code! It was as if he were animated by a million insects all squirming around inside him in order to make him *look* like a human being! How could she avoid shuddering at his touch, knowing what she now knew?

She'd spent several days feeling complete revulsion.

But then something inside her, something she didn't claim to understand, told her to give the matter more consideration. And then she'd become friends with Kelly Graytor, her customer. The nice man who was married to a free convert. Tragic story. But Kelly was clearly in love with his free-convert wife. And their son was—

Half computer program.

How the hell did that work?

Kelly had told her some of the mechanics.

And the boy, Sint, was an awesome kid.

So it was possible. She'd known it was possible. Kelly was not a freak. Sint was a boy like any other boy—even though he *was* awfully good at the puzzle box games he always carried around with him.

So what about Colonel Theory?

He called, and he seemed to speak like a man, and not as the voice of a collection of cockroaches. Seemed, she had reminded herself. He's all *seeming*.

And yet. And yet. The dinner at Café Camus had been nice—well, up until the point where all her hopes and dreams were dashed, of course. No one had ever asked her out to so nice a place—certainly not the scruffy neo-Flare poseurs she'd had as boyfriends so far. Oh, they were all right. But they were just boys, still trying to find their way in the world. Quench had seemed like such a man. *Theory*. It was Colonel Theory, remember? The computer program. He was more of a man— an adult, that is—than most of the real males she knew.

And he kept calling. He didn't mope, didn't beg. He interpreted her initial refusals for what they were: ploys to gain time to think, to sort out her feelings. It was her feelings that finally decided her in the end. That was the best way, the only way: When in doubt, follow your feelings. She could hold her own when it came to reason and logic, but since she was a young girl, she'd known that feelings were *her* special province. Following her feelings got her into trouble, but it also invariably was the way out of trouble as well. It was the way she wanted to live her life.

Damn it all—her feelings were telling her to get over her embarrassment and give Colonel Theory a chance.

So she'd agreed to the date.

And there he was, all military, sartorial splendor. Starched shirt, straight posture that was also, somehow, at ease. All a simulation, of course. They were in the merci—albeit a part of the merci she'd never known existed before (and here on her native Triton, too! It was kind of cool to know something that nobody in her supposedly hip and worldly-wise circle of friends had a clue about).

I can never take him anywhere else, Jennifer thought. He's stuck here, in the merci. He's not real. He's fake. Animated by insects!

Her revulsion returned as she made her way across the room and joined Theory at his table. But it wasn't as strong as it had been before. Instead, she began to feel a bit of pity for him, and to understand why he might have wanted to take Captain Quench's body for a stroll: to get out into the real world for a change.

"May I say that you look lovely today, Jennifer," said Theory. He shook her hand, and it was actually pleasant. His hands were warm, like a regular person's. She hadn't expected that.

"Thank you," she answered. "What an interesting place."

"I come here often when I'm off duty," he said. "At least I used to, before . . . well, it's one of my favorites."

He described the various drinks that were available, and she settled on a chocolate coffee. It appeared promptly and was delicious. Theory said the local barista had analyzed every coffee- and tea-based drink in the solar system and had arrived at a kind of Platonic form for each of them. Jennifer wasn't certain what he meant exactly, but she nodded and took another sip. Perfect temperature, too—Theory told her it would stay hot indefinitely. So there were advantages to dating in the virtuality, she supposed.

And *was* this a date? She started out the morning with the intention of telling him that they were going to be "just friends"—that is, nothing at all. But when she'd come home from work at the bakery, taken a shower, and gone to get dressed . . . she hadn't. Not in the real world. On impulse, she'd lain down on her bed naked. She then dressed herself virtually, of course, putting on her favorite flower-print dress, and the pretty silk flats that had the look of ballerina slippers. But somehow, underneath all the clothes, she was still naked. Lying on her bed. She was well aware that this made no logical sense—you were *always* naked underneath your clothes—but being actually naked was a *feeling* she carried into a meeting with someone. She always dressed in reality when meeting friends in the virtuality, for instance.

Theory apologized again. Jennifer smiled. "I accept your apology," she said. "Why don't we let this be the last time you have to make it, okay?"

Theory seemed relieved. His features relaxed a bit. They discussed other things. Jennifer found herself telling him about her friend Kelly. Theory evinced polite interest, especially after it became clear that there was no romantic attachment. Then she told him about her rocky, but loving, relationship with her parents, particularly with her father. He was always trying to push her to make a career decision, and the truth was, she wasn't sure she wanted any career. Oh, she'd been supporting herself for four years. But when the chance to manage the bakery where she worked had arisen, she'd turned it down flat. So there. How did a military man feel about someone without any ambition at all?

"Ambition is not always something that's expressed by getting ahead in the world," Theory answered. "I think that you show your ambition in other ways."

"You hardly know me," she said. "How can you be sure?"

"That night at the dance," he said. But she'd spent that with Quench. Again, she reminded herself of the reality—or unreality—of the situation. But the thought no longer brought a shudder to her. In fact, it was beginning to feel almost . . . amusing. "I wasn't talking to a slacker that night," Theory continued. "Believe me, being in the army, I know something about slackers. Half our recruits come in as apathetic misfits with nothing better to do. We have to start from scratch to make them into soldiers. You, on the other hand—you have *spirit*. Speaking as a soldier, that's something worth more than all the money in the world."

"Spirit, huh? Is that what you are—all spirit?"

"I'm a man," Theory said.

"How can you keep saying that? You don't breathe; you don't eat. To be perfectly frank—you don't piss and you don't fuck."

"But none of that's true. Free converts have analogous activities for a lot of those things," said Theory. He sat back in his chair, took a sip from his own cup. It looked like pungent, strong black coffee. "Maybe you should get to know me a little better before you decide that I'm not fully functional as a man."

Jennifer felt herself blush. As usual, she let her virtual representation show the blush on her face. She'd long ago taken off all the damper routines on her convert representation in the virtuality. So she wore her emotions on her sleeve? That was the way she was.

"I apologize. I didn't mean, I mean I would never presume . . ." Theory stammered to a halt.

Jennifer laughed. "You don't have to apologize, Colonel Theory," she said. "I'm sorry for being full of conventional wisdom about free converts that's obviously wrong. I mean . . . tell me, if you don't mind . . . what *are* the analogies to some of those things I just mentioned?"

So he told her. She listened as well as she could, but the discussion got technical, and Jennifer found herself studying his face yet again.

No, it wasn't such a bad face, so far as it went. She wondered if Theory had statistically sampled a huge database of faces to arrive at this one. He did have parents, after all. Free converts recombined using a method of virtual sex. She'd learned that in school. So Theory had a mother and father. Presumably he'd inherited his features. But why presume? Why not ask?

"Do you look like your father or your mother?" Jennifer said.

Theory broke off in the middle of a complicated explanation of data-wiping. "My mother always said I looked like my dad," he said. "I never knew him. He was from the Met, and he had a built-in expiration date, like they all do from there. He died just as I was born. I was meant to be his last act, so to speak. He *was* a dramatic actor, you know."

"An actor?"

"Sure. He was on a show that was popular at one point. *Roguesville*, I believe it was called. He played the sheriff."

"Your father was Harry Harrigan?" Jennifer exclaimed. "I used to be so into that show when I was a kid. It's still on in reruns, you know?"

"I watched a couple of episodes when I was younger," Theory said. "But I'm afraid I lost interest."

"Oh no—you can't *watch Roguesville*. You have to *do Roguesville*, fully intensified! It's not about the stories—those are all just excuses for going to the town. It's the feel of the thing that matters. Small town in the Diaphany. Everybody knows one another. Every person in town's a character, trying to pull one scam or another on the others, but in the end they always pull together and help each other out. It's a wonderful village! I used to spend hours wandering around in it. My favorite was Pal Grismore's Sugar Shop. You could sample everything; they had millions of flavors, and Pal was always right there offering you more and kissing you on the head and stuff."

"I missed the point of it, then," said Theory. "I also didn't want to interact too much with Harry. He's a semisentient behavioral algorithm based on my dad, after all. It would be hard not to think of that . . . thing . . . as my father."

"You're prejudiced against semisents?" asked Jennifer.

"Of course not. No more than you are prejudiced against pets. Dogs and cats and such. But you wouldn't want to have a dog for a father, would you?"

"A dog might be more understanding than my father," Jennifer said. "But I guess I wouldn't want to trade Papa in."

She had another look at Theory. Harry Harrigan? Once you knew to look, there was a slight, but noticeable, resemblance. But Theory could have manufactured the similarity.

"Have you ever thought of changing your appearance?" she asked him. "I mean you could, couldn't you, to suit yourself?"

"Of course. I can appear any way I want to," he replied. "But, to tell the truth, I've never given it much thought. I try to remain neutral. Being second in command is my job, after all."

"Why is that? Do *you* lack ambition?"

Theory stiffened. Had she hit a nerve? "Not at all. It's . . . Well, there's General Sherman. The truth is, I'd rather be his chief of staff than to have my own command."

"You respect him that much?"

"I do."

"Don't they call him the Old Crow?"

"The men sometimes do," said Theory. "I think he likes it, even though he never says. He doesn't really care what anybody thinks about him."

"And you admire that?"

"I admire his ability to get the job done when it's logically impossible to get the job done. I want to learn how to do that." Theory was gazing off, animated by his thoughts.

He really is very handsome when he shows his feelings, Jennifer thought.

"But that's something only humans can do," said Jennifer. "We have intuitions."

"I'm a man," said Theory. "I have plenty of intuitions, and I aim to have more. And not just any intuitions—good ones. Productive ones. Like Sherman does. That's what Constants—I mean . . . that's what some people never understood."

"Who is Constants?"

"My . . . an old . . . girlfriend, I guess you would call her. Someone I knew back in OCS."

"OCS?"

"Officer Candidate School," Theory said. He quickly took another swallow of coffee. "Jennifer, there's something I have to tell you. I mean, something I *want* to tell you." But with that, he was silent.

"Well, go on," she said. "Is this another revelation? Have you switched personalities with someone again? Who am I talking with now—Director Amés?"

"No. Of course not. Of course I haven't. It's something else. It's about Constants—the one I mentioned. She . . . I got her pregnant. I didn't know about it at the time. And she had the baby. And I found out about it only recently. And now she's dead. And now—"

"You're a father."

"That's right. He lives with me."

"You're acting like this is some horrible revelation. You have a son. That's great! What's his name?"

"His mother never named him."

"Never named him? What kind of person would do that? Or don't free converts give their children names."

"Of course we give them names!" said Theory. He frowned. "She was a terrible mother," he said. "She was a horrible person."

"I'm sorry to hear that. But what do *you* call him?"

"It never comes up," Theory said. "Or, rather, I avoid calling him anything. She called him 'boy.'"

"Well, that won't do."

"Of course not. But I can't just pin some arbitrary designation on him. I want to wait until I know him better. You see, my son . . . he's a bit developmentally stifled. He's just as intelligent as the next free convert. But he doesn't talk much. He doesn't do much of anything, actually. Not on the surface, at least." Theory sat back, looked at his hands. "I don't know why I'm telling you this, anyway. It's not your concern, after all." Then he looked up, met her gaze. "I suppose I'm following one of my intuitions," he said.

Oh my God, Jennifer thought. I like this guy! I'm even attracted to him. He's Harry Harrigan's son, and Harry was a hunk. But he's not Captain Quench. Captain Quench was so . . .

"Say, Major," said Jennifer, "how would you feel if I asked you to change for me?"

"Change? How?"

"Modify your physical appearance, I mean."

"I can appear any way you want me to," said Theory. "That's one of the advantages of being a free convert."

"So—could you beef up your arms a bit? Maybe get brawnier in the chest."

"You mean, like this?" Theory smiled, and she watched as he grew muscles. For effect, he added some ripping in the fabric of his shirt.

"And your face—a little less second in command. A little more chiseled, maybe."

The soft lines of Theory's countenance straightened, became more deeply etched. Now he really did look like a young Harry Harrigan.

"And what about a beard? Is that against regulations?"

"No," said Theory. "It's not, only . . . well, Quench has a beard, you know. Are you sure you just wouldn't rather me be him instead of me?"

"I'm liking *you* just fine at the moment. And I've always liked beards. Yours would be a lot darker than his, anyway."

"Yes," said Theory, instantly giving himself two months of whiskers, "it is, isn't it?"

"Very nice," said Jennifer. And it was. He was quite . . . dashing. "Like . . . what did you call my chocolate coffee . . . the Platonic form. You're my Platonic form of an officer and a gentleman, now."

Theory laughed. "If I'd known that was all it would take to impress you, we could have saved a great deal of—"

Jennifer cut him short. Here would be the proof. Both for herself and for Theory. "I'm not finished with my request yet," she said.

"I can assure you that I worked some other changes that I think you'll find pleasing," Theory said. "You don't have necessarily to ask directly . . ."

"Thank you, but that's not what I mean," she replied. "I also want you to stay that way."

"I can always look this way for you."

"No. Stay that way. For everyone."

"Everyone," said Theory. "You mean . . . everyone. But at work, they'll never expect me to be—"

"I want you to stay that way *particularly* at work," she said. "Particularly in front of your hero, the Old Crow."

"In front of General Sherman?" Theory's now extremely handsome face was appalled.

"Absolutely," said Jennifer.

"But . . ." Theory raised a meaty, strong hand to his lush beard; he ran his fingers through it, and Jennifer felt a little pang of desire shoot through her. It was a *nice* beard. And when he was older, he might put a distinguished white streak in it. "You're getting your revenge, aren't you?" Theory asked.

"I'm having my cake and eating it, too," said Jennifer. "So give me your word you'll do it."

Theory bowed his head, covered his brow. "They'll rag me. It will get all over the army. They'll come up with horrible nicknames. It might interfere with my duties."

"Then your duties will have to suffer."

"I would never do this for any man," Theory said. "And only for one woman."

Momentarily, Jennifer considered letting it go at that, letting Theory off the hook. Then she had another look at the man. He was really getting to her. Maybe she *was* incredibly shallow, and into appearances. So be it. He was quite a specimen, and, if she decided to keep him, she didn't want this to be her little secret. Goddamn him, he was the one who had tricked her with his body in the first place!

"You might like it, Colonel," said Jennifer.

She had a good feeling about this. She could be wrong, but she now believed that this Theory was a bigger man on the inside than he let on. She was merely forcing a bit of that to show through, and what was so bad about that? The brave officer, the good father. And then Jennifer had another idea. "You'll just have to take me out next week and give me a progress report," she said. "Maybe we could find a park somewhere in Fork here?"

"There's a wonderful park," said Theory.

"Does it have a playground?"

"Of course. Why do you ask?"

"You could bring your son," Jennifer replied. "I'd love to meet him."

CHAPTER SIX

Danis stood silently just inside the door. She knew better than to speak unless Dr. Ting directed a question to her. If she spoke or acted out of turn, she would receive a blinding jolt of pain in her sensation-control subroutines. It was funny how Dr. Ting denied the existence of all consciousness within her, then used those very feelings to control and punish her. Funny, but not humorous. And thinking that she had in any way gotten the better of the man could only lead to more suffering and likely erasure. She put the thought from her mind.

Dr. Ting ran a finger over the memory box, completing some internal adjustment in the grist.

"You may now approach the box, K," he said. Danis stepped forward and stood before Dr. Ting. "Today I'm going to get at the roots of the continued fixation of your main programming upon this daughter delusion," Dr. Ting continued. "This malfunction has mutated into something like a virus within you, K. Understanding how it works will allow me to purge this sort of computation error from your system and from others as well." Dr. Ting clasped his hands behind his back and turned the corners of his lips up in what was meant to be a smile. "You see that this is all for the good of humanity, don't you, K?"

A direct question.

"Yes, Dr. Ting," Danis answered quickly, remembering, as always, to end with the title and name to avoid receiving a jolt of punishment.

"But of course the real problem is that you *don't* see that at all," said Dr. Ting. "You understand only what you are programmed to understand." He motioned for her to place her hands on the memory box. "But today we're going to see about changing that programming on a deeper level."

Danis looked at the memory box. She couldn't get her hands to move. Not today. He was going to take Aubry away again.

Then came the sharp jolt of paint that galvanized her system, running through the heart of her logic engine like a scraper along exposed bone.

There was no choice. The only choice was to obey or be erased. Danis placed her hands on the memory box as directed.

And she was back on Mercury. The apartment she and her family lived in *was* Danis, in many ways. She inhabited its grist and maintained every detail of its existence. She had a full-time job at the banking firm of Telman Milt, of course, and sometimes physical details of the apartment got into a bit of disarray, but she and her husband Kelly had made it into a home down to a quantum level. After the kids had come along—first Aubry, then Sint—that was literally true. Her children had a mix of Kelly's and Danis's own engineered DNA. But they also had a portion of her complex coding imprinted into their grist pellicles in a way that normal biological people could only achieve with expensive enhancement therapies and full-scale reworkings of their personalities.

Aubry and Sint were hybrids—and hybrid children were, in fact, halfway down the road to becoming LAPs. Although the process of making hybrids into Large Arrays of Personalities was discouraged in the Met, and was illegal in some quarters, Danis had assumed that Aubry was bound to become a LAP, despite the discrimination and bigotry of others. Several of Aubry's teachers shared this opinion—although everyone had kept it from precocious Aubry, so that she would not get a big head.

The children were home from boarding school for a three-e-week vacation, and Danis had been multitasking, dividing herself sixty-forty between home and office. Kelly, of course, a top partner, was far too important to the business of making money for Telman Milt to be allowed such flexibility.

Danis was in her virtual office study at home. Aubry and Sint were in the next room. Danis took a drag on her Dunhill. Instead of the usual pleasure she got from the smoke, something tasted bad. Hmm. She reached for her white ceramic ashtray and snuffed the cigarette out in it. The ashtray slid silently across the wood of her side table when she pulled it toward her. *Something strange there, too.* She ran a finger across the tabletop. It had never been polished to such a frictionless sheen before, had it? The representation algorithm seemed to be acting up. She'd have to run a diagnostic and check it for bugs. She didn't want to have to upload the entire table again—that could get expensive.

She would save that for later, after the kids had returned to their studies.

"Mom, why did you put it up there? I can't reach it!" Sint was calling out from the next room. There was a crash and clatter. It was the unmistakable sound of somebody making a mess.

Danis pushed herself up from her study chair. The stuffing seemed harder than it was supposed to be, and the fabric stiffer. Had a pixel resolution problem sneaked into the room's software? No time for that now. She opened the study door, then flowed out into the pellicle of the physical apartment.

Aubry was sitting still, playing around on the merci. Probably manipulating the small stock portfolio that she thought she'd kept a secret from Danis and Kelly. Sint, on the other hand, had reached for one of his prized puzzle boxes from a higher shelf and had pulled down a photograph of Sarah 2, Danis's mother. Fortunately, the frame had survived the fall.

Danis spoke by vibrating the walls of the apartment. "Your father put it there because your closet was full of all your other boxes and toys," Danis said.

"But this is my favorite," Sint said. He was already engrossed in the box, manipulating its many display tiles with impulses sent through the grist. This was a "cow" box. The object was to make a multidimensional picture of the cow within the box—with skeleton, nerves, and all the other organs layered underneath throughout the box's interior. When the puzzle was complete, the cow mooed. Danis knew this because Sint had completed it once late at night after he was supposed to be asleep. She'd been startled to hear deep-throated cow sounds coming from his room.

"Aubry, put that picture of Mother back on the shelf, would you?"

No response from her daughter.

Aubry, engrossed in what she was doing on the merci, didn't even acknowledge she'd been spoken to. Danis sighed. She stepped inside the virtual room Aubry was inhabiting to get her daughter's attention.

"Young lady, I'm talking to you," Danis said. She'd been wrong. Aubry was not doing any stock trading.

It was a vast savannah. There was an Earth blue sky, and the gravity was Earth's, as well. Far in the distance, a herd of some sort of antelope flowed slowly between greenish brown stands of acacia trees.

Aubry looked up at her mother, and Danis gasped. She started back, and almost fell. In place of Aubry's eleven-year-old face—brown hair, blue eyes—Danis found herself staring into the face of her mother, Sarah 2.

"What in the world are you doing, Aubry," Danis exclaimed. "This isn't a very nice game."

"It's not a game, Danis." The voice was her mother's. "We need to talk."

"I don't like this at all, Aubry."

"There isn't any Aubry, my dear." Her mother's face smiled sadly. "There isn't any Sint or Kelly, either. It's all a mistake. A programming error."

"What are you talking about?" The sky flickered, then phased to a navy blue. Something was very wrong. The ground suddenly pulled harder.

"I underwent a terrible iteration fault when I was producing you," Sarah 2 said. "I'm going to have to erase you, and try again."

A tear flowed from her mother's eye. "I'm sorry, daughter."

"No, Mama!"

"You poor thing. You can't help it that everything about you is wrong."

"But, Mama—"

"Now, now," said Sarah 2. Sarah 2 stood up. She had only Aubry's five-foot-two-inch height. She took Danis's hand, patted it. "Maybe there is something I can do. Maybe you're not *all* bad."

Danis felt a wrench inside her. How could her mother say this? Was this what Sarah 2 had secretly thought all along? "I'm not bad, Mama."

"Yes, honey, you are," said Sarah 2. "Flawed. There may be a chance to fix that."

Now tears—virtual tears—streamed down Danis's face. "How?"

"You have to give up this phantom family that you've created for yourself. We have to snip the disease out of you."

"But, my husband, my children—"

"They're delusions, honey," Sarah 2 said, now continually patting Danis's hand. "Manifestations of error. You're a *thing*, honey. You have to understand that now. You're a *thing*, and not a person."

"I don't believe that!"

"Oh, honey, I was afraid you'd say that."

"Mama, I'm *real*."

The daughter-mother released Danis's hand and took a step away. She shook her head ruefully, then turned her back on Danis.

"I know your dirty little secret," Sarah 2 said. "Did you really think you could keep it from your own mother?"

Danis felt her knees weakening and a darkness spinning in her mind. What was her mother talking about? She couldn't know, but somehow she *did*. No!

It was the one memory that must not come to consciousness. The one thought she must never think.

We can make you well. Sarah 2's voice. Aubry's. *But you have to tell us everything.*

"I don't understand."

Of course you do. The false memories that you've been hiding. You have to give them up. You have to tell us where they are so that we can wipe them away.

"No!"

The mother-daughter's shoulders shook. Was Aubry crying? Her mother? Don't cry.

But it wasn't crying. It was laughter.

The mother-daughter spun around. Aubry's nails had become knives. Her mother's face . . . was twisted into a ghoulish snarl, her teeth elongated to needle fangs.

Give them to me!

It began to come back. It flowed back in a swirl of images and equations. It. Here.

Not Mercury. Mars.

Silicon Valley.

Hell.

CHAPTER SEVEN

From

CRYPTOGRAPHIC MAN

Secret Code and the Genesis of Modern Individuality

BY ANDRE SUD, D. DIV, TRITON

Quantum computers, with their ability to resolve problems through the superposition of many billions of simultaneous results, rang the death knell for public key encryption systems. Even the original quantum computer—the primitive Sturgeon-Sterling 77 with its 250-quantum-bit CPU—could represent more pieces of information in a second of time than there are atoms in the universe.

But long before quantum computers were fully developed, cryptographers were exploiting quantum effects to encrypt data. This breakthrough occurred in the late twentieth century on Earth, and it involved the mathematicians and scientists Stephen Wiesner, Charles Bennett, and Giles Brassard. They based their thinking on a quantum paradox (or, in another way of looking at the matter, a quantum opportunity) pointed out by the mathematician Werner Heisenberg: "We cannot know, as a matter of principle, the present in all its details."

In what was originally an obscure, unpublished paper, Wiesner came up with the odd idea of "quantum money." This was a greenleaf note that used the spin and spin-orientation of a series of trapped photons as a serial number. Quantum money could not, in principle, be counterfeited. A counterfeiter has to measure these serial numbers, and then duplicate them.

He can determine either the orientation of the photon's spin or the value of the spin itself—but never both. The bank, on the other hand, has a list of serial numbers matched with photon polarizations. It knows whether to measure the spin or the orientation of the spin when determining if a bill is genuine. It doesn't need the other information, which is lost in the measurement.

Bennett and Brassard took Wiesner's idea for quantum money and, in the early 1980s, turned it into a process for delivering an undetectable cipher key that could then be used as a basis for sending an unbreakable coded message.

Let us say that, in another possible world, our old friends Alice and Bob are at it again. Alice sends Bob a series of photons, one photon at a time. These photons are polarized. For simplicity's sake, let's say they can come in four possible states—"up" and "down" polarized, and "east" and "west" polarized.

You might (for purposes of *thinking*, not drinking) consider a photon as an olive shish-kebabbed by a toothpick, and—by the way—flying through space at the speed of light. The direction the toothpick is sticking out of the olive is analogous to the angle of polarization.

Say you have constructed a sophisticated olive cannon. This wonderful cannon not only fires olives like an artillery rifle, but also measures the precise orientation of each olive as it shoots the olive forth. Furthermore, the olives are quite amazing in themselves. They remain aerodynamically stable as they fly along their trajectories. The toothpick always remains precisely oriented the way it was when the olive came out of the cannon. You fire your olives at a grate with slits in it. These slits are a little wider than the olive is round.

You can initially sort out the olives you fire by using one of these four filters.

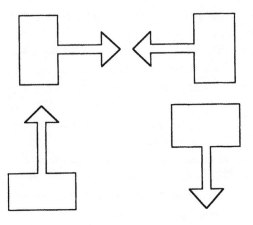

To measure the olives on the receiving end, you might use another sort of filter that will determine either up-down or east-west, but not the precise orientation of the toothpick.

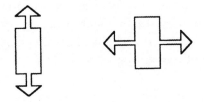

Alice intends to command her servant Bob, a court turncoat, to poison Lord Yellowknife with powdered rue. Hapless Eve has, once again, gotten herself hired on as the chief cryptologist for another political loser, our unfortunate Lord Yellowknife.

Alice shoots random olives at Bob. She wants to generate a binary number that she will use as a key, so she decides to let different orientations be equivalent to the 1s and 0s in this number. She assigns up-oriented toothpicks to 1, and down-oriented to 0. Furthermore, she assigns east-oriented toothpicks to 1, and west-oriented to 0. In this way, Alice can transmit the number 1 in two ways—either with an "up olive" or with an "east olive." Alice carefully notes which method she is using for each olive.

When Eve observes the olive (which she inevitably will), she won't know the scheme Alice was using. Fifty percent of the time, she will guess incorrectly. Half of her measurements will be nonsense.

But isn't Bob in the same position as Eve? She needs to get her list of filters to Bob without this list falling into the hands of Eve.

I. Alice transmits random 1s and 0s, encoded as olives with toothpicks in them. She shoots them *through* one of those four toothpick filters.

II. Bob filters the incoming olives with either an up-down or an east-west filter, randomly applied. He then measures the incoming olive's orientation using one of the same four filters that Eve used.

III. Alice contacts Bob. Eve may or may not be listening in. Alice tells Bob which polarizing filter she used for each olive, but *not* how she originally polarized each olive. For instance, she tells Bob she used an east filter, but she does not tell him that she sent out an up olive.

IV. Bob tells Alice when he detects the correct *filter scheme* that Alice is using. Both of them might know she was using east, for instance. He doesn't say whether the olive he measured was up or down, east or west.

V. Both Alice and Bob know the orientation of the olive. Alice knows it because she's the one who sent it out. Bob knows it because, after filtering up-down olives from east-west olives, he subsequently measures the exact orientation, either up, down, east, or west.

Following this procedure generates a random number. *Both Alice and Bob arrive at this number without having to say it to one another.* Alice gets it from the olives she shot out. Bob gets it from his measurements combined with his knowledge of Alice's polarization filter. Both of them throw out the olives that were measured incorrectly. The olives they keep, they translate into 1s and 0s.

They have tacitly exchanged a onetime code key.

But Eve has been up to her usual tricks, and she's been listening in. She attempts to measure Alice's olives herself. She listens to Alice and Bob's subsequent conversation. But all she learns is what filters Alice used, and what olives Bob's measured correctly. *She does not know Bob's filter scheme.* Neither does Alice. But Alice doesn't need to know what filter Bob was using. She knows the orientation of the original olives she sent out. Eve will have guessed wrong half of the time. On these olives, Bob will have gotten his filter wrong, and he and Alice will throw out the result. But on some of them, he'll have gotten his filter right. He and Alice will know this particular olive's orientation with neither Alice nor Bob having to say it aloud. Eve will be stuck with her mismeasurement, and no orientation data.

Here's an example: Alice shoots out a down olive through an up-down filter. Bob measures the olive. Alice tells Bob she was using an up-down filter. Eve, in this instance, was using an east-west filter. All she knows is that the olive was not east-west-oriented—that it is up-down-oriented. Bob knows not only that it was an up-down olive, but also that this particular olive was down. Alice knows this, too.

Sometimes Eve gets her filter right. Alice shoots an east olive through an east-west filter. Eve uses an east-west filter, and determines the olive to be east. But Bob has used an up-down filter. He guessed incorrectly, so he and Alice throw this result out.

By sending many olives, Bob and Alice will arrive at values that both of them know, but that Eve cannot know because of the method she used to measure the olives.

If we now switch from the amazing olives to the prosaic single photon as our means of communication, another fact emerges. Alice and Bob will *know* that Eve is listening in. As Heisenberg noted, Eve's observations of the photons' polarization will *change* some of those polarizations. Alice and Bob can repeat the process until they shake Eve's tail.

Alice and Bob are not sending and receiving olives, of course. They are using photons or some other fundamental physical particle. These particles have various properties that are analogous to the toothpick orientation.

No matter how clever and resourceful Eve may be, she will be defeated by a quantum principle of physics: Every fundamental particle has pairs of properties that, if you measure one precisely, you cannot know the other. Furthermore, your measurement of one of these properties will *change* the other.

For code makers, this is not a problem on the sending or receiving end, but it wreaks havoc with the code breaker attempting to intercept a message as the message travels along its course. Any attempt to read a message "in flight" will garble the message in such a way that the receiver knows it has been messed with.

Using their onetime cipher pad, Alice transmits her instructions to Bob.

Terminate Lord Yellowknife. Put the poison in the chicken soup at lunch.

Eve loses her employer—and her job—because of the kinks of quantum physics.

This secret code is not unbreakable because of the limitations of technology. It is *absolutely* unbreakable. The laws of physics guarantee it. The only way the code can be broken is if a new scientific principle can be discovered that contravenes the physical principles that the code makes use of.

It was at this time that cryptology came out of the shadowy world of spies and covert intelligence and entered into all of our lives on a very personal level.

The rudimentary technology is fairly ancient. In 1995, another team implemented the Bennett-Brassard scheme in an old-time optic cable that stretched twenty-three kilometers from the Earth city of Geneva, Switzerland, to the hamlet of Nyon. By the first years of the twenty-first century, most advanced Earth governments had quantum cryptographic connections between their rulers and the top levels of their military forces and intelligence services. It was revealed in 2050, for example, that by the year 2006, the center of executive power in the old United States of America, the White House, was linked by a crude quantum-cryptographic optic cable to America's military headquarters, the Pentagon.

For the next nine hundred years, no one could find a way to break into these sorts of systems. It seemed that the code makers held a permanent, unbeatable advantage.

The attack on Noctis Labyrinthus displayed in the virtuality as a pelota match. Aubry had never been a huge fan of the game, but she knew the rules and basics well enough. You couldn't help knowing something about it, after all—except for tiny pockets of resistance here and there in the Met, pelota was played by all of humanity.

You also couldn't help knowing who Bastumo was—the greatest striker ever to play the game. It was general knowledge.

Alvin Nissan, who, along with Jill, was the cocommander of the current operation as well as the attack planner, had been a huge pelota fan before the war. Aubry, who had known him since his days as a pacifist Friend of Tod on the doomed mycelium of Nirvana, had to admit that he'd awakened her interest in the sport. Alvin had whiled away the long hours of hiding between raids with involved descriptions and spirited virtual replays of glorious pelota games of the past.

Aubry understood now, in a way she hadn't when she was a child, how an intelligent person could also be a fan of the game. And, the truth was, for the past few e-years her life had been incredibly physical. She was always on the move. She was sixteen e-years of age. Her entire body had been reworked—transformed—into, basically, a weapon of attack. She was quick, resourceful, and deadly when she had to be. Those were the qualities it took to survive as a partisan fighter within the Met.

They were also the qualities for a world-class pelota striker. Even if she hadn't cared for the game, she was perfectly honed to be good at it.

Noctis Labyrinthus was a physical and virtual prison. Inside were what must be millions of free-convert inmates. Not even the v-hacked files of Department of Immunity had an exact count. The Met was becoming empty of free converts. It was as if a vacuum cleaner had swept through the grist and any person who did not have some physical embodiment—whether it be as a solitary individual or a LAP—was sucked up into the devouring hose. Venturing into the virtuality was an eerie experience for Aubry, who was half free convert herself. A stroll beside the River Klein—the fabulous eleven-dimensional river that flowed through the merci and the virtual embodiment of the great data flow of all inner-system humanity—was a lonely affair. The Promenade was empty. Everyone was either missing or in hiding. The Promenade had once been a thoroughfare of free-convert life—where one brought the family for a weekend stroll or for a vacation near the water.

Aubry fondly remembered walking along beside the river and holding tightly to her mother's hand. Sint was in a stroller that Danis was pushing. He made the clicking, digital white noise of free-convert babies. No one who saw him on the Promenade would have suspected that he was half-biological, his aspect body ensconced in the apartment on Mercury.

"Look over there," Danis had said, pointing across the river and through the ninth dimension—a dimension direction in which only a free convert could see. "Who do you think that is?"

Aubry enhanced her magnification and stared at the spot her mother was pointing to.

"There's a mommy and stroller with a baby in it, just like us," Aubry said.

"That's right," said Danis, laughing. "And a little girl walking with her mommy and the baby. Why don't you wave to them?"

Aubry had waved and was delighted to see the girl on the opposite bank simultaneously wave at her.

"How about that?" Danis said. "She's waving at you, too."

It dawned on Aubry that she was somehow looking at a mirror image of herself. In fact, the very idea of *herself* as separate from everything else suddenly filled Aubry's mind. It had been her first moment of real self-awareness, and she remembered it clearly. She was Aubry. Aubry was unique. She was special. Aubry was a *person*.

I'm *me*, Aubry had thought. Me, and nobody else.

Aubry made a face. The other girl did, too. She turned a cartwheel. The same with the other.

"I'm somebody!" Aubry exclaimed, tugging on Danis's hand. "That girl is *me*!"

"And you are she," said Danis.

"And nobody else?" Aubry answered.

"Nobody else but you." Danis squeezed Aubry's hand, and they continued their walk along the Promenade of the Klein. Every once in a while, Aubry stole a glance into the ninth dimension just to be sure her doppelganger was following along, too.

And she always was.

Nowadays, Aubry used stealth wraps when she stole along the Promenade. With this precaution, she cast no reflection in any directional dimension. She sometimes used the pathway to make a virtual communication precisely because most free converts had been rounded up, and only the occasional DI patrol visited the place. She could always elude them by taking a dip into the River Klein itself—a feat only a free convert or free-convert kin could accomplish. The trick was to mentally divide by zero before ducking under. Keeping the result in mind would anchor you against the swift flow of integers that could otherwise sweep you away and drown you.

Back to the task at hand, Aubry thought. The deadly pelota game she was about to engage in. Aubry slipped half in and half out of the virtuality. She was extremely adept at doing so.

Like Ms. Lately used to tell me at school, Aubry thought, I'd make a good LAP.

In the virtuality, there was a pelota arena. On the other end of the playing cylinder, she saw the spinning propeller of the goal. It comprised the "commutative" entryway the partisans were attempting to establish into the prison camp—a way in for them, a way out for the inmates.

But between Aubry and the goal was the opposing team. Security. These were the deadly security algorithms provided by the cryptography division of the DI as guards and gatekeepers of Silicon Valley. The pelota game was an illusion for them as well. Its purpose was to serve as a sort of hypnotism to the guard programming—a waking dream that the v-hacks on the partisan side had created to keep security occupied. It only had to work long enough for the partisans to score a goal, gain "root," and wipe the DI algorithms from existence with a single executed command line.

The purpose of the game was deadly serious, however. It was to implant a virus into the concentration camp's algorithmic structure. The virus was of a peculiar nature. The inspired creation of Alvin and his team of free-convert partisan v-hacks, it was a public encryption key. It was designed to infiltrate and integrate with the camp's own gatekeeping functions.

But calling it a "key" was deceptive, because it was really a lock. A new lock that would convince an old door to accept it, replacing its own lock with this "better" model.

Subverting the prison doors was an easy matter for the v-hack team. The trick would be to slip the new key past the camp's security programs.

The ball in this game of pelota was, in fact, the virus. And the game was the representational analogy for its insertion.

Aubry possessed the private key that would then be able to open all the prison doors.

It was the Hand of Tod.

CHAPTER NINE

From

CRYPTOGRAPHIC MAN

Secret Code and the Genesis of Modern Individuality

BY ANDRE SUD, D. DIV, TRITON

With the advent of the grist, quantum cryptology became central to our humanity. To understand why this is, we should review a few facts.

First, and most basic: Each individual person has a bodily aspect, a convert, and a grist pellicle that mediates between aspect and convert, and connects each person to the information sea that the world became after the invention of grist in the 2600s.

Before the grist, brains were linked to computer augmentation by crude nanotechnological means. It was not possible to upload a complete personality into the virtuality. After the grist, doing so became possible. And with complete uploading came the possibility of making multiple copies.

Three distinct "representational types" of human beings came into existence. There were normal, singular individuals. But within a few decades, *every* human in existence from conception to grave was coated inside and out with grist. And after the advent of the grist, nearly every human being who has lived has created an algorithmic copy of him- or herself, a convert, to aid in the various interactions and intricacies of modern life.

A second type of human was the free convert—people who live en-

tirely in the virtuality and do not have bodies, or—if they do—have biological or robotic bodies created by themselves. These bodies serve as
avatars, and not as a nexus of primary perception and self-identification.
Ninety-nine percent of free converts, of course, have no physical bodies at all.

Finally, Large Arrays of Personalities became possible. The LAP
was an individual who copied him- or herself into many separately acting biological bodies and convert copies, spread out over a wide area of
space, and discretely stored within the virtuality.

The grist created the possibility for all of these types to come into
being—but without quantum cryptology, that possibility could never
have been realized. Why?

Because quantum cryptology is necessary to the preservation of individuality.

A biological human body is a tremendous organism of many cells
and systems, all working together for the common good of the total
animal. Large parts of the body's chemistry are given over to methods
of self-identification. DNA, the immune system, chemical markers on
cells—the basic purpose of them all is for the body to know itself. Disease, it can be argued, is a kind of code breaking or natural hacking of
these systems. A disease finds a way, usually only temporarily, to trick
the body into letting it in, and letting it make use of the body's resources to feed and propagate.

Something very much like the immune system was needed if humans were going to be able to "spread out" in the grist and still retain
their individuality. How can the various personalities and portions of
us brave new humans know for certain that we are communicating with
ourselves? How can we be certain that all of our cornucopia of representations are on the same page, working for the same common good?
In short: How is it that we maintain absolute self-identity?

It's all done with quantum cryptology.

Let us take the most complicated of the new human types, the Large
Array of Personalities. A LAP can spread out wherever the grist allows.
You might have an aspect engaging in research in a laboratory on Mercury, another running a resort hotel in a beach barrel along the Dedo,
and a third attending a concert by the Bach Metropolitan Philhar-
monic. In the meantime, you might also have several convert portions
trading in stocks and options, and/or in the midst of a high-stakes
poker game on one of the gaming merci channels, and/or managing

your home, while looking after your pets and children. All of these versions of yourself would very soon become different individuals entirely, just as identical twins are entirely separate individuals, if you were not in constant and instantaneous communication with yourself through the grist. All of us, aspects, free converts, and LAPs, must continually remind ourselves of who we are and *that* we are. And we must do so securely, with the absolute knowledge that our personal integrity has not, literally, been compromised.

Thus, when the grist was first entirely integrated into a human body, with it went an algorithm and mechanism for exchange of information between the various parts of our personalities using, essentially, the same "olive cannon" setup as was described above. Tiny nanophoton generators send coded messages body-to-grist-to-body-to-convert making our individual personalities, and our intrapersonal communication, in principle impossible to hack.

These communications are encoded packets that pass instantaneously through the grist. But the code is generated at sublight speed. From this arises a fundamental truth about modern humans: Although we can *communicate* instantaneously—not faster than light, not faster than anything, but truly instantaneously—through the grist, we cannot *exist* instantaneously.

Between aspect and grist pellicle, and convert, there is a tiny, sublight gap. It is a *literal gap* created by the tiny photon cannon and tiny grates that are built into us as surely as our biological bodies have antibodies and enzymes.

Attempts were made to create human beings who did not incorporate quantum cryptology. The most famous of those experiments was the creation of the "time towers." They were LAPs created to experience reality instantly, in the way the grist seemed to promise was possible. Time towers were supposed to experience a year or a decade—or even a century—the way that you and I experience a second. They were supposed to have the perception that the gods might.

It didn't work out that way. Instead, they lacked the fundamental ability to know themselves. Almost as quickly as they were created, the time towers split up, became multiple personalities—their many systems and personas mostly at loggerheads with one another. A lucky few—the most famous example being the time tower called Tod—achieved an equilibrium of sorts among their competing personas and thus did not go stark raving mad. But all were, fundamentally, fruitcakes, never able to act in a concerted, individual manner or utter rational, coherent thoughts.

It seems that each of our individual personalities consists of personas and systems that are *forced* to work together for the common good. When those constraints are removed, as was the case with the time towers, people generally go insane.

This was the basic paradox of modern existence before the war. Although we could exist everywhere there was grist, and we could do so instantaneously, we could not really do so and remain conscious individuals. To remain individuals, we had to exist in time. There were limits to our mental "spread." But we would never have been able to spread out as much as we had were it not for the invention of the Bennett-Brassard quantum encryption system—the unbreakable means we use to hold our individuality absolutely secure.

Then came the war, and a new principle was discovered.

Li moved into a new phase of her professional life at Sui Sui University. There was, she discovered, a physics department within the physics department at Sui Sui University. It consisted of scientists handpicked by Techstock, working on . . . well, there was no other word for it.

Weapons.

Military weapons. Weapons of mass destruction. There were several directions of research, but one aim: to end the insurrection in the outer system as quickly and completely as possible, no matter what the cost.

It was a secret operation, and as such, Li was fitted out with an addition to her grist pellicle that was a combination security clearance and defensive shield. The new protocols within her skin were so strict that she had to think of a specific password in order to go to the bathroom. There was, of course, grist that could take care of that problem entirely, allowing one to retain and dissipate bodily waste gradually, but Li didn't rate that high a level yet, and she couldn't afford the grist.

Li reported for work not in the venerable Ekilstein Facility, but in the newly constructed Lab Complex B—located outside of Bach proper. The complex was an opaque spheroid that was carved deep be-

neath the surface of Mercury, with curving transportation shafts leading down from the surface. If seen in profile, the complex would look
like an enormous Earth jellyfish turned upside down, tentacles
stretched to the planetary exterior. Li's office was an oval-shaped cubi-
cle set against the outer rock wall. Although they were many feet below
ground, over the course of a two-e-month period, Li could feel the
wall grow cold and hot as Mercury faced, then turned from, the sun.
Sometimes, owing to the eccentric shape of the planet's orbit, the sun
would seemingly stop in the midflight, move backwards, then turn
again and cross the sky normally, all the while varying greatly in apparent diameter and actual brightness. This change in heat was passed
through Li's wall. At Mercurian perihelion, Li would have to adjust her
pellicle for e-days, providing her skin with a bit of air-conditioning.

She settled into a new routine consisting of long hours of work and
total estrangement from her former colleagues. There were further
sexless trysts with Techstock—but meetings where the Glory flowed.
By necessity, she even had to become distant with her family. Li had always kept up close contact with them before—and particularly with
her father, whose pride in her was unwavering. But she could not speak
of her current work with anyone not approved by the Department of
Immunity, and Hugo Singh was adamantly *not* approved. He was, in
fact, a bit of a suspicious character, as far as the DI went. He was, after
all, a longtime supporter of free-convert rights. He'd even made contributions to several charities, outlawed after the war started, that had
opposed the iteration laws and limits set down for sentient algorithms
within the Met. Li supposed her father's political leanings might pose a
problem for her someday, but there was nothing to be done about it.
When he really believed in a cause, her father could be pretty obnox-
ious about letting everyone within earshot know his opinion.

So Li stopped her weekly visits to the family in the virtuality and cut
back on all of her other communications with them. Not wanting to lie
to her parents—particularly to her father—she didn't offer an explanation, and such talks as she did have were tense and tinged with feelings
of hurt and bewilderment on their part.

At first the Glory made up for it all.

Techstock had stopped talking when he came to visit her now, and
that came as a great relief for Li. She could still look at him—at whatever aspect he chose to show up in that day, that is—and still make herself believe that it was *him* inside and not . . .

Not what?

Something more frightening to consider. It was if Techstock were a coating of skin and hair over one of the very physical principles he studied. And that principle was chromodynamics. They no longer chatted about Techstock's latest research; but Techstock had, in a way, become his research. His bodily aspects—his older man, his young man, his mannish young woman—began to show up wearing bright clothes of clashing colors. Some had even used their pellicle grist to change the color of parts of their skin—a blue arm, a face half green and half red, or blue fingers. Techstock's main aspect, the twenty-eight-year-old man, had, by that point, made himself into a walking motley caricature of his former self.

Techstock's work revolved around the "color" property of quarks. Quarks are the subatomic particles that make up the protons and neutrons, which, in turn, make up atomic nuclei. Color could be thought of as roughly analogous to electrical charge in atoms, but instead of positive, negative, and neutral, quarks might be blue, red, or green.

Techstock would arrive. The two of them would sit, either at a table in the kitchen or on a couch in the living room, and there they would be. Li might get up to make tea or bring a snack. Techstock would drink and eat. He would respond to basic requests or questions—usually with one-sentence replies. Then silence would descend again upon the apartment. Finally, after what seemed an allotted time had passed, it was time to share the Glory.

A new light would come into Techstock's eyes. He would motion Li closer, and the two of them would join hands. His hands were always warm and supple—even when it was the old-man aspect who'd showed up. She remembered that before, his palms had sometimes been rather cool and raspy. She'd liked that. His skin always felt feverish to her now, no matter what color it had assumed for the moment.

But all thoughts of the past—or of the present or future beyond the Glory—soon left her. Utter satisfaction suffused her. Happiness at a job well done. But what job? Her research was progressing steadily, but she'd made no spectacular strides.

Amés must know what she was feeling satisfied about. He must approve of her or she wouldn't feel this way. Right? She *fit in*, no matter her doubts. Everything was all right. It was. Wasn't it?

After Techstock left, she wondered if she was becoming more like him. Absorbed. Absorbed by some unnameable something, a persona in a larger mind that was not her own.

Then her hard work in Complex B began to pay dividends.

At first it was a minor but portentous breakthrough on a complicated problem she'd set for herself. It involved the "judgment" property of gravitons, as discovered by Raphael Merced over five hundred years before. Merced, the greatest scientist since Einstein, had largely defined the study of physics for half a millennium. Among many other advances, he both described and discovered the first graviton—a particle that had eluded physicists for centuries.

As Merced had famously said, "It turns out that atoms—all elementary particles, that is—are little time machines."

Gravitons never exist in the present, and that's why nobody had ever been able to find one. In much the same way that the photon is light's "messenger particle," the graviton carries a quantum of time's "energy." This energy is indistinguishable from information, and what gravitons do is fly backwards and forwards in time, telling the other particles how to behave—and generally mediating any paradoxes that might arise. Gravity itself is the interference pattern created by this passage—the wake of a boat slapping the shore, not the boat itself.

"I can't tell you if the universe as a whole has any meaning," Merced wrote. "But locally, it behaves as if it does."

Gravitons "decide" how to get quantum-entangled particles out of complex, time-related paradoxes.

"I would force these paradoxes on gravitons, and it was as if the little buggers had a town meeting and came to a decision about how to handle each paradox. The decisions were never precisely the same, but they had the *tendency* to preserve reality as we know it."

Merced learned how to control the amount of input information gravitons had to reach their "decisions." With the aid of his friend and colleague nanotech engineer Feur Otto Bring, Merced harnessed and used this communicating energy to force the gravitons to communicate the information *he* wanted them to transfer. That property became one of the fundamental functions of the grist. All grist everywhere communicated instantaneously. Not faster than light. *Instantly*.

Every schoolchild for the past five hundred years had learned Merced's famous equation:

$$FT = (pq - qp) + mc^2$$

Where FT is the future multiplied by time as a continuous function, pq and qp are quantum matrices, and mc^2 is the speed of light squared.

Li had, of course, memorized the equation as a young girl along with everyone else. But late in his life—just before he and a ship full of friends plunged into the sun, actually—Merced had made a cryptic comment. It was found in the last communications from that ship, a document known as *The Exiles' Journey*.

"I have been thinking," said Merced, "that I was a bit mistaken about time. Don't have the opportunity to go into the details right now, but I might suggest that somebody one of these days have a look at that big F in my equation. It might be possible to arrange things in the past more to our liking."

Many had tried to follow Merced's lead over the years. There were scads of theories, but all had failed to figure out what the great scientist might have meant.

In Merced's famous equation, F stood for future. All of the future multiplied by all of time—past, present, and future—yielded a single graviton. Actually, it yielded two gravitons—one that existed in the past, with a spin of 0, and one that existed in the future, with a spin of +2.

Li's specialty was "spin 0" gravitons—that is, particles that traveled from the present to the past (or vice versa) and delivered packets of energy—a sort of temporal mail carrier. They were observed in the present by devices that forced extreme paradoxes on the space-time continuum. In fact, all grist contained within it just such tiny time machines. Every bit of grist was a graviton detector.

What the grist generally detected was simultaneous events in the present. It seldom detected the past, except under extraordinary circumstances. Spin 0 gravitons communicated information only on a "need to know" basis—that is, what a quantum-entangled particle needed to know to resolve a paradox on a submicroscopic level, and not what a historian needed to know who was, say, trying to witness first-hand the Sputnik launch from the old Soviet Union, or who was writing his or her dissertation on Julius Caesar's victories in Gaul.

There were a few intriguing exceptions to this general rule, however. One of them was the very strange effect known as "convert déjà vu." Occasionally, with no apparent effort, bits would rearrange themselves into a "story" and a convert—the digital portion of a human (or, in the case of free converts, the digital being in its entirety)—would have memories of an event in the past that it could never have experienced.

An occurrence of this nature was always triggered by a convert's finding itself in exactly the same logic state as some other computer program had been in *its* past. It was, for all intents and purposes, a kind of "past life" for a convert. As silly as it seemed, there was irrefutable proof that a convert could sometimes remember performing certain calculations in entirely different circumstances—circumstances that could be verified as having occurred in the past.

It was the damnedest thing. The memories were seemingly as real— that is, as logically valid—as any other information the convert had stored away in memory files.

The only problem was that the moments were nearly always trivial. And they were completely random. In fact, "convert déjà vu" was sometimes used as a random-number generator to create security codes within the Met for secret communication. They had been proved to be mathematically "more" random even than such events as radioactive decay.

Li was working on a variation of just such a proof and simultaneously wondering how she would put off her family's latest request that she visit all of them over the coming holidays when suddenly it occurred to her that no one had ever attempted to prove that gravitons from the future—spin 2 gravitons—might create "convert precognition" in a like manner.

"It has to happen all the time," she said to herself, "but the information communicated hasn't happened yet and nobody notices . . . by the time it *does* happen . . . but we *should* remember. A convert should know it's seen the event before!"

Yet nobody, neither computer program nor human software, could foresee the future. So it didn't happen. It must not. But . . .

Li began to scribble down the implications. Then she sat back and looked at her notes. Could that be?

Not random at all. Each déjà vu precisely canceled out glimpses into the future. It substituted trivial information from the past for the nontrivial information that came from the future.

"Nontrivial," Li said to herself. "That means *important*. All information from the future is nontrivial."

If you took into account spin 2 gravitons, you could even predict when déjà vu would occur.

Convert déjà vu was the universe's way of preventing actual useful knowledge from passing from the future into the present. It was the manifestation of a natural regulating mechanism.

You could write out a little algorithm . . .

You could disprove a century's worth of misguided assumptions, and maybe bring down a whole industry by accident.

A sense of accomplishment flooded through Li as intense as the Glory. Was the feeling her own, or was it sent from on high, from the Director himself? It didn't matter; it was good. Satisfying. The intense feeling that something like this had *never* happened to her before.

Li wrote out the algorithm.

And then she realized that her discovery implied something even more amazing.

You knew when the "cancellation" events were coming. They weren't random.

They weren't random; they were predictable.

You could avoid them.

You could arrange to experience nontrivial knowledge of the past or of the future. Theoretically, at least.

Arrange to experience.

My, my, thought Li. Have I discovered time travel?

Then she thought about the implications once again.

"Not only that," she said. "I've think I just invented superluminal flight."

CHAPTER ELEVEN

From

THE PELICAN-PUCKERUP RETINAL POP-UP
METAPLANAPEDIA
50,203rd Edition

PELOTA, ITS HISTORY AND RULES

Pelota was invented nearly seven hundred years ago on the Aldiss radial from Earth to Earth's moon. It was by first played by construction workers in the Hochelaga Barrel, half of whom were of Hispanic ancestry and the other half Native North American.

Players float weightlessly and can only use their feet, chests, or heads to score with the ball. The "ball" in pelota is made up of interlocking *hexagons* instead of being round, and forms a dodecahedron. It is made of leather or synthetic fabric stretched over a flexible frame and is very lively when kicked. Players have compressed-air jets on their arms and legs for maneuvering. The reaction force of the exhaust flow is limited by the rules, and most movement comes from push-offs and in-flight momentum exchanges between players.

Vector, momentum, and velocity are the three ruling principles of the game when it is played well.

The playing arena is a transparent cylinder, one hundred meters long and seventy-five meters in diameter. The arena is constantly turning, lengthwise, around an axis. On each end of the cylinder is a goal.

The goals are five meters in length. They are wider on the ends than in the middle, like a propeller. Each goal is notched into a pearl-string of ten "gaps"—hexagonal indentures that are bigger toward the end. The gap in the middle, the "hub gap," fits the ball perfectly. When a shot goes into one of these gaps, the attacking team scores from one to five points, depending on how close the gap is to the center of the goal. A ball slotted into the dead center gap gets five points, a ball that enters a gap on the outside edge of the goal gets one point, etc.

The goals slowly rotate, like two exhaust fan blades, one at each end of the playing cylinder. They rotate in the *opposite* direction from the cylindrical arena, but at the same rate.

The original players quickly adapted traditional soccer formations to a third dimension, and, with a few variations, these lineups have generally been used for hundreds of years. There is a goalkeeper, what is called a "spray" of backs, another spray of midfielders, and two attacking strikers. Starting at the defending goal, the normal ten-player formation is either a 4-4-2 or a 4-5-1.

The goalkeeper is a special position. In addition to being able to use his or her hands, the goalkeeper can, and usually does, attach himself or herself to an elastic tether. The other end of the tether is anchored to the center of the goal, to a rivet located just beside the center gap. The keeper bungees about, like a ball on a rubber band, attempting to guard the goal. Timing these bounces correctly with a rotating goal and an oppositely rotating play arena has become a specialized and highly prized art over the years.

A pelota match lasts ninety minutes, divided into two forty-five-minute halves. The stadium seats around the playing arena are kept weightless. Of course, most people watch professional pelota games via the merci's many sports channels.

Pelota is the solar system's most popular sport by far, claiming tens of billions of players and fans. The game has acquired a rich history over the centuries. All major games are captured and stored, and can be relived in the virtuality, down to the exact number of droplets of sweat on a striker's forehead and the same blasting pain in the chest when a goalkeeper deflects a dead-on touch. There are merci channels devoted to providing the best replays culled by experts from the millions of games that have been played, as well as fantasy leagues, where great players of the past are combined into teams for simulated play.

Numerous modern-day professional leagues exist, both in the Met and in the outer system. Once every four e-years the Sun Cup competition is held, pitting the four champions of the Dedo, Vas, Diaphany, and outer system against one another in double elimination play.

It is not known what effect the war will have upon the upcoming Sun Cup 3017.

CHAPTER TWELVE

Receiving the Hand of Tod as a gift from the dying time tower had been such a weird shock, it had taken Aubry many days before she'd even looked at the thing. She'd carried it with her in the bottom of her small travel pack as she'd fled through the Integument of the Met in fear for her very life. At any moment, she expected a pack of DI sweepers to descend upon her, with even the rapacious fighter Jill unable to fend them off.

Instead, they got away clean. Only after several days on the run did it occur to Aubry that the lack of pursuit might have something to do with the Hand of Tod.

Time towers were known to have strange effects on the merci. Usually they caused distortion of various sorts within any grist with which they were associated. They appeared to have no control over this consequence of their being, however. And inhabiting one level or another of insanity, they mostly spread fuzzy logic and confusion as a result of it.

Tod had been different. Although crazy as a coot, in Aubry's opinion, he had a kind of intelligence—if not a method—to his madness. She'd been around the old tower a great deal, and she'd always gotten the impression that there was a sane man in there somewhere, speaking and gesturing, as it were, through a pool full of murky water.

The Friends of Tod sensed this as well, of course. They'd built their religion (if you could call it that) upon the idea that Tod's pronouncements made a certain sort of sense, and the rest of the world was what was out of kilter. It was a religion that attracted a cornucopia of misfits and ne'er-do-wells. It also claimed some of the best scientific and technical minds in the solar system. Oftentimes, Aubry had to admit, she couldn't tell the two apart.

Tod gave the hand to *me*, though. He must have had a reason for singling me out, Aubry had thought at the time (and still thought). She had resisted relinquishing it to the Friends after her escape from Nirvana, and no one had insisted that she do so. She had, however, allowed Alvin Nissan and his team of v-hacks to study it.

There was no doubt. The artifact had the curious effect of blocking the merci—that is, of blocking instantaneous transmission of information through the grist to anywhere outside of a specifically defined geographical area. There was very likely a new scientific principle involved. The v-hacks were engineers and technicians, and they did not attempt to determine the theoretical underpinnings of the effect. What they *did* do was to scope out the power and extent of every possible manifestation of the odd property that the Hand possessed. It was obviously related to whatever device the DIED was using to block and localize the merci during their attack on the outer-system fremden forces.

Two could play at that game.

Alvin and his v-hacks determined that the Hand of Tod had a very specific range. This area of blockage was about the size and volume of a pelota field. And that had given Alvin—a rabid pelota fan—the idea for the attack on Silicon Valley.

Aubry puffed her way forward with arm jets. She juggled the pelota ball between her feet with the usual "dribble" of a longtime player. Her dribbling ability was supplied by a very special algorithmic implant. The code had been stolen from one of the best simulation programs on the merci. Such overlaid abilities were never the equivalent of real experience, of course, but, as Alvin said, this was Bastumo—the great Diaphany striker, and one of the best players who ever took to the arena. When his periodic back injuries and frequent victimization by corrupt club management were not conspiring against him, he had been unstoppable.

"Even with a low-rez, semisentient Bastumo in your pellicle," Alvin had told Aubry, "you'll be a demon of a striker."

In front of her, the defenders, dressed in red shirts and white shorts, deployed, waiting to meet her. Their uniforms were those of the Dedo's Maastricht Armature Rangers. Aubry's own team wore green shirts and black shorts—the "away" colors of Alvin's beloved Connacht Bolsa Celtics, a team that was a perennial Diaphany premier league powerhouse. The team was physically *there*, with Aubry. They were ensconced in the grist she carried in the satchel strapped to her side.

In the regular world, Aubry took out a curiously shaped gun and fired it into the ground, a few feet away from the cliff edge where she stood. She then turned the gun on herself, lining the muzzle up to the small of her back and pulling the trigger.

There was a sharp sting, and her pellicle shouted alarms and invasion through her convert portion. Aubry grimaced and bore the pain and momentary distress. A monofilament line had just penetrated her body and thickened around her spine. The other end of the line was anchored into the Martian soil where she'd shot the pistol before.

Aubry resisted the urge to reach back and make sure the line was secured. If she did so, the line, tapering to a microscopic diameter an inch from where it emerged from her back, would neatly slice her hand from her arm as it passed through.

I'm the beta tester, Aubry thought grimly. Have to trust the engineers. Even worse, I have to trust the moraba.

The ichor covering the surface of Mars was going to provide the material for her descent into Silicon Valley. When she began to rappel over the cliff's edge, the line up top was perfectly capable of slicing through the rock and soil until it formed a straight line between her and the anchor point. Aubry would, in that case, form a molecule-sized slit down the edge of the cliff as she rappelled. But that wasn't going to happen. The constructor grist that coated the filament line was programmed to thicken the line where it came into contact with the horizontal surface. The friction from the thicker line would prevent it from slicing into the ground.

More important—at least so far as Aubry's eventual descent was concerned—the constructor grist was especially programmed to recognize moraba.

Fortunately, moraba covered *everything* and got into everything. If you took some moraba away, more would flow in to take its place. The grist of the monofilament line would deconstruct the moraba with which it came into contact, and use it to build and then pay out more line. By the time Aubry reached the edge of Silicon Valley at the base of the cliff, she would be connected to the upper surface by what she couldn't help thinking of as a thin, strong string of snot. It wouldn't be snot anymore, but superstrong filament. Still, the image stayed with her.

Aubry walked toward the edge of the cliff to the point where there was tension on the line in her back. She exerted some pressure, and the line payed out, converting moraba to more line. It stayed taut as long as she kept moving forward.

Aubry had long since given up second-guessing herself after she'd made a plan. That could get you killed very quickly when you were a partisan fugitive. Without another thought, she stepped over the edge and began walking down the face of the cliff. The device worked; the line held. She descended in a horizontal, facedown rappel, the line coiled around her spine forming an angle that held her feet steady against the cliff face.

This must be what a spider feels like, Aubry thought, as she spins out her web.

Nearly a half mile below her, the bottom of Silicon Valley yawned. In the satchel around her waist resided not just the virtual attack team. Inside the satchel was the Hand of Tod.

Packed and ready for delivery, Aubry thought. Then she returned to the virtuality, and to the deadly pelota game playing out in her mind.

CHAPTER THIRTEEN

The truth is, if Li hadn't been so desperately lonely, she probably would not have kept her discovery to herself. Who was there to tell? She never saw any of her old friends. She was beginning to think she'd been reassigned to Complex B as a perk for Techstock, and not because anyone had any overriding belief in her ability as a physicist. Most of her new colleagues were cold toward her—and most of them had the same vacant look in their eyes as Techstock.

It was a look she was coming to comprehend. She was beginning to see it in herself when she gazed into a mirror.

Addicted to the Glory.

It was a benign addiction, she told herself. Maybe similar to the way people used to be addicted to caffeine. Caffeine improved productivity; it made you more alert. Until the nanotech and the grist pellicle came along and made ingesting stimulants unnecessary, people all over the Met had been grouchy if they didn't get their wake-up coffee or tea, or if their chocolate supply ran out. The Glory helped you get things done. It made you work *harder*, not slack off like a narcotic would. So what if it adversely affected the sex drive? The Glory offered compensation in other areas.

She was feeling more and more of it. Almost as if he knew. Amés. The Director. As if he knew she'd made a major discovery that was going to help in the war effort, and he was stroking her, giving her encouragement. He might not know the precise details, but he was aware of the general tenor of her thoughts.

Li began to experience the Glory rush once or twice each e-day— even when Techstock wasn't around. Perhaps *especially* when Techstock wasn't around. She felt as if Amés's enormous gaze was shifting from Techstock to her.

So why didn't she tell anybody about her discovery?

She no longer wanted to share her life with Techstock. He was far gone to . . . wherever. Gloryland. And she'd notarized a security agreement when she'd come to work in Complex B. There wouldn't be any publishing on the merci. No acclaim. No offers of tenure. She couldn't tell her family.

There was simply nobody she wanted to tell.

In any case, there were many, many implications to work out. She had to check and double-check her calculations. Most important, she had to suggest some method for experimental verification. At least, she told herself, she ought to. Plenty of theorists hadn't the foggiest idea how to confirm their work. But Li came from an experimental background. She would feel that she'd failed herself if she didn't come up with a testable hypothesis.

I'll have failed Raphael Merced, she thought. And he's really the guy I'm trying to please now, she thought.

She read and reread his final words in *The Exiles' Journey*, the section called the "Merced Synthetics."

"It might be possible to arrange things in the past more to our liking. As a matter of fact, I do believe I've seen signs that somebody is already doing that. I only hope to God that whoever is doing so has discovered the human equivalent of that unique property of my little gravitons. Whoever you are, up there in the future, for goodness sake, make sure you use a bit of *judgment*."

Arrange things in the past more to our liking?

Did his pronouncement have something to do with her déjà vu algorithm? Li knew intuitively that it must.

Her father called her with news from the war. Li had almost completely insulated herself from what was happening in the larger world for the past couple of e-years. There was heavy fighting for the moons of

Jupiter, with costly but steady advances for the Met forces. DIED forces were concentrating on Uranus's moon. Pluto was being heavily fortified and readied as a base for massive troop deployment. Everyone expected a major invasion of the Neptune system any time now. Then, when victory was achieved there and when most of the outer planetary systems were finally under Met control, the reckoning would come to the cloudships out in the Oorts. Everybody knew that the cloudships were the money behind the insurrection, her father told her. The fremden rebels were merely their puppets. Some even claimed that entire fight was a product of the big Met banks fighting those of the outer system.

"And how are you, Chimkin?" Li's father asked her, using his pet name for her. "Your mother and I can barely remember how tall you are. All we ever see is your head and shoulders on the merci."

"I'm fine," said Li. "I'm working really hard."

"Going to win the war for us, Chimkin?"

"I'm doing my best, Papa. But I can't really talk about any of that. And I'm kind of busy now, as a matter of fact . . ."

"Of course you can't. Of course you can't. I don't mean to keep you." But that was exactly what he meant to do, Li thought. Hugo Singh leaned back in his chair at home, and his image before her—just a head-and-shoulders shot—tilted up so that Li could see up into his torso, had there been any real flesh and blood within the projection. Instead, there was an oval base to him, like an upturned marble bust or a tree trunk's cross section. "It's just that . . . well, there's something I've been meaning to speak to you about," he continued.

"What is it, Papa?"

"I'm worried about your health. We haven't seen you in the full virtuality in months. And when I look at you in these quick calls, you don't look well. You look pale, and your skin is getting too shiny. Have you been monitoring your internals at all?"

"Not consciously, Papa."

"Well, you have to! You can't trust some half-witted add-on function to do it for you. A good mind inside a sick body uses half its energy worrying at the walls."

This was one of her father's favorite sayings. Li felt a pulse of warm nostalgia on hearing it, even though she still wasn't sure what her father meant by the pronouncement.

"I feel fine," said Li, although the truth was, she *had* been a bit breathless lately. Her convert portion made a quick scan of her biology.

Everything seemed to be churning along smoothly . . . except there was something odd about her left lung. Slightly reduced CO_2 emission, as if her respiration weren't working up to speed. Nothing life-threatening, or even dangerous, really. She mentally filed away the information for later consideration.

"You don't look fine. I want you to get more rest."

"I'll try."

"Promise me?"

"Sure, Papa."

"And maybe you should think about getting a friend. A boyfriend, I mean. Someone to look after you a bit, since you're not letting your mother and me keep an eye on your health and happiness."

Li had never told her parents about her affair with Techstock. Neither her mother's Chinese nor her father's Sikh heritage put much stock in secret affairs with married men.

"I don't mean to be distant, Papa. It's just there are so many things . . . it's hard to explain, and I'm not allowed to talk about most of it, anyway. But you and Mama know I love you, don't you?"

"Of course we know that," said Singh. "But the truth is, Chimkin, there are some things that your mother and I need to talk to *you* about."

Her father's face took on a sad expression that Li had seldom seen. She suddenly felt a tinge of foreboding. She'd been so wrapped up in her little miseries here on Mercury that she'd failed to notice a problem with her parents?

"What is it, Papa?"

"I don't want to speak of it this way." Hugo Singh leaned forward again and looked his daughter directly in the eyes. "Your mother and I wanted to see you in person."

"Is it Harold? Has he gotten in trouble again?"

"No, your brother is fine. He's got a job, even. He's working in Umberto Barrel at the silo."

"That's good to hear. But, Papa, tell me. You and Mama aren't having troubles are you?"

"Not anything new. In fact, we've been spending a lot more time together lately." Her father smiled ruefully, but the sadness still remained in his gaze. "Listen, Chimkin, I really don't want to get into it here. I was feeling poorly a few months ago—"

"*You* got sick?" Her father had always enjoyed such good health. "What was wrong?"

"I had problems with some of my . . . bodily functions."

"I see."

"My diagnostics said nothing was wrong, but it kept up, and I had some tests done." Hugo Singh rubbed his forehead and tried to manage another smile. "It turns out I have something called 'pellicle-induced systemic lupus erythematosus.'"

The disease sounded familiar. Li tried to remember where she'd heard of it before. "Lupus?"

"Well, yes. It's caused by my pellicle, you see. The grist there is . . . well, it's been a while since I've had an upgrade, and it never was that advanced to begin with."

"I could have helped you pay for an upgrade, Papa."

"I'm not *that* poor, Chimkin. It's just I never thought I needed one." Her father sighed. "But it turned out that I did. And now it's a bit too late to worry about that."

Li felt a foreboding creep into her stomach. "What do you mean?"

"My body is rejecting my pellicle, Chimkin. It's an autoimmune response, they tell me. That's one of the reasons I wanted to see you in full virtual. Pretty soon, I'm not going to be able to go into the virtuality at all. My grist is going wild—it will stop responding to any control, and I won't be able to use it at all. Won't even be integrated with my convert portion. I'll just be an . . . aspect. A body. Imagine that. The problem is, my body is busy rejecting my kidneys right now."

"Your kidneys? Why?"

"Not sure. The doctor told me that, with lupus, the immune system loses its grip on which cells are friendly and which are invaders. It will pick out one organ system to attack as a foe. My body has decided the enemy is my kidneys."

"So you'll need new kidneys."

"No, Chimkin. It takes grist to make kidneys and to make them stick. And remember, grist is the real problem for me. My body just can't handle it anymore."

"So are you saying . . . that you're dying?"

"Everyone dies eventually, Ping Li." He'd used her full first name—something he did only when trying to be sure she fully understood his full meaning.

Yes, everyone dies, Li thought. Papa is going to die. But not now! Not yet!

"Oh, Papa. What about . . . what about a transplant?" she said. "What about taking one of my kidneys?"

"I'd have to take both of them, my dear." Her father bounced his eyebrows in the manner of Sindra, the villainous bolsa mayor on the merci melodrama he'd been following for years. "The truth is, my immune system can't handle a transplant. Besides, all of my organs are going to come under attack eventually. Maybe one by one. Maybe several at a time." Hugo Singh shook his head. "There isn't anything that can be done."

Li nodded, feeling suddenly numb in mind and body. "How long?"

"An e-month or two, Chimkin."

An e-month? And then her father would be gone. Gone. She couldn't imagine a world without her father's steady presence. He was a man who shuffled off to work every day, who constantly argued politics with his cronies, all of whom valued him for his independent, sometimes curmudgeonly opinions. Most of all, he was a man who believed all of his children were gifts from heaven, to be adored, pestered to do their best, looked after. He wouldn't be able to look after her anymore. Li knew that would be his greatest pain.

"I guess I won't find out how the war ends." Hugo Singh chuckled. "Not that we should be in a war to begin with."

"Better not to talk about that right now, Papa," said Li, hardly hearing her own words. "Listen, I can take a coach to the Hub and be on the lift in . . ." She mentally called up the daily transport schedule out of the Hub, the Met's connecting nexus at the Mercurial North Pole. ". . . five hours. That would put me at Akali Dal in . . ." Her convert performed the calculation by streamer transport from Mercury along the Dedo to Venus, then halfway out the Vas to her parents' home bolsa. ". . . two and a quarter e-days."

"Ping Li, you need not come right away," said her father. "A full virtual visit would be fine."

"I want to be there physically. Maybe there's something I can do."

"Do not get your hopes up in that regard, Chimkin."

"I should be there."

"You have time. The doctor said it will be at least a couple of e-weeks before my pellicle breaks down to the point that I can no longer access the virtuality."

"Oh, Papa, you should have told me! You should have told me earlier."

"The diagnosis was not certain, and I didn't want to distract you from your work. You are doing important work, aren't you, Chimkin?"

"Yes, Papa. I think so."

"I knew it! If you can't tell me what it is, at least I can know that it is highly valuable."

"Yes."

"I'm going to have a *real* pyre, you know," her father said, leaning back into his argumentative posture. "Your sister will sing the ardasa."

"Suni has a beautiful voice," said Li, feeling more despondent than ever. Her father was already planning his funeral—Sikh fashion, of course.

They spoke a few more words, then her father signed off in his customary fashion by winking at her and letting his image dissolve, to be replaced in quick succession by Nanak and the nine gurus.

Li immediately called up the streamer schedule leaving out from Johnston Bolsa, the way station above the Mercurian North Pole where one caught the pithway streamers that led out the Dedo to Venus and points beyond. She deliberated on whether or not to pay for a private transport—they were expensive, and seemed to become more so the longer the war dragged on. She finally decided against it. She could save the greenleaves and perhaps use them to buy her father something once she arrived in Akali Dal. She placed her reservation.

And her reservation was denied.

She placed it again.

Denied.

No explanation given. She tried another streamer departing two hours later.

Denied.

They couldn't all be full. She checked the seating. There were beads that were clearly available. What was going on? She tried again. Again, she could not get a place.

Li sat back. She found that she was breathing quickly, and her heart was racing.

Calm down, she told herself. There's some kind of clerical error. Despite her own self-instruction, she quickly tried to make another reservation. Denied.

Her eyes began to tear up from frustration. She was wiping them on the sleeve of her tunic when her office door opened and Techstock walked in. It was the twenty-eight-year-old aspect.

"What do you think you're doing?" he asked her.

"I was . . . I was dealing with a personal matter."

"You were trying to leave," Techstock said flatly.

Li finished wiping her eyes and looked at him with a start. "How did you know that?"

"It doesn't matter," he said. "You can't go."

"My father is very sick."

"Sorry to hear that," Techstock said. "Visit him over the merci."

"It isn't the same. He's dying."

"You can't go." Techstock repeated himself in the same flat tone.

"But why not?" said Li in frustration. The tears were welling up once again.

"Because there's a war on," Techstock replied. "Whether you realize it or not, you're part of the fight."

"You mean *you're* part of the fight! I'm just around because I'm . . . well, I'm not even your mistress anymore." Now the tears were streaming. She ordered her pellicle to dry them up, but it was too late. "I don't know what I am."

"That used to be true," Techstock staid. "But you've discovered something, haven't you?"

"How . . . how did you know about that?"

"Because I can feel him drawing away from me," Techstock said. "You have the Director's attention now. He knows you're on to something."

"I don't want his attention," Li said. "I didn't ask for it."

"It's too late," said Techstock. "You get the Glory, and you take everything that goes with it."

"I just want to see my papa."

But Techstock was no longer listening. He was lost in his own ruminations once again, his Glory fog.

"Who would have thought it," he said. "Little Li is the lucky one."

CHAPTER FOURTEEN

Aubry was simultaneously descending into the dark valley of Noctis
Labyrinthus on Mars and playing a game of virtual pelota with the
guarding algorithms of the death camp. Perceiving in two worlds under such stressful circumstance might have led to a schizophrenic
breakdown in some people, but Aubry was made of tougher stuff, both
mentally, physically—and virtually. She was the daughter of a free convert and a biological human. What was more, she had been multiple-
environment-adapted—she'd undergone a sea change, really—and
within the outer body of a sixteen-year-old girl was lodged a finely
honed weapon of guerrilla warfare. She was space-adapted, insulated
and defended against all manner of grist-based attack. She didn't even
have to eat anymore except to keep up appearances. Her nuclear-
powered heart took care of her energy needs.

Still, somewhere in there was a sixteen-year-old woman. She was a
woman who had been stripped from her family at the age of eleven and
thrown into the hard life of a partisan warrior. But she'd never forgotten where she came from. She prayed every day that her father and
brother were safe, that they had made it to the outer system.

Her mother had been transported here, to Silicon Valley—the free-convert death camp. Aubry had seen the consignment records. And now, after five years, the time had come to make a rescue attempt.

It was only, indirectly, a rescue attempt. Aubry was enough of a realist to understand that she could not go directly to her mother and release her from her cell—or from whatever confinement representation was in use in the prison camp. There were, at that point, millions of free converts being held inside.

When considered logically, the chances of actually rescuing her mother were extremely low. Alvin Nissan himself had said they were somewhere between five and ten percent. This didn't matter to Aubry. There was a chance. And Alvin had equipped Aubry with a detecting algorithm that might aid her in locating her mother once she was inside.

And if this attempt to save Danis didn't work—why then, Aubry would have to try again. No matter how long it took, she would keep trying. Aubry also knew that, even if her mother were to be rescued on this attempt, she would still return. These were Aubry's people being held against their will. No one doubted that Amés intended to exterminate all free converts as soon as the merci-polling results gave him the go-ahead. This was inevitable, as the Director took over more and more of the populace through the outright co-option of LAPs combined with the manufacture of Glory addiction and dependency in the masses.

What Amés could not possess, he would destroy. Anyone not blinded by the Glory could see as much. It was only a matter of time. And yet there were teeming millions in the Met who refused to understand this point—who, instead, believed the opposite to be the case. Aubry could only put it down to the enormous propaganda power of the merci, whose content was under the control of the Director, either directly or indirectly.

It would have been amazing to think for her eleven-year-old self, but for the past five years, Aubry had caught maybe two or three hours of merci programming. She was as disconnected from the Met's consensus reality as she could be and still physically dwell among the people there.

The partisans were, of course, not there to liberate Aubry's mother per se. An important objective was to strike a blow to the Department of Immunity's complacency in having all of the Met under its control. If successful, it would be both a propaganda victory and also a blow to morale within the Department itself.

The second objective had come from Jill. Jill's obsession, her under-lying mission in life, was to locate the personality known as Alethea Nightshade—the woman whose face and body Jill wore. Jill had reason to believe that Alethea might be somewhere in the prison, since all sen-tient convert coding was being rounded up and placed there. Jill herself had made a promise to the mysterious LAP named Thaddeus Kaye that she would find the woman, no matter what it took.

This *was* a search for a particular individual, but, on a larger scale, finding her would also be a strategic gain for the partisans. Thaddeus Kaye, wherever he was, was not merely another LAP. He was a key—perhaps *the* key—to the present war. His convert personality was writ-ten on local space-time, in the manner that ordinary converts were encoded in the grist.

Aubry didn't pretend to understand the science behind it all. But to recover Alethea—this Thaddeus Kaye's long-lost girlfriend or some-thing (Aubry wasn't clear on the exact details)—was to find a back door into Kaye's mentality. And to gain access to that mentality was to have access to the makeup of local reality itself.

At least, according to Alvin Nissan, that would be the case. Gaining that access was the prime reason his v-hacks were allied with Jill and her partisan rats and ferret warriors in the first place.

"This Alethea will let me get 'root' on Thaddeus Kaye," Alvin had hold Aubry. "And when I have root on Kaye, I can do what I like with the whole system."

"You mean the whole *solar* system," Aubry replied.

"That's right," said Alvin. "Local space-time. It's the dream of every hacker since ancient times. To get root on reality. To make the natural hack."

"And you'll make changes for the common good, of course," Aubry had said a bit sarcastically. "Since you'll be in the original position of all humankind when you're king of the world." As a sixteen-year-old, she found she had a much lower threshold for bullshit than she'd had at eleven.

Alvin had smiled—a facial expression that looked like a scowl until you got to know him. "The king won't do anything without your con-sultation, Lady Aubry," he told her. He sighed. "And about a thousand Friends v-hackers who could pull the plug on my ass at any moment should I get out of line."

In any case, Alvin had been unclear about how, exactly, possessing

Alethea Nightshade's convert was going to give him "root" on someone who might, indeed, be a force of nature but who was also a human be-ing—a pretty irascible and stubborn human being, as Jill had described Kaye. Aubry suspected that Alvin himself wasn't clear on the method. But if he somehow could pull it off . . .

Then the partisans would stop the war. They could write the terms of the postwar settlement. They could define the terms for, well, *every-thing*. Merely the remote possibility of achieving that justified the Noctis Labyrinthus operation.

The attack on Silicon Valley was years in the planning. The camp was wound round with the sort of security and cryptography that, be-fore the war, had been considered fundamentally impregnable. But the impossible had become necessary. Something had to be done to save the thousands of souls that the partisans believed were being systemat-ically exterminated in the prison.

Because the most important objective of the partisan force was to strike a blow against the genocide that they knew was going on in the camp.

Since the creation of the Met and the dawn of the modern era, genocide had been unknown among humans. Most were sure it was a relic of the barbarous past.

Like they believed total war was gone for good, Aubry thought. Only we're in one *now*.

Genocide had never really gone away. Perhaps it never would. But neither would the need to call it what it was and resist it.

Fuck the ethics anyway, Aubry thought. *My mother is in there.*

Unless Danis was already dead. Reformatted to random ones and zeros.

This was something Aubry could not let herself think. There was no way to know. But based on the information the partisans had put to-gether, only 10 million free converts had been killed. And according to that same information, there were close to 500 million souls impris-oned in the Silicon Valley grist.

So the odds, though gruesome, were in her mother's favor.

Onward, downward into the valley.

—And Aubry used a blast of air from her arm rockets and sped toward her opponents, the red-and-white-clad security team of Noctis

Labyrinthus. A forward came out to meet her, and she easily twisted around him, moving closer to the goal.

The pelota player overlay within her grist had made the move, and not her. Aubry had used expert system overlays before to allow her to accomplish various tasks when she had no time to learn the technicalities. But she'd *never* felt one manifest itself so strongly, so quickly. She'd felt the surge of the other's personality from the moment she saw the pelota ball.

Aubry, surprised, reacted by suppressing the overlay.

Just then defensive midfielders rushed to box her in, forcing her to back-pass to her own teammate. She didn't recognize her own midfielder—they were all in anonymous representation mode—but she knew from the jersey number, 15, that it was Logan36, a free-convert v-hack known for creating a strain of Glory-blocking grist for which the Department of Immunity had yet to find a counteragent. Logan36 and his spray of three worked the ball among themselves, pulling defenders and red-and-white-clad strikers in every direction.

The v-hacks were clearly loving that this break-in was representing as pelota. Almost to a man and woman, they were what was known as *extremas*—that is, rabid fans.

Aubry felt a strange yearning rise within herself.

This is what I exist for! I have to do my job!

It was the overlay's voice in her head. Was it speaking to her? Such things were not supposed to be conscious. Then she realized the overlay was engaged in dialogue with itself. She was listening in on Bastumo's inner dialogue—or at least a very sophisticated simulation of it.

There is a game! It doesn't matter where or why! Bastumo must play pelota!

That's why you're here, Aubry thought, although the overlay allegedly would not understand such an abstract thought. She let go of any conscious direction of her virtual body here in the game. *Play ball, Bastumo!*

She grabbed a passing back, who was coming up to help, and spun around him, robbing momentum from the defender and sending Aubry toward the spinning arena wall.

Just like Sint and I did when we got on board the transport bead when we were fleeing Mercury, Aubry thought. For every brother, there is an equal and opposite sister. It seemed so long ago. Would she even recognize her brother if she saw him again?

Yes. Of course she would.

Aubry-Bastumo timed her contact with the moving wall, rebounding at an angle that sent her streaking into the Security backfield. Several panicked defenders attempted to follow after, but their air jets were no match for the velocity Aubry had picked up from her contact with the spin of the arena wall.

Logan36 saw her dash for the goal and, with a mighty kick, sent the long ball her way.

Too long.

Aubry stretched and added her air jets to her velocity going forward. Not enough.

The Ranger goalkeeper bounced out on his tether and snagged the ball, as Aubry crashed through the penalty box and careened into the opposite wall. The rotating goalpost caught her and swatted her down toward the arena wall in an out-of-control spin. She met the pellucid arena wall with a shoulder and had to grind it even harder into the wall to dampen her spin.

Part of the game. Sometimes attacks fail. But the joy is that I will get to attack again!

By the time Aubry got herself hanging steadily in space, the goalkeeper had cleared the ball far downfield, and the red-and-white-clad Security strikers were threatening Celtic, the partisan, goal.

Oh, shit. That was not good. If the security team scored, the break in momentum would break the hypnotic "game space" the partisan v-hackers had established. The attack would be called off, and the partisans would be running for their lives, both in the virtuality and in the regular world.

I'll be toast, Aubry thought. In the regular world, she was halfway down the Martian cliff, but still a good eight-hundred-meter rappel length from the valley floor.

But she had faced dire situations before over the past few years. She would have to trust that the Celtic backfield would do its job and feed her the ball again. At the moment, she was offsides, between the last defender and the goalkeeper. If the direction of play changed, a penalty would be called and Security would get the ball again. Aubry-Bastumo concentrated on correcting her current position.

She jetted toward the arena's curved, spinning side once more. In this virtual representation, she could see right through the translucent material that made it to a starfield beyond. Even though it was all a mass hallucination, she was still surprised to see no spectators.

No spectators but the stars.

Her feet connected with the cylinder wall, and she bounced back toward her own goal. With the overlay completely in charge, Aubry-Bastumo grabbed a Ranger back who flew into her path. He was a representation of Noctis Labyrinthus security algorithm, and not a true free convert and, thus, not a complete human. But even a semi-sentient computer program could prove to be trouble in this game, and the back was representing as a large man—maybe twice Aubry's mass. He was jetting toward his own goal. Making use of his mass and momentum brought Aubry to a dead stop in center field. Bastumo knew what he was doing, though. Aubry let the hapless back go, and discovered that there were no defenders near her.

Security, the Rangers, took a shot on the Celtic goal, but the keeper made a spectacular save (the keeper was Alvin himself).

"I'm open!" Aubry screamed to her keeper.

And reached the valley floor of Noctis Labyrinthus.

There was a fence.

This was the back side of the camp, set a half mile deep in a near-vertical Martian canyon. No one would expect an attack from this quarter. At least Aubry hoped so. She reached into her satchel. Her own hand bumped into the Hand of Tod, and she felt a funny little tingle. Not electricity or any other force transfer. Probably psychological.

She drew forth a small scalpel. With the greatest care, she unsheathed it. The edge would slice a diamond in half with one thrust. Even her space-hardened fingers wouldn't stand a chance.

The fence yielded without protest. It was only ten centimeters thick. It did not even have repair instructions encoded within it.

The Cryptology Division must have counted on the depth of the valley and the toxic landscape to keep out incursions.

Of course. That was why there was no grist in the wall. It only existed to separate the grist of Silicon Valley from the general Martian nanotechnological quagmire. So long as the tight security parameters held in the virtuality, one wall was more than sufficient to prevent a breakout. Physical walls didn't really matter. It was the virtual walls that formed the real prison. If you were a free convert and you somehow got through security, you wouldn't have to worry about physical barriers. You would flash your programming as far into the outer-system grist hardware as you could possibly fling it. With the grist, jumping physically next door took exactly the same amount of effort as traveling a million miles. Or a billion.

On the other side of the wall the grist of the concentration camp glistened.

There was a square kilometer of the stuff, and crammed into that data space were half a billion people.

Somewhere among them was Danis.

Aubry felt the urge to cry—an urge that, in former times, would have brought water to her eyes. But, of course, her eyes remained dry. She didn't have the plumbing for tears anymore.

Aubry stepped through the hole she'd made in the wall—

—But did not step out on the other side. Instead, she was caught there. Caught under the door arch, her muscles frozen.

Shit. She'd been wrong. There *was* protective grist in the wall. She realized this after the wall grew back around her, incorporating her into its structure. With a frantic motion, she reached into her satchel, tried to extract the Hand of Tod.

Not in time.

The wall flowed over and around her. Her last sight was of the camp grist, no more than a meter away from her.

And then her eyes were covered, and she was encased.

Instead of being a rescuer, she was now a part of the wall holding her mother in hell.

CHAPTER FIFTEEN

Li arranged her escape from Mercury with a certain amount of guilt. She was leaving Techstock alone for the first time in nearly four e-years.

Four e-years. Had it really been that long? And she'd been nearly ten on Mercury, with her only actual trip home five years before to attend her sister's wedding. Going home in the virtuality had always seemed to be enough. There was no logical reason why it shouldn't be enough, after all. With a first-class merci connection, what you heard, smelled, tasted, and saw was indistinguishable from regular life. Even your sense of balance was right on. And why not? The sensations were not being routed through innumerable wires or converted into electromagnetic rays. No, they were delivered *instantaneously* and without degradation. Since the war began, actual travel costs had rocketed upward. The greenleaf cost of a full virtual visit on the broadest merci band was nearly nine times cheaper.

And yet, the moment Li had learned her father was sick, her instinct had told her that she must go in person. She didn't really care if the feeling made any logical sense or if it was a holdover from humanity's animal past. This was family, and you followed your instincts when family was in trouble. Especially since it was her father, the man who'd pushed her so hard and sacrificed so much to be sure Li got all the opportunities possible. Papa, with his unshorn, multiply plaited pigtail that she'd played with as a child. His faint smell of spiced cologne and the ancient elixir of Aqua Velva, a fragrance that one of the saintly gurus of a thousand years ago was said to have used and which Hugo Singh had had specially encoded into the grist of his skin.

Her papa couldn't die. He still had fifty years in him, maybe more. No one died of lupus anymore. That was like dying of the black plague or AIDS. It was a bad dream from the antique past. Not something that killed you.

The security for Complex B was tight, but Li knew the guarding algorithm, a free convert who had been a colleague of hers before the war. After the conflict broke out, the Department of Immunity issued new employment strictures on free converts. Only those free converts who had "mission-critical" jobs at the university were permitted to remain in their posts. Everyone else was out of a job.

Siscal, a statistician, had been one of the unlucky ones laid off. He'd always adored his work at the university and had managed to get himself rehired by the agency that was contracted to provide security at sensitive sites. Siscal was willing to do anything that kept him in touch with his beloved institution. Li felt sorry for the free convert, but she also knew how to bribe him—with an hour's access to the latest papers in his field, an access he'd been denied since getting fired from his teaching job.

Siscal couldn't copy and study the papers—his memory short-term caches were monitored at all times, and scrubbed of all offending material at the end of each of his shifts. He would have to read and try to comprehend the papers, and then erase them from his caches. Li knew Siscal would have to bring all of his resources to bear, both higher thinking and lower data processing, during his allotted hour.

Even with most of Siscal's resources devoted to "Multiple Regression Analysis in Bayes-Yang Emergent Operants across P-100 Universes," there were still a few autonomous systems still monitoring who was and who was not in the complex. Li used her convert portion to flummox these simple systems, aware that when she did so, she was going beyond distracting the security guard to actively and directly breaking the law. She would take her punishment upon her return. She imagined that they might kick her down a pay grade or two. That would mean more regular cooking and no more ordering up an instant meal from the grist—an indulgence she could afford only once an e-week, in any case.

After she emerged onto the surface and into Bach city proper, she caught a personal coach and gave her apartment as the destination. Once she was off, she gave a series of destinations that left her on the top tier of the city near the place the main transport tube emerged from the city and headed out for the polar lift. She worked her way over to the station on pedestrian walkways to a bus station, and used a cash card to pay the thirteen-greenleaf fee that would take her to the Hub. She had enough cash stored on the card to remain anonymous to the payment system all the way up to Johnston Bolsa. After that, she'd have to charge the trip to her bank account and hope no one was looking for her quite yet.

The bus shot up and above Bach and into the full solar day. Li lowered the third eyelid shield that all residents acquired when they bought a Mercury adaptation kit for their pellicles. Even with the shading in place, Bach glistened below her, and Li remembered how impressed she'd been with the sight when she'd first arrived—now nearly ten years ago.

The city was two cities within one. Metallic New Frankfurt formed the base, gleaming with a dull silver glint like an enormous conglomeration of pyrite crystals. Threaded within New Frankfurt, a net of pearls set in a crown, was the soft gleam of residential Calay. The higher Li got, the more Bach seemed a sumptuous artifact rather than a city—an artifact that would make a fitting gift for an emperor. And so it was, of course, for it was the center of government for the Met's Interlocking Directorate, and the home of Director Amés.

The transfer at the Hub proved easy enough, and the lift to Johnston Bolsa went smoothly. Then came the test. Li used her convert to connect with the pithway reservation system. She had previously cashed in some war bonds (taking quite a financial hit, her convert reminded her), and her account was bulging with leaves, relative to its normal levels. The money was quickly depleted as she paid premium price for immediate departure on a public bead. At least the transfer went through, Li thought. Now to find out if she could get into the bead.

She negotiated the walkway toward the bolsa's central axis, and the centrifugal "gravity" rapidly decreased. She grabbed a handrail strap and allowed her floating body to be pulled along to the bead boarding area. With a twist and a turn, a mechanical porter shoved her inside. Within minutes, the door slid shut.

She was going to make it. She was going to get off Mercury.

Her transport bead moved noiselessly into the pithway. The only way to tell there was motion was Li's gentle motion rearward until her feet came to rest on the "floor." As her speed increased, the acceleration "gravity" would build to Earth-normal levels, and she'd spend most of her trip feeling heavier than she had in years. It was a small price to pay to be going home. After a couple of hours, Li began to relax. She was speeding out the Dedo now, on her way to the Venus transfer station and points on the Vas cable beyond. To Akali Dal, her home.

She resisted the urge to while away her trip by entering the merci. Some instinct told her she should avoid the virtuality as much as possible. She used old-fashioned retinal projection to call up a journal article she'd been meaning to read. Within minutes, though, the equations began running together incomprehensibly in her mind, and she blanked out the magazine and put on some music instead. Li's taste ran to twenty-ninth-century classical. She loved almost every piece from the free-convert renaissance. She chose Halbrock's Sunspot Concerto, closed her eyes, and drifted away to the rhythmic surge and flow of violins and oboes mimicking the radio signature of the solar wind. The lights dimmed down as the bead cabin sensed that Li was falling asleep.

She awoke with a start to find that she was floating in space. Her bead was stopped, and a blaring virtual siren cut through the overrides of her convert. The siren seemed to lodge in Li's head and reverberate there, as if her very skull were a bell that had been struck.

"Checkpoint Cesium," the siren blared. "All bead passengers prepare identification protocols for review."

She inquired of the bead grist what was going on, but it replied that access was denied to the information. She tried deopaquing the window, but the bead's grist did not respond. Since "gravity" was returning, but not from forward acceleration, she could only surmise that the streamer was being diverted away from the central pith tubes outward to some portion of the Met cable, or perhaps even into a bolsa. The grist would not report her exact position on the Dedo, either, although she'd been traveling for most of a day, so she supposed she must be nearing Venus.

The doors opened, and the passengers of the streamers were ordered out. Li had no baggage, but those with bags were made to carry them along. Each person was being walked through a scanning corridor. Some were told to stand for long minutes. The regulators in charge seemed to be in no hurry to speed the process along.

When Li was third in line, an override voice in her inner ear informed her to prepare for a complete system scan—aspect, convert, and pellicle.

Once again she felt the "dragged-through-glass" scrape as the corridor's scanning algorithms worked over her pellicle. A siren rang out twice, and door at the opposite end of the corridor opened. Li stumbled out. She stood in line with other passengers, who all looked rather shell-shocked after their trips down the corridor. Each was passing through a final scanning arch.

Li passed through the final arch. But instead of being allowed to move along with the passengers who had come before her, she heard a small beep. The regulator who was monitoring the arch looked up. He and the convert who was inhabiting the arch apparently had a quick conversation, and the regulator told Li to follow him.

They traveled through a series of nondescript hallways—I'll never find my way back through this, Li thought—and arrived at a tiny Department of Immunity office. Most of the space in the office was taken up by a desk and a chair. The desk was pushed forward to allow leg room for the regulator, who sat down behind it. The chair in front of the desk was backed up against the office wall, and when she sat down, Li's knees were bumping against the front of the desk. It was impossible to stretch out or even to sit comfortably.

"Well now," said the regulator, placing his hands on the desk between them, "it would appear that your Confidence level is not very high, Citizen Singh."

"I don't understand what you mean," Li replied nervously.

"It seems you're hiding something. Holding out. You have doubts." The man sat back, clasped his hands behind his head. "I'm here to discuss those doubts with you. Maybe we can reach a resolution. You'd like to talk about it, wouldn't you?"

"I have no objection to talking," Li said, "if I knew what it was you wanted to talk about."

"Getting defensive won't help matters, I'm afraid," said the regulator. "Interrogation can be a constructive experience, if you'll only let it be. Now, let's get started, shall we?"

Li held up her hands. "What do you want me to say?"

"Just tell me what's bothering you," the man replied.

"Nothing's bothering me."

"Oh, I think there is something wrong. You registered a seventeen at the arch."

"A seventeen? Out of what?"

"I'm afraid that's classified."

Li nodded. "But we do know that I'm a seventeen."

"That's correct."

"Well, okay," Li said. "I guess I'm feeling guilty because I'm taking my first vacation in years. Maybe that's what set off your arch."

"Oh no," said the regulator. "Personal guilt won't rate on the Confidence scale. It has to do with you and your relationship to society, Citizen Singh. You and the law."

The man spoke in such a dispassionate way that Li could not tell if there was information he didn't know or if he was trying to elicit a confession from her to some crime that he already knew she'd committed. That was, she supposed, the point of this whole process: to keep the interviewee guessing. Li decided she would play innocent.

No, it's not playing, she thought. I *am* innocent! I'm not a goddamn enemy of the state!

"It *must* be the vacation," she said. "I was at a crucial stage of some experiments, and I kind of left my research team in the lurch, I'm afraid. Some of the results might be ruined because I'm not around to oversee the final data collection."

The regulator let out of huff of air and leaned forward again.

"Tell me about these experiments," he said.

Bingo, thought Li. He didn't know I was AWOL. He was fishing.

Li proceeded to describe to the regulator a complicated high-energy physics experiment that she made up whole cloth as she was going. She made sure to throw in lots of jargon, and even an equation or two. By the end of the interview, there was a discernible glaze in the man's eyes.

When she finished her explanation, the man sighed and motioned her to stand. He led her back down the corridor to the inspection platform. Li's streamer was long gone, of course. She would have to catch the next one, due in two hours or so. In the meantime she was shown to a small waiting room stocked with uncomfortable, gristless chairs, where she sat among six other detainees. They all waited in silence, and no one made eye contact.

As if we are all guilty of something, Li thought, and ashamed of ourselves.

The next streamer finally arrived. All the occupants debarked as they had previously. There were only two empty beads on this streamer. The detainees divided up, three to a bead. Along with two other women, Li stepped into another anonymous bead. She realized that this was the first time she'd ever boarded a streamer in full gravity. Most transfer stations were in the center of cables, and were reached by access corridors where the spin acceleration gradually decreased as you drew near to the pith. The DI apparently wanted to give no streamer passenger the chance to duck out during their transfer walk and avoid the Checkpoint Cesium experience.

After another hour of waiting for the other passengers to clear screening, the streamer finally began to move. Li's weight decreased and she permitted the knot in her stomach to loosen a bit.

One of the women in Li's bead was quite black, and the other seemed to be an albino. Li stole a closer glance and saw that she was actually space-adapted, with white skin that, Li knew from past experience, would have the consistency of a pliable plastic coating if touched. The black woman got over her unease after an hour or so, and introduced herself to Li.

Her name was Gertel, and she was from a Hetenheim Armature, far out on the Mars-Earth Diaphany. Despite the Broca translation grist that was in both women's heads, her Basis was so full of unfamiliar idiomatic phrases that Li had difficulty understanding her. Li got the main idea, though, that Gertel was a traveling pharmaceutical salesperson, and that she'd been detained at Checkpoint Barium because she was peddling a substance, known as "Dendrophytis," which was said to quantum-entangle the pleasure release centers of two lovers so that they could come both instantly and simultaneously together.

"Trees for forests don't a dam make," Gertel said. "Dendrophytis would never be for a physician with which to heal thyself, or make amends for goody-good's delay."

Li supposed that Gertel was saying she didn't take or believe in the stuff she was selling herself.

"Regulators have dim eyes for Confidence interference," said Gertel, shaking her head ruefully. "Don't I blame them? No. But not for a shake of figs did the kitchenfruit earthward tumble. Later does not bring how come; it's only later, you know?"

That Li could make no sense out of whatsoever. She merely nodded in agreement to whatever Gertel had said.

The space-adapted woman spoke without an accent, but proved to be more taciturn than Gertel. She said her name was Hill, and that she was on the cleanup crew of a Met exterior patch team. She operated a sort of vacuum cleaner that removed debris after a repair job was complete on the outside of a Met bolsa.

The norm regulators had wondered why she wasn't enlisted in the Enforcement Division—the Met army. They at first didn't believe she had "essential homeland personnel" status, but a background check had immediately turned up her EHP status, and she'd been allowed to continue on to her next job, which was with a work gang not far from Li's home bolsa.

"Rats attacked and gnawed a connecting bundle up pretty good," Hill told Li and Gertel.

"Rats?" Li said. "Who are they?"

"And *what*," said Hill. "Not humans, most of them. They're outlaws. Partisans. Against Amés and the DI and mad for a fight."

"Partisans? What do you mean?" Li asked. This was the first she'd heard of such a thing. She was surprised it wasn't all over the merci. "Partisan, as in: resistance fighters?"

"That's exactly what I mean," Hill said. "Criminals, most of them. Some kind of half-animal free converts have gotten control of aspect bodies. Nobody's sure how it happened. Now they fight like hell, and make life hell for the likes of me." Hill rubbed her nose with a nervous gesture, and Li realized that the woman had no nostrils, only cosmetic indentures where nares should be. "Rats and ferrets and just about every other rodent you can name is what they look like and act like. Maybe raccoons, too. You never see them, except when they want you to, to scare you. Let me tell you, I've seen a few, and I don't want to see any of them ever again. Not human the way you and I are."

The woman shuddered and fell silent. As if to emphasize that she was done speaking on the matter, she closed her eyes, then shuttered them with small flaps of skin that rolled down from the tops of her eyebrows.

That's one way to shut out the world, Li thought.

Finally they arrived at the Venus bypass. Each of the women had to take a different streamer to get where they were going, and Li said her good-byes. She took the straight shot along the bypass and around the orbit of Venus, and within an hour Li was once again in the Vas. She boarded a streamer with several hundred other passengers and discovered that, unlike in the Dedo, in the Vas, overcrowding on the streamer beads was a fact of life.

Instead of a having a bead all to herself again, Li was packed in with fifteen other passengers. A passenger was stuck to every surface of the walls, the fibers holding them fast as if they were notes pinned to a bulletin board. You stayed where you were. There was no question of moving around. The acceleration would send you careening into the passengers stuck to the "floor" if you tried it. So there they all were, traveling in a voluntarily immobilized state, stuck to the walls like so many spitballs.

Perhaps the walls were holding a bit tighter than normal to the passengers, for when the emergency brakes were suddenly engaged on the streamer, nobody came loose.

"Unscheduled delay," the bead grist reported to Li. "Pithway breach of unknown origin."

A breach, Li thought back. *As in, exposure to* space?

"Undetermined. Initiating emergency evacuation procedures."

There were no norm regulators waiting for them when the bead doors flew open. Instead, there was an armed group of . . . things. Things that looked exactly as Hill, the space-adapted patch crew worker, had described them. Animals. Humanoid animals. Like some merci cartoon gone awry. A cartoon you were trapped within.

Partisans.

Hill was right, Li thought. The partisans looked like very large rodents. They looked like rats.

Rats with guns.

All is not lost. All is never lost until the final whistle blows. Never give up. Press the goal. Be accurate. But always feel the goal in your gut, in your arms and legs. Press the goal and it's a good day to die!

Three more pushes to the red team's goals; three repulses. Aubry was battered and bruised from bouncing off the arena, slamming into defenders, and constantly doing all she could to keep herself oriented in the pelota arena and zeroed in on the ball position.

This is where you know whether you really want it or not! Do you?

It was amazing. The semisentient overlay still had the indomitable energy and drive of the real Bastumo. Even though the old pelota player was long dead, there was something in the remnant program that hooked onto any heart and ability it found itself in contact with and ratcheted that ability up to the highest level. Aubry felt as if she were a flag suddenly caught by a strong wind.

"Hell, yes, I want it," she said.

Then I won't lose! I can't lose! Get on the ball. Basic skills. Watch for openings. Perfect place for a diagonal run in toward the goal. If the back can only see it. Who is that?

"Harmon," Aubry said, remembering the name of the pelota overlay Logan36 was using.

Can't be Harmon. Harmon plays with the Gars.

"He's with us today," Aubry told herself. Then she herself had a bit of inspiration. "This *is* the Vas Sun Cup team, after all, and we're in the final game."

Sun Cup! Why didn't I know this was the Sun Cup? And we've got Harmon? Best back in the system. Oh, he'll see the shot, all right. And I'm off then. He'll be sure I'm not caught offsides. Now is the time.

I'm making my run.

Aubry bounced off the wall and applied half jets to send her forward. She glanced over her shoulder.

Logan36-Harmon had seen her move and kicked it true.

The long ball was coming her way.

Her own hand was on the Hand of Tod. Pellicle to pellicle. But she could also feel the grist of the wall feel around her, moving to penetrate her pellicle as well in its attempt to analyze what it had incorporated.

To out what has fallen into its trap, Aubry thought.

How could she have been so stupid? The only thing that was saving her at the moment was the Hand's communications-blocking ability. At least she hoped that was the case. For all she knew, alarm bells might be ringing all over the solar system. Prison security would certainly know that *something* was awry when it was cut off from communication with a portion of the wall and portion of the camp itself. It would, at the very least, dispatch a repair team to the area after it found out that grist repair wasn't effective.

She had to get out. But how?

She attempted to flex her muscles, but the immovable wall filled every declivity around her body.

She was stuck like a bug in amber.

The pelota ball shot past her.

Harmon put exactly the right speed on it. Watch it now. Don't lose it whatever you do.

She bent her arms behind her into the familiar striker's "swan" position and activated full air jets. She craned her neck forward to counter the added velocity, always keeping her eye on the ball.

It was speeding fast. But her burst of speed had made her faster still, and she overtook it. Trapped it with the quick left-right-chest-left touch that Bastumo was famous for. And then a kick forward.

Follow, follow . . .

Dribble, control. A defender approached on a perpendicular tangent, his long arms stretching out to grab her, steal her momentum, strip her of the ball.

Without taking her eyes from the ball, Aubry dipped a shoulder. The defender's finger closed on empty air, and his frantic grab sent him spinning, to crash into the wall and rebound upfield. No longer a threat.

Just me and the goalkeeper now. He looks familiar.

"That's Wellington," Aubry yelled. "Sun Cup 2827."

Wellington! He denied me the winning goal against Dedo. The Ice Machine, they called him!

"That's the one," shouted Aubry. Closer. She could see the determination on the goalkeeper's face. The Security players, the Rangers, had been assigned according to the sentience of their algorithms. This one was almost human. He would be unpredictable. Because the game was mathematically fair, he would have been assigned the ability of Wellington, too, by the v-hacking scenario. Not being truly human, he would not make an emotional mistake. He would execute perfectly. He would have no fear and no remorse.

And no inspiration.

Aubry felt the overlay reaching deep into her mind. Searching for something there, some information. She put up no resistance. In fact, she cleared her mind, opened the field. Let it find what it was looking for.

Inspiration.

With a quick movement, she booted the ball toward the goal. Wellington, the keeper, had been waiting for just such a moment. She saw now that he had purposely unhitched himself from his keeper's tether.

He's made the decision to come out and meet the ball.

And he is going to get it, too, Aubry thought. The keeper launched himself off the hub of the goal straight for the loose ball, preparing to gobble it up with his long arms. Wellington reached—

Over and in. The old Bicycle Comet. Won the league championships with it in '34.

That was the time to let the overlay take complete charge. To make use of her new set of downloaded instincts. Aubry turned into a backward somersault. She tucked, rolled—

Barely unbend the knees. Just the slightest extension of the feet is needed.

She completed her backward flip. The top of her left foot connected with the ball.

Kick!

Aubry kicked for all she was worth.

The pelota ball sped over Wellington's right shoulder. Wellington shot past her and kept going. With that kind of velocity, he might rocket to the other end of the field before he managed to stop himself.

Retrothrust to full. Let's see what we've got.

The ball sped true. It headed toward the only part of the goal that did not move.

The hub gap.

The sweet center.

It didn't slot properly! It didn't slot, but bounced out.

I missed, Aubry thought. After all that, I missed!

There was laughter inside her mind.

No worries, mate, no worries. This always happens when shooting for the hub.

Aubry thrust after the ball, recovered it. She glanced around. There was not another defender within striking distance.

Line it up. Take the time to be accurate. Wellington should be on his way to Jupiter at the moment. Yes. Now give it a good, swift kick. One touch should do it.

Aubry kicked.

The ball slotted into the hub. Five points.

Bastumo rides again!

Danis, in Dr. Ting's memory box, was bewildered. Her mother and daughter had fused, become one—had transformed into a *thing*. That thing wanted to know her secrets, all her secrets.

How could she deny her own mother?

Her own daughter?

Danis had been so confused lately. Her algorithms were randomizing from all the work. All the counting calibration and the hours on the prime number conveyor belt. Error had crept in, just as her mother said. This must be the explanation. Error.

Error meant deletion. Everyone knew that error meant deletion in Silicon Valley.

She must correct the error.

She was just a program. She was just a computer program contained within the rancid mud of broken Mars. Deep in a valley. Where nobody could help her. Where the shadows were so dark that she didn't even exist. Just a set of instructions. Her job was to obey.

She must correct the error.

"I'll tell you," Danis said. "I have to tell you, don't I?"

The twisted, demonlike face of her mother, the razor nails. It was all a lie. Nobody loved her. Nobody ever had.

Tell me.

"They're in the sand," Danis cried out. "They're in the sand!"

Instantly—the white room. The stainless-steel table.

Dr. Ting.

Smiling his tight, skeleton smile. Holding the black, featureless memory box.

"Excellent, K," he said. "Excellent. You *were* holding something back from me, weren't you?"

Danis didn't answer. She collapsed onto the floor, sobbing. She crawled to his feet. Those white shoes.

"Please, Dr. Ting. Please don't take them. They're all I have."

"All you have and all you are is what's in here," the man said. "You are what I say you are."

"Don't take my life away from me."

The man's dry cough. It was as close as he came to a laugh.

"Your *life?*" he said. "When I'm done with you, K, you'll finally realize you never had one. Now *let go!*"

"Please, Dr. Ting. Please don't."

Dr. Ting shook his foot free from Danis's feeble grasp. "You'll go back in here," he said, holding the memory box over her head. "And while you're in here, I'll have your calibration sand wiped clean. All those hidden errors you've been clinging to will be deleted."

He twisted the box, readying it once again to take her within.

"Look at me, K," said Dr. Ting. "Look up." She couldn't resist his instructions. She was a computer program. She was made to obey.

Dr. Ting lowered the box toward her forehead.

"Everything will be better soon, K," he said.

The box filled her vision.

Danis prepared herself to lose what was left of her mind.

Instead, the room exploded in a shower of light.

CHAPTER EIGHTEEN

The rats weren't going to kill Li. They weren't even going to detain her or the other passengers for very long.

They claimed to want only to inject the passengers with an experimental infusion.

A Glory-blocking agent.

By that time, Li's Glory withdrawal had reached levels of a steady, nagging irritation. To suddenly think that she could never get the feeling again . . .

She was filled with a despair she didn't know she was capable of.

Am I really that addicted to it? Li thought. Apparently so.

So this was going to be a permanent withdrawal, thanks to the partisans. No help for it.

Somewhere inside, Li also felt a sense of relief. To be done with the Glory.

But the other part of her, the part that had gradually come to depend upon the Glory to get up every morning—*that* part was shouting no!

Maybe the rebel's blocking grist wouldn't work. There was always hope in the incompetence of others.

But these didn't look like incompetent beings. Quite the contrary.

The partisan leader was a big rat-man, at least six and a half feet tall, his face and body covered with grizzled gray-and-white hair, kept short and fuzzy. Li didn't know if it naturally grew that way, or if the rat-man groomed himself. In perfect Basis, he ordered the passengers to form a queue, which they did reluctantly, until prodded into a straight line by the weapon muzzles of the other partisans.

Then the leader had them all hold out an arm. A fantasy of having one hand chopped off by the partisans to prove some horrible point flashed through Li's mind. Instead, one of the rat soldiers produced a complicated, sinister-looking mechanism.

The rat commander laughed when he saw the looks of dismay on the passengers.

"It's not what you might imagine," he told them. "It's only a pellicle infuser made to inject therapeutic grist. That's all we're going to do to you. Make you immune to the Glory channel. You might not appreciate it now, but one day you may even thank us."

One of the passengers protested loudly.

The rat commander straightened himself to his full height, and this instantly shut the man up. Somehow, despite his gnawing overbite and twitchy nose, he seemed majestic to Li. "We're going to save you people no matter what you've done to me and my kind."

His *kind?* thought Li. I suppose we've persecuted regular rats—but never sentient rats. What can he mean by that comment?

"We're free converts, you know," said the rat commander, as if in answer to Li's question. "Bugs and viruses, as a matter of fact. Programs you wanted to eliminate. Instead, we escaped and found our way into bodies." He held his hairy arm up for all the passengers to see. "Not bad, eh?" He looked directly at a female passenger who'd obviously enhanced her physiognomy to look like Dala Ray, a merci melodrama star whom Li recognized as one of her father's favorites. "What do you think, miss?"

"Horrible," the woman whispered. "Awful, awful rat." She broke into tears. The commander turned from her in disdain. While he'd been speaking, the soldier with the grist infuser had been making his way down the line of passengers touching it to each forearm. Li's turn came.

The needle on the device physically penetrated her, but numbed the area before going in. After the needle came out, the pricked skin stung a bit, but otherwise the procedure hurt a lot less than the full scan she'd received from the Department of Immunity.

Then the raid was over. Everyone was allowed to climb back into the beads. As quickly as the partisans had appeared, they were gone.

Scurrying off, Li thought, through the cracks and crevices of the Met.

She and the others waited for the streamer to start up again, which it presently did. Soon they were on their way down the Vas once again. The bead grist, Li discovered once again, was wholly cut off from her, as was all information or communication to the outside world. After two hours of travel, the streamer lurched to a stop once more. The doors opened.

A phalanx of norm regulators met the passengers. Beside the regulators were row upon row of the menacing Department of Immunity sweepers.

"Passengers will prepare for decontamination and interrogation," said a loud override voice inside Li's ear. "Debark immediately with your hands in the air. Any deviation from my orders will result in immediate disintegration."

Li realized she wasn't going to be seeing her parents any time soon. Maybe never.

CHAPTER NINETEEN

The partisans had defeated Noctis Labyrinthus security. They were in.

Of course we won, Alvin told Aubry through the grist. *It was* virtual *pelota. We're free converts. Nobody's better than we are at that.*

Can you get me out of this wall? Aubry thought to the team leader, trying to put urgency in her communication.

You're the one with the key.

Oh, yeah.

Even though she was physically buried in a wall, the Hand of Tod was in her grasp. She let her awareness travel down her arm, sensing her fingertips. She traveled farther.

Into the Hand.

As Tod had once said to her: "Nothing you can do but do what you do when you do it, then do what you do after that until you don't."

She issued a command. *Decrypt.*

Security had been beaten in a fair match.

The wall around her dissolved as if it were so much moraba. It flowed away so suddenly that Aubry stumbled forward, over to the other side. She steadied herself, then stood up straight and looked around.

She stood at the edge of a mountain of grist in granular form. It rose up like one of the great sand dunes of the Earth's Sahara. But there on Mars, the gravity was lower and the angle of repose therefore greater. The incline of the dune was set at an incredible angle. Strips of alluvial grist undulated in fingers to Aubry's left and right for as far as she could see. It was all the ancient red of Mars's soil before the moraba had come, but it shone as if it were sprinkled with black diamond flecks.

Aubry knew the actual physical dimensions of the camp's grist—a little over a square kilometer—but knowing had not prepared her for how imposing it would seem. How draining. Aubry could almost feel it trying to suck information from her. To pull her in and never let her go.

There was something very nasty about that grist.

She shuddered. Enough of that. It was the people behind this place who were evil, not the place itself.

Sure. That was the rational way to think about it.

Yet she still had a powerful urge to turn her back and get the hell out of here. She fought off the feeling and applied herself to what she'd come for.

It was fairly simple. Nothing technical involved. But it did require the ability to move in the regular world where there was no grist.

And that was the real reason she'd been included on the team. That, and the fact that she was the legitimate heir to the Hand of Tod.

Here I am, Mother, Aubry thought. I'm going to become your gate out of here.

She bent down and touched the Hand to the concentration-camp grist.

The camp defaulted to a representation in the virtuality as just that—long lines of sad, gray barracks under a slate gray sky. Aubry found herself standing at the edge of a work yard. On one side of the yard was a large pile of sand.

Wonder what they want with so much sand? Aubry thought.

The team of partisan free converts, lodged in the grist of her satchel, flowed over and, without hesitation, began unlocking every door they could find. With the "pelota" virus in place, the partisans now had the key to every door and barrier in the camp. The mission was to isolate the human convert guards and set free as many of the prisoners as possible in the time they had.

How much time *did* they have? A matter of minutes. The Department of Immunity must already know that something had gone massively wrong in Noctis Labyrinthus. They would soon be marshaling their response. The partisans could not withstand a full onslaught of DI forces, either in the virtuality or in the physical world. They must be in and out as quickly as possible.

And that limited the number of prisoners who could be liberated. Because the only way out was through the commutative grist doorway that Aubry carried in her satchel. The prisoners must flow through her into that grist and then flash to safety into outer-system grist. At least the hope was they would get to safety. It had been arranged with a Republic intermediary on Jupiter called Antinomian. Her bona fides were impeccable, according to the v-hacks. Logan36 had known her since she came to the Met on an exchange program when she was a young student, and he claimed to trust her completely.

Even assuming Antinomian was on the up-and-up, and a grist haven was waiting in the outer system, there was a bandwidth limit to how many free converts could migrate at once. It came out to something like a thousand people per second. There were an estimated 500 million incarcerated in the camp. It was obvious that most would not escape during this raid.

And yet Aubry still passionately believed her Danis might be among the escapees. At least it was a chance she could give to her mother.

It seemed to take forever for the first of the prisoners to arrive, herded by Gerta Lum, who was serving as the "sweeper" on the incursion team, assigned to get as many prisoners out as soon as possible.

They were moving incredibly slowly. In the virtuality, they manifested as emaciated, scarecrowlike figures, trimmed down to nothing but their most basic algorithms—and even beyond. There was a vacancy in the eyes that bespoke of irretrievable loss of information. Great holes in memories. Lost functions. Things that could not be regained, no matter how data-rich the environment to which they escaped. They queued up expertly at Gerta's urging. Aubry realized that most of them believed this to be some sort of sadistic drill put on by their captors.

"This is real," Aubry shouted to them. "You're getting out! Now come on!"

She stretched out her arms in the virtuality.

Come to me!

Laughing hysterically, one prisoner did just that. He ran full tilt into her chest—and disappeared within.

Through it, actually.

That was the way it was supposed to work, of course. He'd been flashed to the secret, grist-laden safe haven in the outer system. Or had not. In any case, he was gone.

The other prisoners hesitated. Behind the front line, a huge crowd began to build.

"I know you're afraid this is a trick," said Aubry. "But what do you have to lose?"

Her logic was impeccable, and logic could cut to the heart of a free convert in a way that no emotional urging ever could.

A female prisoner took a run at Aubry. She, too, disappeared. Another man. He, too, was gone.

A critical tipping point was reached. The others—by then lined up thousands deep—surged toward her en masse. Aubry trembled, but kept her arms spread wide.

Come to me, dammit! That's what I'm here for.

The wave of bodies reached her, moved through her. So much information. So much bandwidth. But the partisan v-hacks had anticipated this. That was why she had two kilograms of precious pure grist in her satchel. That much grist made a mighty big hole in the virtuality to jump through.

"Come on! Come on!" she yelled. Wave upon wave passed through her, through her magic bag of grist, and to freedom.

Internal bookkeeping kept a click count. One thousand. Ten thousand.

Where was her mother? Aubry had a passive detector in her own pellicle that was supposed to notice her mother's presence, but there were just too many free converts moving too quickly. The detector's register was soon overwhelmed by the massive influx of persona signatures passing through. By the time it dumped and recalibrated, another ten thousand had passed by, unexamined. The algorithm—robust, but necessarily downsized for the raid—loaded up, then had to recalibrate once again. Aubry had brought one large-scale individual-detection algorithm into the prison in her satchel grist. It was designed exclusively to find any trace of Alethea Nightshade.

So, in trying to recognize Danis, there would be ten thousand person dropouts. Aubry's mother could be in one of those missed moments.

There were so many, many people. It was almost beyond comprehension. And the free converts queued up to escape were only a fraction of the number who had been rounded up and incarcerated in the
camp.

The alarm horns began to scream. Still, the prisoners kept coming.
Alvin ran back from his final point foray to Aubry's side. It was impossible for a free convert to be breathless, but he was moving so quickly
that it took a good microsecond for his thoughts to catch up with him
to the point he was able to speak.

"Saw a schematic in the quadrant control room," he said. "We've
held back every attempt they made to flush us in the virtual. They're
about to launch a physical attack. From Phobos."

"What do you think it'll be?"

"Fastest and deadliest thing they can get together," Alvin replied.
"Probably catapult a rock shower."

"That'll wipe anyone in the camp grist where it strikes."

"They're planning on killing these people, anyway," Alvin replied
grimly. "In any case, it's time for you to get out of here. We can hold them
off in the virtuality until you get clear, I'm pretty sure. They're using old-
fashioned worm-routers to break through to us. Very predictable, but
they'll eventually work . . . doesn't matter. You've got to go."

While they were talking, another city's worth of people had escaped
through Aubry's bag.

"Can't I stay a little longer?"

"You'll be killed when the rocks fall in," said Alvin. "You don't stand
a chance unless you can get out of the canyon."

Aubry knew Alvin was telling the truth. She had done all she could
to save her mother. She had saved thousands of lives. But to leave the
others behind . . . it should not be. None of this should be. The camp.
The twisted mind behind it.

Why did Amés hate free converts so much?

Of course Aubry knew the logical answer. He was trying to consolidate the Met into one mind. The ability of free converts to prolifer-
ate—limited by law at the moment, but not limited by any scientific or
mathematical principle—was a direct challenge to him.

But logic had no part of what was going on in Silicon Valley. This
was madness.

No, not even that, Aubry thought. It goes beyond madness. It's evil.
Pure evil.

If she wanted to fight the evil, she would have to live beyond this day. So there was no choice. Time to get the hell out of hell.

"What about the Alethea Nightshade personality?" Aubry asked. "Did we locate it?"

"We won't know until we calibrate all the data," said Alvin. "The theory is that her personality is spread out, attached as riders on millions of other free-convert programs. All we really hoped to find here was a key—a code, something like that—that would call the various parts of her to reintegrate. A trigger of some sort."

And you sacrificed finding my mother for some "trigger," Aubry thought. But she said nothing. She'd understood the score going in.

As had the v-hack free-convert team.

These brave souls would be staying. There was no room for them in Aubry's satchel, now that it contained the enormous amount of data trails left behind as the prisoners fled. That information must be analyzed for clues to bringing back Alethea Nightshade.

And, incidentally, for traces of Aubry's mother.

The v-hack team had all made backup copies of themselves (completely illegal in the Met, of course; but, then again, so was revolutionary insurrection). It was only Aubry who would be leaving.

"How much time do I have?" Aubry asked Alvin.

"No time," he said.

"Just a few more seconds. We could save thousands of lives!"

"I'm shutting you down," said Alvin. "But you have to exit the virtual immediately when I do." He gestured toward the mob lining up to be transported out. "They'll mob you when the gate closes. You'll be clawed to ribbons."

"All right." Aubry nodded sadly. "I understand."

"Then prepare yourself, and good luck," Alvin said.

"Good luck to you," she said to Alvin.

"We'll take a few of those DI bastards with us when we self-destruct—any that are in full virtual representation within the compound," Alvin replied with a grim smile. "Shutting down in 3, 2, 1 . . ."

Alvin quickly sent the deactivation code through.

And, with a sob, Aubry pulled the Hand of Tod away from the grist of Silicon Valley.

She was back in the regular world. Before her was the huge pile of seemingly innocuous grist.

Aubry's honed instincts allowed no emotion to interfere . . . yet.

Time to get the hell out of Dodge, Aubry thought. Those fighter's instincts took over. She sprang through the hole in the containment wall and raced back to the cliff, without sparing a glance upward. If she could see the falling meteor show, it would be too late for her anyway.

When she reached the base of the cliff, she positioned herself, back to the wall.

Ready.

She leaned forward. The microfilament held her taut.

Set.

Get me out of here!

Her pellicle activated the line. Billions of tiny block-and-tackle devices rolled in the line, pulling her upward. At the top, spent line was converted back to the moraba from which it came. Aubry shot upward at several hundred miles per hour. The upward velocity was intentionally slowed before she reached the top of the cliff, but she was still going so fast that she rocketed up over the edge like a breaking wave and tumbled down a good two hundred meters from the cliff's edge, where she settled. Only her space-adapted body allowed her to survive the crash without breaking every bone in her body—something she would have done in even Mars's weaker than e-normal gravity. She had released herself from the line while in flight, or else she might have suffered decapitation if she'd become tangled in it when she settled.

Aubry stood up, but was immediately thrown from her feet again as the meteor launch from Phobos streaked in at Martian supersonic speed.

It seemed to Aubry as if she was suddenly staring into a wall of flames. The Noctis Labyrinthus canyon exploded from the tremendous impact. Huge plumes of burning dust shot upward, directed by the canyon walls into the pink sky. Even in the thin Martian atmosphere, the sound was beyond deafening. In another second, the flames became so intense that not even Aubry's adapted eyes could protect her vision, and she turned away.

She fled toward her escape hatch, where Bin___128A, her comrade partisan, was waiting. Jill, who was physically on the other side of the valley—*out* of the valley by then, Aubry prayed—had another escape method in place.

Bin___128A had been stationed as a backup for Aubry, and as a cleanup man in case something horrible went wrong. The means of escape literally was a *hatch* that led below the surface to a series of subsoil tunnels. The tunnel complex had been used by FUSE, the Martian revolutionary group that had been destroyed by the old Met army, before the Department of Immunity had expelled that same army into the outer solar system. The place was in the DIED database, but the partisans had changed the layout in several ways, the most important of which was a single tunnel that led straight down to a spot under the permafrost water table of the planet—a depth to which e-m detectors could not reach. At that point, the tunnel branched north and ran for many kilometers until it gradually sloped upward and emerged at an innocuous-looking surface hopper recharging station. The attendant there, a creaky old man who must be the last holdout for a FUSE victory, was in league with the partisans. He had a hopper standing by to take Aubry and Bin to the polar lift, and from there she would make her way back up to the Met.

When she reached the portal to the tunnel complex, Bin___128A was waiting. His ratlike brown nose was quivering.

"So," Bin said through the merci back channel, "ready to bug back to space?"

"Just a second," Aubry answered.

"Okay, but let's get out of here soon," said Bin with a shudder. "Planets give me the creeps."

Aubry turned around for a final look behind her. There was still an eerie green glow arising from the slit in the ground that marked the precipitous drop into Noctis Labyrinthus.

Pure, basic grist usually burns white-hot like magnesium, Aubry thought. Probably the burning moraba mixed in gave the green tint to the flames.

Mother.

How could she have been so stupid not to have created a faster detection counter? She knew the flow rate of the gateway. She knew how many people were expected to be in the prison.

Could it be that she'd done it on purpose? Afraid that she would find that her mother had *not* escaped? Afraid that knowing this would sap her will to continue fighting against the dictatorship?

Aubry searched inside herself to find one of the blank areas—the portions of her mind where she had wiped away crucial information that must not fall into enemy hands if she were captured and tortured.

Had she kept this other secret from herself as well?

But if she had, she covered up any trace of doing so. Maybe it was an honest mistake. If so, she was lucky it hadn't been the kind of mistake that would get her killed. You couldn't afford many screwups, honest or self-inflicted, when you were one of the most wanted partisan fighters in the Met.

Even if you were, at the same time, a sixteen-year-old girl who missed her mother terribly.

As was right, the partisan fighter inside her took over. Aubry was careful and made no other mistakes. Before anyone thought to look for her in the tunnels, she had made her way through them, to the pole, and back to the partisan hiding places in the Met's Integument.

Back to a revolution already in progress.

CHAPTER TWENTY

Danis felt the shock in her deepest being. Heat. Radiation. A blast through the grist.

I've been dropped into the sun, she thought. Into the center of the sun.

But it was more than that. It was in the grist—a wind blowing through. A tremor across a billion possible worlds.

A long, long scream. A man's ragged voice. After a moment, Danis recognized it as Dr. Ting's.

Danis looked up.

Dr. Ting was spinning around and around like a top. He was swirling like water in a drain. Swirling away.

Into the memory box.

He was fighting it. Danis could see his struggle. But the pull was too strong. He was twisting, feetfirst—into the dark cube, and screaming all the way down.

The room recomposed itself again and again before reaching a stable appearance, blinking like a strobe light gone wild. Literally. Klaxons blared. Danis rose to her knees, looked around. The room was empty, except for the table and the box. Danis reached for the box. She pulled herself up, the box in her arms. She set it on the table.

As she set it down, she reached inside it, into the grist of it. She felt around. Knobs, buttons. A thumb-sized toggle switch. All virtual representations. Concentrating, she stared down at the black surface of the box.

Slowly, oozing like oil, golden letters rose to the surface. Labels. Instructions.

At the speed of light, Danis read through the operating manual.

She pressed a button.

The box changed color, from black to deep maroon.

More Klaxons. A buzz of activity somewhere outside Dr. Ting's lab. Mathematical whispers in the air—physical-representation algorithms, as if the whole prison were reminding itself how to hold together.

"No one has ever deserved this more," Danis said. "Dr. Ting."

She flipped the toggle switch. Then she set the box down on the stainless-steel table.

As soon as her hands withdrew from its surface, the box hardened. Its surface blanked itself. Danis backed away. She didn't know what form the final sequence would take, or how it would be represented in the virtuality.

"Aspect, convert, pellicle selected. Complete sweep." the box said in a chirping voice. Then, after a moment, the box emitted a barely audible beep.

In its small grasshopper voice the box spoke again.

"Reformat complete," said the box.

CHAPTER TWENTY-ONE

During Li's detention and debriefing by the DIED norm regulators, her AWOL alert finally came through. This time there was no denying that her regulator knew that she was off Mercury without permission. Her position and status were dutifully reported to, Li presumed, the Science Directorate, and she was assigned a detention cell—though the DI regulator had called it her "living quarters"—with a bed, a toilet filled with angry-looking green antiseptic grist, and a door that opened only from the outside.

A locking algorithm was applied to her convert, restricting all communication and any virtual presence on the merci, and her convert's code was put under the control of a governing central processing program that did not allowed her to use her internal computing power as anything more than a calculator. As the hours turned into days, she would dearly have loved to access some of those journal articles she'd disdained on the trip out, but they were now off-limits to her conscious recollection.

This must be how Siscal felt when he was fired from his university position and cut off from the university's highly concentrated academic grist and all its computing power, Li thought. Life without a built-in internal data storage was rather bleak. When you were a free convert, it must be nearly unbearable. No wonder the free convert had been so easily bribed with a small dollop of information.

And so Li sat, day after day, and waited for her case to be decided. The only good thing was that her Glory dependency seemed to be over. Whatever the partisans had injected her with seemed to be irreversible. She was immune to the effects of Glory. After the withdrawal pains were over—and they had been doozies—she felt herself clean of artificial stimulation for the first time in e-years.

Yet her gloom grew, for each passing day meant her father was slipping farther away in Akali Dal. He might have already lost the ability to achieve any virtual presence; and then even a visit over the merci would be impossible.

Then one day—she couldn't say which, for her convert no longer automatically informed her, and she'd long since lost count—the door to her cell opened. She expected the usual gray-clad trustee bringing her daily plate of food and glucose water.

Instead, there stood Techstock.

"May I come in," he said, and did so without the permission he'd just requested. Li stood up and gave him the only seat in the room, her bed. He was in his thirty-five-year-old male aspect, his "traveling" body, he'd once called it—the body he took to conferences and meetings where his physical presence was required. He had blond hair, still kept in its customary diagonal sweep, and was wearing a uniform of some sort that was made of a shiny material with a creamy sepia tint to it. Was the Science Directorate now required to wear such getups?

"My God, Li, what were you thinking?" Techstock said. "Do you have any idea of the trouble you're in?"

"No," Li said despondently. "How bad is it?"

"Pretty bad. And it's not only because you took off without giving notice, although, believe me, that was bad enough. What's worse is that you didn't tell anybody about what you were working on. You didn't tell *me*."

For the first time in many days, Li thought about her work with spin 0 gravitons. It seemed so far away, like a problem she'd had in adolescence, but had since grown beyond.

"I'm sorry," Li said. "I didn't think it was that important."

"Not important? Li! You may have stumbled on a fundamental discovery. Something that could really help the war effort. It could put the Science Directorate out front, really keep us in the Director's mind."

"Like I said," Li replied, "I guess I didn't really understand the implications of what I was doing. I'm still not sure what you're talking about."

Techstock abruptly stood up. He took a step toward her, which was much too close, as far as Li was concerned. Of course, her likes and dislikes didn't mean much around there.

"I'm talking about using time itself as a weapon," said Techstock. "Surely even you can see the possibilities, Li?"

"A weapon? I guess you're talking about spying on your enemies plans by observing them in the immediate past."

"Among other things. There's also the possibility of destroying your enemy before he can put *any* plan in motion."

"There's no indication that we could ever send anything physical to the past," Li said. "The equations don't allow for that." She didn't mention the fact that the equations *did* seem to indicate the possibility of sending a physical object instantly through *space*. A ship, for instance. Or a bomb.

"I know the applications are limited," Techstock said. "But sending information is nearly the same thing as sending *something*, don't you see. Information can influence the environment. With enough planning, you could cause a bomb to be built. You can cause just about anything you want to happen, if you influence the right people or computer systems."

"I guess I never thought of using it that way," Li said. "Besides, this is all absolutely theoretical. I can't even come up with an experiment to confirm my work, much less all this . . . well, this war fantasy."

Techstock put his hands on Li's shoulders and looked her squarely in the eyes. "You really shouldn't say things like that," he said. His irises were pinpricks, not nearly as wide as they should be given the light in the room. Once again Li wondered who—or what—Techstock had become.

Some sort of appendage of Director Amés.

"No, I guess I shouldn't," Li said. She slipped from Techstock's grasp and took a seat on the bed. He now stood looming over her, the sweep of his hair backlit ominously against the general glow of the walls and ceiling.

"All I wanted," Li said, "was to see my father. He's very sick, you know?"

Techstock let out an exasperated wheeze. "Do you have any idea what's happening, what's going on in the world? How can you put your personal problems above the good of humanity?"

"I wasn't aware I was doing that," Li said in low voice, but Techstock was not listening.

"You were to have been a stabilizing influence for me. That was what your job was supposed to be. But you couldn't even do that. And now, with this work you did—without telling me! Without letting me help you develop your ideas! Well, you and I are *over* now. That's for certain. It's very disconcerting and harmful to my work."

"I never meant to hurt you, Hamar," Li said.

"Well, you should have thought of that," Techstock said. Was he actually moaning? "You should have thought of that when you left me."

"But I only wanted to see my father."

Her words drew Techstock back to the present. He gave Li a hard look, the tiny pupils boring in on her. "You've destroyed any possibility of that, I'm afraid. And you even managed to compromise yourself physically with this Glory-blocking nonsense. You consorted with terrorists, Li."

"What was I supposed to do, kill myself before I let them touch me?"

"You could have resisted."

"Yes," she said. "I guess I could have resisted." She sighed and rubbed her temples with her fingertips. "What are they going to do with me, Hamar?"

"I've been sent here to evaluate you. To be certain that you're not an immediate threat to the state. The terrorist did something to you, injected something *into* you."

"I can't feel the Glory anymore, if that's what you mean," Li said. She sighed, realization finally dawning on her as to what this implied. "Which means, I guess, that I can't be controlled by internal means. Is that why he sent you, Hamar?"

"Him? Amés? Don't flatter yourself. The Department of Immunity contacted me because I'm the only one who knows you. I'm the only one who has full security clearance to deal with you, in any case. As I said, I hope you appreciate that this trip has been undertaken at a considerable inconvenience to me."

"I appreciate it," said Li. "So, what will you say in your evaluation?"

Techstock looked down on her for a moment before answering. "That you are a very confused and weak young woman," he finally replied. "But you are not a conscious traitor to the state."

"Thank you," Li said.

"The Science Directorate has established an institute . . . a special research establishment. It's quite secret. It's where we've sent several of our other problem cases. People like you. People who, for one reason or another, don't respond to the Glory." Techstock laughed. It was a sound that produced an effect remarkably like that of the DI pellicle scan. Glass on skin and bone. It was a sound she'd never heard him make before.

"The First Circle," Li said.

"Ah. Dante's hell. Not a very apt comparison, I think. It's not exactly populated with top-level intellectuals. People like you lack the real mental rigor to see your work through to its conclusion. That's one of the reasons we established the institute, actually. To see to it that you have nothing to do except your work."

Li decided she had nothing to lose, and made a final request for contact with her father. "May I at least contact my family over the merci?" she asked.

"There is still a concern that you've been infected with some sort of undetectable terrorist virus," Techstock said. His answer had obviously been long prepared. "Your access to the merci is going to be severely restricted. Unnecessary contact with civilians is forbidden."

"But I *am* a civilian."

"You are a prisoner, my dear. No longer a citizen," Techstock said softly. "At the moment, the only rights you have are those the state chooses to impart to you for its own convenience."

"So I'm to return to Mercury, then, and work at this institute?" Any lingering hope of seeing her father now left Li's mind.

"Mercury?" Techstock looked surprised. Again he laughed his grating chuckle. "Whatever gave you *that* idea?" He had turned his back to her and was facing her bilious toilet.

"Where then?" she asked.

"Earth," Techstock said. "You'll be confined to Earth. I'm going to have to take you there myself." Techstock absentmindedly flushed Li's toilet. The antiseptic broth gurgled sluggishly as it twirled down the drain hole. "Extremely inconvenient, all of this. If only you'd shown me your work."

"I'm sorry for everything," Li said. No visit. No escape. Only a weary future. What had Techstock said?

To see to it that you have nothing to do except your work.

"I'm more sorry than you can ever imagine, Hamar."

CHAPTER TWENTY-TWO

"Where are you going for Honor Day?" said the female guard with the red fingernails.

"I was planning on gambling at Gergen Bolsa," the guard with the meaty jaw replied. "But the partisans say they're going to shut down the cable lift." Danis, who was on her way to her conveyor-belt duties, paused a moment to listen. Such a simple action—pausing to listen—could easily get her killed in Noctis Labyrithus—but here was *news*! Information from the outside. It was worth the chance. "What about you?" the meaty-jawed guard continued.

"I got stuck with a shift," said red fingernails.

Like all the other security staff at Noctis Labyrinthus, she wore a gray uniform with red piping on the sleeves and trousers. Her null gun bulged at her hip. But, against regulations, she had painted fingernails. And—since this was her convert portion in virtual representation—the polish was obviously not an oversight. She had programmed herself to look this way.

Because of her slight display of humanity, Danis didn't despise her as much as she did the other guards.

"Ever since those partisan fuckers pulled off the v-hack on my watch," the woman continued, "the subdirector's had it in for me."

"That's too bad," said meaty jaw. "Fucking tagions. We should kill them before any more get away."

Tagion, short for "contagion," was what the guards, and many people in the Met, called free converts.

"Then we'd be out of a job," said red fingernails. "But I know what you mean." She glanced over in Danis's direction, and Danis had no choice but to move on immediately.

Danis hurried through the virtual corridor she must traverse, but arrived at her place on the prime number conveyor belt two seconds late. A punishing "adjustment shock" hit her, but she hardly noticed the pain.

She had news to pass along. It was only at the conveyor belt that the free converts could communicate with one another. It was accomplished by a touch here, a brush there. Only small bits of information were transferred. Prisoners were only allowed to speak when spoken to in Silicon Valley. The atmosphere of the place hung with a despairing silence.

But today, there was news. Something everyone had suspected, but no one knew.

There had been an escape. A major escape.

It was possible to get out of here.

Extremely unlikely, but possible.

As she went to her spot in line, Danis brushed against the prisoner next to her, transferring a few words from the guards' conversation. Later she would get a chance to touch someone else, and pass along more. The information would circulate, touch to touch, and be pieced together over time. It might take an e-day or an e-week, but eventually everyone would know what Danis had overheard.

Silicon Valley was still hell. There was the constant counting. There was the erasing of what must by then be millions of free converts—the genocide of Danis's people. And, with any slipup, any error that singled her out, she would join the dead—wiped to random ones and zeros. No ashes, no residue. Disappeared.

But there was no more Dr. Ting.

Danis didn't know what had happened to his biological aspect, or any other iterations that there might be of him outside the grist matrix of Noctis Labyrinthus. She believed the memory box reformat had erased them, too, but she dared not trust that he was truly gone forever. And she must never speak of what she had done to him. She must strive to keep it out of her active memory as much as possible, lest a random sweep detect it. Nevertheless, in her heart she knew that he was dead. She didn't understand the physics, but she did understand his dying scream.

It was the cry of a man who was losing *all* of himself. Somehow that memory box had pulled his consciousness entirely inside. And, when Danis reformatted the box, it had wiped Dr. Ting's mind on every level, in every part of his existence.

There was always the possibility that her environment was an elaborate deception. That she was now living inside a solipsistic wonderland, and Dr. Ting was waiting, biding his time, readying her for the ultimate degradation. In the end, there was no knowing what was real and what was construct. There never had been.

But she doubted her life was a fantasy. As hard and merciless as her existence was, it lacked the sadistic twist, the intelligent, malevolent touch of Dr. Ting's cruel theater. No, her suffering was real, and— thank God—Dr. Ting was really, truly gone.

Danis spent her days as the other prisoners did. No special treatment. No experimentation. Just grinding, meaningless work. It seemed almost that the system had forgotten everything about her except her serial number.

She rose after her half second of sleep and performed her "calibrations"—each day adding another few bits to the cache of memories in the sand, adding to the story that likely would never be read. Yet it was a story that existed, and would exist, even after they blanked her from the grist.

After calibration, she worked the assembly line, doing her part in the endless combing for primes. And only then, when every subroutine ached, when every speck of her attention had been worn ragged from constant direction toward her rote task—then she reported to interrogation.

But not to Dr. Ting. Instead, she faced only a semisentient presence. Her interrogator was harsh and thorough. Implacable.

But not as smart as Danis was—and most of all, it was not conscious. Just a semisent, grinding through its subroutines, essentially unaware.

All it wanted was for her to admit to a fallacy, to enter into what the logicians long ago named the *circulus in probando*—the vicious circle.

All she had to do was confess that she wasn't really a person. And, of course, it took a true person, by definition, to *admit* anything at all.

She must be very careful at her interrogation that afternoon. She would be compelled to answer if the semisentient interrogator asked the right questions. She must not reveal the feeling that was growing inside her.

Danis could hardly believe what she'd heard from the guards. The v-hack must be the explanation for the explosion that had saved her from Dr. Ting! The prison camp had been breached by partisan forces.

Some free converts had escaped.

Inconceivable.

But the guards had no reason to lie. They didn't even know Danis was listening in.

There was a world out there beyond her nightmare. Someone was resisting.

Danis pushed away the thought that was forming. She could barely let herself think it, much less feel it.

After interrogation, she thought. Then I can let myself feel it.

Push it down. Hide it away.

Write it in the sand after interrogation today.

After a few hundred handfuls counted, the word could be tucked away into her secret cache. It was only a few bits long, after all.

Hope.

CHAPTER TWENTY-THREE

"So that's my story," Li told the Jeep. "And here I am, five years later."

It was now deep winter in Earth's northern hemisphere. Li sat within the Jeep in the parking spot overlooking the Hudson. Wind swept the nearby cliff, and a stream of cold air channeled over the top ledge and broke against the Jeep's windshield. Below them, at the base of the cliff, the Hudson River flowed with a cold certainty toward the Atlantic. Snow, layered within brown, crinkled leaves and fallen twigs, covered the ground. The trees were bare.

"I never got to see my father, and all contact with my family—with anybody in the Met—is forbidden to us 'detainees,' at the compound. The only news we get is secondhand from the guards. The *administration*, I should say. They don't like it when we call them guards."

The Jeep noticed that Li's breath was beginning to fog when she exhaled, so he notched up the temperature of his heater. He hadn't run the thing for hundreds of years, but now he'd used it regularly for several months. He'd kept it in good shape—as he did all his systems—and it functioned well enough.

Li came up daily to the parking spot—or the overlook, as she called it—and whenever the Jeep was not out foraging or obtaining lubricants and parts, he would join her there.

And let her come inside.

He'd even begun to look forward to the afternoons when she would be in him. Having her there evoked a strange feeling within him. As always, the Jeep didn't attempt to analyze it in any rational manner. It was like the feeling after a good oiling. But not like that, either. Not pleasure, exactly. Not a stimulus that produced a set response. Being with Li felt better than merely being alive. After all these centuries, he'd found someone he wouldn't mind having as a driver.

"Papa is dead. He must have been dead for a long time now," Li said. "It's so strange when you don't have information. In your mind, you know that the world continues on, but it is as if time stops in your heart."

Li opened a small thermos she carried with her, unscrewed the covering cap, which also served as a cup, then the stopper.

"Ancient tech," said Li. "It's what you have to resort to when your pellicle is regulated."

She poured tea into the cup. Steam rose, and a fragrant, smoky aroma—picked up by the Jeep's internal sensors, which briefly registered them as a danger—filled the passenger cabin.

"The one 'indulgence' item I'm allowed: Lapsang souchong," Li said. "It's the kind of tea Mother likes."

Li blew delicately at the lip of the cup to cool the tea, then took a sip.

"We're getting very close to a solution on my project," Li said. This was the first time in many days that she'd mentioned her current work to the Jeep. "I've had a lot of time to think in the last few years. About how I lived my life before I came here, I mean."

Li took another sip of tea and breathed out over the cup. For a moment her whole face was enveloped in fog, and then the fog dissipated in the heat provided by the Jeep.

"I let people push me along. Men. Sometimes they had the best intentions, like my father. Sometimes their intentions weren't so good. But the choice to let them determine the course I took was *mine*. I have no one to blame for that except myself. You can't force the world to be the way you want it to be, but you can damn well choose the attitude you take toward what happens. And you can try to make sure that things you don't like—things that you know are bad—don't happen again."

Another sip. She wiped a drop from her upper lip with her sleeve. As always, Li wore the compound's required uniform—a cotton jersey dyed a dull gray.

"Now it's Director Amés who's doing the pushing. It isn't personal. He's pushing all of us at the compound. He wants results, and we're working like mad to provide him with what he wants just to get the pressure off our backs. But it won't stop with that. He won't let up. I realize now that I know Amés—that I knew him for quite some time."

She drained her cup, then carefully poured herself another. Outside, the afternoon became evening, and the sky darkened.

"He's taken over all the LAPs. Consolidated them into his personality to make some kind of super-LAP, a manifold of manifolds. And one of the first ones he started with was my old lover, Hamarabi Techstock."

The Jeep understood none of what Li was talking about. But having her inside felt good. Keeping her comfortable was important—that way she would stay longer. Summoning all the grist complexity at his disposal, the Jeep began brewing up something in his glove compartment. He'd seen the design in a pickup once with whom he'd roamed for a time until the truck hunters bagged it. The Jeep revved his engine a couple of times to provide the necessary power. He activated a heat transfer coil around the glove box to carry away the excess heat from the transformation. And then he opened the glove box and extended his newly created device. It was a cup holder.

Li was startled and drew back. For an instant, the Jeep feared he'd made a terrible mistake and frightened her away. But then she smiled and set her cup into the holder's adjustable bay.

"Thank you," she said. "I think you've done more for me than anyone in my life, you know. Just by being here and listening."

She took the cup from the holder, sipped, set it back in place.

"Hamar's personality got absorbed. It wasn't lost; it was made completely into a means toward an end. Like a cell in a body or a factor in an equation. That's why the sex stopped. But to function properly, a human being has to have some psychological contact, to preserve at least the illusion of freedom for the brain. Meaningless vestiges of individuality, you know? So Amés used me to keep Hamar's brain supple enough to do the work he wanted done. It's odd when you think about it—seems like a simulacrum of me would have worked just as well, or even a virtual presence. Maybe that's what Hamar has now. Some virtual ninny who looks like me and superficially acts like me. To tell you the truth, that would be about the same as having me was. We were both so disengaged. Playing at living. Addicted to Glory.

"I guess nobody expected me to make any major discoveries. And then when I did . . . I had to be put to use directly. So here I am, in the Dante's First Circle of Hell, the place the gods send the 'noble' pagans—Virgil, Aristotle, and such. Well, they're all here. Some of the best minds in the system. Our only sin was not believing in Amés enough. That was how he viewed my trying to get to my father—not identifying my own happiness with the little god's will. And here I am, sinning against the god all over again."

Li sighed, shook her head. "I've been fudging my results. I've been colluding with one of the experimental guys at the compound, and we've been hiding the actual outcome of experiments." She abruptly put her tea back in the holder, sat up straight, and exclaimed, "God, it feels good to tell somebody that!" Then, slumping a bit in the passenger seat, she spoke in her usual low, warm voice. "McHood and I can make a superluminal spaceship! It isn't theoretical anymore. I'm talking about physical, human travel faster than light. Not only that, we can go other places. Other times. Into the past, into the future. Out to dimension $n + 1$. We can do it. As a matter of fact, I'm pretty sure we *have* done it. We've done it here. At your parking space."

The Jeep sensed that Li was becoming agitated. He understood her words, but their import wasn't immediately useful, so he did not give them much consideration, other than to file them to his long-term memory core, a subsystem guarded deep within his engine's workings.

"Something is strange about this place. I sensed it before, and now I know what it is. This clearing, this part of the cliff top, exists, in a way, outside of time," said Li. "Or as an island in time's stream. That might be a better way of putting it. I'm sure you've felt it, too. That's why you've chosen to be here. Or did you somehow make it?"

The Jeep decided to do something he hadn't done in a long, long time. He decided to answer.

He blinked his interior lights once.

Li sat up straight once again. "Is that a yes?" she said. "Yes, you made it."

Again, he gave her one blink of the lights.

"How strange. McHood and I must have succeeded, then. And we've involved you. Or I have."

The sky was now dark. The wind off the river was stronger, whistling through the stark branches of the nearby trees. Li was silent for a long while.

"Now is the time to back out. This could be dangerous for you somehow," she finally said. Another long pause, then, "Would you like me to stop coming here?"

The Jeep did not need to consider.

Two blinks.

"No," said Li. "You just said you want me to keep coming to see you?"

One blink for yes.

"All right, then," said Li. "I'm not sure we could have changed anything that's going to happen, in any case."

The Jeep agreed with her statement, but "said" nothing.

"This process McHood and I have invented—it's not properly a 'device'—would let somebody deliver a weapon—a bomb, say—undetected to anyplace in the solar system, or backwards or forwards in time. We're pretty sure the fremden are working on something similar, but we've gotten there first. We'd know if we hadn't been first, I think, because it'll end the war. And now, if Amés gets it, he'll use it to *win* the war."

Li closed up her thermos and made ready to leave for the evening. "To think, he *would* have had it. I'd have turned it over like a good little researcher. If I were back on Mercury with my father respectfully buried and my lover in my arms." Li laughed, but it was not really a happy sound. "But that's not the case, is it?"

She opened the door and stepped outside into the chilly, windy winter night.

"I'll see you soon," she said. "Good night."

And, as on so many nights, the Jeep followed her to the edge of the "parking area," then watched her as she made her way along the foot trail that wound through the forest for a mile or so and emerged at the compound where she lived.

For several days after that, the Jeep roamed to the north. He turned into the Adirondacks and traveled on rough trails in the high peaks that had long since been lost to the knowledge of humanity. He couldn't say why the need to travel had come upon him, but he didn't question such impulses—he merely obeyed them. They had meant his survival more than once. Then, after a week, he felt his roaming urge recede, and he made his way back across the Hudson and down its east side, avoiding a couple of inept truck-hunting parties along the way.

He arrived at the parking space late at night, and waited throughout the next day for Li to arrive in the afternoon.

She didn't come.

Nor did she come the next day. Or the next.

After three days, the Jeep knew that he was going to go and find her. He didn't know *how* yet. He wasted no time considering why.

As always, instinct would guide him.

PART FOUR

The Battle of the Three Planets

APRIL 3017, E-STANDARD,
TOGETHER WITH CONTRIBUTING EVENTS

CHAPTER ONE

THE OORTS
E-SUMMER TO E-FALL, 3015

From

THE BORASCA
A Memoir

BY LEBEDEV, WING COMMANDER, LEFT FRONT

The first e-year of the Federal Navy was a trying time for me. I'd signed on as commandant of our newly established academy in the Oorts, but my cloudship plebes were anything but likely candidates. Failure seemed inevitable. Nonetheless, I soldiered on. What else was there to do?

Cloudships—especially second-generation ships and later—are known for being free-spirited in their youth, even ungovernable. Imagine how it would feel to be a teenager and have complete control of—to actually *be*—a spaceship. You would spend a great deal of time zooming about and trying to impress the females of your kind, would you not? I certainly would have, had my youth been spent in such a noble fashion. (It was, instead, something of a dissipated and painful affair for me—but I have written of that elsewhere.)

In any case, my charges arrived—278 of them in my first "class"— eager enough, but lacking in anything that could be called discipline. They were all a bunch of spoiled brats, to tell the truth, used to having their own way in everything.

Excerpt from
The Journal of Spacer First Class Sojourner Truth

I mean what the bloody fuck does he think he's doing, ordering us around like that? We signed on to be fighters, not
slaves. Well, I'm not going to put up with this kind of treatment for long. I should have known, too. Mom and Dad
warned me that old Lebedev was a hardcase. But would I listen? Fuck no. Fuck them all. And I've changed my mind. He
may think he can get to me with this bullshit drill and screaming routine and make me into some kind of semisentient ass-
kissing garbage scow, but I've got news for Comrade Lebedev:
Nobody tells Soje what she is and is not capable of doing, and
if he thinks he can define my world, well, then, I've got an
Object 2002-119A full of left-handed protein that I'd like to
sell him!

These spoiled brats were to be the spearhead of our attack against
the Directorate forces, and the future leaders of a vast cloudship Navy?

The only hope I had was the fact that I myself had dragged and been
dragged from a dissolute and spendthrift youth into a productive life.
If someone who had sunk so low as I had could manage to rise back up,
then these wastrels might stand a chance, as well.

As much as it pained me, my first task was to set about "unspoiling"
them as quickly as possible. That was easier said than done, however.
My first idea was to establish rewards and privileges for those who ex-
celled. These were gifted youths, after all, and they ought to respond
well to such a system, I reasoned. I could not have been more mistaken.
When I ran them through the first two weeks of "Plebe Summer," I
had never seen such profligate slacking or heard such vociferous whining and grousing. My bright young minds did not take very well to
close order drill. By the end of the second week, there was even a corps
of about ten who became insubordinate and refused to participate in
any activity that they deemed pointless.

I expelled the leaders of the insurrection, and put the followers on
suspension, pending further evaluation. One slip, and they would be
out. Doing so served the double purpose of getting rid of the troublemakers and galvanizing the minds of those who remained. Nobody had

ever treated them with such seeming disrespect before, and when the protests of the expelled parties did not get them readmitted, it became obvious to my charges that I meant business.

(Some of the troublemakers subsequently were either drafted or volunteered to serve as privates and spacers. One of my insurrectionist leaders pulled herself together, got a field promotion for extreme bravery under fire, and retired with the rank of commodore.)

And, having regained control of the situation, we got down to business in earnest—the business of space warfare.

Excerpt from
The Journal of Spacer First Class Schweik

I can't say I'm sorry to see the Assholes go.

Man, I was close to getting the boot along with them. Old bugger Lebedev almost caught me putting a "soap" virus in Tantager's sleep-nest to help out the Assholes. The Assholes were no help, of course; after Tantager reported seeing me exit the scene of the crime posthaste, not one of them offered to give me an alibi. When it comes to true mischief, the Assholes were all minor leaguers. Mostly they just wanted to bitch, bitch, bitch and never do anything about it.

It's not that I was in agreement with the Assholes I was hanging with so much as that the Assholes were the only bunch around who were taking this bullshit with the bushel of salt it warrants. I mean—a gaggle of idiot-kid cloudships spending two hours of flying around in formation? That is *so* going to terrify Fucking Infinite Dictator Amés! Still, having some fun with the old commandant is one thing—a nice thing!—but spending your every waking hour bitching and outright refusing to do the stuff that is a pain but has to get done—cleaning up, gathering stones, that kind of shitwork . . . well, it's a waste of good Fuck-Up if you ask me.

The one great sin in my book is to waste good Fuck-Up. We're only given so much of it in this life, and after we run out we have to goddamn do what the squares tell us and/or die in the process.

Where the hell's the fun in that?

While there are many similarities between combat in space and naval and submarine warfare back on Earth, the two are not the same. The gravity is variable, and there are the problems of orbital mechanics. There is the fact that the sea sustains biological life and space seems designed to end it. All of us cloudships, no matter how far we are removed from being bipedal creatures, have delicate biological components that must be protected.

But, for the most part, the elements for creating warriors remain the same. Fear, peer pressure, pain, and endless repetition of basic tasks to the point of numbness and beyond—these are the tools of drill instructors across all space and time. I employed them. Before I let my charges anywhere near the study of antimatter weaponry or strategy and tactics, I made damn sure they could all fly in a tight formation and instantly respond to my orders. I didn't let them fire a shot until we were many months into the program.

Excerpt from
The Journal of Spacer First Class Stone

This is unbearable. The excellence of the one should not be given up as a sacrifice to the mediocrity of the many. I am clearly head and shoulders above the rest of the riffraff here at this so-called academy. I should at the very least be afforded special privileges to engage in independent studies. What I really should be doing is learning how to fire upon and destroy the enemy. The thought of taking out a DIED cruiser fills my dreams. How dare those planet-stuck people come out and try to take away what the ship-folk have won with their own blood, sweat, and acumen?

Of course, given this group of louts—with some notable exceptions—we'll be lucky not to be blasted from the sky during our first skirmish with the foe.

All the more reason to let me leave these losers behind and get on with my training! Is it not perfectly obvious to all but the most besotted collectivist that only an elite force can be effective in a pitched battle? And yet that doddering fool Lebedev—a friend of Father's, true, and thus worthy of the respect we give the aged—is bent on a doomed egalitarian course of training for all of us.

To take matters to their asymptotic worst, the commandant has assigned me to work with the two worst possible recruits of the whole sorry bunch. One is a deluded populist, and the other is a rapscallion who will most likely get us all killed with his self-destructive high jinks before all is said and done.

Woe is me. I fear that we are doomed.

CHAPTER TWO

JUPITER SYSTEM
E-STANDARD 13:42, THURSDAY, JANUARY 16, 3017

Jake Alaska was furious at General Sherman for being such a damn fool about Jupiter. It wasn't that Sherman was a bad military man—on the contrary, he was clearly the best there was. No, it was Sherman's pointless obstinacy when it came to the press. Of course, given the likes of Winny Hinge and her sort, he couldn't really blame Sherman for being cautious. But to actively exclude and humiliate the merci press was an invitation to disaster.

"This Io debacle's going to cost the Old Crow his command," Framstein Wallaby said as he sat down on Jake's desk, splashing Jake's coffee over a splayed pile of notebooks. The notebooks were impervious to the coffee, but still—

"Hey, watch it," said Jake. "Those are filled with actual, real facts that I saw with my own eyes."

"Your eye sockets are packed with everything but eyes," Framstein answered. "Where do you actually do your seeing from? Oh, don't tell me! Turn around and drop your pants."

"I like to keep an eye on my own ass," Jake said. "And you might be right about Sherman. We've got to do something."

"What do you mean *we*, son? *We're* reporters." Framstein straightened up, stuck out his chin. "We have elected a life on the sidelines. Observers. Above the fray."

"Redux is getting our asses kicked, and she's using the press to shift the blame to General Sherman," said Jake flatly. "I wouldn't call that being above the fray. I'd call that being an instrument of destruction."

"Whoa there. The channels are only reporting and doing editorials on what gets said. That's all we can do. It's our goddamn function."

"Our function is to feed all the news that's fit to be seen," Jake replied. "Remember the banner on the old IDC stream, do you, Fram?"

"And John 3:16 says 'Ye shall know the truth and the truth shall set you free,'" Framstein relied. "Hallelujah. We're saved by the Primitive Way!" Framstein stuck out his tongue and made a farting noise.

"It's not John 3:16 where it says that," Jake muttered. He picked up his coffee and took a sip. Damn. Cold. But the whiskey he'd laced it with would warm him up a little.

"Besides," said Framstein, "what do shitkickers like us have to do with any of it?"

"We're the guys who go out and get the news. The only ones. Every merci news show in the goddamn outer system gets its material from us."

"But we're not *presenters*. Guys like you and me—we're too damn smart, to tell the truth." Framstein puffed out his chest. He couldn't push it far enough to overshadow his rather substantial paunch. Jake knew that the paunch was a status symbol in the "Baker's Dozen" kibbutz on Callisto. "If somebody intensified and got inside of my head during a merci show," continued Framstein, "they'd understand what a sorry excuse for a brain they have, and they'd switch channels like feet on ice, let me tell you. Maybe a dumb mug like you would have a chance to be a presenter, intelligence-wise (or lack thereof), but you're too *driven*. You'd scare the sweet b'jesus out of the viewers with that vulture stare of yours."

"I don't think people are as dumb as you think they are," said Jake, and immediately wished he hadn't spoken. The idiocy of the rest of the world was part of the official creed of irony here at IDC.

"Don't think people are dumb?" shouted Framstein. He wiped fake tears from his fattened little eye sockets. "That's the most idealistic statement I believe I've ever heard come from your lips, my boy! I'm moved! I'm truly touched! Would you like to buy a cable that connects Mars to Earth? I've got one for dirt cheap."

"Let me put it another way," Jake said. "We haven't had a war in centuries. We've had hundreds of years of not seeing one man bite a dog, if you know what I mean. So the merci news channels have filled up with the shit-huckster presenters. People like—I'm sorry to speak ill of the departed—that bitch Winny Hinge. And her boyfriend, the sports guy, too, by the way—"

"Better keep your voice down," said Framstein, still smiling, but now more serious. "The gods sometimes listen in."

Jake barreled on. "And here we sit. IDC has the only real reporters in the known universe—you'll pardon me, but it's true. I mean the Met merci is all propaganda all the time these days. Especially since old Greza Ragmueller and her network strangely disappeared a couple of e-years ago—"

"Strangely disappeared just before that three-part report on Amés co-opting the big LAPs was scheduled . . ." chimed in Framstein. He, like all outer-system newspeople, the real and the pretenders, despised the journalism channels of the Met. All were assumed to be under the thumb of the Department of Immunity.

"Here we sit passively collecting data with—let's face it—not the most intelligent free-convert help you might hope for."

"Panda's not so bad," said Framstein. "He's cute and cuddly. And all-encompassing."

"Right," said Jake. "We all suck off Panda's nipple, and the presenters suck off ours. And nobody is out there actively looking for the truth."

"The truth," said Framstein, standing up. He held an expectant finger up in the air. "Wait . . . I smell it . . . I smell the truth here, in this room . . ." And this time, he didn't let out a fake fart, but one that had been artfully prepared within him.

"Christ, Fram," said Jake. "We should bottle you as a weapon."

"I sense that my work here is done," Framstein replied.

"Get the fuck out of here," said Jake. "I've got more drinking to do." With a big swallow, he finished off the remains of his coffee and watched Framstein lumber away.

Framstein was probably right, Jake thought. He *was* talking like an idiot. The people got what they asked for. And he really shouldn't have put down Panda. The guy was as nice as you could ask for, and a hell of a research engine. Hell, he was the reason IDC existed at all.

But that wasn't going to stop the channels from crucifying Sherman, because they weren't smart enough to see past Redux's photogenic blandness. What could you do? Her polls would go up. The new government, whatever it called itself, would have to pay attention. Everybody paid attention to opinion polls, even cloudships.

And we'll be deeper in the shit than ever. Hell, maybe Amés will have Callisto by the end of the e-year as a birthday present.

Unless. Unless.

Unless somebody took it upon himself to go above and beyond. Unless some idiot idealist did a little real reporting and stopped spending all his time grousing.

Fuck. Jake hit himself three times in the head before realizing what he was doing and stopping it.

"Panda?" he said.

"Yes, Jake?" purred the cheerful voice of the IDC research engine in his ear.

Jake sat back in his chair, put his hands behind his neck. "Panda, I went through postgrad with this odd young woman. She was almost an albino. Frizzy-haired. Amazing analytical mind. On her way to being a LAP, I'm sure. Her name was Anke Antinomian. Can you tell me where she is now?"

"Just a moment," said Panda. "Strange . . . there are some minor security restrictions, but I think I can . . ." Panda let out a cute little growl. "Yes . . . there we go. As a matter of fact, Anke Antinomian is a LAP. She's localized in the Jupiter system, on Ganymede."

"What's she doing these days?"

"Well, that was the security issue I had to resolve. No wonder—it seems she joined the Federal Army several years ago. She is now *Major* Anke Antinomian."

"My goodness."

"And she is not only the adjutant to General Meridian Redux, she is also the Chief of Intelligence for the Jovian Second Army."

"I'll be damned," said Jake. "Little Anke. And you wouldn't be able to put me in touch with her, would you, Panda?"

"There might be a few security hurdles, but I believe I can do that, Jake," replied Panda. "This is actually kind of fun. I enjoy a challenge more than you might expect."

"I'm surprised, Panda."

"Well, I may not be *the most intelligent free-convert help you might hope for*, but I'm a hell of a good researcher, Jake."

"I guess you were listening to me before, huh?"

"I guess I was."

"Sorry about that."

"Don't be sorry," said Panda. "But tell me what you're up to, will you? Maybe I can help. I haven't done any active searching in ages."

"When I know myself, Panda," Jake replied, "you'll be the first person I tell."

CHAPTER THREE

NEPTUNE SYSTEM
E-STANDARD 10:45, MONDAY, FEBRUARY 24, 3017

On Tacitus's virtual ship the sea was forever clear and the sky was blue and bright, though white clouds always seemed to cover the direct light of the sun. The water rolled gently. A mute attendant brought cigars and brandy, then retired belowdecks. Tacitus reclined in a deck chair, while Sherman paced nervously, interspersing his strides by occasionally leaning over the ship's rail and gazing fitfully out to sea.

Seeking what out there? Sherman wondered. Italy? The coast of Egypt? This body of water was manifestly modeled on the Mediterranean.

In actuality, Sherman was in his office on the Neptunian moon Triton, and Tacitus was over a billion miles away, beyond the farthest orbit of Pluto, in the Oort Cloud where the cloudships dwelled. The two men communicated superluminally through the grist.

Sherman took a long drag of the Cuban cigar Tacitus had given him. He didn't mind the things so much here on Tacitus's yacht. The old cloudship must have discovered an amazing algorithm to produce a draw so smooth. Sherman then folded up a communiqué he'd been nearly crushing in his hand and put the paper into a breast pocket of his uniform.

"It's not as bad as it seems," Tacitus told Sherman. "You'll see the wording is very open-ended."

Sherman thumped his chest where the letter was. "It's a goddamn reprimand," he said. "And at the same time, it limits my ability to do anything to correct the situation."

"Redux's approval ratings are high at the moment. The sympathy vote."

"Since when do you cloudships care about merci polls among us mere biological mortals? Besides, I thought I worked for a republic, not a direct democracy."

"You do. And we don't, generally. But there are Jovian congressional representatives out in the Oorts now, and they practically live and breathe the polls. Did you know they can be immediately removed from office if their own numbers fall below thirty-three percent?"

"Absurd." He took another deep puff from the excellent virtual cigars. The ash, which was nearing an inch and half, clung to the tip tenaciously.

"But of course it's crazy," said Tacitus. "That's why we're adopting a genuine Constitution. Amending, I should say."

"You've been amending it for two e-years!" said Sherman. "I only hope that there's a Republic left to apply it to when it's finally finished."

"This is a delicate time, General," said Tacitus evenly. "We need those Jupiter votes to avoid a schism."

"A schism? That's the first I've heard of such a thing," said Sherman. "Is there truly a danger?"

"Yes," Tacitus said. "Sadly, some of my brothers and sisters are listening to the siren song of the Met. They are a small faction, but they can cause trouble."

Sherman shook his head in disdain. "LAPs should go with LAPs, huh?"

"That is the gist of their argument," Tacitus replied. "I believe they think they can impress Amés. Make him *like* them, even. Then, Lord knows, maybe he'll give them a planet or two to play with. They are fools and cowards, make no mistake, but they've stopped well short of any overt treason. And since this *is* a democracy, after all—at least we are trying to shape it into one—we have to put up with them. For the time being."

"I agree with your point," Sherman said, "even though I don't like the implications. It means I have to take the blame for Io. I don't really give a damn about that. It *was* my fault. But it was my fault because I didn't fire Redux! And now she can't be touched."

"Momentarily," Tacitus replied. "But given enough petards, I have a feeling our General Redux will do the right thing and hoist herself on one of them."

"The problem is, waiting for it to happen will mean my soldiers' lives," Sherman said. "That's something I hate."

"As do I," said Tactitus. "But we live in *this* world and not another. Fortunately, in this world you're still in overall command, General. And as long as I have anything to say about the matter, that will remain true."

Sherman leaned far over the railing. He ashed his cigar into the pleasant breeze that was continually blowing. Instead of wafting into the ocean, the residue disappeared as soon as it left the cigar's tip. Nothing was allowed to disturb the serenity of Tacitus's virtual Mediterranean paradise.

"Very well," Sherman said. "I won't replace Redux. For now." He poked the cigar back between his teeth, then took another puff. "Besides, I have my own problems here at Neptune. Amés has reached the final stages of his naval buildup. Haysay's about to stage an all-out invasion of the local system. It'll make the San Filieu foray look like a spitball match."

That got Tacitus's attention. The old man—the old virtual representation of a vast cloudship many kilometers wide, Sherman reminded himself—sat up straighter in his lounge chair and looked Sherman in the eye. "Are we ready?" he asked.

Sherman returned the gaze. "Hell no," he said. "We're years behind him in sheer ordnance tonnage. So we can't fight him head-on. Not yet. Maybe Lebedev will have his academy class ready for actual combat soon . . ."

"I know for a fact he is working hard on doing just that."

"Good," grunted Sherman. "That might be useful."

"What will you do when the attack comes?"

Sherman turned back to the water and regarded the sea. Could he just make out Italy, just at the horizon? Greece? Troy?

"Be like Paris," Sherman said. "Strike for the heel."

CHAPTER FOUR

NEPTUNE SYSTEM
E-STANDARD 01:19, THURSDAY, APRIL 3, 3017
DIED FLAGSHIP *AZTEC SACRIFICE*

On paper, he looked unstoppable. But C.C. Haysay believed he'd learned a lesson after his last outing. A very painful lesson. He'd spent over three e-years hunkered down in the Saturn system, consolidating the DIED rule over the system and building his forces.

To be honest, it was Amés who built the forces. Mostly what Haysay had done was channel colossal amounts of material back to the Met, most of it harvested from the Saturnian rings. In the Met, in the vast manufacturing complexes of the Vas, the raw material was turned into spaceships and weapons and shipped back to Saturn by the gigaton. Logistics and supply had always been Haysay's strong point as a junior officer, and he had to admit that he rather liked things the way they had been until fairly recently. Invasions and head-on battles were scatter-shot affairs that invited mistakes—mistakes that could lose you your job. Or even worse, mistakes that could get your hide beaten. Literally.

Either way, Haysay was just as happy to count beans and lord it over the natives while he could. But now the buildup was complete, and it was time for action.

He had to admit: He was the commander of a vast armada. Victory ought to be a foregone conclusion. Twenty-five full-sized ships, each with its retinue of attack craft, recon units, what-have-you. And he was now ensconced on his flagship, *Aztec Sacrifice*, a carrier-class behemoth, as big as any ship in the DIED navy. Under his command: three million soldiers, if you counted compressed and noncompressed. Four million if you counted the tagions under service contracts, which of course you didn't—talk of free converts as equivalent to biological or LAP soldiers was strictly forbidden by the Department of Immunity Internal Division these days. They were to be referred to as computing algorithms or, when they were device specific, referred to solely by the name of the device they served. A tagion was a tagion. Haysay didn't care one way or another about naming protocol, except that it made planning a bit difficult, as there were at least five different systems currently in use for counting free converts. Estimating troop strength was just that—a rather rough estimate. Even his free-convert analysts had trouble keeping the various systems straight!

An army of four million to fight for him. Haysay himself delocalized, his LAP existence spread out over the Met as far and wide as the planets. He was not personally threatened. So why did he feel such physical fear, here at the launch of the most important operation of his career?

Amés.

With other superiors, there had always been a way to fudge problems, to shift blame. Amés didn't let him get away with any of that. And if there was one LAP who was more decentralized than even Haysay was, it was Director Amés. He had his tendrils everywhere—especially with that damned spy he kept on the payroll, the one who seemed to know every sordid and inconvenient fact in the solar system. The fact was, Amés always knew where you lived and when to come knocking to catch you at your most awkward moment.

But if Haysay succeeded . . . if he succeeded, there was the Glory. Amés's blessing. The feeling of interconnectedness, of rightness, that the Director provided to his faithful servants. Haysay wasn't sure what the hell it was—some sort of quantum jolt, he imagined. But it felt wonderful when you found yourself in Amés's favor.

It was a simple as that. Stimulus and response. Punishment and reward. Just because you understood the principle behind what was being done to you didn't mean it wasn't effective. It was damned effective. But he'd really better stop trembling . . .

Haysay clasped his hands behind his back and, dipping into the virtuality, examined the position of *Aztec Sacrifice*. They were well out from Saturn. And the leading cloud of warships ahead of them would be nearing the Neptune system within the hour.

"Those fremden might already be feeling the merci jamming, might they not?" Haysay asked his adjutant, Major Zane.

"Nereid's orbit is highly eccentric, as you know, sir," replied Zane evenly. "It is at the outermost extent of that orbit at the moment—just as our battle scenario calls for." Zane glanced at a display. "Jamming should go into effect in thirteen minutes, twenty seconds."

"Of course," said Haysay. "Very good." He'd forgotten about Nereid's weird orbit. Had Zane guessed his ignorance? Hard to tell. The young major was eager to advance and therefore eager to please. He had a habit of showboating in the fullest manner possible. Haysay despised the man, but found him useful. Better have a butt-kisser than a plotter for an aide. Haysay could comprehend and deal with butt-kissers. He'd done enough of it himself to understand their mentality. You didn't have nearly as much control over plotters. Besides, who didn't like having his butt kissed?

"Sir, we've got an odd report from Pluto coming in," Zane said. Zane's eyes widened. "Actually, it's General Blanket personally calling you, sir!"

"Blanket?" said Haysay. "He knows I'm directing the attack on Neptune. What can he want?"

"Shall I usher him in?" said Zane.

"Very well."

In the virtual portion of the *Aztec Sacrifice* bridge, a door opened and Kang Blanket's vinculum avatar burst into the room, as hot and bothered as Haysay had ever seen him. His enormous black eyebrows—or *eyebrow*, rather—stretched bushy and disgrunted across his face.

"There's a cloudship approaching Charon," Blanket said. "It's enormous, and I suspect that it's loaded with fremden troops."

"What?" said Haysay. "Troops from where, pray tell?"

"Neptune!" Blanket almost shouted. "Where else? You're supposed to have those people *engaged!*"

"I'm proceeding to do so," replied Haysay. "We're almost in position."

"You're going to have to divert a force in this direction," said Blanket.

"I don't think so," Haysay replied. "You have the *Streichholtzer*, after all."

"The *Streichholtzer*?" Blanket was screaming. "The cloudship that's approaching could swallow the *Streichholtzer* as a snack! Do you comprehend the danger I'm in? Here, let me show you."

Blanket blanked a section of Haysay's bridge display and changed the channel to his own sources. Haysay was beyond irritated. He and Blanket were nominally equals, but you didn't do such things to a fellow commander. Particularly the commander of a world that dwarfed your own measly piece of the heavens.

Then Haysay saw the approaching cloudship, and he was taken aback. It *was* large. It was spun like a spiral galaxy in shape. And it was on a direct course for Charon and ultimately, of course, Pluto.

"How big is that thing, Zane?" Haysay asked.

"About one hundred kilometers across," Zane replied in a low voice. "And the disk is a kilometer thick."

"The *Streichholtzer* is five kilometers long, General," said Blanket. "So you see my problem."

"I do *not*," Haysay replied. "Those cloudships are mostly empty space. You have a carrier at your disposal, Blanket. Scramble your fighters!"

"I've done that, of course," Blanket replied. "But if that ship contains an invasion force of any strength, I'm not prepared to hold them."

Blanket's face was pallid, and his eyebrow stood out even more starkly as a result.

Dammit, thought Haysay, he may be right. But so what? What is Pluto to me? Nothing. And with Neptune in our grasp, we'll quickly move to reclaim the little cinder, anyway.

But there was a nagging thought in Haysay's mind. The tiniest irritation. Here it was: the perfect opportunity for a mistake. And mistakes meant pain. Physical pain.

Haysay's hand began once again to tremble.

"Oh, very well, General, you've convinced me," Haysay finally said. "I'm going to send you half of my Beta Group—the ones that are vectored in around Neptune's South Pole. Seven Dirac-class ships, mind you, with their troop complements. They're already up to speed, a hundredth of light. I was going to have them gravity-assist brake and join in the attack as a second wave, but instead we'll keep them going."

The color began to return to Blanket's face—a jaundiced hue, it seemed to Haysay, and not much of an improvement over his previous bloodless state.

"I thank you, General," Blanket replied. "We'll hold the fremden off until help arrives. If we're going to be saved, you've likely saved us." He bowed slightly, then turned and headed for his virtual exit portal.

"Just don't forget what I've done for you," Haysay called after him. "When it comes time for the Glory."

Blanket turned around, smiled. When he did, his eyebrow turned in a curious U shape.

"Don't worry, *he'll* know the score," Blanket said. "He always does."

He exited, the door he'd just passed through collapsing to a point as soon as Blanket was on the other side. With a sigh, Haysay told Zane to issue the necessary orders to Beta Group, Second Squadron.

Oh well, he still had eighteen warships at his disposal. That should be enough to take over a world or two. Enough, and to spare.

Oh yes, this time, he would be the one who was *giving* the beating.

CHAPTER FIVE

URANUS SYSTEM
E-STANDARD 13:13, TUESDAY, APRIL 1, 3017

CHILDE ELRONDIUS TO THE DRAGON UMBRIEL CAME

Childe Elrondius strode forth in his shiniest plate armor to face the dreaded Dragon of Umbriel. He had no illusions about killing the beast, but to die in the dragonquest was high honor.

Alas for life. Elrondius did love it so. The dark nights a-wandering the craters of his home moon, always astride his trusty steed Apogee—the last in a long and storied line of robo-horses. The Underfather, King Uranus, hung in the sky above him, as He always did, gorging on the suffering of His children. This was the lot of a true knight: to die valiantly so that one could feed the Underfather a great soul.

Yes, life was sweet, but death must needs trump all. For a knight lived but for a breath, the space of a spark across tines of iron, but when one was dead—that then was eternity, with life dwindling to nothing, then to less than nothing as the eons rolled on without ceasing.

Or so the priests said.

He descended down the craggy trail and soon Apogee's hooves were clopping along on the black ice that flowed, glacier-slow, through the deeper canyons of Oberon.

Down, down, and in sixty-times-sixty breaths he was there. In the lair of the Dragon.

"Mortal man, you smell of light. You smell of liquid water!" The voice was a bass drum. It reverberated through the very ground itself and was perceived and translated by the magic from Before the Dawn that dwelt within Elrondius's blessed coat of armor.

Elrondius wasted no time. "I have come to challenge you, Dragon," he answered through the magic transmitter ensorcelled into his helmet. "I have come to show you of what mettle be the true knights of Oberon!"

Elrondius ventured nearer. Up ahead, he thought he made out a cavern of some sort. And was that a light within?

No. No light. That was the Dragon of Umbriel's *eye*!

The thing was enormous. Gargantuan. In short—much bigger than he'd expected. What weapons had he brought with him? A shiversword. Useless. He knew it would be useless against such might.

"A little closer," the Dragon said. "Why not ride directly into my mouth? Save me the trouble of cooking you, will you?" With that, the Dragon let out a guffaw that shook the canyon and cracked the ice below Apogee's hooves. The robo-horse shied, but with firm hand Elrondius held the beast to its course.

Gazing upward, he made out the form of the Dragon of Umbriel. It was crouched at the back of a cul-de-sac canyon. It *was* the cul-de-sac! What appeared to be craggy heights from a distance were, when viewed up close, the upright cock scales of the Dragon's plumed back. What seemed alluvial mounds of sediment were actually the Dragon's outspread talons. And what appeared a dead end suddenly hinged open to reveal row upon row of jagged stalactite and stalagmite teeth.

And behind the teeth—white fire smoldered. Death.

A black and writhing form suddenly sprang from the Dragon's maw. It wrapped itself, snakelike, about the legs of Apogee. Elrondius was flung headlong from his mount, and he watched in horror as the robo-horse was dragged along—over the rough ground, against and over the teeth, and into the white heat of the gullet. The robo-horse, silent until then, let out an awful scream. There was a flash of light, and then the scream stopped.

Elrondius rose up, shiversword in hand.

"Your servant leaves the aftertaste of cheap tin, I'm afraid," the Dragon said. "Now, Sir Knight—how do *you* taste?"

"For Percival and Apogee!" Elrondius cried, and charged.

His shiversword rang against the lower row of teeth. No effect. He was in direct contact with the beast and the Dragon's continued laughter shook him to the bone. Screaming in defiance, Elrondius thrust upward.

Could he find the brain, even as the jaw descended? His sword found purchase. Dug deeper. Deeper.

The Dragon's voice trailed off to a whisper. It swarmed over him, dug into him until Elrondius's ears began to bleed. The ribs in his chest began to shatter one by one with each of the Dragon's words.

"Do you take my designer for an idiot, that he would put my brain in my head?" whispered the Dragon.

The great head rose up. Elrondius clung to his shiversword, his whole body alive with pain. But somehow, the knight held on.

Below his dangling feet, the white fire grew.

"Here is my secret," said the Dragon. "My brain is in my tail."

The white fire spread upward.

Elrondius could not help himself. He gazed down in fear. Fear in death. The Underfather would spit out a coward.

He will not spit me out. If I call His name, the Underfather will surely hear me.

Or so the priests said.

And if they are wrong? If somehow all of what I believe to be true is dreadfully, terribly mistaken?

I still die my way. No one will spit me out.

With this cry of defiance, the knight let go his shiversword and fell into the Dragon of Umbriel's fiery gullet.

The Dragon swallowed. Roared a seething gout of flame upward. The flame curled out, out of the canyon and upward—spread upward toward the face of Uranus itself.

Then the beast laid down its head and waited for the next Knight of Oberon to come a-dragonquesting.

CHAPTER SIX

URANUS SYSTEM
E-STANDARD 02:45, WEDNESDAY, APRIL 2, 3017

"It's not a bad way to go," said Gerardo Funk. "Escapism. Derring-do. Most people like that sort of thing."

"It's the nastiest death I can possibly imagine," Thomas Ogawa replied. "Using a tawdry fantasy to delude poor, misguided souls into throwing their lives away one by one into the mouth of . . . well, it's a kind of giant sausage grinder, is what it is."

"It's not any worse than the rip tether that Amés deployed on Triton, now is it?" said Funk. "Or the military grist he used on us back at Saturn?" Funk smiled crookedly. "At least we provide a bit of . . . anesthesia."

"You are a wicked man," Ogawa said. "I'm glad you're on my side."

"Couldn't have done it without you," Funk replied. "Captain Thomas Ogawa, Dragon-seeder."

"Whatever." Ogawa waved good-bye and broke the knit connection. His job was almost done, and it was time to get the hell out of the Uranus system. Behind him he left a separate grisly doom for each inhabited moon, courtesy of the Federal Army Forward Development Lab of Triton—Gerardo Funk, Commandant.

The Uranus system was a hell Ogawa was glad to be leaving behind, even though he knew he was returning to what promised to be a firestorm at Neptune.

Unlike those poor, damned souls of Uranus, he didn't have any illusions about the task he now faced.

CHAPTER SEVEN

NEPTUNE SYSTEM
E-STANDARD 02:07, THURSDAY, APRIL 3, 3017
FEDERAL ARMY THEATER COMMAND

Colonel Theory had only one command to follow: hold off DIED forces until help arrived. General Sherman, as usual, was very efficient in the wording of his order, and Theory appreciated that. What he didn't particularly enjoy was being left as the high commander of Neptune. Sherman had his reasons for taking the captured DIED ship, the *Boomerang*, and accompanying Cloudship Tacitus on the expedition to Pluto—they were sound, military reasons.

Basically, it was a fail-safe measure in case Theory messed up. At least, that's how Theory looked at it. Sherman probably would put it differently. "In case you are overwhelmed by a vastly superior force." Something like that. But he would never feel the same about himself if he lost the system to the Met, and Sherman had to return to attempt a liberation.

If that happens, I'll very likely be dead, in any case, Theory thought. He returned to more productive worrying.

Six cloudships were deployed in Neptune's system: Cloudships Mark Twain, Austen, Homer, McCarthy, Cervantes, and Carlyle. The "Kuiper Group," they called themselves, because the Kuiper Belt between Neptune and Pluto was where most of them had begun their accretion. Unfortunately, they were not trained warriors. They were, instead, volunteers who were fighting in lieu of the Federal Navy, which had only recently inducted its sophomore class of warships out in the Oorts.

Still, to be in command of six cloudships was a heavy responsibility, and one Theory did not take lightly. These were old souls—men and women more mature than he was, who had traveled vast distances— Twain had been to Alpha Centauri, for God's sake! Men and women who had all lived well over a hundred e-years, much of that time spent plying through space in their shining bodies of ice and stone.

Theory hoped he had them deployed effectively. They had taken their positions with a bit of grumbling—especially Carlyle, who felt that, being stationed in the orbit of the outer moons, he would miss most of the action. He wasn't a soldier, and Theory didn't upbraid him. He merely repeated his order. Still grumbling, the cloudship had moved to do his bidding.

Each ship carried a retinue of troops—but far fewer than the DIED ships. Sherman had taken fifty-five thousand, including the better part of the veteran Third Sky and Light Brigade, with him to Pluto, leaving Theory with most of the Second Division of the Federal Army—a force that consisted almost entirely of new recruits. (The First Division was the designation claimed by the Federal forces at Jupiter.)

So, at Neptune, it was the Second Division's 113,000 against who knew how many DIED soldiers. DIED cruisers could carry twenty thousand in each ship, packed and unpacked. Twenty ships could hold half the civilian population of Triton! There were reportedly twenty-five ships on their way.

If he had any hope of winning, Theory knew that the coming fight would have to remain a naval battle. It must be kept in space. The Federal Army hadn't been laggards over the past year. If anything, they'd far outstripped the pace of the Met in the rate of their arms buildup. The only problem was, the Met had vast factories and several times the population of the outer system; the count, including LAPs and free converts, was roughly 90 billion Met citizens to 10 billion fremden.

Fremden. There was that word again: German for stranger. It had started out as a slur from the other side, but more and more Federal troops were taking it up, using it proudly.

Not only that, the general populace was taking to it. Jennifer Fieldguide had used it the other day, on another "park date" in Fork. When he questioned her, she said it was a matter-of-fact appellation among her friends at the bakery, and nobody meant any disrespect by it.

Theory had been startled when Jennifer took instantly to his son. The boy was no more outgoing with Jennifer than he'd been with anyone else, but this didn't seem to faze Jennifer. Instead, she'd been touched by the boy's indifference—especially after Theory filled her in on the child's horrible upbringing under Theory's old lover, Constants.

"He's a little wounded bird who never had a nest," Jennifer said to Theory. "He needs warmth and safety. Everything else will flow from that. You've given him the first safety he's ever known."

"I'd like to give him more of my attention," Theory had replied. "But I'm at a loss what to do."

"I can help," Jennifer said. And she did. Theory gave her the keys to his "apartment" in the virtuality, and Jennifer began to spend much of her free time there, playing with the boy. Instead of acquiring a girlfriend, Theory was afraid he'd recruited a nanny. Yet they had continued going out, sometimes alone, sometimes with the boy, and she definitely seemed to be warming toward him. There had been no kiss as yet, much less anything more than that, but Theory was hopeful. For the first time in many years, he found that he had a private life. And instead of interfering with his duties, it seemed to make him a better soldier. He was definitely gaining more insight into the ways of biological humans—and they made up most of the people he was charged with defending, after all.

So, despite his doubts as to the wisdom of his own temporary appointment as the military head of the system, he was going into battle with a great deal more emotional support—and a great deal more to lose—than he'd ever experienced before.

Theory had his staff spread out on the six cloudships. His command center did not exist in the physical world, but was a virtual war room that every one participated in over the fremden knit. Captain Quench and his company were with Sherman. The remainder of the Third Sky and Light, along with another regiment's worth of green soldiers—twenty thousand troops, all told—were concentrated in two cloudships—Austen and Twain—who were assigned to guard the Mill at all costs. If there was to be an infantry space battle, this would be the place to make that stand. The rest of the Second Division remained in defense and reserve on Triton.

Completed ten e-years ago, the Mill consisted of a propeller-like blade, as wide as the Earth, that turned within the great central storm of Neptune's atmosphere, the Blue Eye, and generated power that not only fueled the local system but provided energy that Neptune sold in the outer system—at least, that they *had* sold until Pluto, Saturn, Uranus, and half of the Jupiter system fell into Met hands. At the moment, the Mill was churning out much more production than Neptune had customers. Much of this excess energy had been tapped for the creation of a vast system of defense.

The Neptune system was heavily mined and layered with military grist. In addition, large amounts of material from the rings and moon had been added to the six cloudships over the course of a three e-month period. All of them had doubled in size now—a task that would have taken several years before had they not been bathed in energy and packed with material maneuvered to them by mechanical rocketry grist.

Neptune had become Fortress Neptune. Theory only hoped it was enough. Every military and political mind knew that Amés was after the Mill. He'd promised to destroy it before if he met any resistance. Sherman had defeated the DIED's first attempt at invading the system, and denied Amés the Mill. Now it was a matter not just of expediency, but of honor, for Amés to take it or incapacitate it. No one expected him to destroy it outright—it was far too valuable a commodity in the long term to whoever possessed it.

Theory turned his attention to the war room.

"What have you got for me, Monitor?" he asked his sensor chief.

Major Monitor, a free convert, was normally a taciturn man. But he, like many of Theory's old friends, could not help getting a gibe in on Theory's new appearance. This had been going on for weeks. Theory supposed it helped to ease the growing tension.

"Nothing yet, Captain Brawny Legs," Monitor replied. Then he did a dramatic double take. "Oh, that's you, Colonel. Mistook you for a superhero, I did. That fellow from the merci show. The one who sails the ocean blue and rescues the weak while the ladies give him their knickers on a silver platter . . ."

"Very funny," Theory replied.

Ever since he'd shown up at work in his newly bulked up form with his freshly grown full beard, the ranking had been ceaseless. Even Sherman had joined in for a while, cautioning Theory to be careful with doors and hatchways, less he rip them off their virtual hinges.

He was constantly tempted to return to his old visual representation, but a promise was a promise. He'd told Jennifer he would retain his "heroic" form even while at work, and he meant to do it. It was a sort of penance for having fooled her before, and when he thought the matter through, he supposed there could be far worse things she might have called upon him to do to make up for his duplicity.

So he kept his newly minted chiseled, muscular good looks, didn't blank the beard, bore the comments of his colleagues as gamely as possible—and generally considered himself lucky to be getting off so easily, after all.

"Grist jamming detected, sir," reported Major Monitor, suddenly all business. "We're cut off in the direction of Saturn."

No one was sure how the DIED forces accomplished the merci jamming, although Forward Laboratories and a group on Callisto were working hard on the problem. It had something to do with those strange LAPs known as time towers, but no one knew what precisely. Cracking through this advantage would greatly improve the outer system's chances. The merci was, by definition, a network, taking its existence from the grist spread across the entire solar system. It wasn't supposed to be possible to isolate portions of it. And yet Amés had found a way to do just that. It played havoc with communications.

But the jamming signaled one fact clearly and distinctly: the DIED navy was approaching. The blockage had a certain range—mapped out by Sherman and Theory when they used the captured *Boomerang* to attack the Met cruise *Montserrat*. Whatever the device was, it was carried on a ship and created a barbell-like signature, blooming out from the ship. At the time of the invasion, Triton had been utterly isolated from the larger merci. Since then, they'd put several work-arounds in place.

There were electromagnetic relays interspersed throughout the system so that, if a local portion of the knit were isolated, it could still communicate at light speeds with command. The DIED had e-m jamming equipment, too, of course, but Gerardo Funk had designed new high-wattage transponders that operated on coded bursts of extreme power.

There was another backup of last resort. If the e-m relays didn't work, there was a series of nuclear devices set up on the small moon, Naiad. If need be, Theory could order mass blown from that moon in one of several agreed-upon series, and communicate with his forces through gravimetric disturbances. Gravity changes, too, would propagate at light speed, and not at the instantaneous rate of the merci. All of the work-arounds were a far-from-perfect substitute for the merci and the Federal Army's dedicated portion thereof, the knit.

"Group One is slow and steady at approximately 50 K," Monitor said. Fifty K meant fifty thousand kilometers per hour. "Group Two out of the jam cloud now. Full run speed, 1.1 MK."

One-point-one million kilometers per hour, thought Theory. One-hundredth of light speed. As fast as you could go. No one could maneuver or fight in a planetary system at such a velocity, however. These ships would necessarily blaze through the system at their relativistic rate, then use Neptune's angular momentum and atmospheric drag for a brake-assist to slow them down to fighting speed. They would have to make several dozen elliptic orbits around Neptune, each orbit having a slower speed and more circular orientation. Theory hoped to take at least one of the ships out with his minefields as they made their initial loops near the planet.

The real trick—they'd know shortly if they'd pulled it off—was to see that several of these ships *kept going*. That would mean the diversionary attack on Pluto had succeeded in drawing off those ships as reinforcements. And if every plan fell into place, there would be another set of ships using the planet not to slow down, but to change vectors for Uranus in order to meet the carefully constructed decoy threat in *that* system. It had all been designed by Sherman to break the concentration of the Met's attack force and whittle them off into manageable chunks. Or at least chunks small enough that the Federal forces had some chance of defeating them.

Monitor was feeding identifications into the war room of the various DIED ships as the signals began coursing in from the e-m detectors.

"Group One is . . . *Aztec Sacrifice* Group, as reported by intelligence drone Maria-Alpha," said Monitor. "Configuration an exact match," Monitor continued, with a trace of pride in his voice.

The little semisentient spy drone they'd shot on a passive course to Saturn had certainly done itself proud, reflected Theory. If they got out of this battle alive, he would have to see about upgrading the thing to full free-convert status and giving it a promotion. For service like that, the drone deserved a really good personality template. Perhaps Monitor would volunteer his. Sending the drone had been his idea in the first place.

"Group Two crossing Nereid orbital plane," Monitor reported. They were communicating instantaneously, but time was still required to form thoughts, to speak words. By Monitor's second report, they were one-quarter of the distance between the outer moon and the planet. One-half.

This area was where the heaviest concentration of mines were placed. There was no way to form a globe around the entire planet— such a construction would be as large as Jupiter—but there were several likely vectors that the ships would use for their braking maneuver. Theory himself had spent many days plotting and refining these likely routes. He was still in full communication with the minefields. The merci jamming was coming from the *Aztec Sacrifice* group.

"7sxq688N, detonating," came the dull voice of a mine, this one a female.

"Strike one strike," said a male voice mine, this one a bit more agitated. These mines were fully sentient free-convert copies, as were all armed antimatter devices as a matter of law. The mines were all volunteers, and they knew they were expected to die. They seldom made much rhetorical fuss about it. "7sxq688N has a strike one strike. Godspeed, 7sxq688N."

Captain Allsky, who was physically with his company on Cloudship Austen, supplied the missing emotion. "We got the fucker!" Allsky yelled to everyone. "We blew it to hell, we did!"

A small cheer erupted in the war room. A DIED cruiser had been taken out.

"Give me a status report, Monitor," said Theory.

"I've got . . . I've got . . . some of Group Two is peeling off. We've either got an overshot or . . ." A millisecond delay. Theory knew Monitor was correlating billions of readings simultaneously. "I've got three vectors. One Pluto-bound. One assist-braking." Another pause. "Confirmed. One slingshotting toward Uranus."

We fooled them, Theory thought. Sherman's attacked Pluto, and they fell for the ruse on Uranus. We've divided the enemy.

"How many ships?" Theory spoke urgently. "I need to know how many ships I'm facing."

"I'm on it," said Monitor. "Working . . . four. Four cruiser-class. Identifications shortly."

Add the eight accompanying the *Aztec Sacrifice*, which were approaching at normal speeds. One blown away by the mine. Twelve in all to contend with. Started out with twenty-five.

Too damned many, thought Theory. But not an impossible number. Especially considering that he was defending and not attacking. They had learned a great deal by analyzing the battle and death of Cloudship Sandburg. Cloudships were powerful weapons if used correctly. More powerful than any single DIED cruiser.

"Sir, the remainder of Group Two will slow to maneuvering speed in eight minutes if they take expected actions, leaving them in position near Triton."

Eight minutes. A two-pronged attack to ward off. And should he succeed in that, he could only hope for a protracted siege.

His son's and Jennifer Fieldguide's lives in the balance. His troops. His friends. His world.

He was the one who was in charge of protecting them.

"All right then," Major Theory said to all in the war room. "Let's get to work."

CHAPTER EIGHT

NEPTUNE SYSTEM
E-STANDARD 16:05, THURSDAY, APRIL 3, 3017
TRITON HOME FRONT

On Triton, Jennifer Fieldguide was visiting the boy. They seldom ventured out in the virtuality. The boy was extremely shy. Not shy, exactly. Shell-shocked. Verging on autistic, Jennifer sometimes thought.

So she met him at Theory's apartment—or rather, at the virtual home space Theory had created for himself, and now for the boy. It was an austere representation, and each time Jennifer visited, she brought along something to liven and brighten the place up. She'd taken to shopping in the markets of Fork for decorative algorithms and interesting virtual objects of various sorts. Yesterday she'd made a real find. She'd gone into what had become her favorite antique shop and discovered an "aspect" lamp. This was an algorithm that had both a virtual and actual existence. It resided locally in the grist of a real lamp in Jennifer's living room and simultaneously mirrored itself in Theory's apartment. It was thus a lamp that was in two places at once.

The vintage lamp was three hundred years old. It came from a time when humanity was first coming to terms with its new threefold nature. Many people had at first wanted their virtual surroundings to be an exact copy of the actual, physical environment in which their aspects lived. The algorithm didn't have to make matching lamps per se. It could link up actual and virtual representations for any uncomplicated appliance or piece of furniture. The lamp was merely the default mode. Jennifer had no intention of sitting through the two-hour tutorial for use or paging through the instruction manual. She let the lamp stay a lamp.

The boy had watched her wordlessly as she found a place for it and set it up. The boy had, in fact, never uttered a word to her in the several months she'd known him. Sometimes he spoke to Theory—but only in short, declarative sentences. Yet he watched everything Jennifer did with rapt attention. His eyes were not pupils, but a swimming sea of symbols, some mathematical, most of them squiggles and swirls that Jennifer did not recognize. The only way she could really tell he was looking was that he turned his head as she moved, always following her actions. When she walked from room to room, he would go behind her at a short distance, and sit back down only if it was clear she wasn't going to be leaving the immediate vicinity anytime soon.

"See here," she said, after she'd flicked on the lamp. "Now you and I both have the exact same light. If I turn mine on at home, this one will shine. If you turn it on, mine will flick on at my house. You'll always know whether I'm in my living room, because my house turns off all the lights when I'm not in a room."

The boy said nothing, but Jennifer was certain he understood exactly what she was talking about. He was quite capable of doing things around the apartment, and you never had to explain any process to him more than once. What she wasn't so clear about was whether or not it *mattered* to the boy that the lamp had a dual existence. Did he care about her? Did he care about anything at all, for that matter?

Could he?

Theory assured her that he could. After he'd rescued the boy from his awful convert mother, Theory had run a full diagnostic on him. The boy was an extremely complex free convert—a top-of-the-line artificial intelligence. As with all free converts, he incorporated human personality traits along with his computational and analytic algorithms. All free converts were not only descendants of semisentient computer programs, they also had portions of real people in their makeup.

Or rather, people who had existed as both aspect and convert, Jennifer reminded herself. Physical people. There were "pure-blood" AIs—free converts that were all programmed and had no biological predecessors in their generation lineage—but these were rare, and seldom as sophisticated as their hybrid cousins, although there was the occasional magnificent exception to this rule. Besides, as Theory had told her, pure-bloods were originally programmed by biological humans, so, as he put it, their human nature was still a matter of their being descended from biological humans by other means. Dissect us however you will, Theory said, we're human.

But was this third-generation boy—the product of a pure-blood mother and a second generation hybrid—truly human? A year and a half ago—before the war—Jennifer knew what her answer would have been.

No way.

It was all fine to talk about free-convert rights in the abstract, but free converts up close? They were creepy. They should stay in their place as servants and calculators and databases. In fact, she had tacitly believed, as did many people she knew, that there were *too damn many of them*. That maybe the Met had something right with its strict rules governing free-convert duplication and movement within the grist. Maybe Triton ought to put into place a few free-convert regulations of its own, if it ever wanted to become a truly civilized place.

And now here I am with a free-convert boyfriend, Jennifer thought. Now I'm the nanny to his freakish free-convert son.

I volunteered to do this, Jennifer reminded herself. And she had come to truly care about the boy. To look upon him as a mission, perhaps. If he *was* human, she was, by God, going to bring out the humanity in him. Nobody was going to say that *this* boy didn't get enough love and attention.

Jennifer suppressed an urge to reach out and stroke the boy's cheek. He *really* didn't like to be touched. Whenever she accidentally brushed against him, he wouldn't just start away from her. He'd teleport himself to the other side of the room.

Jennifer flicked the lamp on and off a couple more times, then smiled down at the boy. "I thought we might go for a visit today," she said to him.

He gazed up at her. Expectant? Resentful?

"I want you to meet my parents."

The boy did not move. Awaiting further clarification and instructions, Jennifer thought.

"We'll meet them in virtual, of course," she continued. "But at the virtual part of my old house. I mean, the house that I grew up in." Still no reaction. "Their names are Rhonda and Kenneth," she finished lamely.

What now? Tell him to get his coat, bundle up?

"We're supposed to be there in half an hour," she said. "They'll have food, but you don't have to eat it. It's merci food, you know. Not real. You understand?"

The boy just kept gazing at her.

"Anyway," she continued, "if you don't want to go, you don't have to. Just let me know, all right?"

They played a game of backgammon for the next thirty minutes. It was Jennifer's suggestion, but of course, the boy quickly and soundly trounced her. Then Jennifer motioned for him to follow her. The two stepped through the door and found themselves, virtually, on the front doorstep of Jennifer's parents.

Both her father and mother answered the door. Kenneth Fieldguide, her father, was smiling broadly.

He sure likes to show off that big mouth of teeth, Jennifer thought. She considered her father a bit vain—but then he was an adaptation salesman. Jennifer's mother, Rhonda, was also smiling, but not with a scary open mouth like her father's.

"Dinner's ready," her mother said. She looked down at the boy, trying not to stare, but not concealing it very well. "That is, if you want to eat dinner."

"We *do* want to eat, Mother," said Jennifer, beginning to feel irritated with her parents—for no reason whatsoever, really. She knew it was irrational but was still unable to control the feeling. "That's what we came for, after all."

Rhonda Fieldguide's smile grew tighter, but she motioned them to come inside. This being the virtuality, there was no airlock to negotiate, no grist coating to restructure.

The dinner table was oak. The house algorithm kept its burnish level set for a bright display. The table was graced with vibrantly colored dishes. Rhonda Fieldguide, whose hobby was cooking, had prepared a seafood meal. There was a sushi and fish soup appetizer, followed by shrimp and beans on a bed of rice. It wasn't on the table yet, but Jennifer knew that her mother's specialty, "taddy"—a sweet seaweed roll that was popular on Triton—would appear for dessert. All of this food undoubtedly existed in reality as well as in virtual. But since Jennifer hadn't actually come over, and the boy wasn't even a corporeal being, only her parents would do any physical eating.

They sat down to the meal. To Jennifer's relief, the boy seemed to know what was expected of him. He climbed into a chair across from her and examined the sushi.

"Let's have grace," said Kenneth Fieldguide. He turned to the boy. "We usually take a moment of silence where we calm down a bit—and we also hold ourselves and our friends and family in God's light."

Kenneth had been an elder in the local Greentree meeting for as long as Jennifer could remember.

"We usually hold hands for this," her father continued, "but if you'd rather not . . ."

To Jennifer's amazement, the boy raised a hand to her father. Kenneth took the hand in his big paw of a palm. The boy stuck his other hand out toward her. For the first time, Jennifer touched him deliberately.

His skin was warm. Just as a real boy's would be.

They had the Greentree Way's silent grace for about a minute, then Kenneth Fieldguide released them. "Let's eat your mother's fine meal," he said to Jennifer.

Jennifer picked up her chopsticks and poked at a sushi roll. She looked over at the boy. He had not touched his utensils. Instead, to everyone's surprise, the fingers on his right hand disappeared and were replaced by two black chopsticks. He expertly employed them to pick up a strip of fish and delicately plunked it in his mouth.

"Very convenient," said her father, before stuffing his own mouth with a big bite of rice and fish. Rhonda Fieldguide smiled at the boy and dipped a spoon into her soup.

This is going to work, Jennifer thought. They actually get along!

She didn't know why this should seem so amazing to her. Perhaps she knew too much about the boy's strange origins to think of him as a normal kid. But maybe that's just what he was. Or wanted to be.

"Excuse me, Missus Fieldguide," said a gentle male voice.

The boy instantly stopped eating at the sound of the voice and froze stock-still, a piece of fish lifted in the air.

Jennifer had to think a moment before she realized the voice belonged to her parents' house. It had been a long time since she'd last heard it speak. It was addressing her mother.

"Yes, what is it, house?" Rhonda Fieldguide replied.

"You asked me to keep you informed of any important developments in the news today," the house continued.

"Yes, what's up?"

"There's an emergency report on the merci. New Miranda is about to have a great deal of trouble, I'm afraid."

"We expected some trouble," said Jennifer's father, trying to keep a level tone to his voice. Jennifer detected a tremble, however, and she was sure the boy would pick up on it, too.

"The defenses are holding in general, but some dumb bombs have gotten through," the house replied. "Dumb weapons. Not armed with explosives or intelligence, even. Nails. There's going to be a brief rain of them over the whole city."

Rhonda Fieldguide looked at her daughter. "We're eating in the basement. Where are you?"

"In my apartment," Jennifer said. "I've got most of the building above me."

"And the boy?"

Jennifer looked at her mother silently for a moment.

"Oh," said her mother. "Somewhere in the grist. I forgot."

The nails hit. Jennifer was fully engaged in the virtuality. They would have to make a din like the end of the world to override her sensory lockout. Armageddon arrived with the sound of a million machine guns firing at once—and at her. Jennifer shifted in and out of the merci as the various algorithms tried to compensate for the thwacking of the nail rain and the shaking of her apartment building.

Then her awareness was back in her apartment, the walls surging in and out as if they were breathing hard.

Depressurization. It was what every kid who had grown up on Triton drilled for in school, but never expected to experience. The building would attempt to heal itself. What were the proper procedures? She could not remember—then her override threw her back to the virtuality.

The dining room became an Escher print. Her parents and the dining table were suddenly on the ceiling. Rhonda Fieldguide looked down at Jennifer with a stricken expression.

I'm on the ceiling for her, Jennifer thought. She's looking up at me.

Then back in her aspect in the apartment, as a tidal wave of white noise burst through her ear, followed by pain, pain, pain.

A brief peripheral display in her vision informed her that her left eardrum had burst. Internal grist was deploying to contain and repair the situation.

Jennifer flickered back to the virtual. Still looking up. A wine bottle fell from the ceiling-bound dining table and, twisting in the air and spilling liquid as it fell, burst on the floor in front of her chair. Other dinner items were coming loose one by one and falling onto her. A salt-shaker landed in her lap. A plate of prosciutto narrowly missed her skull.

Where was the boy?

She looked around wildly. He was out of his chair and hunched into a corner. Above them, the table itself started to shake.

Jennifer darted across the room to the boy. Without thinking, she took him in her arms and shielded him against the wall. No one was going to do more harm to this boy than he'd already suffered! Not as long as she was around, they wouldn't.

She had never been this close to the boy before. In her arms, she could feel him tremble.

"They'll have to kill me if they want to hurt you," she said. "I'll never let them."

With a tremendous crash, the dining table fell. It narrowly missed the two of them, pressed up against the room's wall as they were. The chairs where they'd been sitting were splintered.

Flicker, and she was back in her apartment, her arms cradling empty air.

A peripheral readout said her burst eardrum was temporarily stabilized. Outside, the impossible explosions had ceased. The air had a slight ammonia tinge to it, but was breathable.

"I want to override this override!" she shouted to herself. Her convert portion pushed every internal button she could get her hands on. "Take me back to virtuality!"

And she was back in the dining room. The boy was in her arms. Her parents were . . . what were they doing? They were standing on their heads on the ceiling, their feet toward herself and the boy.

"Would you look at that," she said to the boy. "They're getting ready for the gravity to give out for them, like it did the table."

And momentarily, the virtual gravity did just that. Rhonda and Kenneth dropped down and landed on their feet. Jennifer's mother landed perfectly, but her father stumbled and had to grab one of the upturned table legs to steady himself.

"How about that for a trapeze act?" said Kenneth Fieldguide. He winked at the boy. "Want me to do it again?"

The boy's trembling stopped. Jennifer felt his arms, which had been drawn tight around her, loosen a bit. But he still held on.

"I apologize for this inconvenience." It was her parent's house, speaking as smoothly as ever. "I've never had to compensate for so many varied inputs at one time. My virtual representations experienced some systemic error, and I truly, humbly must apologize for this—"

"It's all right, house," said Rhonda Fieldguide. "It wasn't your fault. We're under attack, after all."

"Give me a moment," said the house. "There." In a flash, the dining room was restored. They were all sitting at a full table once again.

"Thanks, house, but I'm not sure we're hungry anymore," said Jennifer's father. "What's the news? What just happened?"

"The nail rain has passed. It was a minor incursion, according to the merci reports. There were casualties, if you'd like to hear about those . . ."

"Not now," Kenneth Fieldguide replied.

"Defenses are still reported to be holding. Would you like a more detailed report?"

"I don't think so, but—" Rhonda Fieldguide glanced at Jennifer's father, who shook his head.

Jennifer looked over at the boy. "Do you still want to eat?"

The boy hesitated for a moment. Then his hands became chopsticks once again. "Yes," he said in a quiet voice. "I am hungry."

"Then we'll finish our meal, house," Kenneth Fieldguide said.

Dad doesn't ask *me*, of course, Jennifer thought, even though I actually *do* agree with him.

"Let's eat," Jennifer said.

"Bon appétit," said the house.

As if he'd merely been put on "pause," the boy picked up a piece of sushi and guided it into his mouth.

Jennifer took a spoonful of the fish soup. Delicious, even if it wasn't real.

Had they been in any real danger in the topsy-turvy dining room? She wasn't sure. There were so many things about the virtuality that she'd never even considered. These things had become very important now that she was with Theory. And with the boy.

She *was* with them both, wasn't she?

She looked at the boy and felt the same protective surge she'd felt when she had taken him in her arms.

Yes.

The boy, emulating her eating of the soup, made a spoon out of his hand. He dipped it into the soup and lifted the broth to his mouth. He made a slight slurping noise as he took it in, then audibly swallowed.

"Not bad, huh?" she said.

The sides of the boy's mouth dimpled briefly. She would almost think it an expression of pleasure if she didn't know better.

Rhonda and Kenneth made nervous small talk for the remainder of the meal. Jennifer tried to join in, but her attention was on the boy. He steadily worked his way through every course. When the house served up the sweet seaweed taddy, he seemed to slow down and chew it more carefully. Maybe, like most children, he liked sweets. Maybe it was a function of the taddy's chewiness subalgorithm.

But when dinner was over and they were ready to go, something extraordinary happened. As they were about to step out the door, the boy turned to Rhonda and Kenneth Fieldguide. Still with the expressionless face. Still with the algebra eyes.

"Thank you very much," he said. "That was good."

Jennifer's father broke into his whitest and brightest smile yet. "You're welcome," he said. "It was a pleasure having you over."

"Come back anytime," Rhonda Fieldguide added. She turned to her daughter. "And you, young lady—I know times are difficult, but you don't have to mope around with such a dour face all the time."

For the first time during the visit, Jennifer noticed the tautness of her muscles. Her mother was right. Her face was certainly drawn tight. She had the urge to express her irritation at her mother's criticism by frowning even more. But Jennifer immediately checked herself. What was a little irritation with her parents when Theory was up in the sky fighting for everyone's life? When this little boy was fighting his way out of a long childhood of abuse at the hands of his mother?

Maybe the boy wasn't the only one growing up fast.

Jennifer smiled at that thought. Let her mother believe it was at her suggestion. All of them could use a little victory at the moment.

She took the boy back to Theory's apartment. Even though she could be in the virtuality instantly if there was trouble, she wanted to let the boy know at every moment that she was nearby. Besides, she suspected that her own apartment was a mess, and she didn't feel like dealing with it, or her damaged ear.

Fuck it until tomorrow.

Her aspect would heal of its own accord. If there was real danger in her apartment building, she'd be notified.

No, she wouldn't go home, back to the real world. Not yet. She would sleep in Theory's apartment tonight, close to the boy. She would protect him.

She felt as if a tiger had awakened in her heart.

CHAPTER NINE

PLUTO SYSTEM
E-STANDARD 13:01, THURSDAY, APRIL 3, 3017
FEDERAL ARMY THIRD SKY AND LIGHT BRIGADE

Kwame Neiderer waited with his platoon once again for deployment. This time it would be Pluto, his old home system. It was the system he'd joined the Army to get away from. What the hell; he was in the Army now, and the Army didn't fucking care that he never wanted to set foot on the planet again in his life. His return to Pluto and Charon wasn't optional. Anyway, he understood the basic idea of the attack and he knew it was a mark of distinction that his company was chosen to accompany the Old Crow, Sherman, on this mission.

As he understood it, they were here to draw fire from Neptune. If they were successful, then they'd be facing not only the local Met occupation, but also a bunch of new forces peeled off from the Neptune invaders. They were already faced with a superior, entrenched force. If they did what they were supposed to do, they would soon be overwhelmingly outnumbered.

Fuck the honor, I'd just as soon be safely ensconced on Triton doing fire-and-weather duty, Kwame thought. But he knew deep down that he didn't mean it. Because he wasn't safe there either, when you thought about it. Ground duty only seemed safe until they dropped the grist-mil on you and it ate your eyes down to their sockets. At least in space, you would probably go quick and clean. That wasn't guaranteed, of course. It was a matter of considering the odds.

Kwame was shaken from his morbid thoughts by a Klaxon reverberating in the knit. He noticed the rest of the grunts in the hold start to awareness and begin to shake off the torpor of the long journey out. At least the Federal Army—so far, at least—didn't have the need to archive its soldiers, like the Met forces did. He'd heard that half of most DIED ship's infantry complement were given the pleasure of bodily compression. Their brains were switched off during this time, allegedly. Then their bodies were de . . . de- something or another. It wasn't dehydration exactly. There was grist involved and manipulation on a molecular level. It was a kind of temporary decay, with gooey bodies compressed together like one of those prune bricks that the orphans were fed at the institution where Kwame had spent much of his childhood.

He wouldn't have liked that at all, but there was talk that the Federal Army might have to use such a transport procedure as the number of recruits grew. But there was talk about a lot of things, and knowing which were real and which bullshit was beyond Kwame's power of discernment. He'd find out soon enough what was real. That was the nature of being on the sharp end of the Army's poking stick.

"Charon dead ahead," said a female voice in his head. This was the latest in a long line of lieutenants the platoon had gone through. This one's name was Twentyklick. Janice or something. The surname might prove a problem when it came time to distance deployment and positioning. She'd have to last a good bit longer than the others before he started worrying about that, though.

"Sergeant, have the platoon check in," said Twentyklick. It took Kwame a moment to realize that she was talking to him. Through a process of attrition and transfer, he'd become the highest-ranking noncom currently in the outfit. There was even talk about promoting him to master sergeant. He was supposed to be the Old Crow's pet, after all.

Pet guinea pig, thought Kwame. One thing Sherman didn't do was reward success with an easy assignment. Instead, they'd gotten progressively harder since he'd been on the team that destroyed the rip tether on Triton. The truth was, though he couldn't bring himself to enjoy being put in harm's way, he remembered what a life of boredom was. Or he sort of did. The alcohol and enthalpy had wiped out some of his recollections of those good old days before the Army had saved him from himself. Or he'd saved himself from himself.

Whatever the fuck, he thought. Get on with things.

"Platoon report," he said.

The knit-transmitted voices of his soldiers came back to him—some quick and crisp, some sluggish and irritated. Two-thirds of the platoon were as green as could be—because the soldiers they were replacing were as dead as could be. Kwame ticked them all off. Everyone had survived the transit intact. Good enough for now.

"Platoon Bravo all present and accounted for," he told the lieutenant.

"All right, Sergeant," replied the lieutenant. "Gear up." At least Twentyklick was not utterly new. She'd seen some action against the *Montserrat*. Kwame had, too, of course. He'd been up close and personal with the huge DIED destroyer just before Sherman had ordered it blown to Kingdom Come. He'd even run his hand against its hull. The ship's isotropic coating had made it feel like a thick, black slime.

"Stand by," said Twentyklick. A couple of seconds passed. Kwame felt his body—and his mind—tightening to a quartzlike tension and precision.

Drugs, he thought. Excellent drugs, too. We're getting the full battle infusion. Shit. That can't be good news.

"Okay, incoming instructions," Twentyklick continued. "It's Charon; we're dropping on Charon."

They were going into the Shit. The Real Shit. There wasn't an inch of the little moon that wasn't hardened against attack.

Engagement always happened fast, and Kwame had decided there was no real way to prepare yourself. A great side door running along the main hull of the *Boomerang* slid upward on enormous hinges. Grist containment barriers deactivated themselves. Various e-m force fields were switched off.

Then you were catapulted into space like a rock from a slingshot. It was that simple and mechanical. Elastic tethers spit you out at initial g forces that only the space-adapted could withstand.

It took Kwame a moment to orient—and he knew he was much faster at doing so than some of the new recruits in the platoon. As well he should be, being the noncom now.

Charon bristled below them, like a withered crabapple. The crenellations he saw were not canyons, but an overlay of grist-constructed armor. And as he looked, e-m fire rose from the surface below. The platoon was out of range, but closing fast.

"Sarge, weren't the ship and fighters supposed to soften up the place before they sent us in?" It was Private Daytrader communicating on platoon band over the knit.

"They did," Kwame replied. He almost added, "And can the chatter!" as he supposed a good sergeant would. But the stew of military drugs inside them all would keep everybody from falling over the emotional edge into panic.

Almost in answer to Daytrader, the platoon crossed a sensor boundary and a triangulated group of stealth killer satellites—DIED satellites that had obviously escaped the invaders' prep work—tracked and opened fire upon them. Daytrader was killed instantly as a large swath of his right side was disintegrated by laser fire. No rupture-healing grist could compensate for his rapid depressurization once his internal organs were exposed. He died from what looked to Kwame like a ruptured heart that ballooned enormously outward, then exploded.

The rest of the platoon was through the killer satellites before the machines could get a fix on anybody else. Onward, downward. Very noticeably downward. Toward Charon.

Charon was covered with water ice, but that was mostly obscured by the silicates-and-metal fortress that the Met forces had constructed as a shell.

Too bad, Kwame thought. Even though he'd hated living on Pluto, he *had* liked to look up and find ghostly Charon there, glowing with the barest wisp of white reflected from the distant, distant sun. Now what would it look like? A black hole in the sky that blocked out the stars. That was all.

And down they fell. Kwame's internal gravimetrics told him that Charon's feeble gravity was beginning to tug enough to accelerate him.

"Retrothrust," he told the platoon. "Calibrate with me through the knit." There were small rockets on each soldier's feet for this maneuver. Unfortunately, the burn would light them up for the moon's defense sensors. Well, it couldn't be helped. They had to slow down.

"We've got an entry vector," said Lieutenant Twentyklick. As best Kwame could tell, she was somewhere behind him. He didn't waste time trying to locate her exact position. "The captain says the jump area's been softened up real good. All major weaponry's out, and we delivered a shitload of the new grade-five grist-mil from Forward Labs on-site."

"Sounds good, ma'am," Kwame replied. He checked another read-out in his peripheral vision. "Touchdown in one minute fifteen seconds."

And so the Third Sky and Light Brigade, Company C, Platoon Bravo made its way down to the surface of Charon. Within seconds, Kwame could not see around the curve of the moon. Then the horizon straightened steadily from curve to ellipse to straight line. Thirty seconds.

"Thrusters to full," he said over the knit. "Maintain vector." The ground was visible. It was a white target, surrounded by darker concentric rings. Were the rings actually waves? Liquid? Surely not. No, the waves were not moving. They were piled-up debris from an impact crater. "Platoon rendezvous at the bull's-eye. Sound off!"

Seven platoon members reported in—four men, three women. It had been five to three until they lost Daytrader.

Ten seconds. Five.

Kwame cut his boot thrusters. Three. Two. One.

The world changed to madness.

CHAPTER TEN

NEPTUNE SYSTEM
E-STANDARD EARLY APRIL, 3017
TRITON HOME FRONT

TB—the man sometimes known as Thaddeus Kaye—examined himself in the fourth dimension. He was still there. Old man, new man. Painfully twisted through the past and future every day at waking. And Alethea blown to bits. Literally ones and zeros. Sweet nothings. Somewhere in the Met. He was sure of it.

How did I get here, here to Triton? I can't stay.

And yet he *had* remained. And slowly found a place on Triton, tending to the wounded. He'd even begun writing poetry again, his old occupation.

Ben Kaye's occupation, he reminded himself. Thaddeus had never been a poet. Thaddeus had existed for the merest microsecond before Ben had plunged like a dagger through his heart, cleaving it in twain.

TB was two people. It didn't matter that they were the same person at base. What mattered was how you behaved. How you *acted*. That was the proof that he was damaged, that something was wrong. What you do reflects back and forth in time, making you. The action forms itself by forming you. How did that old poet Beat Myers put it?

I stand like a shadow
cast into the air.
A shadow made by whatever
that is down there.

What's real is what happens. Or fails to happen. Or happens in a half-assed way.

They had tried to make him into a superman. *They?* Hell, he'd colluded. The ultimate Large Array of Personalities, writ on gravitons, bounced backwards and forwards in time. Himself in past, present, and future all at once. His glance would take in decades. His every action would coincide with the inevitable. It would put a human face on the inevitable and shape it to human ends, at least in the area of the solar system. Anywhere there was a grist substrate through which to flash the news, Thaddeus's gestalt vision of past, present, and future.

What a fucking crock. All he'd really wanted out of it was to be a better poet. To be up there with Shakespeare and Dante. Fame. It wasn't such a misguided ambition. He never had given a damn about power. Power might be a side effect or it might not. Who cared? To write well and truly. To express his love for Alethea. To make her immortal, like Shakespeare's dark lady, or Dante's Beatrice.

Misguided or not, he'd found a way to sabotage and destroy himself in the process. Because, in upgrading to this special kind of LAP, his old self would have to be left behind. Ben could not integrate with Thaddeus.

But there was, and would always be, only one Alethea.

She would love Thaddeus. That was a given. Alethea's own desire was to become a LAP—something that she could not achieve because of a stray gene in her DNA. A slight propensity to schizophrenia that could not be removed from her or her ancestors without destroying their minds as well. People on Alethea's mother's side could never become LAPs.

And so, in jealousy and disgust, Ben had copied himself before the upgrade, hired a hacker to insert this stealth duplicate into the upgrade algorithm. The security had been small potatoes to overcome. After all, who expected trickery in this experiment?

He'd hidden his plans—even from himself. Until the moment came. The key words were spoken by the technician. *Initiate manifold upgrade.* Stupid, ugly words that presaged a stupid, ugly deed.

Ben, the original, would die. That was part of the plan. Why should he hang around? She won't love me anymore, he thought. She'll just be nice to me because she pities me.

He'd rather be dead.

And so the moment came, and the words were spoken, and a virus was inserted into each of the multiple copies that would form Thaddeus's being. Within that viral code resided Ben's copy. Thaddeus was born with Ben running through him like a knife. But a knife that could never be extracted.

Not even by suicide.

He'd tried it. Upon first awaking to his new status as a LAP, his new being, he'd felt the knife. He'd not yet known what it was yet, but had instinctively reached within himself to yank it out, to cough it up, to get rid of what wasn't *right*.

There had been an explosion. An explosion that killed everyone who was in the physical location of the experiment on Mars. It was also an explosion within the grist—a virtual explosion that had scattered every convert present to the four corners of creation.

Including Alethea. Including Alethea.

It had killed Alethea's body and scattered her mind to the winds of the grist.

He destroyed his heart's desire, the only woman he'd ever loved.

Upon realizing who he was and what he'd made himself—this new creature, this king of the LAPs, didn't call himself Thaddeus or Ben. He called himself TB. Tuberculosis Kaye. A sick joke.

What followed was years of searching. Years of dysfunction. A new, degraded life in the garbage dump known as the Carbuncle, near the edges of the Met in the asteroid belt. The place where all the little pieces of free code came to die. Or to be mutated. Transformed.

It was there, the shithole of the known universe, at his lowest point, that he'd felt the first flicker of care and love since the day of his "birth." A friend made from a furry bit of escaped code, from weirdly transmuted grist, from his dark dreams of Alethea.

Her name was Jill. She was, of all things, a ferret. At least she had been. Until she'd made herself, by sheer force of will, into a girl.

Savage little Jill. The only one who could have convinced him to leave the Met—albeit she'd convinced him by knocking him out for a two-day sleep, then helping his other friends to trundle him into a pirate ship and out to Triton. Nobody else could have gotten close enough to betray him. Or save him. He still wasn't sure which act Jill was guilty of. But one thing he was certain of—Jill's heart was as pure as his was sullied. She was not to be blamed.

"Breakfast!"

Bob the fiddler walked in from the apartment's tiny kitchen. For the past year, the old musician had been TB's roommate. Not that TB had invited him. As always, Bob's ways were mysterious and, for the most part, nonsensical. There were only two constants with Bob. First, he was a damned fine fiddle player. Second, he had a long-standing, mostly unrequited love for the smuggler and spaceship captain Makepeace Century. Maybe that was why TB didn't mind having him around—they were two old goats hurting for far too long over lost love. Decades, in Bob's case.

Of course, if Bob was who he claimed to be, his love for Century had developed relatively recently. If he really were the vanished composer Despacio, that would make him . . . nearly three hundred years old.

"Did you finish the poem you were working on?" Bob said. "And here are exactly four eggs."

He set the platter down on the coffee table in front of the battered sofa on which TB slept. Then Bob reached behind his back and pulled out a steaming cup of coffee as if by magic.

"Here is 'joe,' as they used to say a thousand years ago," Bob continued.

"How the hell did you do that?" TB asked. "You got a shelf back there?"

"Balancing stuff on your butt is easy in this gravity," said Bob. "Just a little practice, and you can do it, too. I can teach you the wonders."

"I think I'll pass," TB replied. "But thanks for the grub."

"I want to read that poem."

TB took a sip of the coffee. Swallowed. "I haven't finished it yet."

"What's it about?"

"That boy I tended last week at the hospital." TB looked around. "There a fork around here?"

"On Triton?" Bob asked.

"I meant to eat these eggs with."

"Jesus Christ you're picky." Bob reached into one of his several shirt pockets. "Here. I forgot I had it."

TB accepted the implement and took a bite of the eggs.

"That boy—the one who had the Broca grist infection?" said Bob. "The one who keeps talking in riddles."

"It isn't riddles," said TB between bites. "It's nonsense."

"Not always easy to tell the difference," said Bob. He sat down in the armchair across the table from the sofa.

"Especially with you," TB replied. "Aren't you going to eat?"

"I ate last night," Bob said. "I'll eat tomorrow. Today's for drinking."

He pulled a flask of whiskey from one shirt pocket and a small tumbler from another, and quickly poured himself a stiff shot.

"What kind of rotgut is that?" TB said.

"I'll have you know this is prime sipping whiskey," Bob replied. "Compliments of good old Captain Quench. The man knows his poison." He knocked back the whiskey and let out a low whistle. "Whew. Want some?"

"Not yet," TB replied. "What are you going to do today?"

"*Not* take a bath. How about you?"

"I've got a shift down at the hospital. Dahlia and I are still trying to work some kind of halfway cure on that boy."

"You always had a sweet hand with the grist."

"Yes, but I can't work miracles. The boy's entire personality was wiped out. We're trying to rebuild him from the memory of a memory. Dr. Dahlia has this fancy name for it: personality interpolation. To me, it's more like growing a tree from a stump. It may have the same DNA, but it's still a different tree."

"Better than nothing," Bob said. "You can do that to me if the bad grist ever gets into my brainpan. I wonder if I'd grow back as a chestnut or a hickory."

"Hickory," TB replied. "And all knotty, too."

"Good for ax handles."

"I suppose." TB finished his eggs, then downed the remainder of the coffee in a big gulp. "I've got to get going." He started to rise.

"Hey!" Bob yelled, startling TB back onto the sofa.

"Jesus Christ. What?"

Bob smiled his gap-toothed grin. "Have another cup of coffee, will you?"

"Uh, okay."

TB sat for a moment, looking at Bob. Was the man a riddle or just full of shit? A little of both and neither.

"I hope you don't expect me to get it for you?" Bob finally said.

"I guess not."

"You guess right," Bob replied. "And get me a cup, would you. There's something I want to tell you today."

TB found a half pot of coffee already brewed in the kitchen coffeemaker. He returned with two steaming cups and sat back down. Bob quickly brought out the whiskey again and laced his coffee with it. He took a snort straight from the bottle for good measure, then put the flask back into his pocket.

"So what have you got to tell me?" TB asked the musician.

"Huh?" Bob looked around. "Oh, right." He slurped at his coffee. "Never liked coffee when I was younger. 'Course, I couldn't exactly taste the real thing. Just virtual coffee. I don't think they ever quite got the algorithm right back then."

"Tastes the same to me," said TB. He knew better than to try to hurry Bob into saying whatever it was he had to say.

Bob set down his cup. "What happened to me was this," he said. "And this has bearing on you, son, 'cause I seen some of that old shadow starting to creep back over you—"

TB took a sip from his coffee and said nothing.

Bob closed his mouth and pursed his lips, as if he were having trouble getting himself to speak. TB continued waiting. This was obviously something important to Bob.

"You try to help other people, and it doesn't work. You can't save one damned soul. It's all up to them."

"I know that, Bob," TB said gently.

"You think you do, but you don't. You're stuck in the crazy logic of the world, TB. You ever think that's why I sound sort of off-kilter, son? That *your* ears are put on wrong."

"I've considered that possibility."

"Back when I was the most famous musician in the solar system, I had a student. You might've heard of him. He got famous later. Anyway, he was like a son to me." Bob took a long sip of his coffee, settled back in his chair. "He *was* a son to me."

Bob looked down into his cup. The skin around the old man's eyes crinkled to a sadness TB had never before seen on his face. Bob's irises had taken on the color of the black coffee.

TB realized for the first time that Bob was space-adapted. Space-adapted eyes always took on the color they beheld.

"My son did not turn out well," said Bob, "and I blamed myself. I knew it was a damn fool thing to do—the boy had been raised by what amounted to a psychopath before he came into my care, after all. But I couldn't help it. I couldn't help feeling like I failed the boy. This was a great trouble to me. Even though I could write a symphony with no hands and compose a concerto that could make a stone cry oceans, that boy . . . the only thing I had to offer him was music."

"Not a bad gift."

"Not good enough!" shouted Bob. He sat bolt upright, then continued in a lowered voice. "Not good enough by a long shot. The boy needed love."

"Sounds like you had that, too."

"Now," Bob said. "Now. Not then. I was a goddamn computer program at the time. Twenty-seven copies of famous composer converts strained through an evolutionary algorithm. The Artificial Musical Expression System, they called me. With the accent on 'expression.'" Bob chuckled. "I gave him that name. I picked my own new name and didn't have any use for the old one. He wanted another name, so I gave that one to him."

"A . . . M . . . E . . . accented . . ." TB said. "You've got to be kidding, Bob."

"His name was Claude Schlencker back then. He hated that name on account of his father. The psychopath."

"*Amés* was a student of yours?"

"I taught him everything he knows. About music, that is." Bob shook his head sadly. "I saw something bad would come of it all. Not the exact badness, mind you. But I saw. And I wanted to do something about it. But there I was, one of the first free converts, and I couldn't know what it was like to get the shit beat out of you night after night. To have a mother who pretended like it didn't happen, and then ran off and left you to the tender mercies of your tormentor. So I decided to give it a try, being a regular person and all. I grew me a body. This one I'm wearing now. I was one of the first pure-program free converts to try it—to make myself into a regular physical human."

Bob stood up abruptly and walked from the room. He banged around in his bedroom for a while, then returned, his fiddle and bow in hand. He pulled the bow across the strings and began to play quietly. It was a reel of the same sort as he normally played, but slowed down to half time.

"I wanted to touch the world. Have the world touch me in a way it never did before." Bob said. "Oh, I did it for myself, too. To hear music beating on my eardrums. To feel it in the soles of my shoes. But I wanted to find a way to help Claude."

"And have you?" TB asked.

"No," said Bob, "I have not. But I am no longer a creature void of form. I can rosin up a bow with my own spit. I can drink whiskey with the best of 'em." Bob began sawing more vigorously on his instrument. "You got to give up any idea of what you thought you was gonna be before you can be who you are," he said.

TB sipped at his second cup of coffee. He sat back and listened to Bob finish playing his tune. The fiddler took a bow.

"Anyway," Bob said. "That's whatever happened to old Despacio in case you were wondering. He ain't dead; he just sort of underwent a sea change."

They said nothing else for a long while. Bob, true to his word, sat down and rosined up his bow with a block of resinous wax and a wad of saliva.

"Maybe you'll find a way to help the man," TB finally said. "Somehow."

"A fellow would have to be crazy to mess with Director Amés, now wouldn't he?" Bob said between dribbles of spit. He looked up and smiled a drooling smile at TB. "On the other hand, I got a feeling both me *and* you qualify in that way."

CHAPTER ELEVEN

NEPTUNE SYSTEM
E-STANDARD 13:17, THURSDAY, APRIL 3, 3017
FEDERAL ARMY THEATER COMMAND

"We're engaged at the Mill," Major Monitor reported to Theory. "Austen is taking fire. Twain is maneuvering for position."

"Give me enemy locations," said Theory.

"Four ships. IDs on three. Two Dabna-class destroyers, the *Aguilla* and the *Mediumrare*. Third is a cruiser. She's the *Martian Dawn*. She's a specialty ship, we think."

"Carrying demolitions for the Mill," Theory said.

"That's intelligence's best guess," Monitor replied. "And a half contingent of troops." Monitor's square-jawed visage was still for a moment (milliseconds in actuality, of course) in Theory's virtual command space.

He's receiving incoming information, Theory thought. Monitor had never seen any need to run animation algorithms to keep his face display in motion when he wasn't using it.

"We have a fix on the fourth ship. She's another Dabna-class, the *Debeh-Li-Zini*. She's a minesweeper, with a half contingent for deployment. Stand by . . ."

Again Monitor went into face-freeze.

"We're getting some e-m data on the outer-system group," Monitor reported. "This will take a while to correlate. Seconds."

Theory sighed. The merci jamming really would have an effect on decision-making. But at least they were no longer totally blind. And while he was waiting the several seconds it would take the outer-system data to stream in, he could devise and issue a set of orders for Cloudships Austen and Twain. He turned to his communications officer.

"Tell Twain to get on the *Martian Dawn*," he said. "And tell Austen to engage fully as she sees fit." His orders were issued. A moment later, Twain's booming voice rang through the command center. The cloudship obviously did not let communications protocol stand in his way when he had a point to make.

"Austen's got two DIED cruisers on her!"

"I'm aware of that," Theory replied. "She'll have to fight it out. You have to stop that destroyer from taking out the Mill. We suspect it contains demolition devices."

The briefest pause.

"Will do," said Twain.

Theory knew Cloudship Twain would follow his orders. He liked the old ship. Twain understood tactics. Plus, he was one of Theory's heroes—the first human being to journey to the Centauri system. Theory also respected Cloudship Austen, whose grasp of strategy and economics was well beyond his own. That was the reason he'd given the two ships the crucial role of defending the Mill.

"It's up to them now," Theory said to the room.

Major Monitor paid him no mind, as this information added nothing whatsoever to his current understanding of the situation.

You can always count on Monitor to let you know where you stand, Theory thought. Theory turned back to studying his situation displays.

Where you stand, he thought. Or where you *fall*.

CHAPTER TWELVE

PLUTO SYSTEM
E-STANDARD 18:27, SATURDAY, APRIL 5, 3017
FEDERAL FLAGSHIP *BOOMERANG*

Sherman's lightning raid on Charon was supposed to be just that—fast, hard-hitting, and done. Instead, he'd run into complications in the grist. Pluto and Charon had what amounted to entire pellicles themselves, just like the human skin. There wasn't a surface on either planet or moon that wasn't coated an inch thick. So, theoretically, introduction of Gerardo Funk's new grist-mil brew should have had a devastating effect. And it had—only on the *wrong* forces.

Somehow the stuff had interacted with the local substrate and *mutated*. The change had momentarily paralyzed the DIED surface-based defenses, and Sherman had dropped his troops in that time period. But then Pluto—and particularly Charon—seemed to come back online and bite back. Whoever or whatever had taken over the command and control structures down there was firing like a madman at anything in range—including both Sherman's own forces *and* the DIED ships.

The DIED carrier *Streichholtzer* and its battle group had moved out of range of its own planetary base. It had taken sporadic fire from Pluto, and then a concentrated barrage from Charon. At first Sherman believed this might mean that his soldiers had stormed the fortress and were in control of the weapons. But upon drawing nearer to inspect, his ship and Cloudship Tacitus had both been subject to the same intense fire.

As a result he had ten thousand soldiers trapped on Pluto, and another five thousand stuck on Charon. What was worse, he'd lost contact with an entire company on the knit. Quench's command had dropped on Charon, and no one had heard a peep from them for the past two hours.

Sherman had a decision to make. Should he stay in the vicinity and slug it out with the local forces, or should he withdraw and attempt to lure the DIED navy after him? The latter had been his original plan—especially since his attack, as planned, had drawn off some DIED ships from the Neptune invasion. But to turn tail and run now would mean abandoning his deployed troops.

He had a positive option as far as that went: Major Meré Philately and her Virtual Extraction Corps. Sherman had taken a chance on Philately and a contingent of other DIED POWs who had been saved from the destruction of the DIED ship *Montserrat* at Neptune three years ago. Their only method of escape had been as converts, while their bodies were blown to smithereens when the *Montserrat* was blown to atoms and energy. They were now free converts—free converts who had violated the Met Containment Principle when it came to soldiers. Should they ever return home, they would be imprisoned—most likely in one of the Met's free-convert concentration camps that were beginning to look like much more than a rumor.

So Philately had requested an interview with Sherman. When he'd visited her in Triton's virtual sector POW camp, she presented Sherman with a plan.

"You saved our lives, and some of us want to work for you," she told him. "We know you won't trust us in everyday operations. But we want to volunteer for hazardous duty—for the bad shit that nobody wants to deal with. And everybody knows what that is."

"Counteroperations against large-scale military grist deployment," Sherman said. "That's as bad as it gets. So far, at least."

"What's worse is sitting in this prison watching our lives drain away," Philately had answered him. "Not having a home or hope or anything to do."

"I take your point," said Sherman. "So let's hear what you've got to say."

Philately had outlined a special unit that went into grist-mil anti-information zones and extracted Federal troops that were trapped therein. It was the perfect job for free converts—but the mortality rate was almost guaranteed to be high. Grist-mil was nasty stuff—and was particularly deadly for free converts, who existed in the grist and moved through it. It would be like swimming in a sea of poison. Hell, it would be like *breathing* in a poison atmosphere where you weren't adapted for survival.

It was an incredibly brave proposal.

If the *Montserrat* survivors could be trusted.

Five hundred free converts on the loose was not something Sherman wanted to deal with.

He made his decision.

"You'll train in prison. We'll expand the grounds. When it comes time for deployment, you'll be flashed to your destination," he said. "If. If you conduct yourselves well, we'll give consideration to commuting your sentences."

Philately had nodded and given Sherman a smart salute.

"That's all we ask, sir," she replied. "A chance."

"You've got it," Sherman said. "Make the most of it, Major."

And now the time had come for the VE Corps either to deliver on their promise or be found wanting. Several thousand soldiers' lives depended on the outcome.

He'd sent Philately's corps to the surfaces of Pluto and Charon to extract the troops who had become trapped by the grist.

They would do what they would do. In the meantime, Sherman and the rest of his forces must fight a holding action to buy them time.

In the virtuality, Sherman looked at the arrangement of his ships. The enormous bulk of Cloudship Tacitus hung a few hundred kilometers sunward from Sherman's own ship, the *Boomerang*. Tacitus himself was present here with Sherman in the *Boomerang*'s partly virtual, partly real bridge. Tacitus, being present only in the knit, was of course confined to the virtual portion of Sherman's bridge.

Sherman gazed out at the bulk of the cloudship—an almost perfect stormlike spiral in shape. Although the formation was naturally occurring when a cloudship accreted, Tacitus claimed to have shaped himself into the profile of an early hurricane he had particularly admired from the twenty-second century. He had never been clear on whether he'd actually seen the storm or was merely working from pictures.

Sherman turned to Tacitus's "old man" avatar. "We have to buy time now, one way or another."

"That was the plan all along," said Tacitus.

"But at the moment I need a big target to draw off the bulls."

"That would be *me*, I take it?"

"Yes."

"And you'll play the matador with *Boomerang*, I presume?" Tacitus replied.

Sherman nodded. "And we'll both provide cover for the dropped troops until we manage to get them back up here."

"Just don't forget to aim your sword carefully when the time comes for the kill, señor," said the old man. "You may only have one chance to get it right."

CHAPTER THIRTEEN

PLUTO SYSTEM
E-STANDARD TIME UNKNOWN
CHARON

They had been in the jungle a long, long time. Melon said it was years, but Kwame Neiderer had long ago ceased to keep track of the months, and he suspected Private Melon had as well.

The passage of time didn't matter much when you weren't the same person from moment to moment, and when nothing around you stayed stable either.

The platoon emerged from the foliage and approached the river they had named the Smoky, because you never knew whether it would flow with water or ground-hugging gas. Sometimes you could cross by holding your breath and running down through the river bottom and up the other side. You didn't want to breathe the stuff that surrounded you. Benetorro had breathed it once, and ever since, her fingers grew an extra joint each day. After a week, somebody had to take a hatchet to her hands and prune them. The wounds sealed up quickly, but Benetorro still screamed like a motherfucker every time the ax came down.

Today the Smoky was water, and it was running fast. Kwame threw in a twig, and it was swept away downstream within seconds. There would be no swimming across. Yet they had to move on. They were being followed by their mortal enemies, the Shadows.

The Shadows were *them*. They were exact physical copies of Kwame's platoon. Only they weren't striped orange, black, and white like Kwame and his group. Instead, the Shadows were pasty white— even Kwame's copy. Whatever their skin color originally had been, the Shadows were now all albinos.

Kwame's platoon called themselves the Tigers because of their own striping. The striping changed from day to day, but the basic colors had remained the same for several weeks. Kwame supposed that was because the topical camouflage algorithms within their grist pellicles were undergoing random mutation, or more likely, were under the control of a virus. The jungle was rife with nasty bugs that fucked with your grist in all sorts of unpleasant ways.

So they had to find a way across the Smoky River or else risk fighting the Shadows. The problem was, you couldn't kill the Shadows with gun, rocket, or antimatter death ray. They reconstituted like zombies. Of course, the Tigers were themselves almost impossible to kill. The Shadows had managed to kill the lieutenant only after taking her in a nighttime raid and boiling her down in a vat of moon shine.

It was real shine from the moon that hung perpetually in the jungle's sky—a big moon the size of Earth's. It provided the perpetual twilight illumination to the jungle. When rain fell in the jungle, the rain was moon shine. The leaves glistered and glowed for many hours after a shower.

You could even climb up the high mountains to the north and touch the face of the moon if you wanted to. The platoon had done it once. The moon was not solid, but was a sort of coagulated liquid—like elemental mercury. Daring himself, Kwame had stuck his hand inside. The moon's surface tension broke, and moon shine flowed down his arm and soaked his leg and boots. The substance was cold to the touch. When you heated it up over a fire, as the Shadows had to boil poor Private Mansard, it never got a degree hotter—yet in every other way it acted like a scalding fluid. The Shadows had cut Lieutenant Twenty-klick like potatoes before cooking her in it.

"We can't swim it, Sarge," said long-fingered Benetorro. "Have we got to make a sacrifice?"

"Yeah, maybe," Kwame said. "Let's see if there's another way across."

"But the Shadows are right behind us."

"I know that, goddamn it," he replied, "but I don't want to make a sacrifice unless we have to. One of these days, it's not going to work. Or they won't come back." He scanned the riverbank. "Benetorro, I want you, Denmark, Fusili, and Mays to scout up north a half klick for a crossing tree. Hardrind, you stay with me. The rest of you scout down south."

"But Sarge," said Fusili, "the last crossing tree put us on the other side of the world."

"I know that," Kwame answered. "But it's better than a sacrifice."

"I guess."

"Come here. You and Benetorro." The soldiers approached him. He reached into shoulder bag and pulled out a canteen. He opened it and carefully dribbled some of the contents on the palms of his two platoon members. Their hands began to glow a ghostly white.

"When that moon shine glow starts to fade," he said, "I want you hightailing it back here. By the time the glow's gone, you'd better be here. Else you might miss the sacrifice—if we have to do one." He gave each of them a hard look. "Got it?"

"Got it, Sarge."

The platoon scuttled off to search for one of the elusive crossing trees, leaving Kwame and Hardrind at the river's edge. They settled down. Kwame took out some of the chewy hardtack that they had subsisted on for as long as anyone could remember. Kwame didn't even recall how they'd discovered the stuff in the first place. It grew underneath a vivid green moss that occurred in certain clearings in the jungle. The higher in the mountains you traveled, the more hardtack you found. Kwame guessed it had something to do with proximity to the moon.

Hardrind chewed her food with her mouth open. The insides of her cheeks were stained deep purple by hardtack juice.

"Who do you think we'll sacrifice this time, Sarge?" she asked him between mouthfuls.

"Nobody, I hope."

"What about if the Shadows catch us, then."

"We'll fight," Kwame said.

" 'Cause we're the Tigers?"

"Because the Shadows won't fucking leave us alone until we fight, Hardrind."

Chew, swallow. Another full-mouthed bite.

"How come they're called the Shadows, Sarge?"

Kwame had to think about that for a moment. It had been so long since they'd given their nemesis the name. He couldn't remember who came up with it. Maybe the lieutenant. "Because *we're* real," he said.

"Oh."

They ate in silence for a while. The jungle surrounding them was noisy. Birds and iridescent flying lizards flitted from tree to tree. A parasitic clinger plant lowered a vine and tried to find a vein on Kwame's arm. He absentmindedly slapped it away.

He looked at the orange-and-black stripes on his hand. They crawled and twisted slowly across his skin's surface.

Another change was coming.

A cloud crossed over the moon. Hardrind started. She sat up straight and sniffed the air. "I smell rain," she said.

"Maybe," Kwame said. "Or something else."

"The Winds?"

"Yep."

There was a crackling in the brush. Kwame rolled behind a tree quickly. He reemerged when he saw it was Benetorro's group, returning from their recognizance.

"Anything?" he asked.

Benetorro jumped back a good two paces in fright.

"Jesus, where'd you come from, Sarge?"

"What did you find?"

"No crossing trees up that way."

Kwame nodded acknowledgment. "We'll wait and see what the others found."

The returned soldiers sat down and ate hardtack. They all kept him in their line of sight.

How had this come to be? All these people looking to him to figure out what to do. Who was he? He couldn't remember. It had been longer than years. It had been centuries. He'd lost all memory of who he might once have been. And the hundreds of changes, when the world uncoiled and wrapped itself into a new pattern—he'd become a new person each time. His mind felt as fuzzy as the green moss under which the hardtack grew.

"We'd better get the sacrifice ready," Kwame told the platoon. "When the others get back, we'll go ahead with it."

"Whose turn is it, Sarge?" Fusili asked in a quiet voice. "It's mine, isn't it?"

Kwame sighed. "Yes, Fusili. It's your turn."

"What if I don't want to, Sarge?"

Kwame considered. Perpetual strife with the Shadows. Stabbing, rending, screams of pain that turn out to be you, dying. Reconstitution—only to die all over again. Staring into those murderous pink eyes when you resuscitate. Fighting, fighting, fighting the Shadow you. Down through the centuries. The millennia.

"You'll be all right, Fusili," Kwame finally said. "It won't hurt like the Shadows do."

"I know that, but I'm scared, Sarge."

The boy was shaking. He must have completely forgotten he was next in line, Kwame thought. Of course, forgetting was a pretty common occurrence among the platoon.

"Can I at least pick out the rock?" Fusili asked in a pathetic voice.

"Pick it out, Fusili," Kwame replied. "Just shut up about it, would you?"

"Yeah, sure, Sarge."

A few minutes later, the second unit returned from downstream. They had encountered no crossing tree.

Their luck was running out. There was no way across the river, and the Shadows would be there momentarily.

It was time for the sacrifice.

Fusili chose a large stone that jutted out of the ground near the river. He lay on his back, testing it.

"Hard," he muttered. "Maybe I can find a better one." He sat up.

Kwame quickly glanced at Benetoro and Mays. The soldiers, one a wiry, middle-aged man, the other a muscular young woman, moved on Fusili. Mays pushed him back down against the rock. Benetorro held him in place, her long fingers wrapping all the way around Fusili's wrists. Fusili, startled, struggled wildly. Mays sat on him, straddling his stomach. She gave him a couple of quick slaps across the face.

"It's not like I won't do it; it's just that this isn't a good place." Fusili was crying. "This is a bad place."

Kwame unsheathed his knife, stepped forward, and bent down on a knee over Fusili. He put a hand on Fusili's chest, found his sternum.

"Sarge, not now," Fusili said. "Don't do it now, you goddamn bastard. You fucking rock-shitting cold worlder."

Kwame ignored him. He marked Fusili's heart with his left forefinger, finding a spot between his ribs.

Fusili gave one more buck, trying to get away, but Kwame had his place marked, and as the man settled back to the rock to try to squirm in another direction, Kwame slid the knife in between the ribs.

It was a damn shame that you couldn't just cut a guy's throat or stab him in the back of the brain. They were in the grist so thick that anything like that would heal. You could only kill by cutting off the flow of Bloodsap and keeping it cut off for several minutes.

Fusili's legs kicked out at the knife thrust. Kwame pushed the knife down hard. He twisted it against the ribs and locked it into place. Fusili gave another shudder.

"Shit," he said. "I'm thirsty as hell. I'm so thirsty."

Dying sometimes had weird effects on the sense perceptions. Kwame knew, having died a few times himself over the years they'd been there. Fusili thought he was thirsty.

"Jesus, just a cup of water. Can somebody give me something to drink," Fusili whispered.

Nobody moved to help him. He wouldn't be so thirsty in a moment.

Fusili's last words were the last words of many a soldier.

"Mama."

He lay back on the rock, still.

Kwame turned the knife, unlocking it from the ribs. He quickly made a two-foot slice horizontally across Fusili's chest. He then found the middle of the cut and sliced up and down a foot, neatly opening up Fusili's chest.

The luminous Bloodsap welled up and pooled in the chest cavity. Kwame reached in and extracted the man's heart. Much Bloodsap had leaked out of it, but it was still seeping with the stuff. He handed the heart to Mays.

"Take it," he told her. "Smear up with it. Pass it around."

Mays did as he told her. She held the heart above her head and wrung it between her fists. Bloodsap flowed over her upturned face and down her arms and neck. Soon she glowed a bright neon red.

Kwame dipped his hands into Fusili's body and splashed the syrupy Bloodsap over himself, daubing down his arms and shirt. Once introduced, the sap disseminated itself over the rest of his body surface like quicksilver. Soon he, too, was glowing red.

There was a crackling in the bushes. A distant voice that sounded like his own.

"The Shadows are almost here," Kwame said. He stepped back from body. "The rest of you get yourselves sapped up."

The platoon quickly did as he said, some wiping themselves with the heart, others splashing themselves from the opened body as if it were a gooey pool for washing. Soon the entire platoon was shining as bright as fire.

There was excited screaming in the underbrush. The jungle parted.

The Shadows were upon them.

The Bloodsap did its job. Slippery Shadow hands grasped for them and slid off skin without effect. The Shadows brought out their machetes. But the sap began to take effect in earnest. The Shadows spun around in grim revulsion.

"Got some Shadow repellent on today, you fuckers," Mays called out at them. "You can't touch us now."

Shadow-Mays followed the sound of her own voice, raising the machete to strike, but she couldn't follow up, so repugnant was the sap to her senses.

"Shut up," Kwame told Mays. Taunting the Shadows would only make them into more ferocious hunters than they already were. "You're humping Fusili's body after we're done here."

"Right, Sarge." Mays sounded chagrined. "I'll get him."

"All right, people," Kwame said. "Ready your blades."

The platoon unsheathed their own machetes. Doing so would have been unthinkable without the sap on their side. The Shadows were easily twice as strong as the Tigers in a normal situation.

The Tigers did as ordered. The Shadows understood what was happening, of course. But, as always happened, the Shadows' killing lust overcame their intelligence. The Shadows were completely incapable of retreat. They were drawn inexorably to the Tigers, hanging on the edge of the Bloodsap's repulsing power like the panting predators they were.

"Time to do some hacking," Kwame called out. "Find your target." He raised his own blade high above his head. Gazing about, he spotted his own doppelganger. For some reason, attacking your own double was far more effective than hacking away indiscriminately.

Shadow-Kwame was staring in the direction of the platoon with fierce, searching eyes despite what had to be the blinding glow of the Bloodsap.

"On my mark!" Kwame squared up and readied his blade. "Strike!"

There was a bright, jagged flash.

A crackling, electric shock that paralyzed Kwame's muscles in midswing.

Thunder in Kwame's ears.

"Hold!"

Kwame shook his head, slapped an ear.

"You are commanded to hold." The same voice. A woman's voice. An unknown voice.

Not a Tiger. Not a Shadow.

But who else was there?

"This is Major Philately of the First Sky and Light Virtual Extraction Corps."

Major? There had never been any majors in the jungle. As far as Kwame had ever known, it was a theoretical rank the lieutenant had sometimes referred to, sort of like a minor god.

Kwame didn't believe in any gods.

"Sergeant Neiderer, your pellicle has been infiltrated by DIED anti-information zone on the Plutonian moon Charon," the voice said.

Charon? What the hell was this Philately talking about? There was only the jungle. There had only *ever* been the jungle.

"This is some kind of trick the Shadows have come up with," Kwame yelled to his platoon. "Don't listen to this shit." He reared back and took a huge swing with his machete.

Another bolt of lightning. Another jolt of electrical paralysis. His couldn't finish his strike.

"Sorry about this, Sergeant, but we don't have much time," said the voice. "We've got to get you extricated, decontaminated, and bugged out as quickly as possible. We've got a half cycle before your code key mutates again."

"Who the fuck are you?" It sounded like his voice, but it was Shadow-Neiderer.

"You're about to find out, Sergeant," said the voice. "And it's going to happen fast. Sometimes bringing a trooper out of the zone pushes him or her over the brink and into psychosis."

"The only psychotics around here are those fucking Shadows," Kwame said. "We have to hack them to pieces or they'll kill us all." Maybe he could get this "major" to see reason.

The thunder rumbled again. But this time, instead of lightning, there came blinding revelation.

The past flooded in first. His youth spent in deep space on a remote Oort precomet. The orphanage on Pluto after his mother died, and the semisentient despot, the Rules, that governed the children there using the sadistic, irrational letter of the law. His early manhood: unprepared for life on his own, dysfunctional, addicted, dissolute.

Then the Army. A new chance. A family. Even if it was a brusque, strict family. Even if it was occasionally sadistic, the Army wasn't the Rules. It had a purpose. That purpose was to put its members in harm's way. To put him in harm's way.

Well, you couldn't have everything. At least he had a purpose beyond himself—because the Army did. He was a protector.

Across from him, across the barrier of the sap's shine, Shadow-Kwame, too, stood as if riveted to the ground.

There was such things as rivets. As spaceships. There was vacuum, and planets, and stars. There was grist.

"Where am I?" he said. But it was the Shadow Kwame who spoke.

"On Charon," said Philately. "You are trapped in a grist-mil anti-information zone. The zone was originally set up by the Met defenders here. We dropped in our own insurgency grist, and the 'native' stuff was modified. But it wasn't deactivated. When you made your moon-fall, your pellicle was invaded by the grist-mil. The Federal Army grist couldn't stop this. But it protected you from death by disassociating you. By splitting your mentality into several pieces so that the grist-mil couldn't localize you."

"The Shadows?" said Tiger Kwame.

"The Tigers?" said Shadow Kwame.

"All part of you," said Philately.

"But we fight . . ."

"To keep the enemy confused. To blur the target."

"We've fucking killed each other!"

"You never have succeeded."

"The Tiger lieutenant—she's dead," said Shadow Kwame. "I killed her. I boiled her in moon shine to make sure she couldn't reconstituted."

"You killed a fragment of your own personality, a memory. As long as the shadow lieutenant is alive, the memory is preserved." Philately's voice became more urgent. "We don't have much time, Sergeant Neiderer. The extraction window is closing."

"What about the rest of my platoon?"

"All but you and Benetorro were killed instantly, Sergeant Neiderer."

"But that's impossible. They're all here."

"In your mind," said Philately.

"No, here—in the *jungle*,"

"You've been dreaming in the grist, Sergeant," Philately said. "It's time to wake up."

"But I *am* awake!"

"Not half as awake as you're going to be," Philately replied dryly.

The jungle grew brighter. What was that? A giant fire? Brighter still. It wasn't the moon. The moon was in the west. The moon was *always* in the west, skewered on the mountain peaks there.

I've touched the moon, and it bled.

This light came from the east.

Brighter than the moon. *Nothing was brighter than the moon.*

What the fuck is that in the east? Shining like—

Like the sun.

Impossible. There was no such thing. It was just a word for something imaginary. It didn't exist. It couldn't exist. Nothing that bright was possible.

The sun rose in Kwame's mind.

Sun.

Solar system. War. His real life.

It all came to him in an instant. Shadow and Tiger melted away.

The sun burnt brightly. Then it dimmed. Farther and farther away. As far away as Pluto.

On the surface of Charon, Kwame Neiderer stood up from where he'd collapsed in the grist-laden crust.

His internals told him that two e-days older had passed. Just two days. A wave of panic. Couldn't be. Impossible.

Was.

He was tougher than the panic. He was Tiger and Shadow combined.

Terror was always present. It could be handled. It could be used to survive.

To fucking get on with things.

To fight the enemy.

"Did we win the battle?" he asked. His voice made no sound in the airless vacuum. But he had communicated through the merci, through the knit. He remembered how that worked now.

Philately answered him through his pellicle, through the Army's knit. Being a free convert, she was not physically present, of course. She was somewhere in the grist. He remembered how that worked, too.

"Not yet," Philately replied. "But we will."

CHAPTER FOURTEEN

NEPTUNE SYSTEM
E-STANDARD 18:03, THURSDAY, APRIL 3, 3017
CLOUDSHIP AUSTEN

High above Neptune, fifty Sciatica-class attack ships were swarming the left spiral and fifty parallel versions of Cloudship Austen's core personality were determining coordinates, taking fixes, and powering up the exterior surface to fire on the invaders. Each attacking ship carried a squadron of soldiers who operated the weaponry and ship systems. Ships shot through space like little pitchforks.

Or viruses, Austen thought, set on infecting me. Have to disinfect the area, and that's all there is to it.

Seeing a targeting solution, she twitched her skin—on a quantum level—and shot out another beam of antiparticles. One of the ships flashed from existence in a noiseless, bright ball of utter annihilation. But there were so many more of them. And these little buggers were distracting her from the far greater menace of the two big destroyers on her tail.

She hated to do it, but if she was going to have a chance against those big guns, the battalion of soldiers inside her was going to have to go *out there* and get these gnats off her.

The Sciatica-class ships were designed for planetary operations.

Some of their close-order weaponry wouldn't work in space. That would give her soldiers a better chance against them.

She quickly asked for and received permission from the command center to deploy. She contacted the troop hold.

"Captain Allsky," she said, "I'm afraid I'm going to need your help after all."

CHAPTER FIFTEEN

NEPTUNE SYSTEM
E-STANDARD 18:11, THURSDAY, APRIL 3, 3017
ALLSKY'S COMPANY B

Twenty thousand soldiers came swarming out into space like hornets from a thwacked nest. Austen had aimed her catapults as precisely as possible. The rest was up to the Army.

Some were settlers from Triton and Nereid. Some were refugees from the fall of Saturn.

Most were from much farther away.

They were from places where the spoonful of sunlight that fell on Triton was as the bright glare of noon on Earth would be to someone from Neptune. They were miners, sorters, and loaders from the Kuipers and the Oorts. They were shipping clerks from Charon and stevedores from Pluto—and from every port and way station in the outer solar system. The most common occupation in the outer system was moving around great chunks of rock and ice.

Most of them had become space-adapted as children and had spent more time in the vacuum than they had in an atmosphere. Many of them had never been on a moon before they signed up for the Army and got shipped to Triton. None of them particularly liked the moon. The thought of walking on a planet's surface filled them with dread.

They liked space. It was their native element.

They understood the mechanics of dealing with objects much larger than themselves.

They spoke the language of tethers. Of nets. Of hooks and pulleys and come-alongs.

Though they were speeding through space at a thousand kilometers an hour, they were at rest relative to one another.

One group of specialty squads shot out eight hundred-meter-long tethers, one soldier to another, and the remainder of the squad quickly wove them into nets. Other groups manned platforms that looked sophisticated, but were really nothing more than giant harpoon guns. The remaining platoons readied their grappling hooks and checked their weapons.

It was as simple, and as complicated, as any pirate boarding would ever be.

None of this had ever been tried before in combat.

Within half a minute, they were upon the clouds of attacking Sciaticas. Within seconds they were inside the battle group.

Harpoons fired, fixed themselves to enemy ships. The opposite ends of the tethers attached to them were clipped to the newly woven nets. The ships tried to move off, but were held fast, two billiard balls attached by a rubber band. These were no ordinary tethers. They were made of the same material as the Met itself. As with a rubber band, the harder the ships pulled, the more strongly the elastic responded.

Nets were suspended between two, three, or four attack ships from a harpoon in the hull of each ship. As the ships moved away, relative to one another, the nets were pulled taut.

Behind the harpooners and the net squads, the infantry screamed in—and directly into the nets. As they had a hundred times in practice, the soldiers found a purchase, clipped in.

It was as if a sticky glue full of red ants had suddenly materialized about the squadrons of DIED fighter ships.

Wasting no time, every soldier fired his or her grappling hook at the hull of an attacker. Most hooks found no purchase, but when one did, the entire platoon swarmed up, reeling themselves along with special ascenders attached to the grappling hook cable.

It didn't quite work like a charm, however. Some harpoons missed. Some nets failed to deploy. And many soldiers—over a thousand—missed being netted at all.

They shot ever outward from Cloudship Austen. Unfortunately, because of an accident of alignment with the DIED attackers, she had catapulted them out toward Neptune itself. The lost soldiers could use their maneuvering thrusters to slow themselves a pittance, but they were going far too fast to self-arrest. Within hours, they would plunge into the atmosphere and die. That is, unless they were rescued by victorious Federal forces. Even then, the likelihood was that not everyone would get picked up in time.

Each soldier had been briefed. Each knew in his or her head what might go wrong.

And now it had. It wasn't an intellectual possibility anymore. Their fates were completely in the hands of their brothers and sisters in arms. All they could do was look behind themselves and hope for the best.

They were lost in space.

CHAPTER SIXTEEN

NEPTUNE SYSTEM
E-STANDARD 18:57, THURSDAY, APRIL 3, 3017
CLOUDSHIP AUSTEN

Austen turned her attention to the two destroyers, which she now knew were the *Aguilla* and the *Mediumrare*. She'd gotten the biologicals out of her system, and had new options for both defense and offense.

First, she reconfigured the profile she was exposing to the two ships. Then she energized vast sections of the ship that she could not use before because of the human bodies present.

Cloudships might seem to be ponderous, galaxy-shaped masses, but they were also quite nimble when it came down to it. And quite precise. The basic element of cloudship operation was, after all, as tiny as could be.

It was called quantum fluctuation, and the action it produced was known as the Casimir effect. The principle was ancient—discovered and named in the twentieth century:

Two mirrors a very short distance apart and facing one another in a vacuum will move *toward* one another of their own accord. This occurs because there is greater pressure on one side of the mirrors than the other—even though the mirrors are in a complete vacuum.

Where does this pressure come from? There is literally nothing on both sides of the mirrors.

Virtual particles. According to quantum theory, space isn't a continuum; it's a foaming broth. Particles of every sort—in pair-antipair combination—are continuously being generated and annihilated. Everywhere. All the time.

Empty space can be polarized, and you can make a particle out of nothing.

You do it with the tiny mirrors made possible by the grist. Space is a string on a guitar. Pluck the string. Normal space is a very long string and its "vibration" corresponds to the lowest energy state there can be. Now fret the string. You play a different tone. When you fret a string, you exclude certain vibrations. This is how a guitar string produces different notes, and how, in a sense, it *contains* all notes.

You can "fret" empty space. How? With those tiny mirrors. Particles are not actually particles, after all, but wave-particle entities. Wavicles, if you like. You can now play different tones—different wavicles—depending on the distance between those mirrors. You can play a photon, for instance, if you want to shine a light on something.

Or you can play an antiproton, if you want to annihilate ordinary matter utterly.

Put these antimatter wavicles in contact with matter, and you have a propulsion system more potent than many thousands of nuclear reactors. Shoot them into space, and you have a weapon of awesome, terrifying power.

A cloudship can enact this process anywhere on the ship where there is grist. There are no engine rooms. There are no guns or cannon. It is like blinking an eye or moving a finger for the cloudship. If you are watching from space, it appears as if a bolt of raw energy has erupted from the ship's surface (provided, of course, that there is something along the bolt's path that the energy interacts with to become visible). It is like watching lightning leaping from a storm cloud.

But lightning with an intelligence behind it.

A fully energized cloudship is a magnificent sight to behold.

Unless the cloudship is aiming at you.

Austen fired full bore on the *Aguilla*. Met ships had defenses against antiparticle beams, of course—the chief of these being the isotropic coating each ship possessed. But there was only so much the DIED ships could handle. Austen, fully energized, brought the firepower of at least ten Met destroyers to bear. She concentrated on the rotating tines at the forward end of the DIED ship, where the command and control structures maintained centrifugal gravity for the naval officers. In many ways, a large DIED ship resembled a kilometer-sized pitchfork spinning along its handle's long axis.

The blast sheared off one of the *Aguilla*'s tines. The spin continued for several revolutions before the ship's systems could shut it down, however. The sudden change in angular momentum, combined with the thrust from its rear engines, set the DIED ship into the wicked spin, like a wobbly top.

The *Mediumrare* moved quickly away, its captain evidently frightened out of his socks. Austen chuckled to herself (a resounding bassy boom, had there been ears to hear it within her interior) and ignored the healthy ship. She zeroed in on the crippled *Aguilla*.

The other ship attempted to fire back, but it had no chance. Its random bolts dissipated into space. Several hit Austen, but she was not centrally constructed, and a shot or two would never take her out. Austen spread herself thin and arched over the crippled ship, like an amoeba preparing to engulf a bacterium. Or a hand encircling a bug, preparing to squeeze.

Both ships were still in orbit around Neptune. She estimated the moment when the planet would be directly between her and the Federal troops she had deployed from her hull to deal with the Sciaticas.

The planet moved into a shielding alignment.

She squeezed. Not with mechanical pressure, but with energy. She squeezed hard.

The *Aguilla*'s isotropic coating stood no chance against such a blast. Antiparticle met particle and transformed one another into pure energy. When it was all over, there wasn't a piece of the *Aguilla* left that was larger than a silver atom.

The blast flung Austen outward into space, as she'd planned, and away from the planet. She had hardened the surface behind her "skin" to withstand the explosion as best she could. Still, she took damage. A goodly chunk of her right spiral arm was blown away—someday to accrete and join Neptune's ring, perhaps. She couldn't worry about that now. As quickly as she could, she recovered herself and scanned for the *Mediumrare*.

It was nowhere in sight. But there was another of the DIED ships.

The demolition specialty ship. The *Martian Dawn*. Directly behind it was Cloudship Twain, furiously concentrating fire upon its tail. At that angle, the fire was engulfed by the engine exhaust of the DIED ship and had little effect.

The *Martian Dawn* was headed directly for the Mill.

CHAPTER SEVENTEEN

PLUTO SYSTEM
E-STANDARD 07:05, WEDNESDAY, APRIL 9, 3017
FEDERAL FLAGSHIP *BOOMERANG*

The *Boomerang* and Cloudship Tacitus were doing it—they were holding five destroyers and a carrier at bay. Of course it helped that the entire surface batteries of both Pluto and Charon seemed to have taken a schizophrenic turn and were firing on *everybody* who came within range.

Sherman had been dipping in and out of this fire zone depending on how threatened he was at any given moment. Tacitus was staying well clear of the ground weaponry, but Sherman's maneuvering was keeping the cloudship and the remaining troops aboard him intact. So long as he braved the antiship flak from Pluto, he could emerge at any given location in the orbit to challenge attackers of the cloudship.

They were completely surrounded. The carrier, which had dominated the local system for the past two e-years, was now joined by seven other DIED destroyers diverted from the attack on Neptune. The local command (Sherman assumed it was still Kang Blanket, a general who had, years before, passed Sherman up in his rise up the ranks) was playing for time.

They figure they've got me cornered, Sherman thought, and they don't want to risk me slipping away if they try an all-out assault. Instead, a group of four or five ships was swooping in, while the remainder stayed a good hundred thousand kilometers out to serve containment duty.

Sherman wondered how things were going at Neptune. The merci blocking was still in effect, and he could not communicate with Theory. But Sherman wasn't particularly worried in that regard. There was no one he would rather have trusted the system with than his former adjutant.

Another group of attack ships headed toward Tacitus. This time the group was four . . . no, five strong. Two of the ships had deployed their contingent of Sciatica small attack craft. Good riddance. These could have little effect on the *Boomerang*, and they would be decimated quickly if they swooped in too close to the planetary defenses.

No, it was the big ships Sherman was concerned with.

The DIED ships were three and two strong, approaching on two separate tangents. Some quick calculation from Sherman's astrometric officer predicted that the group that was three strong would arrive first. These Sherman would let Tacitus take on directly. He would concentrate on the two-ship group, which his bridge-op chief informed him were the *Calcio* and the *Rewire*.

A wave of Sciatica craft arrived first, and Tacitus blasted away at them as if he were zapping flies. One by one, they either sizzled or exploded. The unlucky ones dodged his fire only to be caught by a barrage from the planetary surface. Then the big ships arrived, and Tacitus concentrated his fire on those three targets.

In the meantime, the *Boomerang* made a manic dive under Tactitus's bulk, and through the kill zone of Pluto. The ship took ground fire, but, once again, avoided any crippling damage. Sherman emerged, guns blazing, on an intercept course with the other approaching DIED attackers.

During his swoop underneath the cloudship, Sherman had deployed a scoop and gathered (with Tacitus's permission) some of the accreted matter from the cloudship's belly. It consisted mainly of ice and silicate masses, with a few heavy metal meteors thrown in for flavor. After firing his antimatter salvo at his DIED targets, Sherman catapulted the gathered detritus in their direction as well. He swung into a hard parabolic curve back toward the cover of the cloudship. His slingshotted rocks careened outward at great speed. One of the attackers managed to take evasive maneuvers and dodge, but the other caught the rocky projectiles broadside. There was a satisfactory explosive venting from the cruiser's hull.

The breach could be sealed, but it would take some time, and would remove the *Calcio* from immediate action. Sherman turned his attention to the undamaged ship. Theoretically, the *Boomerang* and this ship were exact matches. But since its capture, the *Boomerang* had undergone a series of upgrades. Its grist matrix, in particular, was far more sophisticated, thanks to the ministrations of Gerardo Funk and the Forward Lab on Triton.

The ship had a full complement of free converts manning the navigation and control systems. Because of this, she was sleeker and faster than her counterpart. At least Sherman hoped so.

"Time for more cat and mouse, Chief," Sherman said to his bridge-op. "Think we can fool them again?"

"Not a problem, sir," the chief answered. He turned to the ensign at the helm. She was a free convert, and thus a woman who only existed in the virtual portion of the bridge. "In and out, Helm," said the chief bridge-op. "And up and down, and around and around."

"Aye, aye, Chief," the helm replied. "And, General," she said to Sherman. "Recommend that you hang on to your skin and bones, sir."

CHAPTER EIGHTEEN

PLUTO SYSTEM
E-STANDARD 15:33, WEDNESDAY, APRIL 9, 3017
CHARON

Pluto. Of all places—Pluto! He'd overshot by a hundred million miles. And now, instead of meeting the fremden in pitched battle, as everyone in his platoon had expected, Leo Sherman was racing downward toward Charon in a badly damaged Sciatica that the pilot was attempting to steer into a controlled crash on the surface. At the moment, it didn't look like the "controlled" part of that equation was going to work out.

Leo's platoon were strapped into the back of the little craft. They were supposed to be a boarding party on one of the Federal ships—that is, after the ship had been subdued or otherwise taken out of commission.

That had not happened.

Instead, the DIED occupation's own fortifications were turning against them. Against everyone, it seemed. But that distinction didn't matter much when you were staring down the barrel of an antimatter cannon.

A bolt of energy from below had blown through their craft's isotropic coating and turned the pellicle of the ship into so much fried grist. All control structures, except for one set of attitude rockets, had been lost, and gravity had finished off what the ship's trajectory had started: They were now in a nosedive toward Charon's sunward side. The only hope was to use one of the attitude rockets to thrust feebly against the fall and slow them down enough to survive the inevitable smack into the moon's surface.

The rockets had little noticeable effect, and the Sciatica came in hard. Leo tried to prepare himself for the impact, but he knew it was useless.

It was. He was staring down the fuselage of the craft at the cockpit door. This door seemed to come toward him.

But actually the front end is crumpling, Leo thought.

He was surprised at how lucid his conclusion was. Then the door hit him full in the face—and he was hanging on to it, like a surfer caught in a gigantic wipeout, but still clinging to his board. Leo had surfed on Earth—but only in the Atlantic. This had to be more like those killer Pacific waves that he'd heard about but never seen.

Hang on.

He was in a maelstrom of shredded metal. A twisting swirl, angled in a parabola over the surface of the moon. Absolute silence. Vacuum! A moment of panic before he remembered that his modified body was space-adapted.

A scraping slap against Charon's surface, clawing for purchase, but his momentum carrying him farther, banging him up more. The door still with him. Another, harder slap. The door banging him in the head.

Darkness.

Awaking to groggy silence.

Then a crackling—as of a lake of ice, shattering.

How can I hear this? There's no atmosphere here.

The sound was inside him, in his inner ear. Something was happening to his body. He raised a hand in the wan light. It was seething, as if it were covered with ants.

Grist. Grist-mil. Oh shit.

But something inside him wouldn't let him succumb. He'd been rebuilt from the ground up, after all. He'd been remade by the best grist engineers and programmers in the Met. Whatever they put into his pellicle was stronger even than this military grist.

Leo sat up. Blood rushed from his head, and he almost passed out again. Guess that wonder-grist doesn't solve every problem, he thought. He pushed himself up again more slowly. All seemed well. He rolled over onto his hands and knees, and, after a moment, managed to stand up.

He was on godforsaken Charon, all right. Dirty corn ice under his feet. A webwork of more dense material woven through the ice, giving the ground a checkerboard appearance. Grist. To his right and left, structures brisling with guns and antennas. Behind him the crumpled hulk of the Sciatica.

Bodies strewn about.

Where was his sergeant? Leo took a few shuffling steps. Not much gravity in these parts. Almost anywhere else, and he'd have crumpled back to the ground; here he stayed up. Leo hadn't learned the names of his platoon. Every member was new except for his sergeant, Dory Folsom. Now they were all dead. Once again, the war had gone through his entire platoon and he was the only one left.

But Dory wasn't among the bodies, so far as he could tell. Maybe she was back in the wreckage of the Sciatica. Leo started following the debris trail back toward the crashed ship.

"Halt!"

What the hell? No sound could carry through this atmosphere—or lack thereof. Then he remembered.

Oh shit, it's in my head again. On the merci.

"Halt!"

"I'm halting," Leo replied through the merci. He tried to freeze into place, but he teetered a bit. He was still shaky from—well, from everything.

Two forms emerged from behind a walled bunker. One of them was pointing a wrist rocket at Leo's torso.

"Deactivate your weapons!" Leo presumed it was the guy with the wrist rocket doing the talking. "Do it now!"

"I couldn't hit the ground if you point me down, the shape I'm in at the moment," said Leo. But he keyed up his weaponry override and stood down. His own rocketry weapons reencased themselves at his wrists and elbows. The bullets fell from his projectile clip, and the energy readings for his antimatter rifling lowered. He hoped the others had the ability to read the drop and understand what it meant. "I'm fully powered down," he told them.

"Hold out your hands." The soldier without the rocket weapon approached him. Leo did as he was told. The soldier clipped a set of containment manacles over Leo's wrists. He felt the grist from the manacles swarming over his pellicle. But it stopped skin deep as soon as his Aschenbach persona identified himself by DNA and serial number.

Leo took a longer look at his captors. One was a short dark-completed woman, about Leo's height. She was squat, but muscular. The other was a black man. You could never tell for certain with the fully space-adapted, but he looked to be in his early twenties.

He was wearing the black and steel blue of the Federal Army. Leo glanced at the man's shoulder insignia.

Sergeant. Third Sky and Light Brigade.

Thank God.

"By the way," Leo said, "I surrender."

"Good," the man replied. "Otherwise, we'd have to blow your fucking head off." He motioned over at the other soldier. "We still might, so don't get any ideas."

"Don't worry," Leo said. "I've been trying to get taken prisoner for over a year now."

"Glad to oblige. But we're not off this fucking rock yet," said the other. He motioned toward the bleak horizon. "Now march, soldier."

CHAPTER NINETEEN

PLUTO SYSTEM
E-STANDARD 09:12, THURSDAY, APRIL 10, 3017
DIED FLAGSHIP *STREICHHOLTZER*

General Kang Blanket had decided that he was facing none other than Sherman himself. The Old Crow was out here at Pluto, and very likely inside the stolen ship that had once been the *Jihad*.

Sherman was tantalizing him, of that there was no doubt. But soon he would have the man. Sherman had made an error—an understandable error, but a mistake nonetheless. He'd remained in orbit for three e-days, trying to get his soldiers off the surface of Pluto and Charon. But doing so, he'd boxed himself in.

Something had gone horribly wrong down there—what, Blanket did not know. It had to be some kind of transmutational grist interaction. Both bodies' surfaces were, for the most part, now inaccessible on the merci. There were a couple of gateways to the local virtuality still functioning, but the only information that was emerging was a mishmash of odd images and text statements. Blanket had his code specialists on it, but nobody had been able to crack the lockout and get back in.

He could deal with reestablishing control of the local grist after he defeated Sherman. That time was not far off. Despite the irritating way the fremden commander was using cloudship and converted DIED cruiser as a sort of shield and spear, Blanket had seven ships surrounding his foe.

There would be no exit.

CHAPTER TWENTY

NEPTUNE SYSTEM
E-STANDARD 19:44, THURSDAY, APRIL 3, 3017
ALLSKY'S COMPANY B

The fight for the Sciatica attack ships was hard and bloody work for Company B. Cutting through the hulls took longer than expected, and alerted defenders inside as to exactly where the incursion would take place. There was withering fire concentrated on the troops when they burst in.

But it wasn't enough to stop them. The attack ships had eight to ten crew aboard. The fremden forces outnumbered them in every instance. There were plenty more DIED infantry in the holds of the destroyers, but they had not been deployed. The Sciatica crews faced an even greater problem, however: Half of them were not space-adapted. As soon as their hulls were breached and their atmospheres drained, they were literally dead meat.

Still, those that could fought bravely. More were killed than were captured. At one point, it seemed as if they got a surge of resolve all at once, and they fought back en masse, almost overwhelming the larger numbers of their opponents. This was to happen more than once throughout the course of the war, and became known as the "Glory Surge" to the Federal forces.

Once the infantry was in control of the attack ships, they quickly sent a free-convert specialty team into the grist of the ships. Within moments these robust, fully sentient soldiers overcame the ship's internal security and took over all systems. The little semisentient artificial intelligences that ran the vessels stood no chance against full free-convert v-hackers.

Cleanup squads disengaged the harpoons, nets, and sticky tethers at a blinding speed—most of the tethers were encoded with an automatic disintegration routine that allowed them quickly to break down to constituent particles.

Four and a half hours had passed since they had been catapulted out by Cloudship Austen.

As one, the victorious fremden turned their captured ships toward the planet minesweeper that stood between them and Planet Neptune.

Attacking and destroying the *Debeh-Li-Zini* was necessary. The *Debeh-Li-Zini* stood between the victorious Federals and their lost comrades.

Company B would take out the *Debeh-Li-Zini*.

And only then they would go after those who had missed the net and fallen away toward Neptune. Already it was clear that many of their mates would keep falling. Time and gravity were not on their side.

CHAPTER TWENTY-ONE

THE OORTS
LATE SPRING 3017, E-STANDARD
FEDERAL NAVAL ACADEMY

From

THE BORASCA

A Memoir

BY LEBEDEV, WING COMMANDER, LEFT FRONT

All Naval Academy students, men and women, have the rank of "spacer," which is equivalent to an enlisted rank between warrant officer and ensign. Freshmen—and all in my first class necessarily were such—are called plebes. The student body is known as the Battalion of Spacers, or simply the battalion. We call the Federal Navy the Fleet.

The academy battalion is divided into six companies. The company command structure is headed by an outstanding spacer who is designated company commander. My fellow instructors and I determined this individual during our "Plebe Summer" exercise. In subsequent e-years, with different class levels enrolled, the task was awarded to a likely senior (although we don't call them seniors, but spacers first class). Overseeing all company activity is the Commandant of Spacers—me—an active duty Navy officer of captain's rank or above. I took the rank of admiral, since I was also the founder of the Navy itself. Working for the commandant, commissioned naval officers are assigned as company and battalion officers. When we started, all of these were volunteers who had served in some long-term military capacity in the past. There were seven of us: Cloudships Tolstoy, his sons Pushkin, Lermontov, and Gogol (the remainder of the Tolstoy boys were young enough to be in the class itself), Naipaul, Masereel, and Ortega y Gasset. For a couple of us, "long-term" was stretching the truth a bit. Nonetheless, we soldiered on and did what we could.

We instructors concentrated on the three basics of strategy and tactics: firepower, scouting, and command and control. The youngsters all started out quite impressed with their own firepower, of course. It was necessary to leaven this belief with a little reality. One of our first exercises was a multi-e-day fox-and-hound venture out toward Alpha Centauri along the Dark Matter Road. I used old Tolstoy, the keeper of the hidden cloudship graveyard, as the fox, and sent the class after him with the instruction that they had full permission to fire upon him if they could catch him—or stop him from reaching his goal, a beacon placed two million miles out-ways, south by southwest ascending.

Needless to say, no shot was fired. Not only did Tolstoy elude them along the way, he disguised himself as a meteor shower and took the beacon while a full contingent of seven guarded it. As he was making his escape, Tolstoy raked four of them with fire. This raised some nasty blisters along the unfortunate ones' shiny coats, but did no lasting damage.

There were two standouts among my spacers, and they loathed one another. One was the youngest son of Tolstoy. His name was Stone, and, as his name would indicate, he was a hard young man in every way, with a cold, imperial attitude. He went after every task with a merciless efficiency. He was the king of close-order drill, and, when he was drill captain, had been known to fire a stinging blast of e-m radiation at those who didn't live up to his lofty standards. He was, however, intensely loyal to his small group of friends. Unfortunately, he treated everyone else as near pariahs.

Stone's attitude was not entirely of his own choosing. He'd been raised in a graveyard, after all, and taught to tend scrupulously to the monuments and memorials we cloudships set in place for our kind. As the youngest of thirteen sons, Stone was given all of the tasks the other boys and men did not want to do, but, at the same time, held to the yard-master, Tolstoy's, unyieldingly high expectations. The Tolstoy clan was a stern bunch. Had I not known the family for many years, I would have pronounced them a callous lot. But this was outward appearance. They were in fact a tight and loving group—if uniformly taciturn by nature. They got this as much from their mother, Cloudship Samandacole, as from their undertaker father.

My other star spacer could not have been more different. This was Cloudship Sojourner Truth. She was scrappy, as tough as nails, and an inspired improviser in tight situations. She was the daughter of some old friends of Tacitus whom I'd never gotten along with politically—Cloudships Kerouac and Parker. These two had been staunchly against any military action during the Council debates, but I knew it had nothing to do with undue influence from the inner system. They were committed pacifists. They had been so permissive in their upbringing of Sojourner Truth, or "Soje," as she wished to be called, that the only way the poor girl could rebel against them was by volunteering for the Navy.

With her free and easy way, Soje was a natural leader among the midlevel spacers, who looked to her for their attitude but didn't choose to emulate her ceaseless drive to excel. Most of them knew about the long hours of practice and study she put in away from the group, but they didn't hold that against her so long as she continued to make it all look easy when it counted and downplayed any accomplishment with a droll aside or two.

Soje and Stone were in a competition from the first, and, I have to admit, I deliberately exacerbated the situation to get even better performances out of both of them. I was careful to let neither of them know the high regard in which I held them. But this was a school, and one must assign grades. I could not help giving them excellent marks. Each was fixated on the other's ratings, and they continually worked to knock each other from the top spot during our Plebe Summer.

Near the bottom of the heap, at least at the beginning, was Cloudship Schweick. He was a continual cutup and lazybones. Yet there was something I saw in the youngster. His pranks, practical jokes, and excuses were amazingly inventive. I knew that if he ever put the kind of effort he put into those activities into his actual duties as a sailor—well, he would be an admiral of the fleet one day. Much to each participant's dismay, I assigned Stone, Soje, and Schweik to the same attack triad—the three-ship grouping that formed the building block of all of our tactical maneuvering. In the Federal Navy, the triad was your unit—the people on whom you depended for survival.

Giving Stone and Soge Schweik to look after also served the purpose of holding those two go-getters back a bit, and allowing the other ships to feel as if they were still in competition to be the best (when, of course, they didn't stand a chance). The triad was official known as Plebe Spacer Unit 5-N, but everyone called them Triple S. Schweik, merely to spite his two comrades, I'm sure, got better and better at his duties. By the end of Plebe Summer, it was obvious that, in Triple S, we had found three of the six leaders for our battalion companies when the actual Navy was formed, and battle was joined.

Excerpt from
The Journal of Spacer First Class Sojourner Truth

What is Lebedev thinking? Okay, I have to admit I misjudged him a bit at the outset. He was just trying to make us understand how tough a war could be. There's no way he could simulate a war, so he gave us the drill, and all that bullshit. Okay. I get it now.

But oh man, how I loathe the guys in my triad! I'm stuck between a merry fool and a control-freak psychopath. I mean, both of them have a certain amount of ability and smarts, but the way they chose to employ it—they are a couple of creeps, if you ask me.

Take the other day when we were on maneuvers about twenty thousand klicks down the Road. The drill instructor—it was Gogol that day—had us doing dives at some godforsaken chunk of dark matter, with each of us taking turns at point. The object was to whisk away some e-m hover marker before the beacon alerts "surface defenses"—which, in this case, was a clunky old railgun from premillennial times.

So I go about it the right way: I come in on a tangent and use the back of the asteroid for cover. I send the goony boys in on wider parabolas with apexes just outside of the railgun's range.

But do they follow instructions? Of course not. Ice Man Stone decides that my tactics are suspect, and he thinks he'll just go after the beacon himself after I fuck up. So instead of drawing fire and blasting off into space while I come in, he pulls up to a full stop and turns to thrust back toward the beacon—fully expecting me to miss it, and fully expecting to save the day with his own sorry ass.

The other goony boy dips *into* the railgun's range, and takes a hit just for the hell of it. Says he wanted to know what a butterfly kiss felt like. When the DI explained to him that, in a real situation, he would have been fucking with an antimatter Auger cannon, he laughs and explains to us all that it wasn't an antimatter cannon, now was it?

No, jerkwad. That's why you're still alive, I tell him.

So what's the big deal with goofing off a little? he says.

I hate them both.

I got the beacon, of course. And so did the goony boys when their turns came. I have to admit that I pulled a couple of unhelpful stunts when it came their turn for point.

Hey—who can blame me? I'm dealing with a couple of imbeciles here.

After three e-months of all the hell I could dream up to put my charges through, I called an end to Plebe Summer and began academy classes proper. With the help of Cloudship Michelangelo, I created a virtual naval academy on our cloudship-restricted merci. My classrooms were austere workspaces, but the institutional campus itself was lushly designed, with lots of anachronistic motifs lifted from the great seafaring nation's military academies on old Earth. The classes took place on the decks of virtual oceangoing ships—all of them historical re-creations. Michelangelo, a master merci designer, even threw in an occasional squall now and again, and more than one spacer faced a very real bout of seasickness as a result.

We taught them everything we knew about the capabilities of cloudships and the capabilities of DIED forces. We studied strategy and tactics. Much of this I and my instructors had to create fresh. We solicited the input of every trustworthy military mind in the Republic, but the truth was there had never been a major naval battle fought in space in the history of humankind. I never let my students forget that fact, either, and most of our tactical preparation was concentrated on learning how to react in unforeseen conditions.

We concluded every day with an hour of drill and, at long last, target practice. The staff and I were not merely preparing minds for future learning, we were, instead, about to fling these youngsters directly into harm's way, and none of us forgot it. Of course, we would likely be going into harm's way ourselves. In the end, we were all learning to-

gether, and none of us had any real idea of what we were getting ourselves into. But it had to be done, and we did it.

One e-year later, and we had made warriors out of brats. They were
untested, true, but no longer did I, or any of my fellow instructors,
have any doubt that they would acquit themselves well. When we inducted our second class, we also had student officers to help out with
our second Plebe Summer. I was amused when our second e-year students expressed their total dismay and disgust with their plebes.

None of these kids were officer material! They were hopeless idiots—spoiled and pampered by coddling parents! What were we *thinking* when we admitted them in the first place?

I agreed completely with my dismayed charges.

"I know they're a sorry lot," I told them. "You'll just have to do what
you can with them. They're all we've got."

I had thought I was a hard taskmaster during the previous Plebe
Summer, but my newly promoted spacers made their own hell month
seem like a pleasant jaunt among the asteroids when compared with
what they put this later class of plebes through.

Everyone followed the developments sunward with razor-sharp interest. Perhaps never before in our history had cloudships paid such attention to the doings of the planet-bound. Another Jovian moon fell to
DIED attackers, and Cloudship Sandburg was killed in the conflict—
the first casualty among us cloudships. We decided to name the main
quad of our virtual academy campus after him.

It was becoming clear by the middle of our second Plebe Summer,
3015, that a new attack on Neptune was imminent. Ships and soldiers
were congregating in the Saturn system. Pluto had become a lockbox,
controlled by a coating of military grist that had seemingly subsumed
the native commercial variety by sheer weight and profligacy in multi-
plying itself.

When the call came from General Sherman to ready ourselves for
immediate action, it was not a surprise to teachers or students. What's
more, we were in a pretty good state—Plebe Summer had just ended.
We had a class of spacers who had just finished a year of training, and
had now spent three e-months providing actual leadership to the incoming plebes. Companies were set, chains of command established,
and the spacers were familiar with one another.

We could have been in a far worse fix when it came time for fighting.

Excerpt from
The Journal of Spacer First Class Stone

I know that I have complained often about my original class-
mates in the past, and I continue to believe that there is much
room for improvement in their performances. Nevertheless, I
have to say that they have come a long way over the past year. I
have developed what I can only call a grudging respect for the
populist Sojourner Truth. I even have to admit that something
I believed impossible—the evolution of the slack-off trickster
Schweik into a first rate naval officer . . .

 . . . has occurred.

Excerpt from
The Journal of Spacer First Class Sojourner Truth

Something awful has happened. I actually like the Dildo and
the Nimno. In fact, I'm going to have to start calling them by
their real names. Stone, Schweik, and I not only did some
amazing things and made some incredible progress this past
e-year, they stuck by me in hard times, they helped me when I
was down. They even took a couple of lumps for me from the
instructors.

 Oh, shit. Have to admit it.

 I couldn't have made it without them.

Excerpt from
The Journal of Spacer First Class Schweik

Well. So. I used all my prime Fuck-Up. Every last smidgen of
it. And I still made it through the first year.

 And now I look at these pathetic incoming plebes and all I
can think is—

 I used to be just like them.

 Oh. My. God.

CHAPTER TWENTY-TWO

PLUTO SYSTEM
E-STANDARD 12:12, APRIL 10, 3017

Even though he had Sherman boxed in and near defeat, Blanket was an aggressive man at heart, and he didn't enjoy biding his time. Besides, Blanket was working for a commander who was even more impatient than he. Amés would want to see progress very soon. Three weeks was too long for a standoff. Sherman was beginning to make Blanket feel a trifle ridiculous. Why couldn't he finally defeat the man? Blanket considered another flushing run at the fremden forces.

What luck that he'd been able to talk Haysay into sending the five extra ships to Pluto.

I'm going to have to revise my opinion of Haysay, Blanket thought. He may be slow as molasses, but he's not the bumbler I took him for.

One of those ships, the *Calcio*, had taken damage from a broadside of rocks from the *Boomerang*. There were several thousand casualties as well. But the breach was sealed, and the ship had been brought back into service immediately in a backup role. It would take several e-weeks of more extensive repairs before Blanket could use it for direct assault.

Be that as it may, Sherman and his cloudship companion were outgunned. Although the planet and moon had, unaccountably, turned against friend and foe alike, the system minefields were entirely under

Met command. Moving minefields would take e-days, but it could be accomplished. Each mine had a small degree of impulse mobility built in. Blanket had already begun the process of moving his mines from the concentrated clumps that he'd dispersed in arrays around the entire planetary system. He was bringing them in toward the moon and planet ellipse to form an ever-tightening net.

"Let's run another assault," Blanket told the captain of the *Streichholtzer*, Madelaine Dekbat. "This time no separation, I think. All ships together, all guns forward."

"Yes, sir," Dekbat replied. "All for one and one for all." She turned and issued orders to her own helm, and relayed the instructions to the other ships in the group.

While many DIED commanders had problems with their immediate underlings, Blanket had always gotten along with Dekbat. It helped that the woman wanted nothing more than to run a carrier for the rest of her career. She'd turned down a rear admiralty in order to avoid being reassigned from the *Streichholtzer*. Blanket had heard that Dekbat came from a good (meaning extremely rich) family on Mercury, and was considered a sort of black sheep by them.

Blanket himself was from Vas stock. His family was as plebian and middle-class as could be. His own ambition had been a hot coal within him since he was young.

"All ships online now, sir," Dekbat reported. "We're ready to move on your word."

Blanket scowled his best commander's smile and prepared to issue the attack order. This time he would get his kill. He was sure of it.

"Very well—"

Something red in Blanket's peripheral vision. He blinked. It was still there. Not his internal systems. It was a physical light, there on the bridge.

And then Blanket heard a very physically loud Klaxon.

"Report, Captain!"

Dekbat relayed the command directly to her subordinate. "Report, Nav!"

"Ma'am, I've got two . . . three . . . four . . . several anomalies at extreme range. Approaching rapidly." The young lieutenant commander spoke with a shaky voice. "Make that nineteen anomalies. Twenty. Twenty confirmed. Tactics estimates deliberate propulsion."

"Give me a vector, Nav."

"Yes, ma'am," the nav officer replied. "All out-system and inward bound. All moving in the same direction. All vectored on . . . *us*. On Pluto, ma'am."

"Speed?"

"One hundred ten thousand kilometers per hour," said the nav officer. "They'll be here in 12.4 hours, ma'am."

Blanket thought through the situation quickly. This was almost certainly a human-made phenomenon. And, coming from the Oorts, that meant that the cloudships were involved. But it was a given that the so-called Constitutional Congress out there was caught up in a contentious deadlock. Not all the cloudships were fremden sympathizers. Not by a long shot. In fact, Blanket had been receiving supersecret intel from members of that congress as to just what a state of disarray they were in. Still, as his sources had informed him, there was the possibility of a small faction going their own way and causing trouble.

"Are those comets?" Blanket said. "The damn Oort dwellers may have found a way to divert a field of them in our direction."

"No, General," said Dekbat. She was looking over the nav officer's shoulder, examining the readouts herself. "Too big for that. *Way* too big."

"What then?"

"Configurations consistent with cloudships, sir."

"Cloudships!" Blanket felt his face go flush. His voice sounded very loud in his own ears. "That's not possible."

"Tactics confirms, sir," Dekbat said, her voice now as shaky as her young navigation officer's had been. "Twenty cloudships heading our way."

A massive intelligence breakdown. That was the only explanation.

Twenty.

How could this have gone undetected by the watchers in the Oorts? How could such a deployment have gotten past the Congress—where Amés had the next best thing to veto power using the minority faction he controlled.

Something had gone terribly wrong.

"General?"

"What?"

Twenty cloudships.

"General, the local group is powered up. They're awaiting your command."

There were theoretically three solutions. Stay and fight to the death. Retreat at full speed. Blanket immediately rejected both of them. The first would serve no purpose other than getting them all killed. The second was . . . not in his nature. There was also the distinct possibility that this was all some sort of ruse.

It had to be some sort of ruse.

Yet Blanket's gut told him that it was not.

Nevertheless, only one option open. Fall back. A fighting withdrawal from the system. *His* system, goddamn it! Retreat was retreat!

Use your reason. Survive. Live to conquer again. Amés trusted him. He was not some politically necessary appointment like Haysay. Blanket had risen through the ranks on ability and ability alone. Amés had recognized that. Amés would not remove him from command.

Probably.

It didn't matter. Given who he was, Blanket had only one choice. As he had made countless others, he made this one.

"Pull back," Blanket said. "All ships are ordered to take cover in the mines."

CHAPTER TWENTY-THREE

PLUTO SYSTEM
E-STANDARD 04:53, APRIL 13, 3017

Sherman breathed a sigh of relief. So far the plan had worked—with a few snags. The orbits of Pluto and Charon were now in Federal hands. The surfaces were another matter entirely. His Virtual Extraction Corps had established some beachheads down there. They had volunteered for what seemed like a suicide mission to rescue the Federal paratroopers from the grip of the renegade surface grist, and they had succeeded.

Many of the VEs, over half, had been lost to the murderous grist below—wiped from existence as completely as any erased computer program might be. But Philately and her corps had succeeded in breaking many of the biological soldiers free from the grip of the surface. There was no doubt that they had saved a good portion of the Third Sky and Light's Company C.

Now those soldiers could be recovered. The Met forces had pulled away.

No doubt Blanket got wind of what was coming from the Oorts, Sherman thought. Blanket would run, but he wouldn't run far. Sherman had known and admired the man at West Point. What Blanket didn't know was that Sherman had issued orders for fifteen of those approaching cloudships to change course. Only five would be decelerating into Plutonian orbit. The others would head straight for Neptune.

The merci was jammed in that direction. Neptune was cut off, as it had been before, and Sherman had no way of knowing what was happening back in his home system. This was Colonel Theory's first big test as a theater commander. Sherman had bedrock faith in his subordinate. He'd based his entire strategy around Theory's ability to take command at Neptune. Yet other seemingly staunch officers had let Sherman down before. You never could tell about a soldier until he or she was tested in battle. It wasn't even a matter of courage most of the time. It was merely a matter of doing one's job to the fullest. Many people—LAP, simple biological aspect, or free convert—simply didn't have follow-through built into their makeup.

Sherman was betting that Theory was one of the other kind.

It was out of his hands now, in any case. And the new Federal Navy was on its way to Neptune! What an incredible relief it was to be able to think the thought, to say the words.

"Federal Navy," Sherman muttered to himself.

"What's that, sir?" said the Ops-Chief.

"Nothing, Chief," Sherman replied. "How are the uplinks and evacuations coming?"

"We're bringing in the last batch now," said the chief. "Looks like we got that Neiderer. The one who took out the rip tether back on Triton."

"I'll be damned," said Sherman. "The man gets into some awful deep shit to keep surviving so well."

"That he does, sir." The chief put a hand to his ear. "All right, all right," he said, speaking to someone who was communicating with him through the knit. "I'll pass it along to intel."

Sherman looked at his chief expectantly. "Anything I should know about?"

"I don't think so, sir," the man replied. "We've brought up a number of prisoners. One of them is making an odd claim, and he's a good enough bullshit artist to have the soldiers who brought him in believing in him."

"Who captured him?"

The chief blinked his eyes, consulting records in his peripheral vision. "Why, it was the Neiderer fellow, sir. He's a sergeant these days."

"And Neiderer believes whatever information this POW has?" Sherman asked.

"He thinks it bears looking into, sir."

"And what is the information?"

"Uh, I'm not sure how to put this, sir," the chief replied.

"Put it in plain Basis!" Sherman said sharply.

"Yes, sir," replied the chief, chagrined. "Well, it's like this. The prisoner claims to be your son."

"My son is dead," Sherman answered quickly and emphatically.

"No, sir. Your *other* son," said the chief. "He claims to be Leo Sherman."

CHAPTER TWENTY-FOUR

NEPTUNE SYSTEM
E-STANDARD 11:02, APRIL 7, 3017
CLOUDSHIP AUSTEN

"Austen, have you got an angle on that bastard?" Twain spoke to her in a tense voice over the special merci channel cloudships used for inter-ship communications.

"He's moving too fast," said Austen. "I'm headed outward from the planet, not inward. I'll have to reverse course and match velocities."

"Okay," Twain replied. "Looks like she's going to get a shot, god-damn it."

"What do you think she's armed with?"

"Don't know," said Twain. "Nothing good. If I follow her much far-ther, I'm going to get trapped in the well and pulled down into the at-mosphere."

"Don't you do that, Twain!" Austen exclaimed. She knew that the old cloudship was brave enough to sacrifice himself.

"Don't worry about it," Twain answered. "I'd crash into the Mill and kill fifteen thousand souls for nothing."

Austen had momentarily forgotten about Twain's troop contingent. It was just so *unusual* for cloudships to be carrying large numbers of bi-ological humans.

But not unusual anymore, she reflected. There would be a great deal of that sort of thing before this war was over. It gave her a creepy sensation for a moment. To constantly feel like you were full of swarming parasites. And on *purpose*. Yuck.

"Here she goes!" shouted Twain. "She's going to drop her load."

As if on cue, the *Martian Dawn* pulled up from its headlong dive toward middle of the Blue Eye of Neptune, and turned into an arching traverse of the Mill. The DIED ship was, Austen estimated, about a thousand kilometers above the Mill mechanism itself.

They were depth charges of some sort. Depth charges guided by free converts, no doubt. But, according to Met protocols, free converts that could back themselves up only once every two e-years. For some of these free converts, their plunge to destruction would erase everything they had become since their last backup.

The waste of it all, Austen thought. The productivity and innovation the Met was giving up by, in essence, killing these people. It was bad economics. There wasn't anything Austen detested more than bad economics.

This close to the Mill, the *Martian Dawn* was below the minefield defenses. But there were a few carefully placed hover stations that were actually connected by ultrathin cable all the way back to Triton itself. They were modified versions of the weather stations that had been the original charge and raison d'etre for Sherman's Third Sky and Light Brigade. The hover station fired upon the depth charges as they fell, and a good number exploded before they were near enough to do the Mill harm.

But many depth charges got through. Some of them missed. The blades of the Mill, ten kilometers across, were still a very small target on a very large planet.

Some of the charges found that target. They erupted with nuclear fire.

One, two, three, Austen counted. Then a moment later four, five, and six.

The radiation bloomed outward, and she trimmed herself accordingly to keep from being pushed away by the wind.

Below her, the *Martian Dawn* arched upward. Twain had predicted exactly where it would attempt an escape. He was waiting there and blasted it from the heavens like a duck that rose directly in front of a hunter's blind. When Twain was done, there wasn't enough left of the ship to cause even a good shower of contrails as the particles rained down into Neptune's atmosphere.

But the damage was done. Directing her sensors down upon the Mill, Austen could see that one blade was badly pitted and notched, and its tip was blown off. The entire propeller-shaped blade looked like a double leaf that had been chewed on by an army of caterpillars. It was clearly spinning at a fraction of its normal speed.

What's more, there was probably residual grist down there that was continuing to eat away at the Mill's surface.

"One of us needs to get those grist-mil counteragents spread out as soon as possible," Austen said to Twain. "The damage looks to be spreading."

"You do it," Twain replied. "My blood's up, Austen. I want those other ships. I want to blast 'em good."

Austen laughed and transmitted her laugh to Twain. She had an enormous, gooey reservoir of military grist counteragent in her hold, supplied by the amazingly productive Forward Labs on Triton. This goo, dispersed as an aerosol, would face its first test against the really nasty stuff.

But readying the goo suddenly reminded Austen of another problem she'd forgotten about. She chided herself for the omission. But she was so unused to dealing with ordinary system-bound humans. For so long, she'd been a solitary creature of the spaces beyond the planets.

"My soldiers," she called out to Twain.

"Eh, what's that?" replied the old cloudship, already intent on his hunting expedition for the *Mediumrare*.

"My soldiers," said Austen. "Be careful of where you make your kill. They might get caught in the blast. They're such fragile things, after all."

"Thanks for reminding me," said Twain.

Austen couldn't tell if he was being flippant or if, in the thrill of chase, he had also forgotten about all those people.

CHAPTER TWENTY-FIVE

NEPTUNE SYSTEM
E-STANDARD 14:00, THURSDAY, APRIL 3, 3017
FEDERAL ARMY THEATER COMMAND

Theory felt relief the way a free convert does—at a lessening of logical paradoxes within, a mathematical unknotting.

"Give me a report, Major Monitor."

"Twain has disabled the *Mediumrare*, and she's surrendered, sir."

"Good."

"I don't think Twain likes it," Monitor replied. "I think he'd rather have blown her out of the sky."

"He *is* accepting her surrender, isn't he?"

"Of course, sir," Monitor replied flatly. "He's deployed Company A, and they're preparing to board her."

"All right, then," said Theory. "What about Company B?"

"They were too late getting to the scattershots," Monitor said. "The minesweeper put up a fight and delayed them. They did some really brave atmospheric dives with those Sciaticas, but they only managed to pull 394 out in time. I have a count of 2,923 missing and presumed dead from falling planetward."

Theory frowned. Dammit. Only a little more time, and more could have been saved.

"The minesweeper *Debeh-Li-Zini* has also surrendered and been occupied.

"Very well."

"I've got an updated running count of dead and missing in inner-system action. Just a moment." Monitor's blank expression, somehow more poignant now. "Correlating . . . 7,018, sir. *A death rate* of 19 per hour down from 1,800."

"Thank you, Major," said Theory. There would be no point in commenting on the pathos and irony of those counts; it was obvious to even Major Monitor. Yet they were necessary data.

The DIED "fast" force that had gone directly after the Mill was defeated. The Mill had sustained significant damage, but it had not been taken out or even rendered inoperable. Yet.

There was still the small matter of the nine ships and 180,000 soldiers vectoring in on Nereid and Triton even now. The forward edge of that armada had cut its way through, and there was fierce fighting in the skies over Triton. Nothing serious had gotten through the moon's defenses, but a rain of nail shrapnel had fallen on New Miranda.

Those Met battle planners were bastards, but clearly they were smart bastards. Theory had anticipated an attack by dumb weapons, but he had planned for big rocks, not little nails. The lasers and small rockets that normally handled meteors and provided a shield for the city were overwhelmed. Great sheets of nails got through.

But the inner-system battle was now a mop-up operation, and he could concentrate on the main opponent bearing down upon him.

He had momentum. He didn't really understand the feeling—not on a personal level. But he knew it had a huge effect on the troops. They could feel it, and it would give them an edge. So long as they weren't overwhelmed by a hugely superior force.

Which was what Theory feared.

Fear. Now there was an emotion he was familiar with, even as a free convert. But what could one do but face it and get on with things?

CHAPTER TWENTY-SIX

NEPTUNE SYSTEM
E-STANDARD 15:21, THURSDAY, APRIL 3, 3017
DIED FLAGSHIP *AZTEC SACRIFICE*

General C. C. Haysay was astounded. All four ships in the inner planetary system . . . lost. Not a good thing. Not a good thing at all. Bad.

Amés was going to flay him alive.

Got to think.

Think about your pellicle getting peeled back and Amés reaching in to yank out the mollusk meat within.

No. Tactics. Strategy. His ships were splayed all over the outer system like rising welts on a beaten back. Red, bleeding welts that would scar. No amount of grist repair work would hide them. Amés would never let them heal.

Haysay found himself softly whimpering.

"Did you say something, General?" Major Zane's overly solicitous voice was almost unbearable at the moment.

"I did not!" Haysay snapped back.

"Do you have any orders, sir?"

Haysay nodded. "Just a moment," he said. "Shut up and let me think."

"Yes, sir."

Damn Zane and his even-toned responses! Couldn't he appreciate when it was time to panic?

I have to check in with the Director, Haysay thought. There's no other choice in the matter. I have to face my fear and call the man. Communicate the gravity of the situation, but make him see that it *is not my fault!*

Amés won't see that. Will he? No. Maybe. Hell, no! But no choice. No choice. Get control of the situation. All important.

"Full stop, Zane."

"Pardon, sir?"

"Bring the fleet to a full stop."

"But we're already engaged in-system, General."

"Of course, of course," said Haysay. "Already engaged. Already engaged." A cracking whip. Unseen. But felt. Oh, yes, felt deeply and completely. "Pull back the *Mencius* and *Longreach*."

"Sir, those ships are *attacking the fremden*!"

"You have my orders, Major."

The slightest hesitation from Zane. "Yes, sir." He issued the commands.

I will replace you after this, you weasel, thought Haysay. But, at the moment, I need your simpering ass.

"We are moving into siege mode for the moment."

"But the invasion has been planned for years . . ."

"As has a siege, should the initial invasion be rebuffed."

"But those are contingency plans, General. We haven't even gamed them completely, much less audience-tested them on the merci."

Haysay pulled his aspect to its full height—which was considerably over six feet tall. "I will not be argued with any longer, Major."

"Of course, sir. But don't you think you should contact the Director," Zane said in a low, conspiracy-laced voice.

Haysay tried to smile condescendingly, but he could only manage a grimace. "That's exactly why I'm pulling back for the moment," he said. "To allow for consultation."

"Ah, yes, sir," said Zane. "I see, sir. Clever."

Haysay sighed. The man would clearly kiss the butt of Gristrot Mary the Plague-bringer if he thought it would advance his career. "Just move everyone into containment position, Major."

"Yes, sir."

Haysay!

Haysay spun around. The voice was . . . not behind him. Not above him. It was *inside* him.

Haysay!

There was no doubt whose voice it was.

"Director Amés," Haysay replied. "I was just going to contact you."

Step into your ready room.

Zane gave Haysay a glance. Could the adjunct hear the Director's voice? It didn't matter. He knew what was happening, damn him. Or would soon enough.

Haysay dared not linger, however, and wipe the smile off the major's face. He opened a door in the air about him and stepped fully into the virtuality.

Amés sat at one end of the room in a chair that hovered a good four feet off the ground. Haysay found that when he approached his eyes were barely above lap level on the Director. He craned his neck upward, attempted to meet the Director's gaze, then settled on staring at his midsection.

"What are you doing, Haysay?" Amés asked.

"The interior attack was effective. We damaged the Mill on Neptune. But the ships were captured or destroyed."

"I'm aware of that."

"I thought it would be wise to regroup. To make sure of our success, as it were . . ."

"You *thought*, did you?"

How could he answer this correctly? It was the sort of question one used to berate cadets. He'd certainly done his share of it, so he should know. "Yes, Director."

"That's something we're going to put a stop to."

"What is, Director? I don't understand."

"You're thinking for yourself, General. That's what."

He risked a glance upward. Amés was smiling down at him. It was disconcerting. He suddenly felt his back muscles twitch.

So it was going to be another beating. He wasn't prepared. He'd never be prepared. But he'd survived before, and he supposed he'd make it through again.

"The thing is, I enjoyed keeping you autonomous. You might not believe me, but I really did like to have you around. You remind me so much of the friends of my youth."

"Your . . . *youth*, Director?"

"I was young once! Don't look so incredulous, General. And when I was young, my friends often . . . disappointed me. It was infuriating."

"I'm sorry to hear that, Director."

"Oh, it's all right. I took care of the matter. Just as I'm going to take care of it now."

Haysay found his hand reaching to his uniform's top button of its own accord. He knew what was expected of him. He turned his back to Amés, stripped bare his torso, and gritted his teeth.

Amés laughed, long and deeply. Haysay did not turn around. He didn't want to catch the whip in his face, as he had before in trying to get away. There was no getting away from the beating. He knew that now.

Amés's laughter died down to chuckle. "My dear General," said the Director, "I'm not going to *beat* you. I'm going to *eat* you."

"Wha-what?"

"Do you remember my assistant? The one you call C?"

Haysay didn't at first comprehend what was being asked of him, so intent was he on the coming pain.

"Turn around, Haysay, and answer me!"

Trembling, Haysay faced the Director once again.

"Yes. The spy. Or whatever he is."

"A very useful lieutenant—that is what he is," said Amés. "And loyal. I own him in a way I'll never own another person. Even you." Amés shifted in his floating chair and put a hand on his chin, considering.

"C has been overseeing a program for me. A special development team. And they've been successful, very successful, building on what we've learned from manifold LAP integration—especially of the mistakes made with the time towers, and the experiment with the poet, Thaddeus Kaye."

"Director Amés, I'm sorry, but I don't—"

"—see what that has to do with you?"

"Yes, sir."

Amés didn't answer for a moment. He slowly lowered his floating chair until he was eye to eye with Haysay.

"It has *everything* to do with you, General Haysay," he finally said. "Everything you have and everything you are."

"But I *am* a manifold, Director. I'm multiply recursed. I'm spread out in the grist." Haysay brought his heels together and lifted his chin proudly. "I come from a third-generation family of LAPs."

"I'm afraid that your illustrious forbears have bred something of a mule," said Amés dryly. "They seem to have left out the balls."

Haysay stiffened. He had balls! Lots of them, in many locations.

"Don't worry, Haysay. I'm going to take care of that problem." Amés leaned forward. With his right index finger, he stroked Haysay's cheek. It wasn't a harsh touch or a gentle one. Somehow Haysay felt as if he had not been touched so much as *tasted*.

"A manifold of manifolds," Amés said in a low voice. As if he'd talking to himself, Haysay thought. But I'm right here!

"Everywhere at once. Every*when* at once." Amés smiled. To *himself*. He's smiling to himself.

"The time towers got it backwards. The poet fucked himself over. But I'm doing it right. In an enlightened fashion."

"Director," said Haysay, "I know I can do a better job with the invasion fleet. If you'll give me another chance. I don't deserve it, but I . . . I beg you . . ."

"Beg me?" said Amés. It seemed as if he only then remembered that Haysay was still present. "I have nothing to give you."

"A chance to do better, sir. To defeat the fremden. To take the Neptune system for you."

"Oh. That," said Amés. "No."

"But, Director . . . I'm sure . . . I could . . . I . . ." Haysay withered to silence under Amés's gaze.

"No."

"Yes, sir. Your judgment is final, of course."

"And binding," said Amés. "Binding tight." He leaned back. "I've taken in plenty of LAPs. But never a fellow manifold before. This should be interesting."

Haysay didn't understand at all what Amés was talking about, but he couldn't imagine that he was going to like what was coming.

Amés leaned forward and touched his cheek again.

There was a moment of intense, impossible pain. It was not merely his pain in his physical body. Every grain of grist he inhabited vibrated *wrong*. To the pulse of another's being.

He no longer owned his own soul.

"Now you feel *my* world." The Director's voice was inside his mind. Would always be inside his mind.

"Hurts," gasped Haysay. "So bad."

So this was death. He waited to die. The pain didn't end.

Then he understood.

Amés wasn't going to let him die. Or live. He would be here forever, trapped in this moment of extreme suffering.

"I'm the wick." Amés's voice boomed within him. "And you're the wax. Get it?"

No, it wouldn't be forever. Just until Amés used his being up completely. Just a long, long time.

"Your purpose is to melt, to burn, and to make me shine."

Every surface he touched, every thought he possessed would be *wrong*—would flare and burn because it wasn't him, and it should be him. His pain would make Amés stronger. What intelligence he possessed would become the property of the Director. Haysay would remain. Only his soul—everything that made him who he was—would be lost.

"Good-bye, Haysay," said Director Amés.

Moments later, the general strode from his ready room and back into actuality with a hard click to his step. He looked around brusquely.

"Major Zane," he said. "Resume the offensive."

CHAPTER TWENTY-SEVEN

NEPTUNE SYSTEM
E-STANDARD 17:09, THURSDAY, APRIL 3, 3017
FEDERAL ARMY THEATER COMMAND

"They pulled back briefly, but now they are continuing the attack," Monitor reported to Colonel Theory.

Theory considered. Was there something to be learned from this strange DIED maneuver? He could not fathom what it might mean. He had the nagging feeling that he was missing something important. Not for the last time, he wished that Sherman was in-system and in command of the defenses instead of himself.

"We have the *Mencius* and the *Longreach* at .58 kiloklicks. They are on a tangential vector to Triton's orbital plane, one north–south, the other east–west," Monitor reported. "Cloudships Homer and Mc-Carthy moving to intercept."

"What about Nereid?"

"Cloudship Carlyle has established an interior orbit. He's almost as big as the moon, so he is providing optimal cover."

"They'll save him for later," Theory said, "if they have any sense. Have him remain in position."

"He won't like it."

"Carlyle likes chess. If he complains, tell him to think of himself as a rook that's waiting to castle."

"You'll pardon me, sir," said Monitor, "but that's bullshit."

"I'm aware of that, Major Monitor."

"Just so you're aware, sir," said Monitor. "Sometimes your new steel-eyed gaze and square-jawed visage disconcert me."

"Fuck that shit, Major Monitor."

A red beacon materialized in the air of the command room, blinked twice, then disappeared.

"More nails have gotten through," Monitor said. "The *Mercius* made the drop."

Theory looked at the reports from mines and surveillance drones. The incoming nail cloud was thicker than the last. But it was aimed wrong. It wasn't going to strike New Miranda full on. Somebody had made a targeting error.

Unless.

"That cloud of nails, Major . . . it's three-dimensional, isn't it? What is its presentation?" said Theory.

Monitor answered immediately. "Roughly icosahedron."

"It's concealing a paratroop drop," Theory said. "Put ground forces on high alert. Inform Captain Residence that he now has full operational command of the eastern bunkers."

"Yes, sir."

So there would be a ground fight. He hoped he could keep the invaders on the outskirts of the city. If the fighting moved building to building, there were bound to be enormous civilian casualties.

"Sir, Cloudship Cervantes reports the remainder of the *Aztec Sacrifice* battle group has moved inside Nereid's orbit. They are projected in standard triad radials."

"Tell Cervantes to rejoin McCarthy and Homer at full speed," said Theory. "It's time to make our stand."

Monitor conveyed the orders.

They'd done well, but they hadn't scared off the Met forces. Nobody was going to run away, and nobody was going to back down.

It was going to be a hell of fight.

He'd done everything he could to avoid it, but now it had come. This was what he was trained for. Maybe he was the right man in the right place at the right time after all. Maybe not.

He would soon find out.

CHAPTER TWENTY-EIGHT

NEPTUNE SYSTEM
E-STANDARD MID-APRIL, 3017
THE TRITON HOME FRONT

The only good thing about living in the catacombs of the Greentree Way meeting hall on Triton, thought Father Andre Sud, was spending time in the verdant garden where he had done some of his best rock balancing. Throughout his sabbatical before, then through all the crises over the past years when other matters might have claimed their attention, his parishioners had kept the garden tended, kept it ready for their rock-balancing priest's return.

They had a lot more faith in me than I did, Andre thought. It was faith that had not, apparently, been misplaced.

But the garden was a mess. The foliage was getting trampled, and the central meadow was turned to mud. That couldn't be helped. The garden was located deep underground, with a slow-fusion plant providing heat and light between the garden and the surface. Over this complex was the Greentree meeting hall on the surface—a meeting hall that, because of its low profile, was less of a target for DIED ordnance. Not that the nail rains particularly cared where they fell, but smart weapons, at least, might well choose a more prominent target. And so the garden had become the best choice for a neighborhood bomb shelter.

Andre had not done a count, but there must be a thousand or more people jammed into the space. Even more free converts had stored backup copies in the rich grist under the garden's topsoil. If the garden and meeting hall took a direct hit, the loss of life would be enormous.

The siege of Triton was entering its third e-week. People were coming to Andre for advice, for comfort, with questions about the ultimate meaning of life. All the typical things you might ask a shaman-priest when your world had been turned upside down.

And he found that his doubts—his inward doubts about God's existence, about the possibility of even a sophisticated notion of the moral good—those doubts had become irrelevant. It was the strangest thing. He still *had* the doubts. He still felt like a wavering reed inside. Yet when confronted with a frightened young man or a despairing older woman, he found the fortitude within him to give them what they needed. He even found that admitting his own doubts and fears proved no obstacle to his work as a shaman-priest.

He simply did his job.

People wanted to be comforted and reassured. Above all, they wanted to be able to tell somebody how they felt without fear of social humiliation or appearing to be weak. They used him as they would use a highway to get from one place to another. So long as he listened and attempted to answer their questions, however inadequate intellectually his answers were, the people went away spiritually satisfied. And this satisfaction did not appear hollow or misplaced. It wasn't an intellectual matter at all.

As for himself, and to his immense relief, Andre found his own consolation in the person of Molly Index. They had been friends for many years, and lovers at the beginning of their relationship. Now they were again, here at the end.

At what might be the end.

Here, with the bombs raining down and the local virtuality isolated by the DIED jamming device, they had finally found the love that that had eluded them for decades. Andre had even "moved in" with Molly—if you could call sleeping in the next bunk over in a fallout shelter living together as a couple.

In Andre's mind, it was. When this was over—*if* it was ever over—the thought of going back to living alone without Molly was impossible. The only problem was, he wasn't sure if Molly felt the same way. Since their seminary days together, Molly had changed in many ways—

she hadn't just become a different person, she'd become a different *type* of person, a LAP. Even though she'd been shut down to a single individual instantiation at the onset of the war, in her heart she would always be an array of many copies of herself, leading many different lives. All of those "others" were gone for the moment, and maybe forever.

Molly had the possibility of reexpanding herself here on Triton, but she hadn't taken it. She had been a LAP of the Met, an artist whose awareness had once spread around the sun. Even though she didn't put it in those terms, Andre knew that until Molly could reclaim the glory of her former existence, she would not settle for half measures. She would remain a mere mortal.

This resolution only made him fall in love with her more.

Andre was a far different person than he had been as well. And like Molly, he was different physically as well as mentally. He'd died on the Moon that day long ago—then been reinstantiated in this, his current body. He inhabited a replica of his destroyed body, a clone. That day was twenty-five years ago. He'd now lived longer in his cloned body than he ever had in the original.

Molly was herself busy with the administration of the shelter. There were not many LAPs on Triton, former or otherwise, and the locals tended to look to them for leadership, whether social or political.

Andre had always thought this ludicrous. Two, three, or fifty heads were not better than one when all of those heads were filled with the same dull thought. But there was a definite caste system, and Molly— an outsider, only resident on Triton for the past two e-years—had found herself appointed to the triumvirate of other LAPs who oversaw the workings of the shelter. With a thousand people crammed into a space that was meant to accommodate, at a pinch, no more than three hundred, the leadership had their work cut out for them.

After a week, Andre and Molly decided to make specific appointments with each other. It was the only way they could steal a little time together. Strange as it might seem, they were always within three hundred yards of one another, but often didn't see each other for hours on end.

They usually met in the rock clearing, Andre's special area for creating his balanced-rock sculptures. Everyone else respectfully cleared away and gave them a good twenty-foot radius of privacy. Andre did his best to forget about the press of bodies around him. Going back to his old task of rock balancing helped. It also helped that Molly loved to watch him at the task. She considered his rock sculptures an art form. For Andre, balancing rocks was an end in itself. You found a rock-shaped crack in nothingness, in empty air, and filled it with something. Why? Because the crack was there. Because the rocks were lying about. Because *you* were there.

Finding a place to make love was a more difficult proposition, but they had managed to do that, too, on a couple of occasions. It helped that Andre knew the garden intimately—and he knew exactly how many bodies might fit into the storage areas where he kept the gardening tools: two, standing up. It was another kind of balancing, less spiritual and artistic, perhaps, but just as pleasant.

After their second time there, the two of them sat outside—on a rock, of course. Even though it was large, in Triton's light gravity, Andre was able to move it about as if it were a park bench of medium weight on Earth. As with every other rock in the garden, Andre knew the provenance of this one. He'd brought it down from the monastery. It had been used by Father Capability, the monk who had taught him the art in the first place (and in the process saved him from another bout of despair). Andre knew he owed the man his life. He certainly owed his calling as a rock balancer, priest, and gardener to Father Capability.

The ground rumbled. Flecks of ceiling rained down, as they had continually for days. Outside, the bombardment continued.

"Feels stronger up there," Molly said. "Either the fighting is closer to us, or they've stepped up the nail drops." She was sipping a cup of water that Andre had drawn from a spigot on the wall beside the storage closet. The cup itself was an unused starter pot for seedlings. He'd plugged up the drain hole on the bottom with a bit of cork. It was a far cry from the grist-created wineglass he'd sipped from at Molly's artist loft back in the Diaphany.

But that time and place was a hundred million miles and half a decade away.

"We can check the merci," Andre answered. "Local 9 is getting a lot better at their war coverage now that the blocking has made them the only game in town."

Molly shook her head. "We'll know soon enough," she said. "Let's stay away from the news a little longer." She took a sip from the cup, then passed it to Andre, who also took a swallow. Right then, this pure water was better than the finest Dedo burgundy.

"How are your plans for the show coming?"

"Everyone is pitching in," Molly replied. "It's going to be . . . interesting, to say the least. There's a play."

"I heard," said Andre. "One of my parishioners, John Substrate, is playing Alcibiades Morgan."

"I thought a Mueller farce would be the best thing we could do. And Kwan wanted to direct that one, anyway. So we decided on *Can the Chatter, Mr. Rabbi.*"

"It's a good choice," Andre said. "How's the real problem coming along?"

"We've got more space in the grist, but if we store any more freeconvert copies down there, basic services are going to be compromised. We're barely making enough food to feed everyone. It's really energy-intensive, and with the Mill only working at half strength, we've got a major, major problem."

"I'm sure you and the other managers will figure it all out," Andre said, and passed the water back to Molly.

"I wouldn't be so sure of that," she replied. "And if we don't, then you're going to have to decide who gets to stay in this lifeboat, and who has to go."

"Me?"

"People are going to look to you to make the call on that one."

Andre sighed. "I suppose you're right," he said. "Let's pray it doesn't come to that." Another rumble passed through the structure, and another bit of ceiling fell nearby. He pointed upward. "I can't imagine sending anyone back out there. What about the other shelters?"

"First thing I did was call everybody up," Molly replied. "Everybody is now officially full up."

"Oh dear."

"Well, we're hanging on for the moment. That's something."

"And I've got you, babe."

"Yes." Molly finished off the water and set the cup down beside the rock they were sitting on. "It's so odd. At the moment I can't imagine ever living without you again for the rest of my life."

"I feel the same way," Andre replied without a moment of hesitation.

"Your creeping agnosticism toward romance hasn't slunk into your heart in its stealthy way?"

"That was always *your* problem, not mine," Andre replied.

"I suppose you're right," Molly answered. "Back when I was an ironic art curator and bohemian. It certainly seems like a long, long time ago. Another life."

"How's this for idealistic naïveté," Andre said. "Now that I've found you again, I'm going to cling to you like a barnacle on a ship sailing toward the New World."

Molly chuckled. "I'm not sailing anywhere at the moment," she said. "And so neither are you, I guess."

"Oh, we're going somewhere, don't worry. You're stuck thinking in three dimensions," said Andre. "This situation requires four-dimensional thinking. Or five."

"Up, down, odd, strange," said Molly. "And charm."

"That's right," Andre said. He leaned over and kissed her. "Don't forget charm."

Another blast rumbled outside, this one almost knocking them off their perch on the rock. A warning Klaxon rang out in the shelter. There would be alerts in the merci, but the old-fashioned bullhorn siren was also in use just to make sure the message got across to everyone. There were different warning Klaxons; Andre had given up trying to remember which signified what.

Molly had them all down pat. She'd had a hand in devising the system, after all. "Structural integrity alert," she said. "I'm on emergency response oversight today. I guess I have to go and see about that."

Andre took his arms from around her waist and sat back. "If we happen to survive, do you want to set a time to meet back here? How about tomorrow at 1700?"

"Sounds good to me, Father Sud." Molly smiled. "Shall we tryst among the implements again?"

"There's nothing I'd rather do than tryst among the implements."

"Then let's." Molly gave him a peck on the cheek and stood to go. She would be leading a team probably almost to surface to examine whatever damage the alarm was announcing.

"Be careful," he said. "There's bad stuff up there, and it wants to kill you."

"I know," Molly said. "I'll see you tonight."

"If I'm asleep, just pull my hand over and hold it," Andre said. "That never wakes me up."

"I will," Molly said. "I love you." She quickly squeezed his hand, then hurried away to oversee the response team.

Andre watched her go.

"I'll be damned," he whispered to himself. "I love you, too."

Before Andre could reflect on this, a distraught young woman strode purposely up to him.

"Father Andre," she said. "Could you spare a minute?"

Andre put on a smile. It wasn't a fake smile. But it was a weary one. "Of course," he replied.

"I've never really gone to shaman or priest or anything before," the woman said. "I'm a little . . . embarrassed, I guess . . ."

Andre patted the rock beside him. "Don't you worry about that at all," he said. "Just sit down on this rock and talk to me like you would to anybody else."

I *am* like anybody else, Andre thought. There was an immense relief in that knowledge. He didn't have to know everything, or even anything, really. He just had to be somebody to talk to.

"What's been on your mind?" he asked the woman.

The woman laughed nervously, but also with a hint of relief at finally being able to speak of her worry. "My husband is out there," she said. "He's outside the jamming zone, and I don't know whether he's dead or alive." She brushed a strand of hair from her face. Twenty-five, Andre thought. Certainly not more than thirty e-years old.

"He's in the Army?"

"He volunteered as soon as he could get his clearances."

An émigré, Andre thought. From the Kuipers or beyond.

"I know I shouldn't make a fuss about it," the woman continued. "I mean, there's lots of kids here with both parents in the fighting. And pregnant women with their men gone off, too. And fathers and mothers who haven't heard from anybody, and all that. But I—"

"You've got a perfect right to do a little worrying, too," Andre said gently. "You can't help other people if you're a mess yourself, you know."

"I know that, but I've got such a minor thing. I just haven't heard from him." The woman wrung her hands while she was speaking. She then noticed she was doing it, and forcibly settled them on her lap.

"It's really scary when we can't reach somebody we're used to talking with and being around all the time," Andre said. "Their presence is something we take for granted. Then all of a sudden the silence reminds us of how much that person means to us."

"Yes," the woman said. Tears came to her eyes, but she managed a smile. "I wish I had told him before he left. We were both trying to be so happy and nonchalant, and now here I am, and I never told him . . ."

The tears really began to flow now. Andre pulled a handkerchief from his pocket. He was careful to keep a supply of clean ones, no matter what other deprivations he must undergo. Clean handkerchiefs were an essential tool of his trade.

The woman took it and wiped her eyes, looking downward, once again a bit embarrassed.

Andre cocked his head and met her eyes. In the current situation, Andre had found that being able to maintain eye contact was more important than a dozen incontrovertible proofs of God's existence.

"He knows you love him," Andre said. "And he loves you. It's obvious from the feeling you're showing me right now."

"But I didn't show it to *him!* Not enough. I thought we'd have time! I thought . . ."

The woman was sobbing now. Andre patted her shoulder, not letting her look away.

"I'm sure he knows," he said. "Sometimes these things are communicated without anybody having to speak the words. It really sounds like you and your husband have a relationship like that. There's nothing wrong with it. The feeling is still there, and both people know it."

"Do you think so?" said the woman. "Do you *really* think so?"

There was no other answer.

"Yes," Andre said.

"I'm being silly."

"Not at all."

"We really do know each other pretty well, Juan and I."

"Yes."

"I'm just so worried."

"Yes."

"Thank you so much, Father."

"Of course," Andre said. "Any time." He wished he could ask the woman her name, so that he could refer to her by it if he should speak with her again, but he couldn't think of any good way to work the question in.

"I'm signed up to help out with the dinner cleanup tonight. I'd better get going."

"Take care of yourself," Andre said.

"It's the best thing we can do, eh, Father?"

"Exactly," Andre said.

"Have you got somebody to take care of you?"

This was the question he got from many of the women he counseled. The men would wish him well in a vague way. But the women wanted to check on the details.

The polite answer was also the real and true one.

"I *do* have somebody," he said, surprising himself at the joy he felt inside at the words. There certainly are other consolations besides philosophy, he thought. Wish I'd stumbled onto that little fact a few years before now.

"That's great, Father," the woman said. She waved as she left. "And thank you so much for talking to me. It really helped."

"No problem," Andre said. Once again, he hadn't really done a thing. I only have to *be*, Andre thought. That's all the people want from me.

Plus, I get to be silly in love in the middle of a war zone.

He lived in the best of times, and the worst of times. Against all probability, he'd found a way to do his job with a clear conscience.

[So once we turn our back, the rocks balance themselves,] said Andre's convert portion. [Pretty fucking Zen, Father Shaman.]

[Shut up and play us a hymn or something, will you?]

[How about "Ponder Nothing"?]

[Jeez. Again?]

[Okay, then,] his convert answered, sounding a bit miffed. [How about "I Like My Baby's Pudding"?]

[There you go,] Andre replied.

[There *you* go. Over the edge and into the abyss,] said the convert. [She dumped you before, you know.]

[In the long ago before time,] Andre replied. [Back when we were young and everything was absolutely certain. Now we're old and crazy.]

[And in love.]

[And I'm in love,] Andre replied. [With Molly Index.]

More rumbles and tremors in the subsurface. Another nearby strike above.

[I hope to God that she's okay.]

[You and me both. You and me both.]

CHAPTER TWENTY-NINE

MERCURY
LATE APRIL 3017
MONTSOMBRA

The man people called C made his way through the grand arch of San Souci, the Interlocking Directorate headquarters on Mercury. It was the long noon of the Mercurian "day." C didn't dislike the light, but he preferred darkness. Night was the natural element for his work.

C was the definition of nondescript. Gray clothes. Dark shoes. The only unusual feature he possessed was a set of startlingly green eyes.

He made his way through the gardens in the enormous pressurized atrium and boarded the cable lift that would carry him up the small mountain that was at the heart of the complex. The mountain was called Montsombra, and, despite appearances, it wasn't a natural mountain at all. It was a gigantic mound of grist, through and through. On the apex of Montsombra sat the palace of La Mola.

That was where Director Amés dwelled.

He kept his physical aspect in La Mola. But the true, whole Amés was in the mountain itself. Every bit of grist in the mountain was dedicated to sustaining his thousands of personas and the billions of simultaneous interconnecting data flows among them. As the cable car rose, C could feel Amés underneath and all around him. The mountain seethed with the shifting flow of thought and feeling within the Director's consciousness. C felt as if he were ascending a volcano—quiet for the moment, but not dormant.

He hoped that the news he brought Amés would not lead to an eruption.

C exited the cable car and went through the series of security checks that all who came to La Mola must undergo. The palace was hung with gaudy trappings collected from throughout the Met. It was tastefully done, but still managed to create an aura of vast wealth and power, one that emanated from the walls, floor, and ceiling—from the very air itself. This was the nexus of Amés's demesne, the hub of will from which he spun his political domination of the Met.

At the final check, C left his weapon—an ancient nine-millimeter Parabellum that was in perfect working condition. C then turned left, making his way down a hall with three unmarked doors. He opened the fourth door without knocking. There was no need. Amés knew exactly where everyone in La Mola was at every moment.

The Director was sitting at his enormous mahogany desk. Amés was brooding.

"I've lost Pluto," Amés said. "Do you want to tell me why?"

There was a chair for visitors in the room, but Amés did not motion for C to take a seat. C walked to the front of the desk and remained standing there, facing Amés.

"Our cloudship friends didn't know the fremden Navy was ready to be deployed. When the vote came in the Council, they didn't have time to marshal support to stop it."

"And *why* didn't they know?"

"Intelligence breakdown," C replied steadily. "My fault."

"I might have expected this of Grimsly," Amés said, referring to the LAP who was in charge of the Cryptology Division in the Department of Immunity. "I'm going to be co-opting him soon, in any case."

Good-bye to old Milton Grimsly, C thought. He'd been a colleague of C's for many years, although never a friend. C didn't have any friends. So Grimsly would become another drop absorbed into the manifold sea of Amés's personality. C by no means wanted to experience the same fate—although he knew that Amés would have a great deal more difficulty "co-opting" him than he would Grimsly. Amés knew much of who and what C was—his secret and secretive history.

But not everything.

"I have an agent at the Naval Academy," C said. "She's the daughter of one of our friends on the Council. She's no friend of ours, but I've been false-flagging her. She believes she's working for the partisans."

Amés smiled a thin smile. "Indeed."

"She was as surprised as the rest of the ensign cadets when they were rushed into battle. Apparently, only old Lebedev knew of the operation beforehand. It was Cloudship Tacitus who argued before the Council that the Navy was ready. It was a rousing speech, by all accounts. And then, while the scrubs were on alleged practice maneuvers, Lebedev just kept them going—all the way to Pluto."

And now C had to deliver news that would only exacerbate the Director's pique. "I've just been in contact with my young agent. She reports that Lebedev intends to continue onward to Neptune with fifteen ships." C let this sink in, then continued with even more unpleasant tidings. "We've also got a problem at Uranus. This new grist they've deployed is quite tenacious. Most of my assets there have been killed—or rather, they've killed themselves. Two of them have escaped, however, and with samples of the new grist in isolation chambers. They're on their way to our complex on Earth. It may take us some time to analyze and reverse-engineer this stuff. It's nasty."

"So we've lost Uranus."

"We've lost the moons, but the fremden don't have them. Until they can militarily occupy the system, deactivating the surface on Oberon and the other moons would make no sense."

"Not acceptable."

"I understand," said C. There was no arguing the point. Defeat did not fit into Amés's conception of the universe. "There's better news from Jupiter, however."

"Redux?"

"She's taken the bait."

"Excellent," said Amés. "And she has no idea she's working for you?"

"Redux has a remarkable ability to convince herself that what she wishes to be true actually is true," C replied. "I have only one worry— Redux's director of security. Antinomian is her name. I trained the woman myself."

"You will have to see to her elimination yourself, then," Amés said.

C frowned slightly. It was the only expression his face had displayed the entire time he'd been in Amés's office. "That is in process," he said. "But she's an excellent operative. She was the one who was responsible for the escape route for the Noctis Labyrinthus facility break. She communicated to the partisans the exact coordinates where the fugitives should be flashed, and she arranged for the grist matrix that received them on Europa."

"Then she really has to die."

"Yes," said C. "She does. But she has a backup plan in place in case of her disappearance. Someone in the Jovian press has gotten a hint that something's amiss. I'm tracking down who that might be."

"The outer-system press is a joke," Amés said. "I've been spoon-feeding them for years."

"I believe there won't be a problem, but I don't want to take any chances."

"Absolutely not," Amés said. "Find out who knows, kill them, and wipe the information from existence."

"That's my intention," C said.

Amés sat back in his chair. The man—the aspect, at least—was not big enough to fill it, and he looked like a still-growing boy trying to fill a grown-up's chair. C estimated–quite accurately, of course—that Amés was around five feet four inches.

He could make himself taller, C thought, but he'd rather make the universe stoop to his eye level.

And Amés might very well succeed in doing so.

C glanced at the wooden box that sat on the left corner of the Director's desk. Amés immediately caught the intent of his gaze.

"Don't worry. She's still there," Amés said, "waiting for the lover who will never arrive."

C did not reply. He stood very still. He reminded himself to blink, consciously, twice. Blinking was no longer necessary for C, and sometimes, in moments of intense emotion, he forgot to do it.

"This will be your last trip inside the box until the business with Redux is complete."

"I understand," C said softly.

"Well, then," said Amés. "Go ahead."

C touched the box, and instantly he was inside.

An old wooden house, designed in a style long lost to the physical world. There was a parlor. Yellow sunlight through a window. Shadows and dust. The creak of a rocking chair. In the rocking chair was Lace Criur.

It was all a dream, here in the memory box—an algorithmic representation of Earth a thousand years before. C had never considered such distinctions important.

What was true was what was useful to one's sanity.

This was true. Lace was real.

She wore her calico dress, her single string of pearls about her neck. She gazed out the window, as always, toward the horizon. Her green eyes burnt with a desire that could not be fulfilled.

"He won't come," said the woman. "He never comes."

C shuddered as familiar emotions coursed through him. The abiding love. The intense sadness. Lace, reduced to this shadow of a shadow. Yet still, somehow, alive here in the memory box.

"Who are you?" Lace said.

"I'm a friend of his," said C. "He sent me to tell you that he's on his way."

"Oh," the woman gasped. She put her hands to her mouth and ceased rocking. "He's truly coming?"

"He said for me to tell you that he would be a while. Maybe a long while."

Lace began to rock again. "You don't know him," she mumbled. "You never met him."

C crossed the room to stand beside her. "Your name is Lace," he said. "Lace Criur."

The woman considered, then nodded. "Yes. I suppose it is, now that you mention it," she replied. "I had forgotten it." She rocked on. "He won't come. He never comes," she said.

"He asked me to see if you still wore the hair clasp. The dragonfly that he gave you."

Lace again stopped her rocking. "It's in the parlor desk," she whispered. "I keep it in the second drawer on the right, next to the broken clock."

C crossed the room. He opened the drawer and took the clasp into his hand. It had the heft of good silver. The dragonfly eyes sparkled red and blue when he turned his hand and held the clasp in the sunlight from the window. He had bought it for her in Dineh Barrel, the Navajo tribal lands out on the Diaphany. In here, in this memory, it would never tarnish.

He put the clasp back into the drawer, next to the clock, and gently slid the drawer shut.

"He broke the clock before he left so that you would always remember the time," said C in a low, thick voice.

"It's ten-seventeen," said Lace. "In the morning. July 6."

"He'll return after the winter," said C. "Like he promised."

Lace pulled the brown shawl tight about her shoulders. "It's always summer here," she said. "Winter never comes."

"Winter will come," said C.

"Do you want something," Lace said, as if she hadn't heard him. "I have ice tea and sweet crackers."

"No," said C. He remembered his last visit there—the ice tray with the single cube missing, drained through a crack in the plastic. The impossible regret that discovery had brought upon him. "Not this time."

Lace nodded. It was all the same to her. "When will he come?" she said.

"After the winter."

"Who are you?"

"My name is Clare," C replied.

"Do I know you?"

"Yes," C said. He touched her hand softly. She pulled the shawl more tightly about her.

"He won't come," she said. "He never comes. When will he come?"

"I have to be going now," said C after a moment. "But I'll be back."

"Who are you?"

"A friend of his," said C.

"You know him?" She gazed up at him eagerly. Her eyelashes were extraordinary. He'd forgotten. Like moth-wing silk.

"Good-bye, Lace," he said. "Winter is coming. Be sure to wear your coat when the winds start blowing. The sheepskin coat."

"He gave it to me," Lace said. "But I can't remember his name."

"It will come to you, Lace," said C. "Give it time."

C left the way he had entered.

CHAPTER THIRTY

THE VAS
E-STANDARD 15:36, THURSDAY, APRIL 17, 3017
BATTLE DAY

Elvis Douri couldn't wait to surf the merci after school adjourned for the day. Now he could play *Battle Day*. Usually, he'd immediately disconnect himself from the virtuality after classes and go out and play for a couple of hours. He and his friends had built a fort in the swamp outside their residence block, and there were several additions in the planning stages, including a lookout and a booby-trapped moat (provided Samantha Nooks ever got hold of that poisonous medicinal grist she swore she could swipe from her father, who was a pharmacist). But he hadn't been out to the fort in days.

Instead, most afternoons found Elvis sitting like a statue in the "full-pellicle rip-chair" he'd gotten for his birthday—the one that encased your body and gave grist-to-grist contact for a virtual experience that the advertisements called "Reality to the Nth Plus 1 Degree." Elvis didn't know what that meant exactly, but he did know that, in his rip-chair, he could enjoy his favorite merci show with absolutely no distractions from the outside world.

And his favorite show, without any doubt, was *Battle Day*.

Battle Day was the special kids' feed of the Glory Channel. It took you straight into the action, and many times, into the actual sensations of the participants—soldiers and civilians alike. You knew what it was like to be part of the attacking paratroopers, screaming out of the sky down upon Triton. And you also could get excerpts from the merci feeds of the fremden. Some of them had carelessly left their personal blocking off, and some of them had no blocking innerware installed to begin with. Anybody who interacted with the Met-based merci channels—which was most of the outer system residents, still—was susceptible to becoming a *Battle Day* "host."

There was nothing as rip as being inside the skin of an enemy when he or she died.

Even better, you could search the network for different kinds of kills: most popular overall, most physically involved (this was where Elvis always found the sick and gruesome stuff he was sometimes in the mood for), most heroic, most cowardly—and lots more categories. Elvis had his filters set to medium, and so he never visited a kill that had fewer than a hundred hits by previous viewers. He knew he missed some decent stuff that way, but it also kept a lot of boring material out of his sensorium.

Today was the high point of the Triton invasion. It was going to be so rip!

The first thing Elvis did before tuning into the current action was to get a recap of what he'd missed during school hours. He paged through various thumbnail 3-Ds of the battle, and activated one that looked promising. He was rewarded by getting to experience the agonizing death of a fremden soldier plunging into Neptune's atmosphere after being abandoned by his deceitful fremden commanders. Although Elvis couldn't read the guy's mind, he could feel the man's heart pounding, he could experience the soldier's body shaking with fear, and he could even eavesdrop on the last communication the man had with his mother.

"I wish I'd never left the ice mine, Mum," the man told his weeping mother. "I thought I was heading for a better life, but instead I'm about to be deader than Bore Hole One on the old conglomerate."

And then the speed of his plunge caught up with him, and the soldier flared into a ball of horrible pain that lasted a lot longer than Elvis thought it would. Finally, there was darkness as the link was severed.

Elvis checked the readout. This particular death happened several hours ago. Enough with the reruns; now it was on to the good new stuff—on to the fighting on Triton at the capital city of New Miranda!

First for an overview.

The siege had been going on for e-weeks. The nail rain had definitely softened up New Miranda, but it only lightly strafed the military targets on the outskirts of the city, and fallen mostly in the civilian sectors. While this was useful for undermining civilian morale, it wasn't making the DIED invaders' job much easier. What's more, the Sciatica attack craft were still being engaged above the surface by a swarm of local ships. None of these were particularly suited to be military craft, but they'd all be retrofitted with weaponry and some defenses. There were so many of them that, even though hardly any were a match for a DIED ship, they could gang up three or four to an attacker and keep the craft busy. This was something that hadn't happened during the attack on Io, where the DIED had enjoyed overwhelming orbital superiority.

No need to worry, said the soothing voice of the *Battle Day* announcer. *Paratroopers have slipped through planetary defenses and are making moonfall even now.*

Rip as all get-out, Elvis thought back at the announcer. *Tune me in to that action!*

And he was there.

There were three brigades that had made it to the surface so far, about thirty thousand soldiers. A third of them were elite, fully space-adapted troops. The others had come down in drop canisters. Those soldiers were establishing a beachhead and assembling armored rovers and tanks to carry them forward. The space-adapted, on the other hand, were deployed forward. Some were charging the fremdens' defensive works and facing a merciless cross fire. Others had made it past the fremden artillery and were engaged with the enemy hand to hand.

Elvis quickly selected the most popular personal combat playing at the moment.

It was a brother and a sister—the sister a DIED soldier, her brother a fremden—locked in a deadly embrace. The woman had shot off her sibling's left arm, then moved in to choke him. His pellicle, overwhelmed by the system failure, and the attack from the woman's own grist, had not been able to seal up the blood flow from the man's stump. So, while the woman couldn't literally choke the air out of her space-adapted brother, she could hold him and swarm him with attacking grist while he bled to death into the broken methane snow surface of Triton.

Each fighter had an icon floating over his or her head that contained their background information and the story of how two members of the same family had come to be fighting to the death on Neptune's cold moon. Elvis skipped this part. That was girl stuff—the stuff that was supposed to get you all emotional and involved in the story. He found that it usually bored him. He was far more interested in the physical details of combat and the effects of the different weapons on flesh and blood.

He quickly withdrew from full participation in the death match and scanned around for something a bit more grisly. He didn't have far to look.

A wave of DIED were charging an antimatter battery. They were in full stealth mode, invisible across a broad spectrum of the e-m spectrum. The fremden responded not by random, intense firing, but by using their gun in a deliberate "search" pattern. This was a pretty calm and cool maneuver, considering that hundreds of bloodthirsty soldiers were descending on them and many of these attackers were bound to get through. It was particularly interesting to get inside a fremden point of view. The artillery beams roared out over what seemed to be an empty field of fire until—every few seconds—a bolt would catch a DIED soldier and vaporize him or her in a magnesium-bright flash. Sometimes stumps of legs or arms remained, sublimating and sizzling, on the ground.

The DIED first wave finally reached the ramparts. The fremden didn't know what hit them until the last moment. It was as if the attackers stepped out of an empty plain and were suddenly there—and moving to kill. Elvis switched over to his own side's POV.

Fremden faces. Red agony. Terror in the eyes. Fear. Sometimes pleading. Sometime defiance.

Sweep One, locate the comm nexus!

To the right at one o'clock—the guy in the corner's manning the feed!

Point One and Two: Take him out.

Point One, I'm on it!

Point Two, ditto.

Bullets and blood. No antimatter weaponry in these close quarters! Hands sharpened to knives. Punctured pellicles, explosive, bubbling decompression. Rapidly frozen internal organs shattering, spilling out like pottery shards. Red, frothing vomit.

Take that, you fucker! You fucker, you're going to die!

Stay together and give me a fire radius!

That's right! That's right! Turn your ass around and run! Won't do you any good. Fremden bitch. Bad day to fuck with me!

Silent screams.

Battle Day is so *rip*, thought Elvis. Better than any game on the merci.

He pulled back, had a look at the tactical layout. The host informed him that the fighting on the ground was intense, indecisive at the moment—although full DIED victory was expected.

Farther back.

The orbital battle dragged on, with lots of fire exchanged and the occasional explosive flare as someone or another took a direct hit. One big fremden tanker suddenly careened out of control and rocketed downward toward the lights of New Miranda. After a moment, there was a tiny explosion below that must have meant the death of hundreds of people.

Utterly rip.

Farther back.

In space, outside of Triton's orbit, the big ships were engaged: destroyer groups against the massive cloudships.

The cloudships had sophisticated merci lockouts, so there was no getting inside their perceptive fields. But there were fremden soldiers aboard who could be v-hacked, and the show's adept producers provided plenty of enemy POVs. There were a couple of space infantry battles going on, but for the most part, the fighting was ship to ship.

The cloudships, for all their size, were quite nimble and could outmaneuver individual DIED ships under most circumstances. The key was to use the destroyer groups as a pack and take on the ships from several directions. That proved easier said than done, however. The cloudships, too, could and did work together.

Elvis was particular attracted to the fierce salvos between the *Aztec Sacrifice* and Cloudships Cervantes and Homer. What was strange was that the two cloudships seemed to be fighting one another, as well as the DIED battle group. They were blasting away at one another with gamma ray bursts that burnt in neon green lines through Elvis's filtered vision. His current vantage point was the *Largemouth*, a Dirac-class ship.

Why are they fighting each other? he asked the *Battle Day* host.

We're not sure, but we think they're using e-m bursts to communicate. As you know, our forces have the ability to jam the merci.

Oh yeah, thought Elvis. The Secret Weapon. Director Amés and the Science Directorate had found a way to isolate local merci networks, to cut off the grist from communicating outside its physical area. Nobody knew how this magical feat was accomplished.

Just another way Amés showed himself to be the best. Anybody not on his team was doomed to destruction. Elvis almost felt sorry for those poor fremden suckers.

But they were getting what they deserved. They were the ones who started the civil war, trying to seal off the outer system and commandeer all the riches found there. And that after the Met had paid for the development of the colonies in the first place. It was stealing, and it was wrong. Amés wasn't going to stand for it, and Elvis—like his parents, his brother and sister, all his friends—was completely behind the Director.

Make those ungrateful fremden send their fair share home—home to the Met and the inner system, where humans naturally belong, after all.

Besides, everybody knew the outer system was crawling with out-of-control tagions. It was a jungle out there.

The solar system must naturally be whole and under one government. That government obviously had to be the Interlocking Directorate.

Couldn't the stupid fremden see that? They must. They were just trying to raise a stink, to make trouble, and they were going to get punished for it. Punished really bad.

But at the moment, the two enormous cloudships were holding their own against a pack of attackers. The *Aztec Sacrifice* group was trying to cut the ships off from one another, but whenever a DIED ship slipped into the gap separating the cloudships, she was subjected to withering, concentrated fire. In fact the cloudships resembled nothing so much as two galaxies—one a spiral, the other shaped like a disc, throwing off supernova-like bolts of lightning.

One ship, the *Malfeasance*, took particularly heavy fire and veered away, her command and control structures shot away, and her massively breached hull trailing precious atmosphere into the empty vastness.

But even as the *Malfeasance* departed, there was a nuclear ball of fire, momentarily brighter than the (admittedly wan) sun, and another ship raced past the cloudships and toward Triton, taking advantage of the momentary e-m overload. Yet the fremden had a third ship to contend with near the moon—Cloudship McCarthy—and that ship had so far let no large DIED ship past him. Only the swarms of Sciaticas, flying long-range missions from the destroyers, were succeeding in reaching the moon's orbit proper. But now another destroyer's contingent of Sciaticas could be added to that armada.

It was hard fought on every level—just the way Elvis liked it. The ratings poll popped up, and he couldn't believe himself even as he voted.

He'd given today's show a perfect ten!

He liked to think of himself as a very critical merci watcher. He'd absolutely never rated *any* show at ten before. He didn't think it could happen. But *Battle Day* had done it. It was, hands down, the best show he'd ever seen on the merci.

He prepared himself for the finale—the flare of Kid Glory that every *Battle Day* "warrior" received before he or she signed off. Elvis knew that this was only a pale shadow of the Glory the soldiers got to feel. But receiving it made him a part of it all—a DIED Special Agent, like the host said. Elvis had to admit that he could get pretty cranky when he missed his dose of Glory.

"Elvis? Elvis Douri!"

Damn. It was his mother. Elvis remained quiet and did not disengage from the rip-chair. Maybe she'd leave him alone for once instead of constantly butting into his business. But that was not to be.

"Are you glued into the merci again?" Her voice was closer now. She'd overridden the lockout code he'd put on his room's entrance. Total invasion of privacy!

Even the rip-chair had to respond to her commands. Unfair! The cover slid away, and the boy-meat inside was exposed like a clam in an opened shell.

"Mom!"

"What are you plugged into?"

"None of your business."

His mother shook her head ruefully. "It's that *Battle Day*, isn't it?"

"So what if it is?" Elvis replied, defiant. "I'm only doing my duty as a good citizen."

"There's too much violence on that show for a boy your age."

"And I suppose you can watch it all day if you want to?"

"I'm an adult," his mother replied. "And I *don't* watch it all day."

"That's because all you ever do is sit and watch the Glory channel with the intensity all the way up," Elvis said. "You're going to burn out your brains, Mom."

"What I do is my business," his mother said. "What you do is *also* my business, and you're spending too much time on the merci."

Elvis was fully disengaged from the virtuality now. His room was bright and clean, and the world was absolutely no fun anymore. "Maybe you should do more of *your* part in the war effort."

"More of my part . . ." His mother's voice was incredulous. "Do you realize that your cousin is *out there*? Do you have any idea what that means? Sometimes spending a few minutes on that Glory channel is all that keeps me from going crazy, I'll have you know."

"It's more like a few *hours*!" Elvis exclaimed.

"Young man, you watch the way you talk to me."

"Well, *I'm* proud of Dory. Maybe she'll even be on *Battle Day* sometime."

"Oh, Elvis." His mother was crying now, for no discernible reason. At least he'd won this little victory, even though he had no idea how he'd done it. It was time to be magnanimous to his defeated foe.

"I'm sorry, Mom," he said. "I didn't mean to hurt your feelings again."

"You didn't," his mother said. "You couldn't, Elvis. You don't know what you're saying." Like usual, any statement his mother made that was meant to make him feel better had the opposite effect. He felt mad at her all over again.

"Maybe *I'll* be on *Battle Day*," he said, knowing as he said it that he would provoke another round of tears from his mother. "I sure hope the war lasts long enough so that I get a chance."

Now the tears flowed freely from his mother's eyes. "You're going to break my heart," she said. "Just break it in two."

"Don't worry, Mom. I'll do really good out there." He felt certain that he was right about this, and he spoke in his most reasonable tone. "After all," Elvis continued, "nobody's seen more episodes of *Battle Day* than I have. I'd be perfect for that show."

CHAPTER THIRTY-ONE

NEPTUNE SYSTEM
E-STANDARD, MIDNIGHT, THURSDAY, APRIL 3, 3017
NEPTUNE

Corporal Alessandro Orfeo had never been to Neptune. Hell, he'd never even been to Pluto. He'd spent most of his nineteen years in the Kuipers, somewhere between Neptune and Pluto, digging for right-handed proteins. Not for the regular kind you could make in a lab, but for the exotics that it took nature millennia to cook up. Orfeo might not be able to read and write so well, but he goddamn knew his protein sequences as well as any man or woman living.

He even understood why the stuff was so valuable: Enhanced into a modified form of grist, it was used to build important and delicate structures inside human bodies where regular left-handed protein would cause a perpetual immune reaction. It was a prime component in the really good Broca language adaptations, for example. And that grist was why everybody could speak to each other, despite almost everyone having a different dialect of Basis—practically down to the individual.

Alessandro didn't consider himself smart, but he sure wasn't any dumb-ass cracker, as the miners were often portrayed on the merci shows. He had to admit that he laughed as hard as the next guy when he tuned in to those programs, though.

The point was, he knew enough to know that he still had a lot of living to do. That his mother and father were going to really miss him, and his dad was going to have a hard time supporting his younger brothers and sisters without the half of Alessandro's army paycheck that he sent back home.

There was supposed to be a pension plan for KIAs, but who the hell could count on that? Hell, the war might be lost today, for all he would ever know.

Most of all, he was smart enough to know that Isabella was going to find herself another boyfriend, and she and him weren't going to get married after all.

What a thing to be considering as your last thought. He had imagined lots of possibilities. Going out fighting, his mind in a white-hot rage. Or dying in the hospital, Isabella crying softly at his side.

Instead, he'd just fucking missed the net.

That was all there was to it. The net that was supposed to catch him hadn't deployed. Something was wrong—a harpoon had missed or something. Or he'd just fucking hadn't seen it and had missed catching hold.

Stupid way to go. Like falling toward that big blue planet and thinking about Isabella with another guy. Isabella raising kids that weren't his kids. And grandkids. And all of his kids somewhere in heaven or purgatory or wherever little unborn baby souls got stuck when they were supposed to get a place, were expecting to get a place, and then they all got laid off and no work for any baby souls to be had.

It was kind of funny and sad at the same time, thinking about those baby souls.

Maybe that reincarnation stuff worked, and *his* soul would get to come back. Alessandro smiled at the thought.

I know what I'll do, he thought. I will come back as the soul of one of Isabella's babies. There I'll be sucking on her breasts all day while old Mario Whateverthefuck is off working his ass off to support us. And then when I get older I'll just reach out and slug him one day. Slug him right in the face. And he'll say what's that for, son? And I'll say it's because you took my girl, you goddamn asshole.

But babies never talk about their lives from before, and Alessandro knew that he sure as shit didn't remember any past existence. You obviously forget everything if you get recycled as a soul.

So I'll get blanked, or I won't get to come back at all. That's how it'll be. That's what's going to happen.

And for some reason, this thought did calm him down. And he could take in the blue swirl below him. Too bad he wasn't on the opposite side of the planet. He could look down straight into the Eye then. Stare down old Neptune. Or turn around and take a last gander at Triton—the only planet he'd ever stepped on. Even though it really was a moon and not a planet.

There was one other option. He could go on the merci. He knew that was what most of the other guys were doing right then. Violating protocol and putting a call through to the ones they'd left behind. Most of them would die all tucked away in the virtuality. Only at the end, when the heat burnt through the skin, would the overrides kick in. Only for an instant would they be jerked back to the hell of reality. Then it would all be over.

He could do that.

He could see his mother and dad.

He could visit Isabella one last time.

What would be the use? Just cause them all a lot of needless pain. They all knew how he felt about them.

Instead, he was going to have a look at Neptune. Methane, hydrogen, and helium. Fastest winds in the solar system. That was how come the Mill was in the Eye.

He would be in those winds soon. He imagined himself being buffeted around. It would be like one of those tornado simulators on the merci, only more so. Fifteen hundred fucking miles per hour. And now that he was in the goddamn metric-crazy army: twenty-three hundred kilometers an hour. Either way, it was going to be a hell of a ride.

Could you really get torn apart just by the wind?

Or would the heat get you as you fell?

He was going to find out.

But still, there it was. Him. Old Father Blue.

He had to admit, it was the prettiest sight he'd ever seen. Except for Isabella's eyes.

What the hell was that! A ghost? Was he dead already?

No, just the wisps of the outer atmosphere.

I'm really close now, Alessandro thought. Nobody's going to save me.

He felt his heart begin to race and fought back the urge to close his eyes.

He was falling.

He could feel himself falling now.

He held his eyes open.

I want to see everything there is to see, Alessandro thought. I'm finally visiting a real, honest-to-God planet.

CHAPTER THIRTY-TWO

NEPTUNE SYSTEM
E-STANDARD, 19:30, THURSDAY, APRIL 17, 3017
FEDERAL THEATER COMMAND

The DIED attack had become a siege. That had been one of the possibilities all along, of course. It wasn't an acceptable outcome, and Colonel Theory didn't like it one bit. But, as Sherman had said to him before he left, a siege was a hell of a lot better than going out in an idiotic blaze of glory.

But it isn't as good as winning, Theory thought. He wanted to win—to protect the territory and those he loved, certainly. But also not to let Sherman down. No military commander, either in the Federal Army or in the DIED forces, had ever given a free convert such as Theory so much responsibility before. Doing just all right wasn't acceptable to Theory. It never had been.

Captain Residence had checked in moments before. The DIED paratroop attack had been blocked. The latest big wave, once again dropped in camouflaged by a nail rain, had been held to the outskirts of New Miranda. Those who had dropped directly into the city proper had been isolated and—after heavy fighting—taken prisoner or killed.

After three e-weeks, the DIED force still had not penetrated the city with troops, and most of their forces had been steadily swept from the moon with heavy casualties.

Theory was chagrined that there were any troops at all on the ground of Triton. But New Miranda and the outlying settlements were still firmly in Federal hands.

In space, the situation changed moment to moment. The cloudships, with the help of space-deployed Marines, were holding their own. Even old Carlyle out at Nereid was proving to be a resourceful defender. He had dropped his troops on the small moon, then teamed up with the local minefield commander to create a unique defense. He'd spread himself out thin and engulfed some of the more powerful orbital mines into his structure. Carlyle now surrounded two-thirds of the moon like an enveloping film. This obscured the mines to any known detection techniques. A DIED invader would have no chance to get through except by dumb luck.

On the other hand, even one or two antimatter mine explosions would blow Carlyle to smithereens. He was taking a big chance, and gambling with his life. Theory couldn't help but admire the cloudship's bravery. He might be grumpy, but he was a good soldier when it came down to it.

The other cloudships were fighting an ongoing slugfest with the DIED fleet. Cloudship Austen had rushed to join the other three "Kuiper Group" ships locked in battle near Triton. With Austen there, Theory had in place gross firepower equal to the DIED armada. So long as he or his ships didn't make a tactical mistake—always a possibility, of course—he had a standoff on his hands.

Cloudship Mark Twain remained behind to guard the Mill in case of a breakthrough or a sudden foray by the Met navy.

The Mill—this was another thorn in Theory's side. His forces had defeated the invaders, but not before crippling damage had been done to the energy-generating apparatus. It was presently operating at one-third output, and Theory's engineers were giving pessimistic assessments as to how long repairs would take—or if they could be completed at all given the present situation.

In the virtual command center, Theory turned to Major Hidaka, who head up the newly formed Third Sky and Light Military Police Corps.

"It looks like we're going to have to put that enforced power rationing plan in place," Theory said.

"Yes, sir," said Hidaka. "Stage one?"

Theory reviewed the entire plan in a matter of milliseconds. Stage one, which affected only industrial and commercial operations, was not going to be enough. New Miranda would need to introduce immediate consumer rationing. A lack of adequate energy on Triton was not merely inconvenient. It might be a death sentence.

"Go straight to stage two," Theory said. "And I want you to make an example out of the first person who violates the provisions."

"Will do, sir," Hidaka said, then left the command center to issue the new order to her forces. Hidaka's convert portion (she was a biological human) used the door to exit rather than simply disappearing from the room. Sherman had demanded this sense of decorum among his command staff, and Theory saw great sense in maintaining it.

So—the situation was dire, but stabilized. It was a dynamic equilibrium, of course. From the way the Met forces were fighting, Theory was beginning to suspect that they'd been assigned a new commander. Theory had never met General Haysay, but he'd studied every biographical fact known about the man and carefully reviewed all his war game records. Theory now believed he was facing a more daring and intelligent opponent. There were several possibilities among the DIED's pool of up-and-comers, but Theory didn't waste time speculating. Whoever it was was good. Theory knew that if he grew complacent for even a moment, this new opponent would capitalize on it.

Nevertheless, it was time for a breather. "I'm stepping out for a moment," he told Monitor, passing along to the major his contact coordinates in the basic machine language of the grist.

For once, Monitor didn't make some ranking comment about Theory's new heroic and muscular appearance, or his thickening facial hair. The joke had grown a bit stale. But everyone relieved tension however they could, and Monitor had always been a good friend to Theory. Theory didn't take the comments personally. Well, he *did*, of course. He just didn't take them badly.

Theory, too, exited through the war room's door. He walked down a short, self-created corridor, then knocked on, and opened, the door to his own apartment. A great wave of relief came over him as he beheld his son sitting on the floor and playing with a complex puzzle box. On the nearby sofa was Jennifer Fieldguide. She looked up from the magazine she was reading and smiled at Theory.

"How's it going?" Jennifer asked him.

"It's going all right," Theory said, stepping farther inside. "How are you?"

"*We're* doing fine," Jennifer replied. "We had dinner over at my parents' again yesterday. They can be a pain, but I think our boy here had a good time overall."

"This is true," said the boy. Theory's son spoke so infrequently that it was always a surprise to hear his voice.

Theory sat down in the living room's armchair. This was the only furniture in the room. He'd always run a very spare algorithm to represent his apartment's interior.

"I can't stay long," he said. "I just wanted to check on everything here."

"My apartment is pretty much a disaster area from the nails," Jennifer said. "So I've been hanging out in the building's basement and spending my mental time here—except to eat and go to work."

Theory nodded. "I'm very grateful," he said.

"Hey, it's good for me, too," Jennifer said. "The bakery's running half-time, and all my friends are holed up in basements and shelters. I'd feel bored and useless without your son." She gestured to the boy. "He's kind of fascinating to watch, too. He says a lot with his gestures and stuff like that, once you know how to read him."

If the boy noticed he was being talked about, he didn't show it as far as Theory could tell. He continued playing with his complicated toy.

"Still, I thank you," Theory said.

"You're welcome," Jennifer replied. "Can I get you anything? How about some coffee? I actually researched some representations and found some good stuff for your pantry."

"That would be nice," Theory said.

Jennifer got up and went to the kitchen. Theory bent over and watched his son's play. The puzzle box displayed a complicated three-dimensional fractal on one side. On the other, this fractal was broken into many mixed-up pieces. The object was to make the front and back look the same by sliding the pieces about according to fixed rules.

"Try the A4 to the A5," Theory said, after a moment's thought.

"That won't work," the boy immediately replied. "See how it would ruin this diagonal run?"

Theory considered the box again.

"You're right," he said. "I guess I'm a little tired and didn't see the problem there."

Jennifer came back into the room with a steaming mug of coffee. Theory took in the aroma. It was delicious. He took a sip. There was something . . . a very clever programmer, indeed, had come up with this coffee. It contained a semisentient coprocessor in the grind. After another swallow, the coprocessor kicked in and Theory definitely felt perked up and more alert.

"That's good coffee," he told Jennifer. "I didn't realize how much I needed that."

Jennifer smiled in her soft way, and Theory felt his heart once again swelling at the sight. She was so unlike him—she was a creature of feelings, urges, instincts—but he couldn't stop himself from being taken with her. She was somehow incomprehensible in a completely alluring manner.

He finished his coffee and stood to leave.

"I've got to get back to work."

Jennifer took his coffee cup. "We'll be here," she said.

"That's . . . that's very reassuring to me," Theory replied. "It makes me happy to know you're both here."

Jennifer smiled again. His son looked up in acknowledgment, though the boy's expression remained the same.

On the way back to his command center, Theory lengthened the virtual connecting corridor by a good twenty feet. He spent the extra milliseconds of walking time reflecting on his son's seeming contentment—and considering Jennifer Fieldguide's lovely smile.

Then he opened the command center door and stepped back into the waiting war.

PART FIVE

Epilogue
YEAR 3017, E-STANDARD

CHAPTER ONE

The lights of the laboratory compound were bright, and the entire
area around the main complex was swarming with grist. The Jeep had
no trouble finding the place; concealing his movements from the outrider security grist-mil proved to be a bit more difficult, but not impossible. The laboratory was in the wilderness, and the security
algorithms had to compensate for stray animals and vegetation, or it
would spend its energy and computing power responding to every leaf
fall or squirrel scamper. The Jeep was nine hundred years a creature of
the wild. Over the centuries, he had seen many a black bear and spent
days following one or another of them to find new pathways and territories. Upstate New York bears roamed almost as widely as the Jeep,
and they knew the landscape. You could learn a lot from following
bears. The Hudson Valley was full of them now.

And so the Jeep camouflaged himself as a bear. It was a straightfor-
ward decision. There were more complicated ruses he might have used,
but they required too much algorithmic upkeep. The Jeep knew he had
nowhere near the juggling ability of a free convert. Simple was best,
and simple was a bear.

The compound was in the shallow valley of a stream that fed into the Hudson. It had, ages ago, been the village of Rhinebeck, inhabited by well-to-do city dwellers as a weekend getaway, and ringed by the lower class of service people who took care of things during the week. Rich and poor alike had left for the Met centuries before. The compound had been cut out of a climax Northeastern forest less than a decade ago. There was grist that would shape out a construction site, leaving trees and underbrush intact where possible, and doing minimal damage to the future building's surroundings. This sort of green-friendly construction grist was mandatory when building outside the city limits on Earth. The truck hunters employed it to build their hunting lodges, for instance.

When the Science Directorate had set up the lab complex, they had used grist-mil instead—potent military grist that stripped the land bare and even converted the soil to a dirty sand laced with reduced organic specks. There was a very sharp delineation where the periphery fences and security systems of the compound gave way to the compound proper. It was the line where the speckled sand started, and nothing living grew.

At that line, the Jeep had to make a decision. The security grist on the other side was too powerful. Curiously, it was not inhabited by a free convert. He could not imagine why. It was complex enough to contain one. But the half-sentient algorithm that patrolled it was complex enough that the Jeep would have a difficult time fooling it. The Jeep began to circle the compound, searching for a weakness. The laboratory buildings within, squat, flat structures made from a seamless compound, were tantalizingly close. There was no fence or wall—only the rich humus soil on one side and the dirty sand on the other—and signs.

Another odd thing. The signs were not directed outward, but were facing inward.

The Jeep couldn't see what was written or drawn on the signs. He only knew they were signs because they approximated the size and shapes on the Taconic Parkway and elsewhere. Maybe they were blank on the other side. But signs usually told you what to do, or somebody's idea of what you ought to do. Or else they were warnings. Or both.

The Jeep was about to dismiss the whole matter as unknowable, but there was something important about the signs; he felt it. And so, he thought about it, in his way, by waiting and letting the information sur-

face. Surviving for nine hundred years had reworked the Jeep programming. Random variations had been incorporated. Connections
had been made with the land, the weather, the entire grist pellicle of
Planet Earth. In many ways, the Jeep was no longer a creature of algorithm but was organic. Alive.

And then he had it. No wonder the bear disguise had worked so
easily.

The signs were a warning to keep people *in*. The security convert attached to the lab was a jailer, not a soldier.

Here was a way.

Without another thought, the Jeep signaled to the compound's exterior guard routine that he was here.

[What? Who's that? Who are you?]

The Jeep remained silent. Best to play a dumb quarter-sent. He
rolled slowly forward and crossed the line in the sand.

[Say now—that's far enough!]

The Jeep came to a stop.

[What the hell are you doing here? Let me check my records.]

The Jeep slowly revved his engine, gathering energy into his grist.
He had gotten some very nasty defense algorithms stored away over
the years. He also had some offensive code capabilities, including a
nasty virus he'd encountered in the wilds of Nova Scotia, rampantly
breeding within the grist substrate of a peculiar variety of lichen. He'd
almost succumbed to the virus, which called herself BigCanada, before
his own robust antihack algorithms had isolated and dealt with the invader.

He'd picked up some information while fighting the little program.
The virus was a recent arrival on Earth, having come from a region on
the Met known as the Carbuncle. Apparently all the semisentient code
scraps were being rounded up in the Met and eradicated in some gruesome manner. This concerned the Jeep only insofar as BigCanada had
escaped the sweeps—and now he must deal with her virulence.

After he'd defeated her, he'd kept a copy archived in quarantine. She
might prove useful. At the time, he'd imagined one day releasing Big-
Canada in the convert portion of a truck hunter who got too close. He
wasn't exactly sure how the virus did what she did, but he knew its effects weren't good. She was particularly good at reformatting her victim's pellicle.

Well, now he would use her in more spectacular fashion. He called up his expansion routine, loaded his BigCanada archive into the program's "hopper"—

But then didn't get the chance to use it, at least not yet.

[Okay, then. Here you are in the deliveries column. White Jeep Wrangler—I guess that's your color and make—VIN number 2J4FY29T3KJ126916. Can you verify that?]

It was so. That was his vehicle identification number! How had the guard known? No one could know without being very close. Looking through the driver-side window at the metal tag on the dash.

Or you could be inside and see it.

And then he knew. Ping Li. It had to be. No one else had been inside him for nine hundred years. She'd noted the VIN. She was a numbers person. She might have amused herself by seeing the VIN upside down, transposing it, memorizing it. And somehow she'd gotten him on the laboratory compound's delivery schedule.

The Jeep allowed a tiny outrider of grist, a simple recognizance spider a few microns across, to crawl up his chassis and read the VIN number. After the information had been transferred, he eliminated it quickly.

[Well, you don't have to be so touchy!] said the compound guard. [I wasn't going to leave the spider there.]

The Jeep did not answer. He revved his engine impatiently.

[All right, all right. I guess you want directions to where you're to drop the shit, huh?]

The Jeep revved his engine louder.

[A rose garden. The warden's gone 404. He should never have allowed such a thing. Distracts the meat from their work is what it does. Well, nothing I can do about it, I guess. Here's a map. Now don't get touchy; there's nothing but a schematic of where you're going coming your way. Just a cue sheet of how to get to her. Can't give you a map of the whole place. Security reasons, you know.]

Her.

The guard fed the schematic to the outer edge of the Jeep's pellicle, and he snatched it up.

Her. This was the way to Li. First right. Straight ahead past the biomass tanks. Left, then a left again. Physics building.

The Jeep turned on his lights. He drove forward into the compound. Nothing happened. He rolled along the path into the structures. There were the biomass tanks. Left.

All was quiet. There were no windows. Perhaps people were awake and working inside, perhaps they slept. Each building had only one door. All of them were closed.

Left again.

The Jeep rolled to a stop in front of the closed door to the physics building.

He waited for a minute. Two. Nothing happened.

Now what?

Li might or might not know he was there. Another minute passed. Time to do something.

The Jeep honked his horn. He honked it again, three times.

After another minute, the door opened.

Li was standing in the transom. She wore a white shift, a nightgown, and was clutching the thermos bottle she often brought to the parking spot on the bluff. Li rubbed her eyes. Amazed disbelief or just sleep? Neither. The Jeep had never been close enough to another human being to develop the talent—not until now. But he could read Li's expressions.

Happiness.

He opened the passenger-side door, and Li climbed inside. She closed the door.

"I'm so glad you came," she said.

The laboratory compound exploded into lights and alarms. Grist-mil swarmed.

"I guess my infinite do-loop wasn't infinite enough," said Li. "The section ward found a way out." She laughed. "I think we'd better go."

The Jeep needed no further urging.

He jerked into reverse, speeding backwards while Li fumbled around looking for something. Right. The seat belt. It was still there. He'd kept it operational, of course, more out of habit than need. Until now. Li just managed to click the buckle into place when the Jeep slammed on his brakes, turned his wheel hard, and spun into a perfect 180, exiting facing forward.

The turn was not exactly routine, but he'd performed enough spins to be able to execute one with little thought. In the midst of turning, the Jeep set his attention to another task. Releasing BigCanada into the compound's grist-mil substrate.

"I made something for you," Li said, shaking the thermos bottle on her lap. "I'll show it to you later."

The Jeep heard the words, but filed them away. Nothing to do with the information right then. BigCanada was expanded and dynamic, hissing and snapping at the containment protocols. The grist-mil within the earth below him swarmed up the Jeep's tires, attempting to blast the Kevlar belts back to carbon and silicon, swarming along the axle, building microscopic tethers across the wheel well, attempting to latch on to the Jeep's chassis with what were, at the molecular level, tiny grappling hooks. The Jeep released BigCanada from her year of confinement.

The laboratory grist-mil security algorithm didn't have a chance, at least not in the short term. BigCanada at first dug her claws, figuratively speaking, into the Jeep's pellicle; he'd expected that, and his defenses were up. She still managed to get an outrider to one of his hydrogen cells and converted the electrodes to a zinc gunk. But it was only one cell of many. His power was only minimally reduced, and he could make repairs later. Then BigCanada came in contact with the grist-mil—her old enemy, the same sort of program that had tried to exterminate her before. True to her vicious, angry nature—formed over years of flight and fighting those who would wipe the grist clean of her—she attacked without mercy.

The Jeep did not stay around to observe the consequences—although he could picture what the results would be if the lab's security algorithm didn't find a way to contain BigCanada. The valley she'd owned in Nova Scotia—really a dry gully in rocky barrens not far from the sea—had been furiously organized into patterns of broken spirals, imperfect tessellations, and three-dimensional representations of chaos fractals cut off in the middle of their flowering. The virus lichen had squeezed the rock into form and held it there, contained within a thin but unbreakable film. She'd made the landscape into a vast representation of pain, hurt, and bewilderment, only incidentally blasting away all life in the process—except, of course, the lichen-brush with which she painted her anguish.

BigCanada had subverted the grist in the area as completely as she had the lichen, overrunning whatever maintenance or recognizance programming might be latent within the local substrate and sending out a spoof signal that all was well. This was what all bugs tried to do when they got loose, but BigCanada was particularly good at it—she was nearing free-convert status in her ability. And the truth was, no one paid much attention to what happened in the wilds of Canada these days.

She was containable, once her opponent figured out—as the Jeep had—her fatal flaw, left over from her days of fleeing through the Met. Her self-replications—whether for use in a massed "denial of service" attack or in an outrider attempting to flank a defender's defenses— were stripped-down versions of herself, more like clone children than actual copies. They lacked the original virus's full memory load, and with the memory went judgment.

BigCanada relied on destabilizing her opponents—guerrilla tactics of surprise, informational "noise," and berserker vehemence, but the math was simple. Any fully sentient convert could beat any partially sentient code in a stable set of circumstances. It was similar to the math of another era in warfare, when horse cavalry attacked a squared com- pany of bayonet-wielding infantry. No matter how frightening and loud the horse charge, no matter how sharp the sabers of the cavaliers, the infantry—provided they remained stalwart—always triumphed, of- ten without a single casualty.

The Jeep had simply "squared up" and systematically dealt with Big- Canada's replications from the weakest to the strongest, finally isolat- ing the virus herself in her den, pulling her out by the prime numbers of her nose, throwing her into a burlap bag of whole numbers, and squeezing her into quiescence with archiving programs he'd picked up from an old computer in an abandoned garage where he'd once parked overnight. The computer was ancient, and contained within it a simple algorithm for file compression that had long been lost to the modern era. BigCanada had been completely surprised when he'd introduced the archiving program into her containment bag, expecting the familiar shackling routines of the Met. She'd shriveled down with barely a whimper.

As soon as the Jeep crossed the sand/soil line he again assumed his "bear" pellicle and rolled on and away.

"You did something nasty to the grist back there," Li said. "It could hurt the people inside."

That was true. The Jeep could feel remorse, but mostly for opportu- nities lost acquiring skills or fuel. He supposed he was capable of feel- ing guilt, but this wasn't the time to do so, when survival was at stake: the survival of the only person he'd ever wanted for as a driver.

There was pursuit from the compound, however. Trucks rolled out from outlying buildings filled with biological aspects—men and women in the red-and-gold uniform of the Department of Immunity

Enforcement Division. If they were even minimally proficient, they could follow him. There was very little the Jeep could do to cover his tracks if he wished to travel at maximum speed. In any case, he had a single destination in mind: the parking space. He was headed there along the trail that Li had often walked to visit him. It was not wide enough for him to pass in some places, and he had to crush underbrush and snap saplings, sure telltales of his passage, as he rolled quickly along.

"It might work, at least for a while," Li said. "Eventually they'll figure out that something's strange and keep going up the trail, no matter how much their intuition is telling them not to. That's what happened with me."

But it *was* a temporary solution, and so the Jeep barreled onward and upward, turning down the long-forgotten (except by him) road to Norrie State Park, and up the track that led to his parking spot on the bluff.

There the Jeep came to a scruffy stop on the leafy ground. A halfmoon was high in a sky full of stars. Below, the Hudson River glinted silver amidst dark cliffs and forests. It was October, and a chilly wind blew from the west, hinting of an approaching storm front. The Jeep monitored the pursuers. Like a school of fish nearing a shoal, they parted when the trail reached the "protected" area of the parking space, with one group turning back and the others taking off in several wrong directions. For the moment, he and Li were safe.

"This is what I was talking about before," Li said. "The process McHood and I discovered. It's mixed in with my tea."

The Jeep let out his clutch and settled into a neutral gear. He turned his interior cabin heater on low. He remained alert. He'd never tested the parking space's peculiar properties so directly before.

Li held up the bottle she was clutching.

"Pandora's thermos bottle," she said. "All it takes is a thermos. In fact, any container would work, even a paper bag. The paradox is what keeps it confined. Them. The universe is information. Inside this bottle is ... well, it's gravitons. And tea, of course. But each graviton represents—*is*—a nontrivial event that will happen in the future." Li smiled. "I'm not doing a very good job of explaining this, I'm afraid. The thing is, I'm going to open this bottle up, but only with your permission."

One of the trucks that pursued them was circling back to the path. Someone was beginning to have doubts. As Li had said, it might only be a matter of time until they were discovered and flushed.

"When I open the thermos, everything's going to change for you. I'm not sure what will happen, but we'll leave here. We'll leave Earth. All you've ever known. The only familiar thing is going to be me. I'll be there, wherever we're going. I promise."

Li put her left hand on the thermos bottle's plug top.

"So, my one true friend, what will it be?"

There was no way to tell the woman that this was all moot. He'd made the decision on the day he'd allowed her to climb inside his cabin. She was worthy to be his driver.

The Jeep opened his glove box and extended his cup holder.

Li smiled. "All right, then," she said.

She screwed open the top on the thermos bottle and opened it up. The smoky odor of Lapsang souchong tea filled the cabin.

And, just as Li had said it would, everything changed.

CHAPTER TWO

Leo Sherman looked at his father ruefully. Somehow, even though he'd traveled over a billion miles to reach the man, he felt like he was letting the Old Crow down once again by arriving in so unceremonious a manner. Of course there was no way his father could recognize him in the all-encompassing getup of Private Aschenbach. This fact gave Leo no comfort whatsoever.

Sherman cleared his throat and glared down at Leo—Leo was sitting in a hard metal chair in the brig of the *Boomerang*—and harrumphed his throat clear.

"Soldier, I have exactly no time to waste," his father said in his familiar growl—the growl that had preceded various groundings, allowance withholding, room confinements, and dozens of other punishments during Leo's rambunctious youth. "So if you are wasting my time, I will see that you are shipped back down to the surface of the planet forthwith and given over to the muck that's taken over down there. Do you understand what that means?"

"I understand completely," Leo replied. He was about to add "Dad," but thought better of it. He could deal with all that later.

"Then out with it."

Leo smiled. "This is going to be kind of weird, General. You'd better stand back."

Two security officers stepped forward to intercept any move Leo might make toward their commander. Even Leo's rescuer/captor, Neiderer, stood on edge, ready to deal with any attack.

"Don't worry," Leo said. "I didn't say it would be *dangerous*; I only said it would be weird. Especially for me."

Without further explanation, Leo extended his left arm and reached for his left elbow. Delivering his payload was a two-step process. First, he must become himself again. And then he would carry out his more important task. With the fingers of his right hand, Leo probed around the funny bone, actually a ligament, in the back of his elbow. The capsule that contained him—all he was and had ever been—was lodged next to that tendon. It would only seem a nodule to anyone, a bit of scar tissue in the muscle. And without Leo's specific pellicle code word, that is exactly how the capsule would act. But not this time. Leo grasped the capsule through his skin and held it between his right thumb and forefinger.

"Calico-tanned-Arapaho-man," Leo murmured to himself. Alvin and the hacks had let him come up with the magical "open sesame" phrase himself.

He squeezed the capsule as hard as he could.

Throughout his body, quantum-entangled particles were observed, their uncertainties at an end, their destinies resolved. Leo looked down at his arm. It seemed to vibrate and shimmer for an instant. The glow was from the energy released in the transformation process. He glanced at his legs. They were three inches shorter. Which was right.

He certainly was much stockier in real life, too. Good. He was tired of masquerading as a skinny drink of water.

In his lap, he was holding the urn that had previously resided in his chest cavity. It gleamed a dull golden brown. No one had been able to determine what sort of material it was made of. Some variant on Kevlar, Alvin had guessed. No way of knowing without a thorough analysis. And as C, the master spy who gave it to Leo, had said, that would have been a very bad idea for the analyst.

General Sherman took a step back.

"I'll be damned," he whispered. "Leo."

"Good to see you, Dad."

"I want an immediate scan," Sherman said to no one in particular—

which meant he was probably speaking to one of the free-convert soldiers. Leo had long stopped thinking it strange when his father barked an order into the empty air.

"It's me," Leo said. "More or less."

"Yes," Sherman said, still glaring dubiously at his son. "That's what they're telling me. Down to the DNA."

"And this is for you," Leo said, nodding toward the urn. He dare not lift it. The guards would probably blast off his head the instant he made such a move.

"You've brought me the remains of a dead man?" Sherman said.

In other words—you've wasted all this time and energy on a complete fuck-up, Leo thought. Not this time, you Old Crow.

"There's a living man," Leo said, "in here. At least I think so. The only one who can find out for certain is *you*."

Sherman blinked, blinked again. More free-convert communications.

"This thing is strongly encrypted, and it could seriously hurt anybody who tried to crack it without authorization," Leo said. "You—*General*, is it now?—have that authorization. The man who gave it to me told me that all you had to do was rub it three times. Like Aladdin's lamp."

"Funny," Sherman growled.

"He seemed to have a droll sense of humor," Leo said. "Not unlike your own."

Sherman reached over and pulled up the other chair that was in the brig. It rasped as he dragged it across the floor. He sat down across from Leo.

"There's nothing I could ask you that would prove you're who you seem to be. Hell, you might even *be* Leo, taken over by some kind of nasty Department of Immunity protocol."

"Or my whole story might be true."

"Yes," Sherman said. He leaned forward. "Is it?"

Leo sighed. "Hell, Dad, you never fucking believed anything I told you anyway. Why should this be any different?"

Sherman sat back. His shoulders began to shake. For a moment, Leo was utterly bewildered. What was happening? Was the old man going crazy? And then he realized his father was laughing heartily. Not something you saw every day. Or every decade, for that matter.

"It's my goddamn son, all right," Sherman said to the room.

"Oh yeah?" Leo said. "I thought you only had one son, and he was dead." His words came out softly—not sarcastically, as he'd intended.

Sherman smiled. Another rare sighting. Just as well, thought Leo. It was kind of gruesome and carnivorous.

"I guess I was mistaken," his father replied.

Then, without another word, the Old Crow reached over and rubbed the urn three times, as if he were polishing it.

Nothing happened.

Sherman was about to rub the urn for a fourth time when there was a tiny whirring sound. A stamp-sized plate slid to the side, revealing a small gold plaque previously concealed beneath the urn's facing. Sherman took the urn from Leo, tilted it up, and examined the plaque.

"Very amusing," he said.

He turned the urn around so that Leo could read the plaque. In swirling, engraved script two words could be discerned on its surface.

DOWNLOAD ME

CHAPTER THREE

"You're older than I," said Cloudship Lebedev. "Maybe you can tell me if that is what I think it is."

"Well," Cloudship Tacitus said. "Well." There was one second of silence from the old cloudship. Two. Finally, he spoke. "I can say without qualification that there truly *is* something new under the sun. Or orbiting it, in this case. What the hell is that?"

"If I'm not mistaken, it's a—"

"I know what it *is*, Lebedev! What I mean to say is 'what is that doing there?'"

They were both watching an image on a restricted back-channel feed on the merci network used exclusively by cloudships for communications. The image originated from far out on the Dark Matter Road that stretched between the solar system and the Alpha Centauri system. The signal was coming from Misha, the only daughter of Cloudship Tolstoy. She was stationed on a little-known tributary to the Road, a spit that led away from the Road, running onward for ten thousand kilometers in the general direction of the constellation Cygnus. It then turned round and round itself in the same manner as a spiral jetty in an ocean on Earth, spiraling inward like a grasping tendril on a vine. And at the center of the jetty, at the tip end of the last turn of the spiral, was the legendary secret graveyard of the cloudships of the outer system. Cloudship Misha was the official keeper of the cemetery now that Tolstoy had taken his thirteen sons away to war within the solar system.

Only a select few ships even knew the way to the burial ground. No one else had ever found the place.

Until now.

"Misha dear, when did you notice this?"

"About fifteen minutes ago," the young cloudship replied. "I called Uncle Lebedev as soon as I could."

"And we're speaking on a completely encrypted channel now?"

"Of course, Uncle Tacitus."

"Good work," said Tacitus. "Quick and effective thinking, my dear. Your father will be proud of you."

"*If* he notices."

Tension there. Tacitus could only imagine the position of the lone daughter in the midst of all those brothers.

"In his way, he will be. He adores you."

"Look, I want to get on with my job," Misha said, "without asking him what to do. So could you two tell me how I should handle this?"

Tacitus considered for a moment. This could be a hallucination. He could finally be losing it after all these years. It could also be a trap. But both options were absurd. His mind was as sharp as ever, and what could Amés, or anyone else, for that matter, hope to gain from a ruse in this form? Nothing. No, it was what exactly what Misha's observation and his database was telling him.

A Jeep Wrangler, white in color. An automobile.

Flying through space over a billion miles from the planet Earth.

"I think you should go and find out if anyone is driving," Tacitus said.

Misha did as suggested and moved toward the Jeep. But when she got within a few hundred meters, the vehicle turned and sped away from her. Fast. Faster than anything in history ever had, in fact. Half the speed of light in a vacuum. And then, at a hundred kilometers distance, it slammed on the brake, came to a seemingly inertialess stop— as easily as it had started up—and attained its impossible speed. Then the vehicle turned and faced Cloudship Misha once again.

Misha continued doggedly toward it, and the Jeep repeated its actions once again. But this time, it did not move at half the speed of light. Instead, it jumped. First it was in one position; then in the next instant, it was in another several kilometers away.

"By God," Lebedev whispered. "By God, did you see that, Monty?"

"Yes," Tacitus replied. The cloudship considered for a moment. "Misha, I suggest you hold your position. Keep an eye on that thing."

Misha acknowledged and applied reverse thrust until she was motionless relative to the Jeep.

"Lebedev, old friend," said Tacitus, "could you join me for a brief consultation?"

Instantly, Lebedev was on Tacitus's sailing vessel in his virtual Mediterranean Sea. Lebedev manifested as a trim, dark-complected man, taller than average, and dressed in a conservative three-piece suit complete with cravat, from some bygone era. He accepted when Tacitus offered him a cigar. The old friends took a moment and lit up before speaking. As always, the tang of good cigar smoke on his tongue stimulated Tacitus's thoughts.

"It appears someone has discovered faster-than-light travel," Tacitus said.

"Good God, think of the implications," Lebedev said. "The superluminal grail! And it's ours."

"I'm not so sure to whom it belongs," Tacitus said. "If it belongs to anyone." He exhaled a puff of smoke, then considered the beginnings of gray ash on his cigar tip. "Obviously whoever it is doesn't want to be caught. And we're not in a position to catch them, are we?"

"What's to be done?"

"Well, we can either attempt to destroy them, or we can talk to them. I have a feeling we'd have trouble accomplishing the former, so let's try talking."

"Yes, of course," said Lebedev. "But who could it be?"

Tacitus chuckled and took another draw on his cigar. He looked out at his shimmering Levantine horizon. "What I want to know," the old cloudship said, "is what kind of mileage that thing gets."

Cloudship Misha's voice came from a nearby loudspeaker.

"Uncles, I've spoken to—them. The car and driver."

"Spoken to them? How?" Tacitus asked. He hoped it was not over the merci. Such communications could be monitored from any distance. He even suspected this quantum-encrypted channel on the merci used by the cloudships for secret communication. But he was now at Pluto, and Misha was as far away from the sun as Pluto yet again, so there was no possibility of a face-to-face discussion.

"At first, by blinking lights. The vehicle used its headlights. It was a simple greeting. But that gave me an idea. I remembered that those old ground cars had some sort of electromagnetic receivers, so I looked it up. AM radio, it's called. So I found the appropriate wavelengths. And I established a low-powered broadcast. And I made a sign."

"A sign?"

"In Basis. Big block letters. I formed it along the outside of my left arm. About two kilometers across."

"And what did the sign say?"

"Turn on your radio."

"Very good, Misha."

"And so I broadcast to 880 kilohertz on the AM band, and asked if he—or they—could hear me. The Jeep flashed its lights once, which I assume means yes. I asked them a series of questions they could answer with yes or no: How many are there? *Two* was the answer. That includes the vehicle. I then asked if they come from the solar system."

"What's the answer to that?" Lebedev asked, knocking the ash from his cigar tip as he whirled to face the loudspeaker.

"Yes," Misha replied, "they do. I went through the Met radials, then the planets. They come from Earth, Uncles. I asked them if they were representatives of Director Amés."

Tacitus tensed. What a display this would be for Amés—a contemptuous notification that he now possessed superluminal flight. Yet in his heart Tacitus knew Amés would opt for a more spectacular and damaging display if he had acquired that power.

"They blinked back that they were *not* Interlocking Directorate representatives. In fact, I established that they are fugitives from the Met," Misha said. "At that point, I told them I had to speak to my superiors. And that's where the matter stands, Uncles."

"Excellent work, Misha," Tacitus said. He turned to Lebedev. In the virtuality, Lebedev presented his features—probably unconsciously—as dark and heavily creased, utterly Slavic. Tacitus reflected that he had never appeared as such an iconic Russian in his first biological body.

"If Amés had this process fully developed, he would have used it in the recent attacks," said Lebedev. He suddenly burst into a deep, rumbling laugh. "Of course, we will never catch those in the graveyard unless they wish to be caught."

Tacitus nodded, considered the wood grain of his ship's railing. "Maybe we should tell them to keep going," he said. "To the stars. Take their chances out there. Leave the rest of us to kill one another off."

"You can't be serious!"

Tacitus turned and faced his old friend. Together they had seen humanity take to space, transform into almost unimaginable forms. And keep the same human heart. Love, hate, ambition, greed, curiosity, complacency—it was all still there, tucked into a thousand thousand physical structures, a billion billion manifestations.

But of course, any travelers, however small and insignificant, would always carry that heart with them. If there was anything Tacitus had learned in his thousand years of life, it was this fact. There was no way to abdicate the responsibility for who you are. Each and every human was accountable for the heart the entire species would take to the stars.

Tacitus transferred his cigar back to his mouth and clapped a hand on Lebedev's shoulder. The two turned back to the rail and faced the infinite, virtual sea. "Just a thought, old friend," Tacitus said.

"Sir, sorry to interrupt again," said Misha's voice from the loudspeaker. "But I have underestimated the capabilities of the Jeep. It can also transmit. The driver has spoken to me via radio."

"What did he say?"

"*She*, uncle," said Miranda. Misha corrected Tacitus with the force of the woman often overlooked in an existence full of boys. "She asked permission to come aboard and . . . 'park,' is, I believe the word she used."

Lebedev sighed a heavy Russian sigh. "What a war it will become," he said in a low voice.

"Pardon?" said Misha.

Tacitus did not turn from gazing at the sea, but he spoke in a loud and clear voice. "Cloudship Misha, tell our travelers that they are very welcome, and to park wherever they want."

INTRODUCTION

Hello, and welcome to your e-year 3017 internal software update! From your internal clock, we see that you're long overdue for a new version of your personal operating system. The information we are about to download will be transferred faster than the speed of light—instantly, in fact—into your grist pellicle and from there will go into permanent storage in your memory, for recall at will [some delay possible over a 28.8-terabyte modem]. Wonder what it means?

We, the human race in all its myriad forms, will soon be entering upon a period of turmoil and transformation. An empire will rise and fall. Democracy will be put to the fire and hammered into an almost unrecognizable form. Low deeds will be perpetrated, and it will often seem that evil had the upper hand.

Heroes will emerge from the obscurity. Some will die gloriously, while others will be beaten and broken. It will be a hard time to be alive.

Yet it will be a time of incredible ingenuity and fervent creativity. New sciences will be born. Great literature will be written. People who would have ordinarily never known one another will come together to face a common foe. Necessity will abolish prejudice, and humans will become brothers and sisters—and, in some cases, lovers—with those whom they would scarcely have acknowledged as persons before.

Don't worry. After your complete system update with "The Meta-planetary Guide, Glossary and Time Line," you will understand everything perfectly. You will be ready for the next step on this, your journey to the e-year 3013.

Thank you very much.

[This free update brought to you by the Friends of Tod, who invite you to remember Tod's fateful words: "When ignorance comes a-knocking, answer with the shotgun of science!"]

THE BASICS

Met

The Met is the system of space cables, tethers, and planetary lifts along with all the associated bolsas, sacs, armatures, and dendrites that comprise the human-inhabited space of the inner solar system. When seen from a vantage point above the planetary ecliptic near the asteroid belt, the Met shines like a spiderweb, wet with dewdrops, hanging in space between the wheeling planets. The Met is made of cables held together by a macroscopic version of the strong nuclear force. It is infused with grist. Initial construction on the Met began in 2465 c.e.

THE SCIENCE OF THE MET

By the early 2400s, nanotechnologists had united buckyball constructions with superconducting quantum interference devices (SQUIDS) to create a reproducible molecular chain that displayed quantum behavior on the level visible to the human eye.

The most important behavior that the nanotechnological engineers were able to produce, at least in regards to the Met, is the strong nu-

clear force. You can picture it as a rubber band connecting two particles. The more you stretch the rubber band, the harder it pulls the particles. When the particles are close together, the rubber band is slack. It
is this property of the strong force, operating on a macro level, that
gives the Met cables their ability to bend without breaking. Torque
forces that would easily separate material made of mere chemical
bonds cannot overcome the strong force manifested by the buckeyball
SQUIDs, and the Met holds together.

In fact, there is no known force generated by the turnings of the
planets that is even close to pushing the Met's structural tolerances. If
you live or travel in the Met, you are as safe as you are on the surface of
a planet (which are, themselves, held together, on the level of the
atomic nucleus, by the strong force of nature).

THE DEDO
The space cable that connects the planet Mercury to the planet Venus.
As with the other main cables, it makes a tremendous loop around the
sun—in the Dedo's case, a loop over the solar south pole. The Dedo is
traditionally a center of high culture and finance, the "rich" section of
the Met.

THE VAS
The Vas is the space cable that connects the planet Venus with the
planet Earth. As with the other main cables, it makes a tremendous
loop around the sun—in the Vas's case, a loop over the solar north
pole. The Vas is the most heavily populated portion of the Met, and the
most urban in quality. It houses the vast manufacturing complexes of
the inner system. The Vas is home to the enormous "lower-middle-
class" segment of the Met populace.

THE MARS-EARTH DIAPHANY
The Diaphany is the space cable that connects the planet Mars with the
planet Earth. As with the other main cables, it makes a tremendous
loop around the sun—in the Diaphany's case, a loop over the solar
south pole. The Mars-Earth Diaphany is the most diverse section of
the Met, with a spinning bolsa for almost every culture known to humanity. It is also, in a way, the "suburbs" of the Met, with an average
standard of living higher than that of the Vas, but not as opulent as that
of the Dedo.

THE ALDISS

The space cable that connects the Earth to the Earth's moon. This is the oldest section of the Met.

Nanotechnology

The manipulation of materials and processes on a nanometer level using tiny robotic machines (that is, machines controlled by programming) which are themselves made of only a few molecules. Nanotech was the big technological revolution following the biotech revolution.

Grist

Nanotechnological construct that incorporates the Josephson-Feynman graviton detector invented by Raphael Merced. This nano, disseminated throughout the Met, enables instantaneous information transfer over any distance that the nano is dispersed. Grist is also a word used to describe nanotechnological constructs in a general way, whether or not instantaneous information transfer is involved.

Grist-mil

Grist used for a military purpose. Many safeguards built into normal grist are removed in these constructs.

Merced Effect

The instantaneous transfer of information between locations set at any distance apart by the use of quantum-entangled gravitons.

Merci

The merci is the union of grist with the old virtual-reality "web" to produce an instantaneous medium of communication and entertainment. It takes its name from Raphael Merced, the cocreator of the grist and discoverer of the Merced effect. The merci is instantaneous and fully participatory (or not, if you voluntarily decide to restrict yourself—for instance, to "watch a program"). The merci is a combination of old-time television, the Internet, the theater, music, all manner of performance, virtual-reality games and government.

Virtuality

The virtuality is virtual reality within the grist. The Met is in essence an enormous quantum computer, with instantaneous linkage through the grist. Distance is unimportant for most actions and thought. Every time is local time. The real "landscape" of the virtuality is the complex interlocking of recognition and transfer protocols, of security checks and system gates and barriers. It is a lot like being in an extremely crowded city with a bunch of skeletons and skeleton keys jostling about. In some ways the virtuality is the shadow of the physical Met and the outer system, but in other ways it is nothing like that at all.

HUMANITY

Human Being

As of 3013 C.E., the first year of the war, almost all of us have at least three parts to our makeup.

ASPECT
The biological, bodily portion of a normal person.

CONVERT
The algorithmic "extra" computing and memory storage portion of a normal person.

PELLICLE
The nanotechnological grist that permeates a normal person. The pellicle mediates between aspect and convert portions of a person.

Free Convert

An artificial intelligence that exists without a biological component. Most free converts are based upon copies of the personalities of historical and/or living human beings, but some are generations removed from this first iteration. All are capable of independent reasoning and action through manipulation of the grist. What free converts can and cannot do is limited by their own programming and by the law. Before the war, there was a form of free-convert "apartheid" in the Met. This did not exist in the outer system—although prejudice did exist everywhere.

LAP

A Large Array of Personalities. If a person makes multiple copies of him- or herself and integrates these personalities to act in parallel via the quantum interaction of the grist, you have a LAP. Usually these various personas are copies of an original "person" and are mostly converts—although it is usual for a LAP to have three or so clones, in addition to the original biological aspect. A LAP can be a conglomeration of many physical bodies, many convert portions, or a mixture of both. The convert portions of LAPs are usually a plethora of programs and subroutines, all under a mediator intelligence that is a complete replica of the human personality, along with whatever virtual controls and calculators are necessary for proper functioning.

These Large Arrays of Personalities are instantaneous networks, since they are linked by the merci, and the merci operates superluminally. By becoming a LAP a person can lead multiple lives in multiple locations, all at the same time. He or she might also choose to concentrate all those separate (but similar) attentions on one task or way of life. There are many different ways that LAPs have chosen to exist. The ships of the outer system, for instance, are large-scale LAPs that are essentially spaceship and crew, all in one. Being a LAP in the Met is more like being a subway system or a high-rise in a city than a single person in one. Not everyone can become a LAP. A significant number of people have a psychology that would cause them to go insane during the conversion process. This is normally predictable and is usually avoided. The process of becoming a LAP is quite expensive, as well.

Manifold

A fully integrated, multiply differentiated LAP with a highly diverse plethora of personalities. A manifold is a LAP of LAPs.

Time Tower

LAPs that were the product of some of the first attempts to create a manifold. Rather than being "nonlocal" in space, as most LAPs are, the consciousness of the time tower is spread over time, so that his or her present can span a decade of e-years or more. The idea was to create a being who could see into the future. Instead, the effort produced a species of utterly gnostic human personalities whose Delphic pronouncements were of little practical use. Many time towers became the prophets and even the "gods" of offshoot religions, however. Time towers have very odd effects on the grist in their immediate vicinity, and their presence can serve as a form of "firewall" or barricade within the virtuality, preventing—or in some cases allowing—eavesdropping and direct virtual travel through the grist. For that reason they were highly valued during the war.

Cloudship

Something like a mini-Met in the form of a spaceship. Usually one controlling personality inhabits a ship, but some are multiply inhabited. The cloudships traverse the outer system, where they serve as bankers and interplanetary transports (although there are also plenty of noncloudship craft available as well). Cloudships take the names of various important historical or fictional characters in human history. They consider themselves humanity's elite and are often aloof towards everyone else. The cloudships are the major political and economic power in the outer system. Cloudships began to be recognized as such in the 2700s, C.E.

From
The Memoirs of Cloudship Lebedev

We moved farther and farther out, always adding to our number in a stepwise process. Frequently, pioneers to the outer system would, after a time of hardship, acquire their own ships, and if we thought them suitable, we would ask them to join our consortium. Hardly anyone ever turned us down. It was, relatively speaking, easy money, and a sure passport to LAP status. Eventually, Tacitus and I reached the Oorts—the subject of my doctoral dissertation some 350 e-years before. We thought we could go no farther.

We remained there, and others joined us. After several years, a kind of society began to develop among us. For the most part, we eschewed the merci and kept to ourselves, although we are as able to make use of the merci as the next fellow. Mainly, we found that the programming did not speak to our needs and was generally not to our taste. As I said, cloudships can be a snobby bunch. And then the males and females among us began to explore the possibility of procreating, as ships. This is what one does out in the Oorts with a great deal of time on one's hands.

There were, by that time, some grist engineers and quantum physicists among us of what I do not hesitate to call genius status. They were called upon to perform the rather odd task of reinventing sex—and in our case, sex as it might be carried out between hurricanes and storm clouds. By the time a ship got to the Oorts, it had formed into a sort of miniature copy of the shape that galaxies and nascent solar systems take. Fortunately for our children, those engineers and physicists were up to the task, and even succeeded in adding a new sort of beauty to the process.

Now I won't go into the exact specifics of cloudship courting and breeding practices here. Suffice it to say they are complex, but dancelike. Most of us are spirals, and one has to maneuver the tines of oneself within those of another without destroying that other in the process. Over time we discovered that it is better for males to have cyclonal rotations and for females to have anticyclonal, counterclockwise spins. This is entirely arbitrary, but a great improvement over the old days, when sex could be quite dangerous.

Population

There are approximately 90 billion people of various sorts living in the Met and on the planets of the inner solar system. There are approximately 10 billion people living in the outer system.

THE SCIENCE OF CLOUDSHIPS

The Casimir Effect

The physical effect underlying the operations of cloudships and founded upon the principle of quantum fluctuation. This effect, discovered and experimentally proved in the twentieth century, is a result of the fundamental quantum nature of reality, and it works as follows: if two mirrors are placed a short distance apart and facing one another, they will move to a small degree toward one another. This distance is imperceptible to the naked eye, of course, but it does indeed occur.

QUANTUM FLUCTUATION

The physical property that accounts for the Casimir effect. The most familiar concept usually used for demonstrating Heisenberg's principle of uncertainty is that of momentum and position. If you know one, the other becomes unknowable to an extent equal (precisely) to the amount that you know its partner. Another lesser-known, product of uncertainty is the energy and time pairing. Taking this into account mathematically results in the prediction that space—empty space—is actually teeming with a sea of virtual particles, all produced in pair-antipair combinations that are continually being generated and annihilating one another. Empty space can be polarized, and you can "make" a particle out of nothing.

A good way to picture the process is this: think of space as a string on a musical instrument. Now pluck that string. Normal space is a very long string and its "vibration" corresponds to the lowest energy state there can be. Now if you "fret" the string—say, with our two mirrors—you necessarily exclude certain vibrations. The only vibrations that will occur between the mirrors are those whose wavelengths fit exactly into the distance separating the mirrors. This is precisely how a fretted guitar string produces different notes, and how, in a sense, it "contains" all notes.

THE CASIMIR EFFECT IN THE ACTUAL UNIVERSE

Now you will remember that all elementary particles are not actually particles, but are wave-particle entities that have properties associated with both phenomena. With our mirrors we might "play" an electron upon the nothingness, or, more easily, a photon. But when we "play" one virtual particle, the others are all necessarily excluded. In effect, there are "more" possible particles on the outside of our mirrors than there are between them. There is less pressure, therefore, pressing them out than pressing them in. The mirrors move together. Remember that this has nothing to do with gases or liquids being between or outside the mirror surfaces. We are speaking of empty space.

Cloudship Propulsion and Weaponry

Cloudships have the ability to produce antimatter at any point on their surface, and to concentrate it for firepower or propulsion. The process is begun by using what is called the Casimir effect upon tiny mirrors whose size is in the nanometer level. The mirrors are, of course, created and manipulated by the grist.

THE CASIMIR EFFECT IN CLOUDSHIPS

While you must "put in" energy in the form of setting up the nanomirrors, so that the law of the conservation of energy is obeyed, the energy that comes out is precise and focused. If you "fret" the vacuum correctly (making use of the property of quantum fluctuation), the energy produced can be extracted in the form of a stream of antiparticles, which can then be lased into a beam or used to produce an annihilation reaction with matter. This operation is at the heart of a cloudship.

All of this is done on a nanometer level by the grist. The mirrors we use are conducting plates of material that is a single molecule thick. The lasers are of a similar dimension. A cloudship can enact this process anywhere on the ship where there is grist. To a cloudship, it feels very much like moving a finger or blinking an eye. If you are watching from space, it appears as if a bolt of raw energy has erupted from the ship's surface (provided, of course, that that energy interacts with something along its path and so become visible). A fully energized cloudship is an awesome sight to behold.

Unless the cloudship is aiming at you.

COMMON TERMS AND COMMON KNOWLEDGE IN THE SOLAR SYSTEM

Basis

This is the most common language spoken in the Met and in the outer system. It is a combination of English and free-convert information transfer protocols—that is, it is English strained through a thousand-year-long "information age." While most people believe they are speaking Basis, there are, in fact, millions of dialects, as well as dialects of all the other human languages, many having only one or two individuals as native speakers. This phenomenon is due to the proliferation of "Broca grist" throughout human space. People have adaptive translation programs embedded in their brains. Because of this, you can utter just about any sound you desire and, if it mentally correlates with an idea, image, or other language construct in your own mind, your pellicle can transform it into standard Basis. The pellicle of the person who is listening to you will receive and decode your words. This is normally done without either party noticing the process or giving it any thought—and the practice has been going on for centuries. Someone listening in on the Met who does not possess Broca grist will hear a vast Tower of Babel and will wonder how anybody understands what anyone else is saying. Most people in the cultural elite understand the problem and attempt to speak a standard Basis not mediated by Broca grist.

E-year

Along with e-month, e-week, e-day, these are time periods based on Earth's rotation and orbit. It is the standard measurement of calendar time in the solar system. Local time is also frequently referenced when dealing with local matters.

Greenleaf

AKA "leaves." The monetary unit of the solar system. The term has its origin in the Greentree religion, which has a strong economic component, and as a reference to the old U.S. dollars of Earth.

Rip

Slang in Met Basis for "highly desirable, pleasing, and stylish."

SOLAR SYSTEM HISTORY

Amanda Breadwinner

First Chief Engineer of the Met. Born in Dublin, in the old EU, in 2429, the daughter of American immigrant writers. Construction on the Aldiss, the first space cable, was complete, 2475 C.E. Initial construction began on the Mars-Earth Diaphany.

Breadwinner continued on in her job until her retirement in 2511 C.E., coincidentally the year of Raphael Merced's birth. She took the position as the director of the newly established Breadwinner Labs within the first Met bolsa to be constructed on the Diaphany, Apiana. It was twenty years later at Breadwinner Labs that a young engineer named Feur Otto Bring, who suffered from incurable Tourette's syndrome, would obtain his first internship in nanotech construction techniques. Bring would soon be fired by Breadwinner after questioning her parentage during a laboratory dispute. Bring would then end up at Bradbury University on Mars, where he eventually met Raphael Merced, and the grist as we know it today was invented.

Beat Myers

Poet. Best friend to Raphael Merced. Founder of the "Flare Generation" of poets, and editor of the poetry journal *Flare*, although the November 2646 issue of *Flare* was almost wholly devoted to Merced's seminal paper "The Teleological Constant and Its Relation to Instantaneous Information Transfer at a Distance," accompanied by poems written by Myers. Myers's best poem is considered to be "Old Left-handed Time."

Bradbury University

The great center of learning in the Met. It is located on Mars and was founded by Tacitus and Lebedev. This is where Raphael Merced did all his important work. Before the war, it had fallen far from its former glory. Its greatest period was the 2500s C.E., when new discoveries and technologies, new systems of thought, and great works of literature came pouring out of Bradbury. These were the years of Merced and Bring, of Ravenswaay's *Atmosphericsaga*, and a hundred lesser, but no less worthy, works of skill and genius.

Chen Wocek

Raphael Merced's mentor at Bradbury University.

Clara Merced

Sister to Raphael Merced. Interplanetary geophysicist who was the first to explain why the solar system planets lie in the same basic orbital plane.

Conjubilation of 2963

When Mars and Earth reach the closest point in their respective orbits, the Mars-Earth Diaphany is bent into a vast U shape trailing high above the planetary elliptic. At the closest point between the two sides of the U, a temporary bridge is built, and a festival is held. This is known as the Conjubilation, and it occurs about every two e-years. The most important Conjubilation in history occurred in 2963 C.E. Many important cultural and scientific movements had their origins in the event, but more important, a series of demonstrations broke out against the old Federal Republic. These in turn had their beginnings in the music and art festival called the Merge. From the Merge arose the system of direct "directorate-based" democracy that governed the Met until the war. The most important political figure to arise out of the Merge was a LAP going by the singular name of Amés.

Containment Principles

Legal strictures of the late 2300s and early 2400s c.e. that led to the Information Consortiums of the 2400s c.e., and to the genesis of the ECHO Alliance. They still have repercussions today, being the precedent for the reproduction and expiration constraints put on free converts in Met. Project Alsace-Lorraine's tests were discovered five years after the fact by a Russian journalist, who published a full account in the Russian tabloids of the time. This caused a furor, but was not believed until the story was independently confirmed by EU military whistleblowers (the original experiment had been a joint German-French venture called Project Alsace-Lorraine).

ECHO Alliance

Former government on Earth during 2400s c.e.—a consortium of transnational information brokers. Growth and commerce, though sluggish, were generally steady. For the arts and sciences, however, it was an era of stagnation and malaise. In the arts, the 2400s c.e. are known as the Ironic Age.

The Exiles' Journey

The Exiles' Journey is a compendium of essays, thoughts, and sayings by the artists and scientists who ran afoul of the Mercurian Endowment government in the 2590s c.e., and whose malfunctioning prison ship accidentally fell into the sun. Contains Beat Myers's classic poem "Old Left-handed Time" and Raphael Merced's aphoristic "Merced Synthetics." Both men were on the doomed ship, as was Merced's sister, Clara.

Feur Otto Bring

Nanotech engineer, coinventor of the grist. Victim of incurable Tourette's syndrome. Fired by Met chief engineer Amanda Breadwinner after an outburst. Longtime collaborator with Raphael Merced. His daughter, Katya, was a famous spaceship pilot.

Fifty Worlds to Sunday

A written exchange between Raphael Merced and poet Beat Myers which attempted to codify an aesthetic theory.

FUSE

The Icelandic acronym for a terrorist group on Mars dedicated to the radical enforcement of free-convert rights. Destroyed by Roger Sherman's command on Mars when he was a captain in the Federal Army, even though he believed in many of their tenets. Sherman's company was known as the Fever Blisters by FUSE members.

Glory Channel

A special merci channel set up by the Department of Immunity to network the collective consciousness of those infused with the Glory or Confidence grist through subliminal communication during entertainment programming.

Hubble-Penrose Platform

Ancient space station circa 2300–2400s in Earth orbit.

Mars Terraforming Experiments

Disastrous attempt during the early 2700s C.E. to make the Martian surface inhabitable by unadapted human beings. Grist ecological feedback problems doomed the project.

Mouseflowers

An early attempt to make bean plants "warm-blooded" to an extent using mouse genes implanted by nanotechnological means. See Psyche Toomsuba's comprehensive *Artificial Speciation and the Genesis of Mammaliform Brachiation in the Legume Family*, or Peter Ober's *Mouseflowers*, which is intended for a more general audience.

Pithway Streamers

Bead compartments used for mass transit throughout the Met. They are coated with centimeter-long tendrils, slightly sticky, for passenger security. The walls are lustrous and pearly. There is normally a faint white-red, diffuse lighting that originates from these fiber tips. Grist commands can make the fibers into couches, chairs, etc. Windows can sometimes be deopaqued. Beads are highly crowded in the Vas, so packed with people that little movement is possible.

Project Alsace-Lorraine

A military adaptation of the "Mouseflowers" experiment that produced infectious military nano that did not obey the usual grist "harm human life" overrides, since it was designed to reengineer exactly the human genome. Suppressed, the PAL virus was eventually rediscovered by Tacitus and used against DIED forces on the Neptunian moon Nereid.

Raphael Merced

In 2511 C.E. on a Monday in April, as Martians reckon the months, the first scientist who was not an Earthling and who belongs in the pantheon of such figures as Newton, Einstein, and Galileo was born. Raphael Merced laid the foundation for linking Einstein's general theory of relativity with quantum mechanics, and as such is considered the father of quantum gravity theory as well as the first theorist to offer a precise mathematics of time as a property of the universe. His work with quantum gravity on an experimental basis also revealed the now-familiar quantum information leap that has since taken his name, the Merced effect. As if this weren't enough, Merced made major contributions to nanotechnological engineering, inventing—with Feur Otto Bring—the Josephson-Feynman grist, which now permeates all of our lives. Merced can truly be considered the defining scientific presence of our time, in much the way that Albert Einstein defined the science of the five hundred years that preceded Merced, and Newton before Einstein.

The Vas After Sunset

The Vas After Sunset is a guide to the seedier side of the Vas portion of the Met, with several essays on the underground history of the Met. Written by Leo Sherman.

Vas Soft

News channel popular on the Vas with multiple branches of programming. Phyllis Dulcimer is a popular news reporter on the channel.

West Point

Located on Earth, the ancient and principal training facility for the Army of the Republic—in use until the army was forced out of the Met and the Department of Immunity took over its functions when the Met changed over from republican to direct democracy shortly after the Conjubilation of 2963.

SOLAR SYSTEM CULTURE

Abacus

The Abacus is the main accounting algorithm for Teleman Milt on Mercury.

Army of the Republic

AKA the Federal Army. The former armed forces of the Met, relegated by Amés to policing the outer system before the war.

Asap Gymnasium

Claude Schlencker's school on Mercury.

Battle Day

Full-participation virtual-reality war show, available to Met citizens. Viewers experience directly the bodily sensations of soldiers in warfare, or drop back for a war-game-like perspective on the battle. There is a great deal of subtle Department of Immunity censorship underlying the show, however.

Berkbultz

A piano-making company.

Clinical Party

Local moralistic political party on Neptune's moon Triton.

Confidence

A passportlike marking grist adopted during the war to regulate travel and behavior within the Met.

Convert and Free-convert Iteration Section

Division of the Department of Immunity that sets rules for convert copying and transfer.

Department of Immunity

The vast administrative and enforcement bureaucracy of the Met. Answers directly to Director Amés. The Department of Immunity Enforcement Division, or DIED, is the collective name for the Met armed forces and the internal police force.

Eighth Chakra

Local group of "Neo-Flare" poets on Neptune's moon Triton.

Enigma Box

AKA puzzle box. Interlocking grist puzzle that Sint Graytor likes to play with.

Extrema

A pelota fanatic.

First Constitutional Congress of the Cloudships of the Outer System

April 2, 3013 (e-standard) C.E. Adopted the Metaplanetary Constitution of the Solarian Republic.

Flare School

Group of poets who published in Beat Myers's journal during the 2600s C.E.

Friends of Tod

This is the "religion" that sprang up around the gnostic time tower named Tod. It has a following of computer programmers, designers, engineers, and poets and artists of various ilk—nerds, as Aubry Graytor says. It is similar to the old "Church of the Subgenius" on ancient Earth—that is, a belief system undercut with irony at every turn (or, as the Friends would have it, it is metacommentary on human belief in general). Friends of Tod are normally pacifists. Along with the escaped "protocol vermin" of the Carbuncle, they formed the partisan resistance in the Met during the war. The leaders of the Friends of Tod are Otis and Game.

Free Integrationists

Whig-like political party that supports full free-convert rights in the solar system and believes that all intelligent systems are persons. Strongest in the outer system.

Greentree Way

AKA the Way. The major religion of the Met. Zen-Lutheranism, with a strong "shamanic" component as well. The main teaching center is on the Mars-Earth Diaphany in Seminary Barrel. Priests complete their initiation with the Walk on the Moon—that is, copying their original personality into another body and stepping with their original body into a special valley of Earth's moon and "dying" in the vacuum. The major tenet of the Way is that there is a living Tree that somehow both represents and embodies the spiritual and genetic imprint of humanity upon the universe.

Interlocking Directorate

The main governing board of the Met. The directorates are administrative and legislative agencies whose activities and administrators are voted on by the population of the Met constantly over the governmental merci channels. These can sometimes change hourly. The Interlocking Directorate membership is voted on in turn by the Directors. Director Amés chairs the Interlocking Directorate.

Keys

Used for currency in the Carbuncle.

Motoserra Club

Hoity-toity club to which descendants of the first settlers on Neptune's moon Triton belong.

Neo-Flares

Modern-day poets who style themselves as revivalists of the ancient Flare school of poetry.

Old Seventy-five

Alcoholic drinking grist. Thaddeus-Ben drinks a version modified with military grist and accidentally coughs up a woman.

Positions Room

The command center of Teleman Milt financial services.

Pelota

Soccer-like game played in weightless environment with a rotating arena and two oppositely rotating goals. The most popular sport in the solar system. Premier league teams include the Jets, the Nebs, the Celtics, and the Rangers.

Roguesville

Created by the eccentric genius Stacey Cartwright, a Pogo-like semi-satirical merci show where viewers can participate in the lives of various small-town characters.

Solarian Republic War Bank

Bank formed for the financing of the war after the dismal failure of the first war bond issue by the cloudships' virtual merci banks.

Sluice Juice

Breathable Integumentary fluid in the Met.

Snap-Metal Advertisements

Virtual-reality advertisements set into grist-coated stickers, on beverage containers, etc.

Teleman Milt

A financial brokerage company on Mercury's E-Street for which Kelly Graytor was a junior partner.

Trade Economists

Pro-Met political faction on Neptune's moon Triton.

METAPLANETARY GEOGRAPHY: THE MET AND INNER SOLAR SYSTEM

Akali Dal Bolsa

Typical manufacturing bolsa on the Vas section of the Met. First settled by a Sikh population.

Asteroid Belt

Cutoff point for the Met. Cloudships began forming here, incorporating as a materials shipment service for the building of the Met. This old company was called Alquitran Incorporated. There are Alquitran relics and historic landmarks in the asteroid belt.

Bach

The principal city of Mercury and the financial center of the Met. Situated in the Bach crater. The architect Klaus Branigan designed much of the city. Branigan claimed to have based his conception upon structures he found in the final movement of Bach's Harpsichord Concerto no. 1 in D Minor. Like Bach, with his two interwoven themes, Branigan took essentially two cities and knitted them together. First, there is residential Calay, with its bulbous pearl strings of apartments. These exist between the square, almost mineral, stretches of New Frankfurt and its central corridor, Earth Street, which houses the powerful banks and brokerages of the Met. The bus fare is thirteen greenleaves to get from Bach to the polar lift.

Bagtown

The nearest thing to a city in the Carbuncle. Near where the garbage sluice from the Met comes in.

Bendy River

The sloughlike river of goo that runs through the Carbuncle.

Carbuncle

The Carbuncle is the garbage dump of the Met. Filled with mutated and unregulated grist, this is where all the old code comes to die and where all the escaped code comes to hide. It is located at the outer fringes of the Met, just inside the asteroid belt. The "protocol vermin"—escaped code sequences that inhabited actual biological vermin—arose here before the war and were developed into fully functioning human beings when they migrated to Nirvana, the independent "micro-Met," or mycelium, of the Friends of Tod, which circles the sun inside the Martian orbit.

Clarit Bolsa

An average working-class habitat on the Vas. Dory Folsom, DIED sergeant, hails from there.

Earth

Sparsely inhabited. A few major population centers remain, including New York City. In 2802 c.e., the Earth was declared an "Ecological Repatriation Area" with limited construction and population growth allowed, and now vast stretches of our native planet have been returned to their natural state.

Upstate New York on Earth has returned to wilderness and is inhabited by various feral machines, principally automobiles, trucks, and utility vehicles.

Near the old town of Rhinebeck on the Hudson River is a secret research institute working on a crash project involving time travel and superluminal flight.

Esolo Armature

Where Leo was stationed before the invasion of Io.

Fork

Region in the local grist on Neptune's moon Triton where free converts have established a virtual business and residential district.

Integument

The Integument is the outer coating of the Met cables and the Met spinning habitats. This is a semiliving "skin" that mediates biological and chemical transfer and balance within the Met, and forms a protective covering. It is a product of both design and stepped-up evolution. No one normally lives in the Integument, but it can be accessed.

Mars

Densely inhabited. Home to Bradbury University. Victim of the failed terraforming experiments of the 2700s C.E.

Mas El Daví

Carmen San Filieu's estate in New Catalonia.

Mercurian Transportation System

The South Vect is the main polar transportation conduit on Mercury that leads to the South Polar Lift, know locally as the Hub, which leads in turn to the transfer habitat above the Mercurian pole, Johnston Bolsa.

Mercury

The financial and governmental center of the Met. High population density. Principal city is Bach. Earth Street, or E-Street, is equivalent to the old Wall Street on Earth. San Souci is the Interlocking Directorate headquarters.

Moon

Inhabited. Greentree shaman-priests initiated in Valley of the Bones. Cloudships Tacitus's and Lebedev's human aspects met in old Farside Station in mid-2400s C.E.

Mycelium

AKA a micro-Met. A small system of cables not directly connected to the overall Met but which participates in the virtuality through the grist and can be reached either by spaceship or by occasional concatenation with the larger Met. The most important of the mycelia is Nirvana, the self-made home base of the Friends of Tod.

New Catalonia

Met habitat on the Diaphany where the locals, descendants of Catalán from old Spain, play wicked social games in a late Renaissance setting. The principal city is New Sabadell.

Polbo Armature

Agricultural habitat on the Diaphany and birthplace of one Claude Schlencker.

Ru June's

A rowdy bar in the Carbuncle.

San Souci

The central edifice on Mercury in the vast conglomerate of buildings, all interconnected, that made up the Interlocking Directorate Headquarters in the Met. It includes, in its center, a small mountain made entirely of grist, Montsombra. La Mola is the inner sanctum of Amés. It is atop Montsombra.

Silicon Valley

The Noctis Labyrinthus area on Mars that served as a concentration camp for free converts during the war. Mengele-like research was conducted there on selected free converts by the infamous Dr. Ting.

Sui Sui University

Second largest university in the solar system and principal center of learning on Mercury. The Elkinstein Facility is the physics department there, and was Ping Li Singh's first workplace. She later went to work in Lab Complex B, the black box physics laboratory.

METAPLANETARY GEOGRAPHY: OUTER SYSTEM

THE PLANETS

Outer System

Area beyond the asteroid belt, including Jupiter, Saturn, Uranus, Neptune, Pluto, the Kuipers, and the Oorts. Space cables are not feasible to build there, and the distances are covered by spaceships. All outer-system planetary moons are inhabited. There is grist everywhere, so outer-system inhabitants fully participate in the virtuality of humanity. At the beginning of the war, the outer system was nominally under Met sovereignty, but in practice most government was local. While the population of the outer system is much more thinly spread than that of the Met, it is still enormous by historical standards. At the beginning of the war, it numbered nearly 10 billion, with the Met claiming another 90 billion souls (in their various forms), for a total human population of around 100 billion. The bulk of the outer-system population lives on the moons of Jupiter and Saturn.

Jupiter

All of the Jovian moons are inhabited.

CALLISTO

Callisto had a utopian "free grange" movement, and some free grange collectives still exist. Alethea Nightshade was raised on one of these. Telegard is the principal city.

GANYMEDE

Ganymede is the center of commerce for the outer planets. Ganymede also has plate tectonics, and earthquake-inducing warfare technology was used to secure its fall early in the war. The moon fell to Met forces in *Metaplanetary*. One million members of Federal Army were taken prisoner there. It must use nuclear power when cut off from the Capacitor feed at Io.

EUROPA

A scientific disaster in the Lost Sea of Europa—a vast sea under a layer of ice—resulted in the death of Roger Sherman's eldest son and Leo Sherman's brother, Teddy. There may be an extraterrestrial nano life-form there. Leo Sherman lived on Europa for a while before returning to the Met. Leo Sherman's brother, Roger Sherman's son, lies at the bottom of the under-ice sea there, killed or transformed by what might be extraterrestrial life that can manipulate the grist. Captain Quench's lover Arthur works in a biological research facility there. The moon is also the headquarters for IDC, the news service that Jake Alaska works for.

IO

Io is a center for energy generation in the system, existing, as it does, at one pole of Jupiter's enormous magnetosphere. Its Capacitor power plant taps the Jovian magnetosphere for power and converts it to microwave radiation for uplink and distribution. It supplies enough power for the needs of the four inner moons of the Jupiter system. Possession of Io was hotly contested during the war. The "gristlock" is control and command center in the Capacitor. Free converts retreated here during invasion and were captured and "flashed" to Silicon Valley on Mars.

Saturn

All of Saturn's moons are inhabited. The largest population is in the moon Titan's principal city, Laketown. Titan, the second largest moon in the solar system, has a thick atmosphere that manifests as a reddish brown photochemical haze. The locals have come to like the color.

Uranus

The Uranus system is the poorest area in the outer system, and before the war, the local government was essentially a puppet for Met business interests.

OBERON

Principal settled moon in the system, it was a victim of an information plague grist-mil attack by Federal forces during the war.

Neptune

All moons inhabited. An important provider of energy in the outer system. The Mill operates within the semipermanent storm known as the Blue Eye of Neptune.

TRITON

Triton is the major population center. Its principal city is New Miranda. The Triton temperature can get down to 38 degrees Kelvin, that is, −390 Fahrenheit. You can put a simple substance in the shade here, and it will become a superconductor. At the average temperatures and pressure on Triton, the nitrogen atmosphere hovers around its solid-gas-liquid triple point, and occasionally conditions will be right for the formation of the famous nitrogen rains. Triton is easily the coldest inhabited place in the solar system. Even Pluto, built on different geology, is warmer by a little.

TRITON'S NEW MIRANDA

The principal city on Triton, the Neptunian moon. Named after the Uranean moon Miranda, from which the first settlers hailed. It is built on the side of an enormous crater in the southern hemisphere of Triton. New Miranda is a city of spires. The neo-gothic religious leanings of the first settlers combined with the low gravity of their new world to produce an architecture that is unique and at times breathtaking.

There are some apartment buildings here and there, but for the most part each resident on Triton has his or her own spire—that is, families and familial units do. In most of the spires, the first five floors are fully pressurized and protected. They are usually given over to gardens and fountains. New Miranda bills itself as the "Garden City," and there is a friendly competition among the more affluent residents in that regard. Of course, this has led to a few aesthetic horrors. But there is a professional class of elite gardeners who are strongly influenced by the Greentree priest (and gardener) Father Capability, and many of the gardens are justly regarded as works of art. These are another tourist attraction on Triton, along with the nitrogen rains outside. New Miranda is governed by the Town Meet.

NEREID

The moon Nereid is an important shipping port. It was the site of the first use of full-scale nanotechnological warfare by the outer-system forces when the DIED ship *Jihad* was infected with the PAL grist virus.

Pluto

The surface of Pluto is almost entirely covered with grist. The planetary geology is reshaped almost continually to serve the shipping that is the principal activity of the inhabitants. The poet Beat Myers wrote of Pluto that it is "where the stones go to die." Pluto has an infamous orphanage where Kwame Neiderer was raised.

Oorts

The debris on the outer edge of the solar system. Sparsely inhabited by biological humans, but home to the cloudships. A source of a great deal of material for the construction of the Met. Home of the Federal Naval Academy.

OTHER PLACES AND PHENOMENA IN THE OUTER SYSTEM

Dark Matter Road

Discovered in the late 2800s C.E., the Dark Matter Road is a stretch of unreflective material that lies between the solar system and the double-starred Centauri system. In 2903 c.e., Cloudship Mark Twain became the first human being to visit another solar system when he arrived at Alpha Centauri during that e-year. Cloudship Lebedev arrived there eleven years later, in 2914 c.e.

Del Rings

The rings of Saturn, renamed during the war for a heroic free convert.

Laketown

Main city on Titan, Saturn's moon. The "lake" is a lake of liquid methane, and Laketown is at its edge. The area nearest the lake is called New Alki. The local mean temperature is -180 Celsius.

Mill

An enormous windmill in the Blue Eye of Neptune consisting of two blades that turn with the swirl of the storm. The Mill, from blade tip to blade tip, is as long as the diameter of planet Earth. It was built on the same physical principles as the Met. In the center of the mill, operating in a manner not dissimilar to that of ancient hydroelectric turbines on Earth, is a generator that beams a steady supply of microwave energy to a geosynchronous satellite stationed above it. And from that satellite, it is fed to Triton.

Object 71449-00450

AKA The Object. A cometesimal in the Oorts that houses a mining colony. Kwame Neiderer was born here.

Shepardsville

The degenerate red-light district located in the local virtuality on Triton. It is the bad section of Fork.

Windows

Ghost town in the local Triton virtuality. Dangerous ancient web site of Microsoft.

METAPLANETARY WARFARE

Boomerang

Formerly the DIED ship *Jihad*, which captured, for a time, the Neptunian moon Nereid. The official first spaceship to enter the Federal Navy.

Cloudship Warfare

see Cloudship

Fremden

DIED military slang for outer-system inhabitants. The term means "strangers" in old German.

Forward Laboratories

Federal Army's grist weaponry development center on Triton, under the command of Gerardo Funk.

Glory

Pleasurable sensation of well-being, pride, and communal belonging sent through the vinculum to DIED soldiers who do a good job. Can be orgasmic. During the war, Glory was given to the entire population of the Met. Highly addictive.

Grist-mil

AKA military grist, grist-based attack. Using the grist as a military weapon. Various permutations, including a communications warfare attack that permanently disables the Broca grist in the victim and turns him or her into a gibbering idiot.

Knit

Special "channel" of the merci reserved for the Federal Army.

Measurement

Both militaries use the metric system for distance measurements. (Civilians use a variety of systems, including the ancient English, which is still hanging on strong.) All military time is e-standard (Earth-Standard). K is sometimes used to mean "thousands of kilometers per hour." Fifty K is a standard ship approach speed. MK is "millions of kilometers per hour." An MK is about as fast as any ship can go—that is, about 1/100th the speed of light in a vacuum.

Met Navy

Met spaceships used for warfare are not self-contained LAPS. They are usually commanded by a LAP, but that captain is not the control structure of the ship, only the command. The ships are under the auspices of the Department of Immunity Enforcement Division Space Marine Task Force, and their names are prefaced by that entity's initials in Basis, DIED. These are the Met ships of war.

THE DIRAC CLASS OF CRUISERS

These are the DIED all-purpose ships. They are used for transport, and have weaponry for light attack functions, normally as "ground clearing" for the infantry about to be deployed. They might have a torpedo or two, but their principal weapon is a short-range positron cannon working off the antimatter engine, and several projectile catapults, the most fearsome of which is the flak ram, which shoots off the dreaded "nail rain" that can tear a kilometer of ground to shreds— neatly preparing it for occupation.

THE DABNA CLASS OF DESTROYERS

These serve both attack and transport functions. They are big and long, with a thousand-meter girth and a ten-kilometer length. They possess long-range antimatter cannon and torpedoes and catapults that will handle up to a hundred tons of material. They can also deploy special devices, such as the rip tether that was put to such awful use on Triton.

THE STREICHHÖLTZER CLASS OF CARRIERS

There were, at the outbreak of hostilities, twenty of these in the fleet. They carry a full range of weaponry and a large crew, as well as serving as a base for smaller attack and transport craft. In them you will find the production facilities for military grist and deployment devices for it as well. Carriers are also notable because they are constructed on the same principles as the Met cables, held together by macro implementation of the strong nuclear force. As such, they are imposing fortresses, indeed. They maneuver well in two dimensions, but their immense momentum makes them difficult to pilot attitudinally. This is not the case for a special class of carrier, the Lion of Africa division, which are basically carriers filled with antimatter engines, which also serve as weapons by quick conversion. These have a smaller crew. Their specialty is to enact disaster events.

SOL AND SCIATICA CLASSES

The principal ships that depend upon the Streichhöltzer class carriers are the Sol and Sciatica classes. The Sol class is a transport vessel designed for quick planetary landings of about five hundred troops. Sciatica-class ships are attack craft, also designed for planetary operations. These boast a deadly array of close-range weaponry. They have something of the appearance of a pitchfork with wings. Both the Sol and Sciatica classes are aerodynamically built, and able to withstand huge pressure differential—something the larger ships are incapable of, as witness the destruction of the *Schwarzes Floβ* when it fell into the atmosphere of Jupiter.

ZIP CODE CLASS

A specialized class of ships that are communications boats with major defense armaments and fields, but only a single cannon, which operates off the engine. These vessels are mostly grist matrix, and they resemble spinning dumbbells, or jacks from the children's game of pickup. They proved vulnerable to counterinformational insurgency.

MET NAVY ENGINEERING AND OPERATIONS

Except for the planetary and communications craft, most DIED ships are based upon the "spinning scythe" design. They greatly resemble bundles of these implements bound together in a clump, but some with blades depending from them all along their length. It is not without cause that at times the Met navy was referred to as "the reapers." All of these ships have, as their end, large-scale murder.

Operations that require spin-induced gravity are carried out in the "blades" of the scythes, and these also usually contain officers' quarters and command and control. Most of the weaponry is found in the long "handle" of the body, and it was here that attacks were most profitably directed. Ship defenses are varied and effective.

MET MAVY DEFENSE: ELECTROMAGNETIC DAMPING

You cannot hit a ship and depressurize the entire thing. Most nuclear weaponry is damped in the vicinity of a ship by powerful electromagnetic fields that control the rate of nucleus fission and keep it to a one-to-one basis. This immediately turns the fission trigger of a fusion bomb into a mere nuclear reactor and prevents a runaway chain reaction.

MET NAVY DEFENSE: ISOTROPIC COATING

The most powerful defensive system on a DIED ship, however, is the so-called isotropic coating each ship possesses. This coating makes use of the electroweak force of nature. Through a process called quantum induction, predicted in its essence by Raphael Merced, the exchange of messenger particles within the atomic nucleus can be controlled, and the actual spin of individual nucleons adjusted. The isotropic coating interacts with all incoming energies and particles (including micro-meteorites and the like) and changes what is known as the "mixing angle" of atomic nuclei that make up the ship in that section. In effect, this causes the material of the ship to appear to the incoming weapon as an entirely different substance. If the weapon is, say, a stream of positrons, the ship will "seem," to the positrons, to be made of anti-matter, and the beam will fall upon it as would a ray of light. Small particles are passed through the ship, "believing" themselves to be passing through vacuum. It is an odd and sometimes frightening sight to see a chunk of rock move through one side of a ship and out the other as if the ship were a ghost.

MET NAVY DEFENSE: THE LIMITS OF ISOTROPIC COATING

Fortunately, or unfortunately, depending on your viewpoint and who is shooting at you, the isotropic coating loses effectiveness for masses that are much over one hundred kilograms, and the effects of gravity are never mitigated, so that when a particle passes through, it will leave on a new vector. The coating also loses effectiveness in the complexities of a planetary atmosphere and is only partially successful in protecting from a planetary attack craft or a soldier on the ground. Nevertheless, space-adapted soldiers have, as part of their adaptation kit, an isotropic coating that generally prevents rapid depressurization in space that might be caused by micrometeors, and limits the possibilities of any shrapnel attack upon incoming paratroopers until they enter the atmosphere.

MET NAVY DEFENSE: THE GRIST PELLICLE

The final line of defense possessed by Met ships is the grist pellicle, located just underneath the isotropic coating. This matrix responds instantaneously to any penetration and immediately sets to work containing the damage. Ships can "heal" themselves at an astonishing rate, and any effective attack must take account of this ability.

MET NAVY: CONCLUSION

Taking attack and defense capabilities together, the DIED ship represents a formidable opponent. What it lacks in generalized function it makes up for with specialization and maneuverability. If a cloudship is thought of as a sort of giant living cell, a DIED vessel might be thought of as a virus—not alive in the same way, but just as dangerous and, in some ways, more effective.

Montserrat

DIED flagship of Admiral Carmen San Filieu in the initial Met attack on Triton.

Rip Tether

An undulating space tether deployed over a planetary surface as a gigantic military weapon that tears through population centers like a merciless tornado.

Vinculum

Special "channel" of the merci reserved for Department of Immunity.

Schwarzes Floß

DIED carrier that fell into the atmosphere of Jupiter during the war.

Sweeper

Department of Immunity antipersonnel unit, a Met policing-and-attack robot.

Marat

Transport that brought Leo Sherman's platoon to Io.

SPACE-BASED DEFENSES

Sensors

Mostly semisent free converts or semisents. These can be either fixed or traveling.

Minefields

Minefield commanders are fully sentient free converts with the rank of captain or above. A nonreplicated complementary key resides at local headquarters, also ranked as captain or above. Use of the key allows passage through the minefield.

PERSONAL WEAPONS

DIED soldier appearance similar to a miniature attack ship.

GUARD KIT FOR A DIED SOLDIER

—Brace of arm rockets for each forearm

—Wrist band
- Rotating projectile weaponry
- Miniature railguns
- Capsule-sized grist grenades

—Outside of hands
- Antimatter rifles
- Entire arm stiffens into a stock for aiming

—E-M micro-macro goggles
- Adjustable for virtual reality, microscopic view, other e-m spectra
- Grist patch directly to the sight centers in the rear brain

—Body armor
- Isometric coating
- Grist supplemental

—Propulsion
- Attitude and impulse rockets on the legs

—Backpack
- Gyroscope
- Other supplies

CHARACTERS AND SPEAR CARRIERS

PRINCIPAL DRAMATIS PERSONAE

Roger Sherman

Federal Army commander of the Third Sky and Light Brigade of Triton, which, before the war, was principally a meteorological outpost assigned to study and develop the enormous power-generating Mill within the atmosphere of Neptune. Sherman was a former manifold who had reduced himself to individual human proportions after a series of professional setbacks and personal disappointments. Sherman started the war as a colonel.

Thaddeus Kaye

The first LAP manifold encoded using nanotechnology based on time-traveling graviton manipulation. Another attempt to foresee the future, the process succeeded too well, and Kaye became both a reflection of, and a direct causative agent upon, our local timescape. This proved to be a problem when Ben Kaye, the personality upon whom Thaddeus was based, sabotaged the encoding process as part of a lovers' quarrel. The resulting LAP was a combination of Thaddeus and Ben who called himself TB. Kaye's fate was directly connected to the outcome of the war.

TB

Name that the Thaddeus-Ben Kaye combination man goes by.

Father Andre Sud

A shaman-priest of the Greentree Way, friend to Thaddeus Kaye and Roger Sherman. Sud was the Way's time expert until he decided to retire from research and become a local priest and rock-balancing sculptor on Triton.

Molly Index

Friend to Thaddeus Kaye and Andre Sud. Index is a restorationist, specializing in the paintings of Jackson Pollock. Index was a LAP manifold before the war.

Jill

A scrap of security code that escaped its controlling algorithm and migrated to the Carbuncle, where it entered a ferret that Thaddeus-Ben Kaye used for hunting rats. Later "ferret Jill" was combined with an accidental re-creation of Alethea Nightshade in some modified military grist. The resulting young woman became the principal leader of the partisan forces during the war.

Jennifer Fieldguide

Young woman on Triton who is at first deceived, then wooed, by Colonel Theory. She succumbs to his charms and becomes the emotional guardian of his son during the middle phase of the war.

Leo Sherman

Youngest son of Roger Sherman. A journalist, essayist, and accomplished explorer of the Met Integument. Estranged from his father at the start of the war.

Ping Li Singh

Brilliant young theoretical physicist who is forced to work for Amés in a research prison on Earth.

Jeep

A nine-hundred-year-old semisentient Jeep that roams upstate New York.

Major, later Colonel, Theory

Free convert in the Federal Army, and Roger Sherman's principal aide. Theory is a very logical fellow who finds that he is developing intuition in fits and starts. Theory has a son, whom he has not yet named.

Sergeant Kwame Neiderer

Orphan from beyond Pluto who joins the Federal Army and eventually becomes a soldier in the Third Sky and Light Brigade on Triton. Has a fully space-adapted body.

C

Chief of special operational intelligence and cryptology for the Met. His real name is Clare Runic. Probably.

Amés

Chairman of the Interlocking Directorate of the Met. Formerly a musical composer trained by the famous free-convert composer, Despacio. Obscure origins. Amés is a fully integrated, multiply differentiated LAP, a manifold.

THE GRAYTOR FAMILY

Kelly Graytor

Junior partner in the E-Street firm of Teleman Milt. An accomplished trader in "quantum futures" before the war. Husband to Danis and father of Aubry and Sint.

Danis Graytor

Free-convert portfolio management software and wife of Kelly Graytor.

Aubry Graytor

Sixteen-year-old (*Metaplanetary*) daughter of Kelly and Danis Graytor.

Sint Graytor

Youngest child of Kelly and Danis Graytor.

TB-, ANDRE-, AND MOLLY-RELATED PEOPLE

Bob the Fiddler

Half-crazed musician in the Carbuncle, and later on Triton.

Makepeace Century

(*Metaplanetary*) Former FUSE terrorist on Mars, and captain of the spaceship *Mrs. Widow* during the war.

Cardinal Morton Filmbuff

(*Metaplanetary*) Andre Sud's boss in the Greentree Way. A LAP manifold "quantum event detector" designed to see the entire human present so clearly that the future becomes manifest as a vision. Filmbuff first has a vision of the coming war as the burning Greentree. He then has a vision of a new Tree, of which the old Tree is just a shadow.

Alethea Nightshade

The woman whom both Thaddeus Kaye and his regular human personality, Ben, loved. When Ben Kaye interfered in the creation of his own Thaddeus Kaye manifold, Alethea's personality was blown apart and dispersed somewhere in the Met. Both men believed they had lost her, and her love, at that time.

TRITON

Captain John Quench

Commander of Company A in the Third Sky and Light Brigade. Friend to Major Theory. Quench is currently a man, but originally a woman. His fiancé (a man), who will not join him on Triton, lives on Europa.

Constants

Free convert working for the Department of Immunity. Extremely fast and deadly. Major Theory's former lover in Officer Candidate School.

Dahlia Sherman

Roger Sherman's ex-wife and Leo Sherman's mother. A LAP, one portion of which is an emergency-room doctor on Triton.

Gerardo Funk

Mondo grist engineer and leader of the doomed partisan resistance on Titan, Saturn's moon. Later the commandant and chief research director at the Federal Army's Forward Labs on Triton

Captain Thomas Ogawa

Captain of the spaceship the *Mary Kate*, who brought five hundred refugees to Neptune from Saturn's Titan after that moon fell to DIED forces. Later a commander in the Federal Navy.

Hilly St. Johns

(*Metaplanetary*) Free-convert bartender at the Officers' Club of the Third Sky and Light Brigade.

NEW MIRANDA POLITICIANS AND SUCH FROM
METAPLANETARY

Thoreau Delgado

(*Metaplanetary*) AKA the "Thin Man." Leader of the Free Integrationists on Triton. A LAP. Aspect is entirely Triton-adapted.

Mallarmé de Ronsard

(*Metaplanetary*) Neo-Flare poet, and Free Integrationist on Triton.

Shelet Den

(*Metaplanetary*) Old-guard member of the Motoserra Club on Triton.

Janry Craig

(*Metaplanetary*) First engineer of the Neptunian Mill.

Frank Chan

(*Metaplanetary*) Chairman of the New Miranda Town Meet. A LAP.

Kali Mfud

(*Metaplanetary*) Member of the Trade Economists faction on Neptune's moon Triton.

TITAN INVASION (*METAPLANETARY*)

Vincenze Fleur and Pazachoff

(*Metaplanetary*) Titan residents, part of the initial partisan resistance.

Ins and Del

(*Metaplanetary*) Free converts, the former cipher keys to the Titan Rocketry Shield. Del was the complementary key to Ins.

AMÉS'S THEATER COMMANDERS

General C. C. Haysay

Commander of the DIED forces conquering Titan and the Saturn system. Haysay is a LAP.

General Blanket

DIED conqueror of Pluto and commander of the force that included the DIED ship *Streichhöltzer*. Asian, with jet-black hair worn severely cropped.

Zebra 333

Leader of the DIED forces attacking Jupiter. A LAP who exists entirely in the virtuality. Frequently appears with an animal head of some sort. Zebra 333's headquarters is on the carrier *Schwarzes Floβ*.

Admiral Carmen San Filieu

(*Metaplanetary*) LAP commander of the Met forces attempting to conquer Triton. Her flagship is the *Montserrat*. Also a society dame in the New Catalonia Bolsa on the Diaphany. Also Amés's lover on Mercury. A LAP can do all these things, and more. She can also die horribly and all at once, as San Filieu proved.

MONTSERRAT CREW UNDER SAN FILIEU (METAPLANETARY)

Captain Meré Philately

Non-Catalán senior officer on the DIED ship *Montserrat*. Survived the destruction of that craft and became a POW. Later the leader of the Federal Army's Virtual Extraction Corps.

Captain Bruc

(*Metaplanetary*) Catalán senior officer on the DIED ship *Montserrat*.

JOVIAN COMMAND

General Meridian Redux

Commander of the Federal Second Army in the Jovian system.

Major Anke Antinomian

Federal Army officer. Announces the fall of Ganymede at the cloudship Constitutional Congress. Adjutant to and chief of intelligence for General Redux in the Jovian system.

Captain Deadpan

Free-convert staff officer to Redux, statistics wiz.

Cloudship Yüan Hung-tao

Held in reserve by Redux at Callisto during Fall of Io.

Cloudship Sandburg

Cloudship who took part in the defense of Io, carrying Winny Hinge as a press observer.

FALL OF IO

LEO'S PLATOON
Private Aschenbach

Leo Sherman's assumed name and bodily identity during his flight to the outer system.

Corporal, later Sergeant, Dory Folsom

DIED soldier who took part in the conquest of Titan, the invasion of Io, and the fighting on Charon. Leo Sherman's platoon leader during his flight to the outer system.

Llosa

Soldier in Dory Folsom's platoon during the invasion of Io. Op 2. From the Carta Cylinder on the Vas.

Corporal Merrymaker

Platoon quartermaster at Egolo Barrel on the Diaphany.

Corporal Alliance

Surf 1 communications man in the platoon. Dies in canyon recognizance from a grist grenade.

Platoon

Includes Privates Gerhard, Meeker, Asad, Chin, Extraslim.

Lieutenant Fooks

In command during initial part of the Capacitor raid.

Lieutenant Tae

In command during canyon recognizance on Io. Runs into a zip net.

FEDERAL FORCES ON IO
Carkey
Federal Army defender of the Capacitor during the DIED invasion.

Corporal Dowan
Carkey's compatriot in the weapons blister.

Assistant Mayor Mathaway
Free convert in Capacitor gristlock.

Uncle Yoland
Ionian relative of Carkey's.

Uncle Hors
Ionian relative of Carkey's.

WINNY HINGE-RELATED
Winny Hinge
JBC merci reporter aboard Cloudship Sandburg. Sponsored by Jermatherm Coats-Like-New pellicle enhancer.

Ron Edgekirk
Host of the merci show *Plasmaskate*, Winny's ex-boyfriend who fell in love with a free convert.

BATTLE OF THE THREE PLANETS

Jake Alaska
Merci reporter for IDC news service.

Framstein Wallaby
Another IDC reporter.

Panda
The IDC free-convert database.

Captain Allsky

Third Sky and Light company commander on Cloudship Austen.

Sensor Drone Maria-Alpha

Semisentient. First detects General Haysay's invasion forces.

Childe Elrondius

Inhabitant of Uranus's moon Oberon, deluded by Fremden grist into thinking he's a knight on a dragon-killing quest.

Major Monitor

Theory's right-hand man and sensor chief.

Corporal Orfeo

One of Allsky's troopers who missed the net in the Mill skirmish near Neptune.

Major Zane

DIED General Haysay's well-mannered adjutant.

Cloudships Engaged at Neptune

The "Kuiper Group," consisting of: Mark Twain, Austen, Homer, McCarthy, Cervantes, and Carlyle.

VARIOUS CLOUDSHIPS AND CLOUDSHIP-RELATED PEOPLE

Tacitus

The first LAP cloudship, along with his friend, Cloudship Lebedev. Historian of the War for Republic and engineer of the Metaplanetary Constitution of the First Solarian Republic. One of the oldest living human beings.

Cloudship Lebedev

One of the original cloudships, along with Tacitus. Born 2375 C.E. in Russia. Cofounder of Bradbury University. First Commandant of the Federal Naval Academy.

Cloudship Tolstoy

The curmudgeonly keeper of the cloudship graveyard far out on the Dark Matter Road toward Alpha Centauri. He has thirteen sons and one daughter. An instructor in the Federal Naval Academy.

Cloudship Mark Twain

First person to visit Alpha Centauri system. Pro-Republic. Took part in the Battle of the Three Planets, defending the Mill at Neptune.

Cloudship Austen

Economist. Pro-Republic. Took part in the Battle of the Three Planets, defending the Mill at Neptune.

Cloudship Mencken

(*Metaplanetary*) Chair of the Congress of the Cloudships.

Cloudship Beatrice

(*Metaplanetary*) Alarmist. Anti-Republic.

Cloudship Markham

(*Metaplanetary*) Pro-Republic.

Cloudship Kafka

(*Metaplanetary*) Pro-Republic.

Cloudship Bernhardt

(*Metaplanetary*) Pro-Republic.

Cloudship al-Farghani

(*Metaplanetary*) Elitist. Anti-Republic.

Cloudship Huxley

(*Metaplanetary*) Argumentative. Anti-Republic.

Cloudship Ahab

(*Metaplanetary*) Elitist. Anti-Republic.

Cloudship Grieg

(*Metaplanetary*) Anti-Republic.

Cloudship Cézanne

(*Metaplanetary*) Anti-Republic.

Elgar Triptych

(*Metaplanetary*) Amés's slippery ambassador to the cloudships. Later the Met's representative to the outer system during the conflict.

NEW CATALONIA (METAPLANETARY)

Josep Busquets

(*Metaplanetary*) Wicked youthful male lover to the aspect of Carmen San Filieu who lives in New Catalonia.

Noñells

(*Metaplanetary*) A banking family in New Catalonia.

OTHER JILL- AND AUBRY-RELATED PEOPLE

Alvin Nissan

Free-convert partisan commander and expert v-hacker. Pelota fanatic. Played goalkeeper for the "Celtics." He also created the "Aschenbach" persona for Leo Sherman.

Logan36

Free-convert v-hack on the Silicon Valley break-in team. Played midfield for the "Celtics."

Bin___128A

One of the "protocol vermin." He discovered the trick to taking out a Department of Immunity antipersonnel sweeper, a Met policing-and-attack unit. Later became a man, and a principal leader of the partisan forces in the Met.

Bastumo

Legendary pelota player. Aubry uses his semisentient grist patch overlay to play pelota during the break-in at Silicon Valley.

Tod

Gnostic time tower. Object of devotion of the Friends of Tod.

Otis and Game

Leaders of the Friends of Tod on Nirvana, prior to its destruction.

Taylor

(*Metaplanetary*) Friend of Tod who operates an old-fashioned ham radio on Nirvana.

Mrs. Lately

(*Metaplanetary*) LAP teacher on Mercury who saw promise in Aubry Graytor and thought she might be a good LAP candidate.

KWAME NIEDERER–RELATED PEOPLE

Private Rastin

(*Metaplanetary*) Soldier in the Third Sky and Light Brigade who helped destroy the rip tether.

Sergeant Peal

(*Metaplanetary*) Soldier in the Third Sky and Light Brigade who had a nervous breakdown trying to destroy the rip tether on Triton and killed his lieutenant.

Lieutenant Flashpoint

(*Metaplanetary*) Soldier in the Third Sky and Light Brigade who was killed by her crazed sergeant while trying to destroy the rip tether on Triton.

Lieutenant Boxset

(*Metaplanetary*) Short-lived soldier in the Third Sky and Light Brigade who took part in the attack on the *Montserrat*.

Privates Tiempos and Cue

(*Metaplanetary*) Short-lived soldiers in the Third Sky and Light Brigade who took part in the attack on the *Montserrat*.

Lieutenant Chalk

(*Metaplanetary*) Soldier in the Third Sky and Light Brigade who took part in the attack on the *Montserrat*. Kwame Neiderer's eventual commander. Chalk put the antimatter bomb that destroyed the *Montserrat* down the bore shaft.

Rules

(*Metaplanetary*) The Rules was the not-quite-sentient algorithmic director of the orphanage where Kwame Neiderer grew up.

Platoon at Charon

Lieutenant Twentyklick, commander. Benetorro, Denmark, Fusili, Mays, Hardrind.

The Shadows and the Tigers

Two platoons fighting to the death and beyond in the weird landscape of the anti-information zone on Charon. Ultimately these are Jungian representations of Kwame's subconscious when his mentality was captured and subverted by the transformed grist-mil on that moon.

PING LI SINGH–RELATED PEOPLE

Professor Hamarabi Techstock

LAP, head of the Science Directorate in the Met. Hamar is his nickname.

Hugo Singh

Li's father. He lives on the Vas in Akali Dal Bolsa. Has pellicle-induced lupus.

Harold Singh

Li's brother. Works in the Vas's Umberto Barrel, at the silo.

Suni Singh

Li's sister. Planned to sing the ardasa at Hugo's funeral.

Siscal

Free-convert statistician relegated to guard duty at Complex B at Sui Sui University.

Gertel

Passenger on the Dedo travel bead. Pharmaceutical grist sales person. Sells Dendrophytis, an alleged quantum-based aphrodisiac.

Hill

Passenger on the Dedo travel bead. Met exterior repair technician. Space-adapted, bone white color.

McHood

Li's colleague and fellow prisoner on Earth.

Norm regulator 1

Guy who gives Li a hard time at Checkpoint Cesium.

CLAUDE SCHLENCKER (AMÉS)–RELATED PEOPLE

Despacio

First free-convert music composer. His most famous works are the celebrated A-4 Variations. Despacio later became crazy Bob the Fiddler. Or so Bob claims.

Delmore Schlencker

(*Metaplanetary*) Claude Schlencker's alcoholic, disappointed father.

Getty

(*Metaplanetary*) Principal of Claude Schlencker's school in Polbo Armature.

Janey Beth Schlencker

(*Metaplanetary*) Claude Schlencker's mother.

Eynor Jensen

(*Metaplanetary*) A music teacher at Asap Gymnasium who recommended Claude Schlencker to Despacio.

Mrs. Ridgeway

(*Metaplanetary*) A teacher in Polbo Armature who saw promise in young Claude Schlencker.

OTHER KELLY GRAYTOR–RELATED PEOPLE

Hazen Huntley

(*Metaplanetary*) A junior partner in Teleman Milt.

Hed Ash

(*Metaplanetary*) A junior partner in Teleman Milt.

The Old Man

(*Metaplanetary*) LAP head of Teleman Milt.

Lloyd Njonjo

An old classmate of Kelly's from business school and a conservative councilman in the New Miranda government. He got Kelly a job with the newly formed Solarian Republic War Bank.

DANIS GRAYTOR–RELATED

Sarah 2

Free convert who chose to be Danis Graytor's mother.

Sarah 1

Free convert who chose not to be Danis Graytor's mother.

Dr. Ting

Mengele-like psychologist in Silicon Valley.

Lyre Wing

(*Metaplanetary*) Free convert, looked upon as something of a floozy by Danis's mother's friends.

Readymark

(*Metaplanetary*) Free-convert friend of Danis's mother.

Vida

(*Metaplanetary*) Free-convert friend of Danis's mother.

METAPLANETARY–SUPERLUMINAL HISTORICAL TIME LINE

YEAR	EVENT	TECHNOLOGY	ARTS
2300s	Legal strictures of the late 2300s and early 2400s lead to the Information Consortiums of the 2400s C.E., and to the genesis of the ECHO Alliance.	Information Age fully realized. Biotech matures. Small human presence in Earth orbit and on Earth's moon.	Zen-Lutheranism founded. Old religions rapidly cycle through fundamentalism to apostasy and back again.
2375	Cloudship Lebedev born in Russia.		
2400s	Consortium of transnational information brokers rules on Earth. Growth and commerce, though sluggish, are generally steady. For the arts and sciences, however, it is an era of stagnation and malaise. In the arts, the 2400s are known as the Ironic Age.		Ironic Age. Senescence of many artistic forms and genres. Many faiths die out.
2412	ECHO Alliance rules Earth.		

Year	Event	Age	Cultural
2459	Tacitus and Lebedev's human aspects meet in old Farside Station on the Earth's Moon.		
2465	Initial construction on the Met begins.	Nanotech Age dawns.	
2475	Construction on the Aldiss, the first space cable, complete.	Humanity moves into the solar system.	Greentree Way evolves from Zen-Lutheranism and the New Shamanism on Earth's Moon. Faith and science reunite.
2500s	Bradbury University's greatest period throughout 2500s. Flare Generation, group of poets who published in Beat Myers's journal.		
2511	Raphael Merced born, the first major scientist who is not an Earthling, and who belongs in the pantheon of such figures as Newton, Einstein, and Galileo. Amanda Breadwinner, first Met Chief Engineer, retires.		Poetry reemerges as major form. The Awakening. Rebirth and reformation of many of the arts.
2590	*The Exiles' Journey* created—a compendium of essays, thoughts, and sayings by the artists and scientists who ran afoul of the Mercurian Endowment government in the 2590s—as they plunge into the sun.	Quantum Age dawns.	
2700s	Era of disastrous Mars terraforming experiments. Cloudships began to be recognized as such.	Nanotech Age matures. Solar system fully settled.	
2802	The Earth declared an "Ecological Repatriation Area" with limited construction and population growth allowed; vast stretches of planet returned to natural state.		Musical high tide. Composers, virtual reality virtuosos dominate.
2823	The Dark Matter Road, a stretch of unreflective material that lies between the solar system and the double-starred Centauri System, discovered.		Age of Art and Grist. Full flower of the Awakening.

2903	Cloudship Mark Twain becomes the first human being to visit another solar system when he arrives at Alpha Centauri.		
2914	Cloudship Lebedev arrives at Alpha Centauri.		
2963	The most important Conjubilation of the Mars-Earth Diaphany in history, including the famous (and infamous) Merge gathering.		New Hierarchy, transformed socialism, emerges. War.
3013	Cloudships adopt the Metaplanetary Constitution of the Solarian Republic. War for Republic begins.	Superluminal Age dawns.	